THE TRAITOR AND THE THIEF

Andrew J. Luther

www.vanishing-goblin.com

The Traitor and the Thief

© 2022 by Andrew J. Luther

All rights reserved.

The cover of this novel is an original oil painting by Storn A. Cook. You can see more of Storn's artwork at www.stornart.com

ISBN: 978-09953056-8-7

Vanishing Goblin Inc.
www.vanishing-goblin.com

For Nathan

I'm your biggest fan, too.

By Andrew J. Luther

Tales of the Undying Empire
THE TOWER OF DUST
THE SEVERED OATH
THE WITCH'S PATH

Undying Empire: Rebellion
THE SOLDIER AND THE SLAVE
THE TRAITOR AND THE THIEF
THE REVENANT AND THE REAPER

Acknowledgements: As always, I want to thank my wife, Pam, for her support.

Thanks to Bev (yet again) and to Mike for their valuable feedback.

And thanks to Storn A. Cook for another amazing cover painting.

For Nathan

I'm your biggest fan, too.

By Andrew J. Luther

Tales of the Undying Empire
THE TOWER OF DUST
THE SEVERED OATH
THE WITCH'S PATH

Undying Empire: Rebellion
THE SOLDIER AND THE SLAVE
THE TRAITOR AND THE THIEF
THE REVENANT AND THE REAPER

Acknowledgements: As always, I want to thank my wife, Pam, for her support.

Thanks to Bev (yet again) and to Mike for their valuable feedback.

And thanks to Storn A. Cook for another amazing cover painting.

Eighth day of Highsummer,
11 days to the Arrival

Chapter One

THE NIGHT SAT HEAVY OVER YTHIS, AN OPPRESSIVE HEAT permeating the darkness that smothered the vast city on the very edge of the Bay of Ythis. On this, a rare moonless night when the sky was filled with great swirls of stars across its black void, it seemed as if the torches and lanterns struggled against the oppressive gloom that weighed down on the flickering flames. Though the evening was still young, the dark pools of shadow in the alleys, cracks, and crevasses of the city seemed ready to swallow whole anyone foolish enough to be outside the safety of a stoutly locked door.

On the noble estates clustered on the rise at the north end of the city, where stone walls separated the perfectly manicured lawns and carefully tended copses of trees, where the great manor houses perched above the common businesses, tenements, and warehouses below, the great families of the Undying Empire had mostly retired for the evening. As Phana crouched in the shadows of the outer wall lining the estate of the Eorallo noble family, she hoped that no members of that wealthy and powerful lineage were still awake and moving about inside.

On the stone landing in front of the main doors, well inside the circle of light from the pair of lanterns that illuminated the closed and no doubt locked entryway, a handful of estate guards clustered together. She had watched for perhaps half a bell as they shifted nervously, talking in low tones to each other and watching the darkness with wide and fearful eyes. She knew they were supposed to patrol the grounds at regular intervals, but tonight they did not seem inclined to leave the relative safety of the front landing.

The dogs—perhaps picking up on their handlers' unease, perhaps sensing something more ominous—snapped and snarled at each other. Every few minutes, one of the dogs would tuck its tail between its legs and whine as it stared out across the dark grounds, which only served to increase the guards' disquiet.

Something was coming to Ythis. She didn't need to be particularly sensitive to such things to feel the wave building, higher and higher. It was the talk of the city during the daytime, though no one knew the cause, nor when it would peak before crashing down to flood the streets with a new horror, shattering lives and twisting the fates of those who dwelt in the capital city of the Undying Empire.

But everyone believed it was only a matter of time.

Crouched at the base of a wall on the estate of the Eorallo noble family, Phana rolled her neck and tried to ease the tension in her shoulders. She was not immune to the feeling of … *imminence* … that permeated the air. While Ythis was certainly home to its share of both supernatural and mundane horrors, as well as a host of tragic events, this was a new sensation, one she believed she had not experienced before. Yet there was a strange element within it, almost a fleeting familiarity that confused her and set her on edge.

She squeezed her eyes tightly shut and took a deep breath before opening them again. Thinking about the ominous cloud that hung over the city was a distraction she couldn't afford. If she was spotted tonight, the guards' fear would drive their actions. She might be attacked and killed before they realized she was just a normal woman.

Not that she didn't enjoy the added danger. It gave her a thrill to risk everything on her ability to remain unseen while she accomplished the goal she had set for herself.

She moved away from the wall, keeping low and stepping carefully to avoid making any noise. The light from the lanterns would prevent the guards from seeing her out in the darkness, but the dogs might hear her, or pick up her scent. She angled away from the front of the manor and toward the side of the building where she could remain hidden.

Reaching the wall, she ran her hands over the rough bricks, feeling the grooves where the mortar held them together. Typical for a noble's manor, the walls were in good condition and there was little space for her to grip.

The windows into the lower level of the manor, however, were only slightly higher than she could reach by stretching. Looking up at the wooden ledge above her, she uncoiled like a spring and leaped skyward, catching hold of the edge with her fingers. Carefully, so as not to make any noise, she pulled herself up until she could rest her arms on the ledge. Then she paused and listened, both for the sound of the guards approaching from the outside, and for any indication the someone might be awake inside the room.

The windows were covered with ornately carved wooden shutters, closed against the night. The pressure in her shoulders was building as she hung from the window ledge, so she inched to one side before hooking her fingers under the edge of the other shutter and slowly pulling it open.

Luck was with her, and the shutter swung out smoothly and silently. Phana peeked around the corner of the closed shutter, peering into the dark room. In the darkness, she could just discern a small office. A simple wooden desk sat against one wall, a small stone weight holding down a sheaf of papers. A single chair was pushed in against the desk, and two doors led from the room.

The size of the space, and its location on a lower floor indicated this was the office of a servant of the family, perhaps the procurator himself, who managed the estate on behalf of his employers.

Two doors led out of the office, and Phana was sure one of them led to a small chamber where the procurator would be sleeping right now. She hoped he was a deep sleeper.

With little effort, Phana pulled herself up onto the window's ledge and then stepped down lightly into the room. With an ease that came naturally to her, she let herself out of the office into the hallway without making the slightest whisper, closing the door softly behind her.

It took only a moment for her to find the staircase leading down to the cellar under the mansion. There was no guard at the main floor landing, and she silently moved down the stairs to the small room at the bottom.

Phana's eyes quickly adjusted to the deeper darkness down here.

Her ability to see perfectly well in near pitch darkness was something she had never revealed to anyone else. It was yet another thing that set her apart from those around her, and there were enough difficulties in her life these days that she didn't need to add to the pile.

Deliberately turning her mind away from such thoughts, she focused on the task at hand. Three doors faced her, one in each wall. She had no way to know which one protected the prize she sought, but she didn't relish the idea of trying all three. Every door she opened increased the chance something would go wrong and she would be found out.

She moved to the first door on her right and examined it. There was no lock, and the handle was well-worn. This was definitely not the correct door.

The second door, directly across from the stairs, was more promising. This one had a lock, and the handle was worn but had certainly not seen heavy use. A quick check of the third door on the left side revealed it to be the same.

Phana had an even chance to guess the correct door, and she moved back to the one directly across from the stairs. Iadan Eorallo, the head of the Eorallo noble family, loved his wines. He was an insufferable bore about most things, but was a hundredfold worse when it came to wine.

Phana knew that Iadan brought important guests down to visit his wine cellar to show off his collection of rare and expensive vintages and blather on endlessly about this or that grape. Rumors were not hard to come by, as servants loved to gossip about their employers.

If she were Iadan Eorallo, what would make the best impression on a visitor? To make the best show of it, she figured would come down the stairs and straight ahead to the center door.

She was guessing, of course, but she was practiced at putting herself into the shoes of others, figuring out what they might do in similar circumstances. She knelt and set to work on the lock on the door facing the stairs, sure that she had the right portal.

It took her only seconds to release the lock, but she was unable to muffle the loud click as the mechanism released. The sound echoed up the staircase and Phana was sure it had been loud enough to rouse every sleeping inhabitant of the estate.

She rose and moved quickly back to the corner at the base of the stairs. Ears straining to catch any sound, Phana waited to see if anyone came to investigate the noise from the lock. Her heart was beating loudly in her ears and she worried that she wouldn't be able to hear anyone approaching until it was too late.

But she waited, counting out the seconds in her head until a full minute had passed. No usual sounds floated down the stairs toward her.

She returned to the door and slowly pushed it open, slipping inside and closing it behind her. Turning her back on the door, she faced a long room, the air cool and the rough plaster walls lined with hanging amphoras of various sizes and shapes. A small wooden plaque was mounted on the wall above each amphora, engraved with information about the wine stored in the vessel.

Phana moved down the room, quickly scanning the wooden plaques until she found what she had come here to steal. Lifting the small amphora off its hook, she was surprised at how heavy it was. She slid it into her backpack and swung the pack back onto her shoulders.

Turning back to the door, she froze. In the pitch darkness of the room, she saw a tiny flicker of light under the bottom edge of the door.

Someone had come down the stairs and was directly outside the wine cellar.

At this time of night, it was unlikely to be a servant, and Iadan himself would be long asleep. No, Phana decided, the click of the lock must have been heard and the guards had prepared themselves before coming down the stairs to see what might be prowling around the estate.

She was well and truly trapped.

Moving to one side of the door, she considered her options. If she called out and surrendered, the guards would be unlikely to attack her out of hand. But she'd lose the wine and be at the mercy of whatever the guards decided to do with her. They might just hand her over to the Watch, but it was more likely they would beat her first for giving them all a fright on this oppressive night.

She could just burst through the door and try to fight her way past them. She had no idea how many guards had been summoned, though, and at least one—probably more—would have crossbows trained on the door. Phana was fast, but she couldn't dodge bolts.

And then there was the *other* option. Phana pushed that thought away. During the events with Jadir and his sister, Marilsa, Phana had been warned about releasing the ice that lived in her blood.

The young girl stepped back in the shadows and was lost to Phana's sight, but her voice drifted out one last time.

"There is more to your life than you remember, Phana, that much I know. Your power called to me, and it calls to others. Be careful what attention you bring on yourself. Be careful what you bring to Ythis...."

And the suspicion arose in her mind once again—could this overwhelming feeling of doom approaching Ythis be the result of Phana's unleashing of the power in her blood? Was she the cause of all this? And if so, what exactly was coming for her?

She shook herself out of her reverie. She was wasting precious seconds that should be used to figure a way out of this situation. She wasn't going to murder the guards outside the door. And that meant keeping whatever was inside her bottled up.

The sound of a whispered voice floated to her through the door, but she couldn't make out the words. No doubt the guards were discussing which of them was going to investigate the noise they had heard. Even if they had recognized the sound of a lock being opened, there were two doors down here with locks on them, and they would have no idea which room had been breached.

Phana's mind raced through possible options. She couldn't just rush out—that would be suicide. She'd need to wait until they opened the door to the wine cellar, and then use whatever advantages she had.

The door handle was quickly turned and shoved forward, but there was little force behind it, and it swung slowly open. The light of at least one, possibly a few lanterns illuminated the room. Phana stayed in the shadows behind the door, waiting.

No one came rushing through the door—the fear of this night played heavily on their thoughts.

Phana gave the door a gentle nudge with her hand and it began to swing slowly shut again, as if the weight of the door was slowly pulling it closed. One of the guards, holding a lantern, stepped into the doorway and stopped the door's movement with his hand.

It was the opening Phana needed.

Like a striking snake, her own hand shot around the door and grabbed the guard's wrist, yanking him forward. At the same time, she shouldered the door closed.

The guard dropped the lantern, his eyes wide and his mouth open as he sharply inhaled in fear. Phana twisted his wrist and slid behind the man, slipping an arm around his neck and cutting off the scream that was about to come out of his throat.

Instead, she took a deep breath and let out a blood-curdling scream of her own, putting as much rage into it as she could.

The fallen lantern burst into flame as the oil was upended and flowed into a puddle on the floor. The flames were far enough from any wood so as not to set the house itself on fire, and Phana figured the flickering flames would only add to the effect.

The upper panel in the door cracked as two crossbow bolts slammed into it, but the thick wood stopped both bolts from penetrating all the way through. The guard in Phana's grip struggled to pull her arm away from his neck as he desperately fought for air. But she had the leverage and bent him further backwards to prevent him from using his greater weight against her.

She knew she had only seconds to act before those crossbows were reloaded. She was taking a gamble, as there could be more than two crossbowmen out on the landing. But there was little she could do about that now.

Phana spun the guard around to face the door and drove him into it, face-first. She heard his nose shatter and his legs went limp for a moment. Shoving him sideways, she yanked the door open and sent him barreling out onto the landing.

A quick glimpse showed her five more guards out there, two at the base of the stairs frantically trying to reload their crossbows.

The guard she had shoved got in the way of two of his fellows, who realized at the last second that it was their own man charging at them and narrowly averted running him through with their short swords. The one remaining guard on the landing was taken by surprise as Phana bolted through the door, screaming again, and drove her fist into the man's face.

The guard she hit let out his own bellow of fear and backpedaled, trying to get away from the creature that had emerged from the flames in the wine cellar.

But Phana wasn't here to fight. She twisted away and charged toward the stairs. Neither of the crossbowmen had managed to reload their weapons in the few seconds since they had discharged their bolts.

Kicking sideways, Phana swept the legs out from under the closer crossbow-wielding guard and he went down. She leapt over him and sprinted up the stairs as the other guards recovered their wits and realized they weren't being attacked by a monster from the Abyss.

Their shouts told Phana they were now in pursuit of a thief.

Laughing, Phana swept through the office of the procurator and hopped up to the sill of the window. The procurator himself opened the door from his sleeping chamber and caught a glimpse of her crouched on the sill, framed by the open window as she looked back at him.

"Thanks for the wine!" she called out as she dropped from the window and landed lightly on the grass outside.

She was halfway to the estate's outer wall before the guards were able to mount anything resembling a coherent pursuit. Her rope was exactly where she had left it, and she was up and over in seconds, taking the rope with her.

Phana settled into a steady jog, weight of her backpack doing nothing to slow her pace. By the time the guards managed to reach the streets around the exterior of the estate, she was long gone.

Her smile faded as she slowed to a walk and turned in the direction of the Wolf's Den. She had nearly been caught tonight. And yet, she knew it wasn't going to stop her from doing this again soon.

It was another reminder of her restlessness. She needed to be active, to take dares, to flirt with danger, or she'd lose her mind. This city—as vast as it was—felt too small since that night when she turned the tables on her former gang-leader and his men and killed them all. She felt trapped here in Ythis, claustrophobic. But she had nowhere else to go.

Phana needed answers, and there was no better place to get them than right here in this city. She hadn't pressed for an audience with the Wolf yet. Koral had needed time to heal from a stab wound in his leg, and then had been busy with gang-related business. In the meantime, she distracted herself with silly thefts like the one she had done this evening.

She could have been killed. Regardless of what power was inside her, she wasn't immortal, or impervious to weapons.

She could feel her mood turning dark, perhaps a reflection of what hung over Ythis this night. But she didn't want to let herself slip into such a state. She had just acquired a very expensive wine and was looking forward to sharing it with Koral. They would spend the rest of the night together, enjoying the wine and each other.

The smile came back to her face and she continued to the Wolf's Den.

Chapter Two

THIS WASN'T HOW IT WAS SUPPOSED TO HAPPEN. THE GATES of Ythis were crowded from sunrise to sunset with travelers, merchants and their pack animals, farmers and their wagons, nobles with their entourages, and the guards at the gate were too busy to question each person unless there was an obvious reason for suspicion.

If one was trying to avoid scrutiny, that was the time to slip into the city without raising suspicion.

After the sun dropped below the horizon, the flow of people through the gates slowed to a trickle. Even here, near the greatest city of the Empire, it wasn't safe to travel at night. Bandits were a constant threat, and there were other things that lived in the darkness and preyed on those foolish enough to leave the relative safety of local towns and villages, not to mention the great walls of Ythis.

The guards were generally more vigilant once the darkness set in. With fewer travelers to watch, they had time to look more closely at each person, ask whatever questions they wanted, and ensure there was a good reason for the travelers to be out after normal hours.

And there was something in the air tonight, a powerful feeling of dread, as if there was some otherworldly creature crouching in the impenetrable darkness, preparing to pounce on the city and drown it in madness and blood.

Scrutiny was exactly what Laita Naschect had been trying to avoid. But tonight, she knew, the guards would be nervous, waiting for the arrival of whatever might have created this blanket of fear that lay over the night.

Sweat rolled down Laita's back as she looked over the gate, still a few hundred paces ahead. The lanterns hung on poles lining the entryway were small globes of light in the oppressive darkness, barely illuminating the ground directly in front of the large gates, as if the darkness was a tangible thing trying to crush the light under its weight. The massive portcullis had been lowered halfway, forcing anyone riding in a wagon or on horseback to dismount and walk their animals under the heavy iron spikes.

The dozen guards were clustered in two groups, one on either side of the entry. They faced outward, watching not just the road but also staring into the darkness around them in case a threat emerged from another direction.

"We sure we wanna to do this?" Namal said in a low voice. He marched beside Laita, leading the two packhorses, the leads wrapped tightly around his fist in case either animal panicked. Both were highly skittish tonight, ready to bolt at the slightest scare.

He was dressed in simple farmer's clothes and had no visible weapons aside from a small knife at his belt. A salt-and-pepper beard covered his face and his hair had grown unruly since they had left the north. It wasn't the most cunning of disguises, but it was what they had been able to do while on the road. Laita hoped that anyone seeing him would think him nothing more than a man trying to get his goods to market.

She glanced sideways at him.

"We don't have much of a choice. I don't fancy staying outside the walls through the night. It's dangerous enough in the best of times, and right now really doesn't feel like the best of times. I'm concerned about what else might be out here with us."

Pilayni, dressed in simple leather vest over tunic and trousers, a filthy pair of boots on her feet, placed her hand on the hilt of the short sword strapped to her hip and gave a soft snort.

"Whatever's going on, we've been walking *into* it as we got near Ythis. We might be safer turning around and going back, night or not."

Pilayni was posing as the group's hired guard. She didn't look like the professional soldier she was, but rather wore the appearance of a barely experienced sell sword performing simple escort jobs for meagre pay.

Laita glanced back at Addiru and Keynter, each walking beside a packhorse and keeping a hand on their animal to help control it if the creatures decided to panic. Both were watching the darkness on either side of the road, eyes alert. Like Namal, they were dressed in simple peasant clothing and would pass as Namal's sons when they entered the city.

Or so Laita hoped.

Her thoughts went to the other three members of her command squad, who should already be in the city. She had full confidence in each of them to bring their assigned soldiers into Ythis without incident. She hoped they had not experienced the same string of bad fortune that had befallen Laita and her group.

The guards at the gate had by now seen the small lantern carried by Laita and all heads turned to the travelers.

"We're spotted," Laita said in a low voice to the others. "We'll keep going and express our obvious relief at finally reaching the city. Remember, we've been terrified out here in the darkness, and we're desperate to get inside the safety of the city walls."

The others each gave a curt nod and continued moving forward.

Laita watched as the guards ordered themselves, the six with long spears and round metal shields taking position in front of the entryway, the others arranging themselves behind and to either side.

When Laita's group was less than a hundred paces away, one of the guards shouted for them to halt.

The group immediately stopped, and Laita yelled out, putting a note of fear and desperation into her voice.

"Please help us! We've been stuck out here in the dark and there's something … can you feel it?"

"Approach the gate slowly!" one of the guards yelled to them.

They continued on their way, and Laita could feel Namal tensing up beside her.

She deliberately brought to mind the face of Kied, the man she had loved. She thought of his voice, his touch, their fleeting time together in the north, the moment of his death. She let the empty space in her heart open up, let the pain and the sadness well up within her. And then she forced herself not to blink away the tears that came.

They entered the ring of lanterns in front of the gate, and the guard shouted for them to halt again. Laita let out a sob, her tears running down her face.

"Please!" she pleaded once more. "Help us. We just want to be safe …."

"Identify yourselves!" the guard barked at her. Laita twitched at the shouted command and rested her hand on Namal's shoulder.

"My name is Lilsa, this is my father Neillust, and these are my brothers. We're just farmers."

"Who is the girl?" the guard demanded.

Laita looked over at Pilayni, as if she had forgotten about her.

"Her name is Pilayni. We hired her to escort us from Sisty's Crossing to Ythis."

The guards did not relax, exactly, but Laita could see some of the tension go out of them.

"What are you doing out at this hour?" the guard asked, and his words were no longer loud and clipped.

"Our wagon," Namal offered. "We broke a wheel and tried to fix it on the road, and that took too long. I didn't want to leave our food for the market. We were closer to Ythis than Sisty's Crossing, so we grabbed what we could pack on the horses and came here, fast as we could."

Laita was impressed by the tremor Namal put into his voice.

At a nod from the guard who was obviously in command, those other half dozen men without spears came around their companions and approached Laita's group. They did not draw their curved swords, but their hands never strayed far from the hilts. They fanned out and ordered Pilayni to put her sword on the ground. She undid her belt and dropped the weapon and scabbard on the ground and flipped it forward with the toe of her boot.

Laita winced inwardly. Pilayni moved like a soldier, like someone skilled and experienced around weapons. She saw the guards glance at each other.

"Where did you get your training?" one of them asked her, and Pilayni hesitated. Laita tried not to hold her breath. The last thing they needed was to raise the guards' suspicion that there was more to them than simple farmers and a young sell sword.

Pilayni looked over at Laita and frowned, and then looked down at the ground and sighed.

"My older brother," she said. "He … he joined the Legion but was …."

"He was what?" the guard demanded.

"He failed during training and they sent him … he was discharged. He came home and taught me how to handle a sword before he … died."

Laita didn't try to hide the shock on her face—Pilayni's performance was masterful. But Laita used her shock to turn the guards' attention back to her.

"You told me you were a Watchman for a year!" Laita said accusingly. "You lied to us! You … you've never been in a real fight?"

Pilayni looked at Laita and shrugged. "I'm good with a sword—my brother said so. But you wouldn't have hired me if I told you the truth."

"What if someone … some*thing* had attacked us out there?" Laita yelled, letter her voice go from fear to anger. She could see the guards getting uncomfortable as she pointed back out at the darkness. "You wouldn't have protected us! You're not even a real guard!"

"That's enough!" the guard commander said, stepping in. "This is not the place. You can deal with her once you're inside the city."

He turned to Namal as one of the guards handed back the weapon to Pilayni.

"What's on the packhorses?"

"Turnips, carrots, some potatoes," Namal answered.

"Get inside," the guard ordered. "Do not camp in the market square. You are permitted to set up your stall when the dawn bell sounds, but not before."

Namal nodded at him.

"Where did you serve?" the guard asked suddenly.

Laita watched as Namal calmly drew himself up and said, "Fourth Contingent, Dragon Regiment, Tenth Legion."

It was where Laita had met Namal and became his commander,

before she was transferred to the Twelfth and brought him, Saeda, Bor, and Ellend with her.

To Laita's surprise, the guard commander saluted Namal.

"My father served in the Eleventh. Welcome to Ythis. You realize you're lucky you made it, do you? This is not a night be out there," he said gesturing to the darkness surrounding the city.

Namal nodded again, and the guards parted, the spear tips rising to point at the black sky.

Laita didn't let herself breathe a sigh of relief until they were well within Ythis and away from the gate.

The streets of Ythis were never fully deserted, even on a night such as this when the darkness felt alive with malicious intent. Those few souls who were forced to be out and about at this late hour scurried along on their private purposes, furtively eying their fellows, their body language reflecting their desire to be left alone.

Laita led her team through the Market District, heading for an inn just off the West River Road. They stayed clustered together, the packhorses still nervous though slightly less so among the lantern-lit streets of the city than they were out in the deeper darkness. Pilayni kept her hand on the pommel of her sword and carefully watched every shadowy alley.

Laita couldn't quite believe that they had finally reached Ythis, and had made it into the city without incident. The fact that she and her companions hadn't been surrounded and arrested at the gate meant that the other soldiers filtering into the city had so far been success-ful as well. If anyone had raised suspicion—or worse, been caught— Laita wouldn't have made it past the gates.

But her easy arrival indicated that the infiltration was going well, so far. She had tasked two squads with laying a false trail of the con-tingent moving farther up the coast. Some would believe she was fleeing the Empire with her deserters, heading for some other con-tinent where they could become a mercenary company, fighting for the highest bidder.

She wanted *everyone* to believe that.

Unfortunately, she knew her ruse wouldn't fool the entire Legion. There would be those who would realize Laita wasn't the kind of person to run away. They would figure she had a plan and would watch carefully across the Empire for signs of her people. It was only a matter of time before they figured out where she was.

And then Ythis would be locked down and the Legion would come here in force to flush her out.

Her only hope was that she would manage to succeed before that happened. Laita Naschect was going to end the reign of the Undying Emperor, one way or another, and nothing would stop her.

"Do you think any others have made it?" Namal quietly asked her as they walked. She was surprised by the question—Namal had been his usual stoic self throughout their journey to Ythis, accepting her decisions and the seemingly endless string of difficulties they had experienced while traveling down from the north. Was he starting to have doubts about their chance of success?

"Some must be in the city by now," she answered in a low voice. "We were delayed so long getting across the Eullym River that we must have fallen behind."

Namal gave a short nod.

She relied on his strength, his steadfastness, perhaps too much. Without him, she was not sure she'd be able to bring her plan to completion. His presence and support provided the constant reminder that what she was doing was right and just. Namal's moral compass was unsullied by pride or ambition, or even revenge for those who had fallen at that cave in the mountains that contained the gate to another world, destroyed by her hand.

He wasn't doing this for vengeance. Namal followed Laita because he believed that the Emperor was a threat to the people of the Empire. And Legionnaires—even those who had turned their backs on the army itself—protected the Emperor's citizens.

And yet, how could she really be certain she was doing the right thing? Was it even possible to topple the Undying Emperor? Was she leading her people into a slaughter? Should she have fled the Empire, after all, and taken her people somewhere safe?

Knowing that Namal believed in her was a great comfort, but it didn't entirely negate her worried thoughts. In coming to Ythis, they faced more than just the Emperor and his Imperial Guard. He didn't rule alone.

The Church supported him, which gave them the freedom to conduct their rituals of worship, feeding souls and minds to their god Iathephos, who dwelt in the great cavern under the Grand Temple. The power of the Church was vast and terrible.

On the other side was the Five, the great sorcerers of Ythis. They, too, supported the Emperor and acted as a counterbalance to the Church, preventing the priests from becoming too powerful. But they were hardly benevolent. Rumors were that the sorcerers were no longer fully human, and they consorted with demons and other alien entities less powerful, perhaps, but far more numerous than the god of Ythis.

Laita held no illusions that she would be able to fight all three factions. The Church or the Five alone could destroy her force with fell magics. No, her only path to success required that she topple the Emperor before either group could come to his aid.

The thought of the Five sent a shiver of fear up Laita's spine. She was gambling everything on the belief that the sorcerers couldn't just magically scry across the city and immediately discover her and the soldiers who followed her. She simply had to hope that they didn't have some way of automatically detecting any threat to the Emperor and tracking such a threat back to its source.

Finally, there was the Imperial Guard. Highly skilled soldiers who were trained to give their lives in the service of the Emperor. To reach the palace itself, she would have to find a way into and through the Imperial Fortress, a fortified keep that housed the Guard and acted as a bastion against anyone trying to reach the man who ruled over them all.

Her full contingent wouldn't be able to simply attack and fight through the Fortress. She would need to find some way to gain entry in secret, sneaking through as far as was possible before they were forced to reveal themselves. They had to reach the palace without alerting the Guard to their presence or they would be cut off by superior numbers.

And that would give the Church, or the Five, time to come to the Emperor's aid.

She deliberately avoiding thinking about what they would do once the Emperor was dead. There would be no easy way back out. It was impossible that they would succeed without alerting the Imperial Guard, and the full force would respond and attempt to cut down those who had slain the Emperor.

Success meant leading her people to their deaths.

No, she needed to stay the course and that line of thought led nowhere good. This needed to be done, and none of her soldiers believed they would simply walk away when it was over. She would instead concentrate on other matters.

They needed information about the Fortress and about the Imperial Palace. They needed to find out who had made it into Ythis, and who was still coming. They needed to coordinate their force, which would be scattered about the city in order to remain hidden. The logistics alone were a nightmare, and Laita knew that she could lose herself in the details of the planning long enough to ensure that she stayed strong and committed.

The Emperor's days were numbered. For what he had done to Kied, what he had tried to do to so many innocent citizens of the Empire. He was a danger to the people she had sworn to protect.

Laita looked up and realized that they were nearly at their destination. She turned a corner and led them toward an inn where an old friend waited for her.

The first phase of her mission was complete. She was inside Ythis.

And, one way or another, the Emperor was going to fall.

Chapter Three

THE WOLF'S DEN LOOKED LIKE A LARGE AND BUSY TAVERN, but it was much more than that. It was the home of the Wolf, a legendary figure who controlled the vast majority of crime in Ythis after wresting control of the underworld from a collection of the meanest and nastiest crime lords the Empire had ever seen.

Things were different in Ythis since he had taken over ten years earlier. There were no gang wars these days, less overall street violence. The gangs concentrated on making profits by supplying the populace with any vice they could possibly want. The targets of thefts were mostly the nobles and richest merchant families rather than the poor and defenseless.

For the average citizen of Ythis, life was just slightly less dangerous and difficult with the Wolf in charge than it had been before.

Not everyone shared that sentiment, however. The noble families of Ythis had enjoyed the old ways, where the gangs had focused on fighting and killing each other rather than targeting the wealthiest citizens. The nobility continued to put pressure on the Watch to do something about the crime problem, not fully understanding how many individual members of that organization worked indirectly for the very man they wanted to remove.

One of the noble lords had even hired an assassin to eliminate the Wolf. Within a few days, the assassin's body was found hanging from a tree on the grounds of the noble lord's estate. This particular lord had been smart enough to recognize the clear warning and had let the matter quietly drop.

And so, despite its large size and its clientele composed of the most dangerous men and women in the city, the Wolf's Den was perhaps the safest tavern in Ythis.

Phana didn't come here often, despite it being the kind of place where she should feel right at home. She preferred smaller places where she could have a quiet drink and not be recognized by the other patrons.

Despite their attempt to be discrete, it had become common knowledge among the Wolf's people that Phana and Koral Creyss were involved. Koral worked for the Wolf as a troubleshooter and overall expert in smoothing out matters before they might become problems. He was known throughout the Wolf's guild, and within a short time Phana had become known as well.

After her adventure at the Eorallo estate earlier this evening, she was planning on meeting Koral at the Wolf's Den and then leaving with him for some quiet time with just the two of them. Her pace quickened as she turned the corner and spotted the entrance to the tavern ahead.

Despite the importance of this particular establishment, there was little about it to catch the eye. No windows pierced the clay brick walls on the ground floor, and a simple door of dark wood bound in iron was the only visible entrance. No sign hung above the entrance—those who were welcome inside already knew how to find it.

As Phana approached, she saw that Charkel was leaning against the wall beside the door. A large man with knife scars across his face, and muscled arms thicker than Phana's thighs, Charkel was a rather pleasant and friendly man despite his frightful appearance. Phana gave him a smile as she walked up to the door.

Charkel tried to return her smile, but it was clear from his expression that something was wrong. He put out one hand as Phana approached, his palm toward her.

"Phana, hold on," he said in his gravelly voice.

She stopped, her thoughts going immediately to Koral. Had something happened?

"What's wrong?" she asked.

"Look, I'm sorry, but …." Charkel hesitated, a pained look on his face.

"Charkel, tell me what's wrong. Where's Koral?"

"Phana … you … you can't go in."

She blinked at him, not understanding. She took a deep breath and tried to remain calm.

"Charkel," she said with as much patience as she could muster. "Why can't I go in? What's going on?"

Charkel let his hand drop and heaved a giant sigh.

"You can't go in, Phana. You're not, um … well, the word came down…from the Wolf, and you can't … come here … anymore."

She realized her fists were clenched, and she forced them open.

"Why not? What happened, Charkel?"

He shook his head.

"Nothing. It's not … nothing happened. It's just you. The Wolf said that we don't let you in here anymore. He didn't say why. Just that we don't let you in."

Phana tried to figure out if Charkel was joking with her. But nothing in his demeanor said he wasn't completely serious.

"That doesn't make sense, Charkel. I'm meeting Koral here."

"Koral's not here. He's at the Crown."

The Crown and Coin was another tavern out of which Koral normally operated when he was working. It wasn't terribly far from the Wolf's Den, but was far more discrete. Only those inside the Wolf's guild knew it was where Koral could be found if there was a problem that needed to be dealt with. The Wolf's Den wasn't a place to bring trouble.

But if Koral was at the Crown and Coin, it meant he *was* working. He was supposed to be free tonight, so that he and Phana could spend the rest of the evening together.

Charkel was still standing in front of her, an embarrassed look on his face. He was clearly uncomfortable being the bearer of such news. The man had no difficulty tossing out troublemakers or blocking entrance to those who clearly didn't belong. But Phana had always been welcome.

"It's all right," she lied to him. "It's probably nothing. I'll go talk to Koral and find out what's going on."

Charkel's relief was obvious. She saw him unclench his fists.

And then she realized that Charkel had not just been embarrassed to be the bearer of bad news. He had also been ready for a fight, one that he hadn't been sure he could win. He was *afraid* of her.

And Charkel wasn't the only one. Almost two months ago, she had been forced to defend herself against a gang leader—Qudovo—and a bunch of thugs that followed him. He had intended to kill her. Outnumbered and angry, she had done something that she now regretted. There was a power inside of her, inside her blood. She had let it loose and used it to kill Qudovo and the others who attacked her.

Someone had witnessed her summon the power within her, and that person had told others. While most scoffed at the story, which naturally grew with each retelling, there were enough people who believed it had happened to create a certain wariness about getting on Phana's bad side.

She was a skilled fighter, and she was respected for that. But the idea that she could kill a man by filling his lungs with ice engendered fear, not respect.

But now was not the time to be distracted by Charkel's reaction to her.

"Take care, Charkel," she said to him. "I'll see you soon."

She gave him a smile and turned away before he could see how false it was.

As she walked away from the Wolf's Den, her mind raced. Though she had never met the man, Phana had recently discovered that she had been under the Wolf's protection for at least the last couple of years. Before that, her own memory was hazy and led into complete darkness the further back it went.

She had asked Koral why the Wolf had extended his protection over her, but Koral didn't know. And she had been too busy with events at the time to try to meet the Wolf directly.

And now the Wolf had decided she wasn't welcome at his tavern.

She didn't know what the Wolf was doing, didn't understand why he had taken an interest in her in the first place. And she had no way to know why he was now cutting her loose.

Koral could get answers, but she had avoided using him to do so. But it was past time she found out just what was going on. And Koral was her only real way to get to the Wolf.

She worried that this was going to change things between her and Koral. She could lose him by pushing forward. And she might discover things about herself that she was better off not knowing.

She thought of her friend Jadir, and what he had learned about himself from the Wolf. It was knowledge that had been kept from him, that nearly destroyed him, that had changed his life forever.

No, she was being ridiculous. She didn't believe that ignorance was better than knowledge. She had a chance to get answers and she deserved to know the truth about herself. And if the Wolf had those answers, one way or another Phana was going to find out.

Any thoughts of romance this night were well and truly gone as she headed for the Crown and Coin. Less than a dozen minutes later, she approached the entrance to the tavern.

The Crown and Coin was small and well-kept. The owner, Elmther, made sure it was always clean and tidy, and he obviously took pride in his small business. He was also part of the Wolf's guild, and the extra room at the back of the tavern was given over to Koral to use as a private office when he was working.

Koral's smile faltered when he saw the expression on Phana's face as she entered the tavern and strode toward him. He was standing beside the door to his office, speaking to one of the tavern patrons who sat at a table tucked into a corner.

He excused himself from the conversation and stepped aside to let her proceed him into the back room. She entered and, not feeling like sitting, turned and stood with her arms crossed as he stepped in and closed the door.

"What's wrong?" he asked, and she noticed he didn't try to embrace her or kiss her hello. He was practiced at reading people's moods and seemed to understand now was not the time for romantic gestures.

"You tell me," she stated flatly. She waited for a moment, watching his face. But Koral knew how to hide his emotions when he thought it necessary. His face told her nothing. He simply looked at her and waited, silently.

"Okay, that's not fair," she admitted. "I'm angry and I shouldn't necessarily take it out on you."

"Necessarily?" he asked.

"That depends on what you have to say."

"Please tell me what's going on."

She sighed and slipped the backpack off her shoulders, placing it on the small table. The sound of wine sloshing inside the amphora caused Koral to raise his eyebrows at her.

"And what have you got in there?"

"We'll get to that," she replied, not quite ready to tell him about the first part of her evening. There were more important topics to cover first.

"I went to meet you at the Wolf's Den."

A guilty look crossed his face for an instant and then he was unreadable once more. She wondered if he did that on purpose, if he was able to control exactly what he showed her, or if it was involuntary. The thought that he might be trying to manipulate her attitude toward him made her angrier. She forced herself to hold it in check—she had no evidence he was doing anything wrong.

"I'm sorry. I hadn't planned to work tonight, but something came up. I left a message with Nid tell you as soon as you arrived."

Nid was technically the owner of the Wolf's Den and ran the tavern itself. If Koral had left a message for her with Nid, then he had not expected her to be turned away at the door.

"I didn't get to see Nid. I wasn't allowed into the Wolf's Den."

There was no slipping of his expression this time. His face remained completely still, but something in his eyes ….

"What do you know about this?"

"I don't …." he paused. "I didn't think he would ban you from the Den."

"The Wolf? He's spoken to you about me and you didn't tell me?"

Koral looked down at the floor and she could see the muscles of his jaw clench. He looked back up and met her eyes.

"I'm can't exactly repeat my conversations with the Wolf, Phana. Even when he speaks about you, I can't just tell you everything he says."

"You can warn me if I'm about to be cut loose."

"I didn't know that was going to happen. He was just …."

Koral stopped, the sentence unfinished.

"*Tell* me, Koral. You say you care about me, but you're keeping secrets from me. Secrets *about* me. Are your responsibilities more important than that?"

"You don't understand! It's not just about responsibility. It's about … protecting both of us. If I break his trust, then I'm out. Really out, for good. There won't be a second chance. And that will put us both in danger."

The realization surprised her.

"You're afraid of him," she said in a low voice.

"Of course I'm afraid of him! By the Abyss, Phana, he's the head of the one and only criminal guild in Ythis. He treats his people well, rewards loyalty and tries to keep us mostly safe. But he also calmly orders the deaths of those who get in his way."

Koral pulled out a chair and sat down heavily.

"He's the smartest person I've ever met. He sees patterns where the rest of us just see chaos, and that prepares him for nearly anything. He plays the long game, Phana, and he's already years ahead of anyone else. And I'm not going to betray him. It would be suicide."

Phana leaned back against the wall, looking down at Koral. While she understood his own position was difficult, she wasn't sure where it left room for her. Was she just supposed to let the Wolf plot and play with her life because Koral was close to him?

"Am I out of the guild, Koral? Am I cut loose? Has he withdrawn the protection he gave me?"

Koral took a breath before answering.

"Not that I know of. All I can tell you is that the Wolf was talking about distancing himself from you. It started right after that night we helped Jadir and Marilsa."

Phana had never told Koral the whole truth about everything that had happened that night. She wasn't ready to talk to him about what had really occurred. She wasn't sure how he would take it.

And, though she tried not to believe it, she also worried that he would immediately tell the Wolf the whole story.

And that's what it really came down to, when it was all said and done. She cared about Koral, but she had never let herself fully trust him.

"So I don't get into the Wolf's Den. Is that it?"

"I don't know, Phana. I didn't even know he had made a decision about you. I thought it was just him thinking out loud. I thought he'd tell me if he was going to…."

"But he didn't tell you. He did it behind your back."

Koral snorted.

"He doesn't me about every decision before he acts on it."

While that was true, this was something that would affect Koral directly, because of his relationship with Phana. The Wolf knew they were together. It was a surprise that the Wolf wouldn't warn Koral.

And then it struck her. The Wolf didn't fully trust Koral not to tell Phana things he shouldn't.

Shit, I'm acting just like the Wolf.

Koral had never done anything to betray the trust of either of them. But both were holding back their trust, assuming that he would betray the one for the other.

But the Wolf *was* brilliant. If he couldn't truly see the future, he could certainly make some predictions. Phana didn't know what plans he had for her, but at some point, the Wolf would try to use her. And she would fight for the freedom to control her own life.

And Koral would be caught in the middle.

He would ultimately have to make a choice between Phana and the Wolf. And if he was put in an impossible position, neither of them could truly predict which way Koral would go. It was likely Koral himself wouldn't know until the moment came.

She wanted to ask him if he would have warned her ahead of time if the Wolf had revealed his plans. But that wasn't fair, and she knew it.

Phana heaved a sigh.

"So what now?"

Koral shrugged.

"I'll go and find out what your status is. You haven't been in a gang since … well, you don't have an actual position in the guild. Maybe the Wolf just doesn't want a direct link between the two of you."

"Maybe," she said, but there was no conviction in her voice.

Koral glanced at the backpack.

"Are you going to tell me what's in there?"

Despite everything, Phana couldn't hold back the smile at her earlier accomplishment.

"What makes you think I want to tell you?" she said.

"Because you're too proud of yourself to keep whatever you were up to tonight a secret."

She frowned at him in mock anger, but undid the straps on the backpack and pulled out the amphora.

"Wine," she said. "*Good* wine. *Rare* wine."

Koral's eyes narrowed as he looked at her.

"And you acquired this wine from where?"

She grinned at him.

"From Lord Iadan Eorallo's private collection."

Koral's reaction wasn't the one she had been expecting. His eyes widened and he stood up.

"What were you thinking?"

"What do you mean? It's just wine."

"Did anyone see you? Does anyone know you were there tonight?"

Phana thought back to her exit from the estate. The guards probably hadn't gotten a good look at her face in the fight on the landing. She had been moving fast and they were all terrified.

"No. There was a bit of a scuffle, but it was dark and ...."

"What?"

She remembered looking back over her shoulder at the procurator as he emerged from his sleeping chamber. He had looked right at her.

"Maybe one person saw my face. But it was a fleeting glimpse at best. I wouldn't worry about it."

Koral clenched his jaw again and she saw he was angry.

"Iadan Eorallo won't just let this go. He's obsessed with his wine. He's going to pursue this. He'll hire people to find you. He'll throw a chest full of money at tracking you down."

Phana stood up and slid the amphora back into her pack.

"I'm not without skills of my own, Koral."

"You're supposed to be staying out of trouble. This is what, the third theft you've done in the last couple of weeks from an estate?

What are you thinking?"

"I'm thinking that I've had enough of hiding, Koral!"

Her anger was back, and she wasn't going to suppress it any longer.

"I did just fine before the Wolf put me under his protection. I did just fine before you started looking out for me. I don't need a bunch of keepers watching my every move, telling me when I'm doing something that's too dangerous. This is who I am. You can either accept it or move on."

Swinging the pack onto her shoulders, she yanked open the door to find Elmther standing on the other side, his hand raised to knock. He opened his mouth, looking from Koral to Phana and back again.

"Let me guess, you just got a message about me."

She tossed her head at Koral.

"He already knows."

Elmther backed out of her way as she walked across the tavern and out of the Crown and Coin. She knew Koral was watching her go, but he didn't call out after her or try to stop her from leaving.

She wasn't entirely sure if she was happy with that, or not.

*   *   *

THE SOFT GLOW OF THE LANTERN BARELY PIERCED THE GLOOM AS the late night crushed the city under its oppressive darkness. Keynter's low whistle signaled that all was clear, and Laita led the others to the alley that brought them to the stables behind the White Eagle Inn.

Laita had sent Keynter to wake the proprietor of the White Eagle and let him know they had arrived. Keynter was a young soldier, unknown to the upper ranks of the Legion and therefore unrecognizable to anyone hunting for Laita. Anyone spotting him would see a young man in farmer's clothes—nothing unusual or suspicious.

Cedaro was waiting for her beside the stable door. His broad face broke into a smile at the sight of her, his fizzy gray hair sticking out in all directions from being roused out of bed. He took her hands in his and drew her into an embrace, his large belly like a comforting pillow to Laita.

She had to swallow back the sob that wanted to erupt from her as he wrapped his large arms around her.

"Oh, Laita," he murmured to her. "I'm so glad to see you safe."

His deep, gravelly voice brought her back to her childhood, and memories of her parents. She forcefully pushed those memories away before she broke down into tears right here in the stable yard. She let go and stepped back from his embrace, glad the darkness hid the tears in her eyes.

She took a breath before speaking.

"Hardly safe, Cedaro. But close enough now that we're here."

Namal had already led the packhorses into the stable and was removing the bundles from their backs.

"That your weapons and armor?" Cedaro asked Laita.

"We couldn't bring them through the gate in case the guards decided to inspect our goods. We've made arrangements with others who are coming into Ythis by ship. Our gear will be smuggled into the city."

Cedaro frowned at the idea of criminals handling Laita's armaments.

"What's in the bundles, then?"

"Turnips, carrots, some potatoes," Namal replied. "They're yours if you can use 'em. We only needed 'em to get through the gate."

Cedaro nodded at him.

"Let's get you settled out of sight, then."

Once the horses were safely in their stalls, the innkeeper led them to the back door of the inn. He stepped into the hallway that led to the common room at the front, but turned into a side passage with a staircase going down to the cellar.

Laita followed, Namal behind her and the others bringing up the rear. They went down into the cellar, full of barrels of beer, wine, and various pickled foods, and boxes with other supplies for the inn.

In one corner of the cellar, Cedaro stuck his finger into a small divot in the wood beside one of the wooden braces holding up the ceiling. There was a small "click" and the section of wall hinged outward.

He led them into another room behind the disguised door and Laita was surprised at the size of the space. Six bedrolls had been laid out along the back wall, and a wooden table—covered with bread and cheese—and four chairs occupied the room.

"There's enough room for all of you, plus your gear when it arrives," he explained. "That small cask is full of lamp oil for the lantern on the table. Use as much as you need—I have more than enough and get regular deliveries for the inn, so no one is going to notice an extra lantern's worth."

He paused, looking embarrassed as he gestured to one side.

"If you have to … well, there are two barrels placed right beside this door. They're well-insulated so the smell won't travel, but you must make sure you push the lid back down tightly. I'm sorry, it's the best I could do—I don't think this room was designed for hiding people."

Laita nodded and smiled.

"We're soldiers, Cedaro. Barrels are still better than latrine pits."

The innkeeper chuckled and Laita took the opportunity to introduce her people to the man who was taking them in.

"He's an old friend of my family," she explained. She had been cagey with the others before now about who exactly Cedaro was to her.

Namal gave her a curious look.

"Didn't know you grew up in Ythis," he said to her.

"She didn't," Cedaro answered. "I moved here after her parents … um, well … Laita went to live with her aunt, but my sister was living here. Got lucky and bought this inn from a man who was going bankrupt running this place into the ground. I've managed to make a living out of it."

Cedaro motioned to the chairs, and Laita let the others sit and dig into the food. She moved off to one side with the innkeeper.

"You have no idea how much I appreciate what you're doing for us," she said. "This is more than I could have imagined. Did you already have this hidden room before you got my message?"

Cedaro chuckled and shook his head.

"I heard the old owner had a gambling problem. I believe he let smugglers use this room to move illegal goods through the city, to stave off the inevitable problems with the criminals who held his debts. I kept it—just in case I ever needed it for my own purposes."

He looked at her and Laita could see his eyes watering.

"My little Laita," he said, putting an arm around her shoulder and pulling her close. "This is quite the dilemma you have gotten yourself into."

She leaned into the embrace and felt her throat tighten. She knew this was dangerous for her—Cedaro represented her past, her family, the childhood that was torn from her in a single night of blood and death so many years ago. She had walled off that part of her heart for so long, and when she joined the Legion had tried even harder to forget everything that she had known in her youth.

But now she was here, and he was helping her once again. He knew she was a traitor to the Legion and that they were hunting her, but nothing else. But the big man was here for her, no questions asked, though he must be wishing he had more information. She knew he would let her tell him when she was ready, though.

And she wanted to tell him everything that had happened over the past few months. She wanted to sit with him until the sun rose above Ythis and the city began to stir to life around them. But she was worried about his safety as well. If the Legion ever found out that he was helping her, his life was forfeit. They could take him and torture him until he revealed everything.

Not for the first time, fear for this kind and caring man welled up inside her. Was she cursing him to lose everything for a purpose that he had not chosen to fulfill? Would she lose yet another person she loved?

"Is this really a secret?" she asked him. "Does anyone ever come down here anymore?"

"I found this room after I had been here a year. I never told anyone, and even my staff don't usually come down to the cellar. There are probably a couple of criminals still in the city who know the room exists, but there would be no reason for them to think that bringing any stolen goods to the White Eagle was still an option."

Laita knew she should eat and get her soldiers settled. They had long days behind them, and even more long days ahead of them. But she didn't want to let go of Cedaro—she wanted to be that little girl again, just for a few minutes longer.

"I want to tell you," she said in a low voice. "I want to tell you everything. But I'm worried for your safety. Just know that what I do, I do for the people of the Empire. I'm not a traitor. I'm doing what must be done."

Cedaro held her even tighter.

"My dear Laita, I never imagined it could be any other way."

And then he let her go and stepped back, wiping a stray tear from his eyes.

"You need some food and rest," he said, echoing her thoughts. "Sleep, and know that you are safe for tonight at least. We will talk tomorrow."

Laita nodded at him and looked over at her people gathered around the small table.

"I will," she replied. "After all, this is all just beginning."

Ninth day of Highsummer,
10 days to the Arrival

Chapter Four

WITH A TWIST OF THE KEY IN THE RUSTY LOCK, PHANA secured her door. The straps of her backpack dug into her shoulders and the soft slosh of the wine was barely audible inside the amphora tucked into the rough leather pouch.

She had reached her limit of being alone. Last night, after she stormed out of the Crown and Coin and left Koral behind, she had decided she didn't want to see anyone else. No one except Koral knew where she lived—she had been careful never to share that with anyone but him. It was just a small, rented room in a two-story tenement in Low Town, but it was her private place.

After a day spent sprawled on her pallet, thinking about Ythis, about Koral, and about her life—at least what she remembered of it—she was no closer to making any decision about her future. Worse, she was bored. And hungry.

She stepped outside and looked up at the darkening sky, splashes of gold painting the undersides of the clouds to the west, pools of darker blues and purples forming above and to the east. At the edge of her awareness, the faintest tickle of unpleasantness. Like the change in the air before an approaching storm, before the thunderheads are visible and you can smell the rain on the wind. You know it is coming, even if you're not fully aware of it.

With the setting of the sun, the doom was returning to Ythis.

As she stood in the narrow street, the poor and the tired moved past her on their way to whatever homes they had managed to find in this uncaring city, the smell of dust on the air mixing with the ever-present scent of salt water from the bay. She realized now that she had no destination in mind.

She wasn't quite ready to see Koral again. She needed something less intense, just a sense of belonging that had been missing for …

Forever.

For as long as she could remember, she had always struggled to fit in. Back when she was a member of Qudovo's gang, she often went off on her own and did what she wanted. He had hated it. He had also known that he couldn't do anything to stop her.

He had once threatened that he would kick her out of the gang if she didn't start doing what she was told. It was the one threat on which he might have been able to deliver. She remembered the moment she realized how much she valued the company of her fellow gang members. She hadn't wanted to lose them. Her agreement to be less independent had been grudging, but it was something she was willing to do to keep that sense of belonging.

And then Jadir and Marilsa had come into her life. It was an unexpected beginning, and events soon spiraled into something no one could have foreseen. Qudovo had rebelled against the Wolf and the gang was torn apart. And then Qudovo—blaming Phana for everything that happened—gathered those few lackeys who had chosen to remain with him and tried to kill her.

She remembered that night, trapped in an alley with a crossbow-wielding man on the roof and Qudovo and a few others on the streets hunting her. She had taken the only option available to her. Qudovo died from a poisoned crossbow bolt meant for Phana. And then she turned the tables on the others and hunted them down one by one, killing them with the ice that lived within her blood.

Even now, Phana didn't feel any regret at ending those lives. It hadn't been the first time she had killed to defend herself, and she knew it wouldn't be the last. In Ythis, danger was everywhere, and you must always be ready to meet force with force.

But among the former members of Qudovo's gang who still lived, there were those who blamed Jadir and Marilsa for everything that had happened. And some who blamed Phana for bringing the young man and his sister into their lives in the first place.

Despite the destruction of the gang, they had not been the only friends she had in the city. Though she hadn't seen some of them in a while, she knew that the wine in her pack would not go unappreciated. If Koral didn't want to drink it with her, then she'd find others who would.

The streets widened as she entered the Dock Ward, enough for two large wagons to easily pass. Large warehouses with thick wooden beams framing stained clay bricks lined the thoroughfares, with the smell of dead fish competing with vomit, shit, and brine on the thick air.

In a city the size of Ythis, an endless procession of ships from other parts of the Empire—not to mention the dozen large kingdoms of the southern continent and the hundreds of tiny island kingdoms to the east—brought merchants, trade goods, slaves, and wares of every kind. The wharves stretched along the entire width of the city between the great walls that extended out into the dark waters of the bay.

With so many visitors, sailors, dockworkers and those who catered to such people, the Dock Ward was almost a small city of its own, crouched at the base of the long slope that led up from the Bay of Ythis all the way to the hills on which the Nobles' District and the Imperial Palace rose above the common people.

Tucked in among the larger buildings were countless smaller shops and taverns catering to the inhabitants of this Ward. The Red Flag was one of the most notorious.

Named for the bright flag used by pirates the world over to announce their presence to their victims, the Red Flag was owned by the former legendary pirate, Lassadar Schurk, who had terrorized merchant ships across the southern oceans for almost two decades before he retired. A canny ship captain and treacherous adversary to the Imperial Navy that had hunted him across the waters for so long, Schurk was as tough a man as could be found, with a great bellowing laugh, leathery skin, and a dark beard—now with more than a few streaks of gray.

Those who were there to witness the events of that day say that almost ten years ago, Schurk sailed his black-painted pirate ship, the *Endless Deep*, right into the Bay of Ythis and tied up at one of the wharves.

Crowds had gathered, waiting for the soldiers of the Imperial Guard to swoop down on the ship and arrest Lassadar Schurk for countless crimes against the Empire. Schurk calmly walked off his ship and proceeded directly to the dockmaster's office, where they had a private meeting that went on for a good part of the afternoon. When he emerged, Schurk proceeded further up the street to the tavern, which he immediately bought from its previous owner, and changed its name to the Red Flag.

The following morning saw the *Endless Deep* gone from the harbor with no witnesses to its leaving. It hadn't been seen since, and no soldiers ever came for Schurk.

Rumors abounded as to how he had managed to retire in the capital of the very Empire he had raided for all those years without facing any consequences, but no one knew the whole story. Lassadar occasionally regaled the patrons of his tavern with tales of his piratical exploits in years past, but this was one secret he had never revealed.

Phana stepped into the Red Flag and was hit in the face with the smell of spilled beer, old vomit, unwashed bodies, and dried seawater. A dozen men and women from some ship's crew sprawled around a few tables in one corner, and a handful of old, wrinkled former sailors sat at the bar where Lassadar was in the midst of a story about raiding a merchant ship and finding a hold full of slaves instead of the more valuable cargo he had heard would be aboard.

In the corner opposite the ship's crew sat four men and women who did not appear to be sailors. Perhaps "thugs" was the most appropriate word to describe them. They each held a hand of cards, and a scattering of coins on the table glinted among the four clay mugs and the pile of discards. Phana walked over to the table and waited for the hand to be finished.

"Which one of you is getting his ass kicked?" she asked.

The man seated closest to Phana looked up and her, and a broad grin split his freckled face.

"Phana! Always good to see your face," Sotai said.

He reached up and Phana clasped his hand. No calluses on this one. His specialty was not in hard labor or beating people up. But ask him what drug would let you sleep through the night without dreams, or perhaps fuck through the night instead, and he could rattle off a list of names that would make your head spin. Of course, that was usually the point.

The other three at the table didn't seem nearly as glad to see her. Neysi, her dark skin glistening with sweat in this heat, remained expressionless as she gave a curt nod. Ikele, younger and with less confidence, glanced sideways at Neysi and followed her lead. The largest of the four, Danz, simply frowned at her, his great brows drawing together over his dark eyes.

"What brings you down to the docks?" Sotai asked, seemingly oblivious to his companions' reactions.

"I haven't seen you in a while, and I've got something special I wanted to share with my friends."

"Then why aren't you with *them*?" Danz asked in his deep voice, his tone dismissive. Neysi snorted and threw him a grin, Ikele chuckling an instant after.

Phana looked at each of them, one by one.

"I thought I had friends here."

"You do," Sotai said, standing up and pulling over an empty chair from another table. He gave a look at the others, but they met his gaze, challenge in their eyes.

It had been a mistake to come here. She had known these people for years, though she didn't see them very often. Danz had never been particularly friendly, but he wasn't friendly with anyone other than Neysi. The others had always welcomed her. Had word about the Wolf's Den already spread out through the guild?

"So what have you brought?" asked Sotai.

"And what's it going to cost us?" Ikele murmured just loud enough for Phana to hear. An instant later she glanced at Neysi like a beaten dog looking for approval.

Phana's patience was worn thin from the events of the past few days. She had never been one to back down from a challenge, and she certainly wasn't going to accept snide remarks from people she had thought were her friends.

"What is the problem?" she asked. "It's not the first time we've gotten drunk together in here. Why are you being so hostile tonight?"

Danz continued to frown at her, but at least Ikele seemed rebuked by Phana's question. Neysi leaned forward and rested her arms on the table as she met Phana's gaze.

"You bring trouble," she said. "You're bad luck. I heard about what happened with your last gang—"

"You heard rumors," Phana said, interrupting her. "You know the streets have their own truth, and it changes depending on who's doing the telling."

"Maybe so, maybe not. You can't deny your last gang don't exist anymore. You can't say a bunch of them didn't die."

"Some of them at your own hand," Danz added.

"Qudovo had a temper, sure. I don't deny that," Neysi continued. "And maybe you were just defending yourself. But he said you were to blame for what happened to his gang. And what happened to his gang … well, it did happen."

"I did what he asked me to do," Phana said flatly. "He asked me to bring Jadir into the gang …."

She stopped as all of them—Sotai included—raised a hand with middle finger and thumb making a circle, a gesture that was supposed to ward off evil.

"I don't know what gift you brought," Neysi continued. "And I don't wanna know. I want no part of it. Because trouble follows you, and others pay the price for it. We share in your gift, and something bad is gonna come through that door."

She gestured at the Red Flag's entrance.

"And after it's done, you'll walk away fine, but we'll all be dead."

Phana looked at each of them one more time. This time, Sotai wouldn't meet her gaze and just stared at the rough wood of the table's surface. She adjusted the straps of the pack on her shoulders. The amphora hung on her back, a useless weight dragging her down. She should never have bothered with it.

At least it's helping me see how people really feel about me.

She gritted her teeth and stood up straight, looking down at the others.

"I'm not going to apologize for what happened. Qudovo used me to get what he wanted, and now I'm being blamed because he was too weak to handle it. None of you know what really happened, but I'm not going to waste my time explaining it you. You've already made up your minds. Believe what you want."

She turned and walked out of the Red Flag. The sky had darkened fully over the city, and the sense of dread had returned. Maybe whatever was coming would crush Ythis. Maybe that's exactly what the world needed.

*   *   *

THE CLICK OF THE LATCH HERALDED THE RETURN OF KEYNTER. He stepped through the door, and Saeda entered behind him. She looked tired, but her eyes lit up as she saw Laita. She saluted, but Laita leaped to her feet and clasped the woman's other arm in a tight grip.

Keynter pushed the door closed and returned to his bedroll to sit with Addiru and Pilayni, who were in the middle of a dice game, idly wasting time as they waited for their next orders, as soldiers learn to do.

Namal came over and clasped Saeda's arm in greeting before returning to one of the chairs.

"Commander, it's good to see you here in Ythis," Saeda said.

"Thank you. At ease, of course," Laita said, leading Saeda to the table and indicating that she should sit.

Saeda had dark bags under her eyes, and she was thinner than normal. It had apparently been a long trip to Ythis.

"It's good to see you too, Saeda."

"Thank you, commander. I'm glad you made it safely into the city."

"It went well enough, considering this oppressive weight that hangs over Ythis. Have you heard anything about what is causing it?"

"Endless rumors, each one more apocalyptic than the last," Saeda replied. "Some think it's the sorcerers of Ythis—apparently there are six of them now—summoning some kind of all-powerful demon. Others say that the god of Ythis is about to come fully through the portal and consume the world. A few believe it heralds the return of the old gods."

"So no one knows, then."

"Not that I have managed to hear, though it would be unlikely that none of those groups have anything to do with it."

Laita sat back in her chair. It was yet another unknown element that might affect their mission. Not that they had any way to do anything about it at this point. This was not the first such strange occurrence in Ythis, and there was no way to know the cause until something blatant happened in front of witnesses.

Back before she was assigned to the mission in the northern mountains, she had been briefed on a problem in Ythis involving a titanic beast that had appeared in the Bay of Ythis and consumed ships until—so the stories went—the sorcerers and the priests banded together and waged a magical battle against the creature to drive it away from the city. She had been relieved that the Legion hadn't needed to get involved. And there were always more stories about Ythis. Most of them were probably exaggerations at the least, or perhaps complete fabrications.

This was real, though. She had felt it last night and it had returned in force as the sun went down. Still, there was nothing she could do about it.

"We'll focus on the mission at hand," she said to Saeda. "And we'll deal with the unexpected when we have no other choice."

Saeda gave a curt nod.

"How many of our people have made it into the city?"

"Between Bor and I, we've made contact with ninety who have reached Ythis and found a place to stay. They are blending in, and many have found manual labor jobs that allow them to travel across the city and observe the Watch and the Imperial Guard without arousing suspicion."

"Good," Laita said, her mind on the other roughly one hundred who had not yet made contact. She couldn't expect that they would all have reached Ythis by now. They would trickle in over the next couple of weeks, depending on the route they had taken down from the north.

"Any sign of a local resistance group?"

"Nothing so far. We've not been reaching out, though. We're trying to maintain a low profile for now, just in case. But the Imperial Guard has a major presence here. If there is a resistance, I expect that it's going to be small, distributed, and very hard to reach."

It was a good assessment. There was too much of a threat, not just from the Guard but from the sorcerers and the Church. Anyone opposing the Emperor would be paranoid and extremely careful. Her force might have to complete its mission without any assistance from locals.

"Okay, we have several priorities. First, we need to get our weapons and armor. Second, we need to find what information we can on the fortress and the palace, so that we know exactly how we're going to reach our target. Third, we need to keep making contact with our people as they enter the city and get them settled somewhere without drawing attention. The more of us we have here, the more hazardous this gets. And finally, if we can make contact with a local resistance group, we'll do so and see what assistance they can give us.

"You continue to manage the new arrivals—you're doing a fine job so far. Namal will contact the local crime guild and find out where our equipment is being held. Cedaro—he's the innkeeper here—can point me to sources of information on the buildings, and he might be able to help us with the locals as well. I'll take care of those for now."

Saeda nodded and opened her mouth, but then closed it again.

"Speak your thoughts, Saeda."

"They're going to figure it out," she said after a moment's consideration. "It's impossible to hide the trails of so many soldiers. They'll figure out that we came here—or at least that some of us came here. And no matter how big Ythis is, there are going to be nearly two hundred Legionnaires hiding out. If the Legion comes here in force, someone is going to get recognized."

"It's only a matter of time," Laita finished for her. "You're right, it is."

"We might not be able to wait for everyone to reach the city, commander. We might have to launch our assault before we're at full strength. And if the Legion realizes why we are in the city, the Imperial Guard will lock up the Fortress and it'll be nearly impossible to reach our target."

Saeda spoke in a calm and even manner, but her words showed how worried she was about their mission. It all hung by a thread, and one small mistake could spell disaster.

"We've still got a bit of time. Even if the Legion has managed to track some of the squads, they must consider the very distinct possibility that we've laid a false trail. Remember, Ellend has taken a few squads who *are* laying a false trail to the east as well. The Legion won't know which one is our real destination. And even if they figure out we're coming to Ythis, the most likely conclusion is that we're searching for ships to take us out of the Empire."

Saeda nodded again, but the look in her eyes didn't change.

"And if we must launch our assault without our entire force, then that's what we'll do. We're Legionnaires and we overcome terrible odds as a matter of course. If the situation changes, we will adapt."

She leaned forward to look into Saeda's eyes.

"But we still have time. We're going to move quickly now that we're here, and once we gather what we need, I will design a plan that can be executed at a moment's notice. We know what the threat is, and we know our own weaknesses. That's an advantage our enemies don't have."

Keynter, Pilayni and Addiru had stopped their game and were watching her, listening to her words.

They needed reassurance, too. Even more so, because they were not, in truth, part of the command squad. Those three were just common soldiers, and were not generally privy to these kinds of briefings.

During their trip down from the mountains, Namal had privately express his concern with the three others.

"They're young soldiers playing at being spies or some such. It's exciting to them and they don't realize how much danger they're really in."

Laita saw now that Namal was wrong. They knew. They simply chose to pretend it didn't exist. Otherwise, they might not have the nerve to do what needed to be done. And they needed her to remain strong, to remain confident—to remain a leader.

She was no stranger to responsibility, and she didn't fear it. She would be the leader they needed her to be.

And because she knew how small their chances of victory really were.

Tenth day of Highsummer,
9 days to the Arrival

Chapter Five

RELAEL OCHALLUM STEPPED AROUND THE CORNER INTO a dimly lit side passage and leaned against the wall. The smooth white marble felt cool even through his robes. He held his breath and listened carefully, but heard no footfalls nearby. Taking a deep breath, he tried to control the shudders that ran through his body.

If anyone should come upon him like this ….

He closed his eyes and ran through a series of mental exercises designed to bring clarity and focus. Control slowly began to return to him. His trembling hands steadied, and he could feel his heartbeat slowing to its normal rhythm.

Taking a final deep breath, he straightened and turned to face the main corridor. Stepping out, his soft shoes whispering across the polished tiles, he glanced furtively around to make sure no one had noticed his struggle. Only a few young acolytes were scurrying about on various errands, their simple black robes with the white trim hanging loose over their thin frames. They knew better than to pry into the affairs of a priest.

He proceeded to the corridor that curved away from this hallway, his own black robes rustling as he walked. A pair of Church soldiers stood at attention at the mouth of the corridor. Twenty paces beyond them, a pair of heavy stone doors, painted blood-red with golden handles, blocked the path. The soldiers looked Relael over and nodded to him—they knew he had been summoned.

Moving down the corridor to the stone doors, he hesitated. Relael was not, in truth, a priest of Iathephos, though very few within the Church knew the difference. The thought of the god in the vast cavern deep in the earth below his feet caused a gnawing of worry at his belly once more. If he stepped through this door, he might not come back out.

He was finding it more difficult to hide the problem from others, especially other members of his own sect. The priests of the Hidden relied on their mental acuity, and their very sanity, to protect the Church from all its enemies. Anyone within its ranks who displayed any signs of madness were culled swiftly and without mercy.

The members of the Hidden were not true priests, and did not commune with their god. For to do so ultimately, and inevitably, shattered the mind. Mortals could not comprehend the full reality of their deity without losing grip on their sanity. As priests rose through the ranks of the Church, the outward manifestations of their twisted psyches became more pronounced, more visible, and more difficult to manage.

The Hidden acted to guide the leaders of the Church, to perform functions that required a sound mind and careful planning.

And now Relael was about to meet face to face with High Counselor Assirra Untoleu, a legendary figure, one of the founders of the Church at the dawn of the Empire. Some said that she shared the gift of immortality with the Undying Emperor himself. A woman of exquisite beauty and immense power, the High Counselor of the Hidden was the true mind of the Church.

Relael had been a member of the secretive sect of the Hidden for many years, had dedicated his life to keeping the Church strong, both inside and out.

At least until the day he had come face-to-face with a god.

Last year, some kind of great tentacled horror had come to reside within the waters of the Bay of Ythis. It demanded blood sacrifice from any ships entering or leaving the city, and Iathephos had seemingly been unconcerned with its presence.

But the creature had caused no end of difficulties for the city. Too many ship captains had stopped coming to Ythis, not willing to gamble their ships and their lives for the profits they could make here. Other cities had been only too eager to welcome the trade. Relael himself had been tasked by the Church with finding a way to drive it away from Ythis, using whatever methods were necessary.

Ultimately, he been forced to work with the sorcerers of Ythis, known at the time as the Five (now Six), rivals with the Church for power within the Undying Empire. One of the servants of the sorcerer Veylar Dust had figured out the beast in the waters was the offspring of Iathephos—a terrifying prospect in itself. The priests had used the power of their god to convince the creature to leave the waters of the bay and go somewhere else.

During that confrontation, Relael had seen the godling in all its terrible glory—had been directly confronted with the vast, alien power of that being. And in that moment, a seed had been planted deep within his psyche, a seed that had begun to sprout and grow, sending creeping vines of alien thoughts into his mind.

Relael's iron grip on his very sanity was slipping. A rot had begun, and there was no cure, no escape, from the inevitable descent. He knew he wouldn't live long enough to go fully insane, of course, for the other members of the Hidden would recognize the signs soon enough.

He knew too many secrets to be left to his own devices. Upon discovery of his problem, Relael would be slain without hesitation.

His was loyal to the Church and he knew he should report himself to his superiors. He was a weak link in the chain that bound the Hidden to their purpose. He knew his duty.

But he couldn't do it. He wasn't ready to die for the Church, not yet. And so he continued to hide any sign of his problem. Most days were still easy—he hadn't fallen very far yet. But on some days, especially in times of great stress, he found it more and more difficult to function.

He had a feeling today was going to be the most difficult by far.

The massive stone door swung open with the gentlest of pushes, and he stepped into the office on the other side. Two more Church soldiers stood guard here before a second red stone door. To one side, a heavy desk was covered with papers, behind it a bald man in priest robes who was watching him with dead eyes.

"Brother Ochallum," he said with the slightest sneer.

"Brother Shuyaja," Relael acknowledged.

The assistant to the High Counselor of the Hidden was a snake of a man, ready to hold his position over anyone he considered a rival. Of course, this included Relael.

"The High Counselor has requested my presence."

"I am well aware of that," Shuyaja snapped. Relael looked at him evenly, letting no emotion show on his face.

A moment passed between the two men, but Relael refused to give him anything to latch onto. Shuyaja snapped his lips and moved to the other door and rapped softly. There was the faintest murmur from behind the heavy portal.

Even that barely heard utterance was enough to send a tingle down his spine. He gritted his teeth. He could do this.

He *had* to do this.

Shuyaja pushed the door open and Relael stepped across the threshold. A weight fell upon him, the air itself thick with the power of her. He tried to take a breath and the scent of her filled his senses, like nothing else in the world, a heady mixture of flowers and sex and something else he couldn't quite identify.

He felt a stirring in his groin, and he clenched his fists and kept his eyes on the large desk of dark wood that dominated the room. He was dimly aware of the door closing behind him.

"I have a task for you," she said, her voice cutting through his thoughts and bringing him to full awareness of her. His eyes snapped up and he saw the long golden hair, the pale skin, and the eyes that were a blue so vivid he almost winced at the vibrancy of her.

"You will find someone in Ythis for me. She is...."

The High Counselor hesitated and Relael swallowed. Something about her seemed ... wrong. Her eyes darted away from him and around the room, as if she was searching for the right word and didn't know where it had hidden itself. The corners of her mouth tightened slightly and Relael's heart nearly stopped.

But her annoyance wasn't directed at him.

"I cannot give you a name, for she will not be using the name or the title by which I know her. She does not know who she is. She is here in Ythis and she has a power within her, one which she used recently."

Relael's thoughts immediately went to the young witch Marilsa. As if reading his thoughts, the High Counselor gave the smallest shake of her head as she looked down at her desk.

"It is not witchcraft, nor sorcery. It is something else. She cannot have unleashed this power without others seeing it or feeling it. There will be stories, rumors of some kind of unnatural cold or ice. Track down those rumors, find the person who wielded that power."

The tremble began in his fingers and he knew it was over. He couldn't get a full breath in the thick air, and the scent of her filled his head. She was acting strangely, and it was all too much. She could see him, could see his struggle.

But she wasn't looking at him. She was staring across the large office to the shelf of books and rolled parchments against the far wall.

"You may use your contacts, but you must tell no one of the reasons behind your search for this woman. No one, not even other members of the Hidden. Find her and bring her directly to me. Or if you cannot bring her here, then tell me where she is and I will go myself."

He saw her hands, the pale skin stretched over her knuckles as she clenched her fists while they rested on the top of the desk. They stood out on the dark wood, almost glowing with an inner light.

The tremble in his fingers grew stronger and he wondered if his face was showing his distress.

She raised her hand and waved him off, still not so much as glancing in his direction. He spun on his heel and grabbed wildly for the handle of the door, his entire hand shaking. With a desperate pull, he heaved it open and marched from her office.

He dimly heard Shuyaja ask him a question as he crossed to the outer doors, but he fled the room without a backward glance. A quiet hallway, a nook, somewhere out of sight of prying eyes. Regain control, return to his office, send messages out to his network. One step at a time and he could continue to serve her … and the Church.

If some kind of power had been used out on the streets of Ythis, there would be witnesses. Rumors would have already started to spread, and the story would grow in the telling.

His duty now was to find the seed of truth in those rumors, to follow the trail back to the source, to identify the woman who had wielded that power.

She would not be able to hide forever. It was only a matter of time.

$$*\qquad*\qquad*$$

DOZENS OF SHIPS BOBBED ON THE LOW WAVES ACROSS THE WATERS of the bay. Great cargo ships, coastal skiffs, passenger transports, a pair of Imperial Navy patrol ships, and more all anchored off the coast of the greatest city of the Empire, waiting for their turn to use the always busy wharves.

The Legion military transport that had just pulled up to the stone quay was small and fast, a light boat designed to move messages and key military personnel, not full detachments of soldiers. The captain brought his ship smoothly alongside the dock and a cluster of dockworkers grabbed the ropes and secured her to the moorings.

Investigator Hinara Angumu stepped up onto the stone wharf, his four aides following in a line behind him. The ship's crew heaved five heavy packs onto the wharf, and the captain blew three short blasts on his whistle. The ropes were untied and drawn back onto the ship, and within moments the ship was away again, the sails rising to catch the wind and send it skimming toward the entrance to the bay.

Hinara looked up and down the docks at the thick crowds, an endless sea of humanity focused on their next task, their next destination, their next meal. His eyes flickered over the large warehouses, the small shops and taverns, and the stone tower of the dockmaster.

"They are here," he said in a low voice.

"Sir?" asked the young man directly behind him. Hinara turned to his aides.

"They are here," he repeated, loud enough to be heard over the babble of voices around them. "Or they will be, soon enough."

He turned back to the docks to see a pair of Imperial Guard soldiers striding toward him, the crowd unconsciously parting for the armed and armored figures. Their breastplates gleamed in the morning sunlight and their boots were polished to high sheen despite the filth that lay across the great stone blocks of the quay. Both men stopped a few paces away from Hinara and saluted.

"Investigator Angumu?" one of them asked. He was a large man, muscular with short dark hair and a neatly trimmed beard, his skin bearing the faint reddish tint of the western provinces. Hinara returned the salute.

"I am. I take it you are to escort me to the Fortress?"

"I'm Sergeant Danashy," the man replied, nodding. "I have horses waiting for you and a wagon for your gear."

He gestured across the crowded quay to where another pair of Guard soldiers were standing at the corner of one of the streets leading north, holding the reins of three horses. A wagon was pulled to one side of the street behind them.

Hinara motioned for his aides to grab the heavy packs and follow, and they all threaded their way back through the bustle. Hinara pulled himself into a saddle as the sergeant did the same.

"Mount up," he said, pointing at Jiska, the young man who was Hinara's personal aide. The other three Legion soldiers tossed the packs into the wagon and then climbed in as well.

The sergeant rode beside Hinara as they proceeded north into the city. The streets were crowded with people and heavily laden wagons, and the going was slow. Sergeant Danashy spoke loudly over the noise.

"You've been given a room to use as an office in the fortress. A junior Guard soldier has been assigned to help with directions and arranging any supplies you may need. I'm your liaison if you require the help of the Imperial Guard itself."

Hinara glanced sideways at the soldier. The man's manner was professional, but not friendly. Perhaps he resented being assigned this duty. Perhaps he did not realize he had the opportunity to assist in the apprehension of a traitor to the Empire.

"I do have some immediate requests, sergeant, regarding the gates to the city. The renegade former Legionnaires will soon begin trying to infiltrate Ythis, if they have not already started. I do not want them stopped at the gate."

The sergeant glanced over at Hinara.

"Why wouldn't you want them stopped and arrested on the spot?"

"Because you will only catch a few, and then they will look for some other way into the city. No, if there are any traitors already here, I need to know where they are hiding. I will have a few of my men stationed at the gates each day. They are trained to blend in, to look and act like commoners. If the traitors come into the city, my people will follow them and find out where they are staying. We will sweep them up all at once."

They rode in silence for a few moments before the sergeant looked over again.

"I have to ask, Investigator, what makes you think they'll come to Ythis? They can catch a ship out of the Empire from any number of cities along the coast."

"The former commander of the detachment, Laita Naschect, is out for revenge, sergeant. She will not flee the Empire, not yet anyway. She was turned against the Legion by her lover, a man who was subsequently killed in battle. She blames the Emperor."

"And you think she'll come here and … what? Attack the Emperor's palace? She must know that's suicide. Even former Legionnaires won't be able to fight their way into the Palace and reach the Emperor. The Fortress is right there—the entire Imperial Guard would be on them before they could fight their way a dozen paces into the Palace."

As if Hinara needed it all explained to him. This was why the Legion had such a low opinion of the soldiers of the Imperial Guard. They all thought they were the elite military of the Empire, when they were really all just for show. When a war needed to be fought, it was the Legion who was called to action.

Maybe he should explain it to this man, show him how little he knew.

"I do not yet know Naschect's ultimate goal. I doubt she will try for the Emperor himself. Even were she to win through to him, he is called the Undying Emperor for a reason. No, I am sure she has something else in mind. But the force she took with her could cause a great deal of hardship for the city, perhaps cripple it for some time."

"And how did you figure out she was coming here, Investigator?

Did you manage to capture some of her followers?"

The sergeant's tone was casual, but it didn't fool Hinara. He understood the situation well enough to know the man did not believe his conclusions. Hinara's own superiors had been doubtful of his pronouncement that Laita Naschect was coming to Ythis. They had eventually allowed him to come here himself. But, aside from his personal aide and the others who reported directly to him, he was on his own here. He could ask the Imperial Guard for help, but it was up to them to decide how much help they would give and what form it would take.

He could ask, but he could not order. And they were under no obligation to assign any resources to him.

Within the Legion, the prevailing belief was that Naschect was taking her force out of the Empire. She would form them into a mercenary company, perhaps in the southern kingdoms, or on the western continent that was so far away it took almost three months of sailing to reach it. Until Hinara could get real evidence of her presence here in Ythis, his theory was considered, at best, a remote possibility.

"Laita Naschect was an instructor at the main Legion barracks when I joined. She taught me herself, and she was the person who recommended me for the path to Investigator. I know her, and I knew her lover—the barracks was where they met, in fact. They thought to keep their affair a secret, but I was already good at my job, long before I became an Investigator in rank."

"So you don't have any real intelligence that says they're coming here, then. It's just a hunch."

Hinara's fingers tightened on the reins. This bastard was dismissing him without even listening. He imagined punching the smug expression off Danashy's face, beating him until he was broken and bloody.

No, it would not be productive to lose control here, in public, so soon after arriving. He would have time later to take it out on some beggar in the streets, or perhaps a whore. He smiled grimly. There were some advantages to being in a large city like Ythis. No one would miss one more piece of human filth.

Life should be neat and tidy, and this city was a cesspool. It would do him good to get out some of his frustrations later tonight, perhaps tomorrow at the latest. There had been no opportunity to straighten things out while on the ship, and he'd nearly killed Jiska at one point, grabbing the young man by the throat and choking him until he was almost unconscious. It would not do to slay his own personnel, though. He was glad he had managed to stop himself in time.

Frustrations aside, he needed this sergeant to believe him. The man was the key to getting the Imperial Guard mobilized once Hinara found proof that Laita Naschect was here.

He looked over at the man.

"I know Laita Naschect, sergeant. I know how she thinks. And I can tell you with absolute certainty, she is coming to Ythis."

Chapter Six

THE FLY LANDED ON THE SCARRED SURFACE OF THE WOODEN table and rubbed its front legs together. It had no awareness of the doom about to end its short life. It couldn't recognize the danger—could only react and try to escape when it eventually saw death coming for it.

Phana slammed her hand down on the table, crushing the insect.

She wondered how many hands had tried to kill that fly in this tavern. The fly might have lived longer had it picked a different table on which to land.

Are we all like that? Phana asked herself. *Buzzing around in our lives, going from meal to meal, mating when and where we can, always with danger all around us. We manage to dodge death over and over until our lives are snuffed out by the hand of fate that is too fast to escape.*

She picked up her tankard and tipped it up, but only the smallest dribble of ale touched her tongue. She had been drinking since midday, yet she was still too clear-headed for her liking. Maybe she needed something stronger.

She heard the door to the tavern open, but didn't look up. Instead, she raised her hand and stared at the crushed fly on the table. She wiped her fingers on her leggings and considered what she should drink next. Whiskey might do what ale could not.

"Can I sit down?"

Raising her head, she found Koral standing by her table. She blinked at him, not knowing how to respond—his presence was completely unexpected. But he waited until she gathered her wits, shrugged and gestured to the other chair.

She looked back down at the dead fly as he sat.

"I was looking for you yesterday," he said.

She shrugged again, not raising her eyes from the fly's crushed body.

"Look, I—I'm sorry about what happened the other night. I don't have a right to tell you what to do. But I worry about your safety. I can't help it. As good as you are, eventually you're going to run into someone who's better. And if that person has been hired to hurt you …."

The fact that Koral's statement mirrored her own thoughts from a few moments ago didn't do much to help her mood.

He leaned forward over the table and spoke in a low voice.

"The Wolf gave me a message to pass on to you."

Phana raised her head and looked Koral in the eyes. She held her tongue, knowing if she spoke, she would say something sharp and hurtful.

"Phana, he asked me to apologize to you on his behalf. He had intended to get the message to you before you arrived at the Wolf's Den, but other things got in the way. Sometimes events move faster than we'd like."

She crossed her arms and leaned back in her chair.

"Is that it?" she asked.

"No. The Wolf is concerned about you. He says that a connection between you two could be as much a danger to you as it might be to him. He hasn't cut you loose, but he needs the appearance of some distance from you."

"If he's so worried about my safety, then he should realize that pushing me away might just put a big target on my back."

Koral shook his head.

"Officially, you're still part of the guild. But you're already close to him because you're close to me. He just wants it to appear as if I'm the *only* connection. Other than your relationship with me, you're just another gang member he's never met in person."

It all seemed so reasonable, of course. But was it really? Not that there anything she could do about it. The Wolf would do what he wanted. He held all the power.

Koral was looking at her with an expression of such earnestness that she couldn't help but smile. He looked worried that she would refuse to accept his explanation and take it out on him.

He saw her smile and grinned back at her.

It was such an effortless transition for him, from worrying to charming. Again, she wondered if anything he showed her was real. He was too good at controlling his emotions. She tried to crush the thought.

"So what happened to all that wine you acquired?" he asked casually.

"I threw it into the Bay of Ythis."

His eyes widened for a moment and then his shoulders slumped.

"You didn't want it," she accused him with another shrug of her shoulders.

"I never said that," he replied. "I was just worried—"

"The amphora is in my room," she said. He gave a relieved laugh.

Still grinning, he said "You know, I'm not working until later tonight."

Before her thoughts could get in the way, she stood, grabbed his arm, and pulled him to his feet.

"Let's go," she said.

By the time they reached her apartment, she no longer wanted the wine. The instant the door was closed, Phana shoved Koral up against the wall and kissed him hard. In seconds, they were tearing at each other's clothes, all thoughts of the wine evaporating.

Phana pulled Koral over to her bed and threw him down on his back, climbing on top of him as he struggled to kick his trousers off his feet. He pulled her down and kissed her passionately as she slid her hand down to his groin and gripped him hard. He let out a moan as she guided him between her legs and then he was inside her.

She ground herself against him as his hands grabbed her breasts, and she increased her pace, back and forth. She let his hands roam over her body while she rode him, feeling the climax build within her until it peaked and burst as she arched her back and yelled out, an inarticulate sound from deep in her chest.

The next couple of hours were spent on her pallet, ignoring the world outside the small room. At some point they broke open the seal on the amphora and shared the wine Phana had stolen, and then returned to their lovemaking. Eventually, they found they were too spent to continue and Koral fell asleep on his back with Phana's arm draped across his chest.

She stared at him as he slept, watching the muscles of his face completely at rest. He was always on edge when awake, always tense as if ready for a fight. Was it the responsibility of his job that caused so much strain? Was it his relationship with the Wolf? Was it his relationship with *her*?

The Wolf was surrounded by mystery and rumor. Even Koral, as one of the most highly trusted people in the guild, knew little about the man for whom he worked. The Wolf was an enigma, brilliant and ruthless, but also honorable and generous. He was a keeper of secrets, a collector of knowledge, and his goals were an enigma.

And what of Koral himself? Did Phana know the real Koral, or did he guard himself with her the way she saw him do with the other members of the Wolf's guild? At one point, he had been ordered to look out for her. Was Koral making the best of this *assignment* he'd been given?

At least she was confident she had made her own choice to be with Koral. It didn't matter that the Wolf was a master manipulator. It *had* been her choice, no one else's.

And yet, she kept circling back to the Wolf's interest in her. He had plans for her, that much she was sure. He knew more about her, about her past, than she did. She had no doubt that he had answers she needed, and he would hold onto them until it suited him to provide them to her.

In the meantime, Koral was here to ....

No, that line of thought was horrible. She wasn't being fair to the man sleeping here beside her. He had done nothing to give her cause for doubt.

So why couldn't she stop thinking about it?

*   *   *

AS HE WAS GETTING READY TO LEAVE, KORAL CAUGHT PHANA looking at him with a pensive expression.

"What's wrong?" he asked her.

She blinked at him and gave a small shrug of her shoulders.

"Nothing, probably. Well, I think I'm finally hitting my limit of that sense of doom that's been hanging over the city."

Koral was surprised by her words. The feeling of dread had the entire city on edge. The Wolf had told Koral that those sensitive to such things had called it a "wave of darkness and chaos" building over the city.

He'd had no idea that the feeling hadn't had that much of an effect on Phana before now.

"Do you know what it is?" he asked her.

She shook her head and climbed off her bed, grabbing her leggings. He tried not to let himself be distracted by her body, but the way she moved made it impossible for him to hold onto a coherent thought.

"It's like something is coming, and it's big," she said. "I know a lot of people are afraid to go out at night."

He nodded at her as she continued to get dressed.

"Yes," he said noncommittally. "But not you."

"I've been aware of it, but you know how I am. Not much scares me."

He knew if he continued to question her on what exactly she was feeling she'd pick up on the fact that he was hunting for information. He didn't want to spoil the great afternoon they'd just spent together.

"Do you have any idea what it is?" she asked him, and the casual tone in her voice belied the fact she was now pressing *him* for any information he might share.

"Nothing so far," he answered honestly. "But I would bet the Six, or the Church, have more information. If it's bugging people like us, I can only imagine how strong it must be for them."

Phana, now fully dressed, came over and gave him a kiss.

"Be careful," she said. "Don't let it distract you from your job. That's dangerous enough as it is."

Koral grinned at her.

"Someone should take her own advice."

Phana frowned, and he kissed her to take the sting out of his words.

"I promise I'll be careful," he told her. "I haven't survived this long by being foolish."

He left her apartment and headed for the Crown and Coin. By the time he arrived, he was starving. He asked Elmther to send some food into his office, and then made his way to the back room.

A couple of minutes later, there was a knock on the door. He opened it, expecting it to be the serving girl with his dinner, but instead four figures were standing in the doorway. Koral immediately recognized them as leaders of four of the gangs in the city, all working under the authority of the Wolf.

Bejral stood at the front, with the others arrayed behind him. The smallest of the four, Bejral was a weasel who had managed to connive his way to leadership of a gang. They were one of the weakest, least profitable gangs in the city, but so far Bejral had done nothing particular to justify his removal as gang leader.

"Good evening, Bejral. I take it you've come to see me about something important?"

The man nodded once.

"It is. We all wanna talk to you."

Koral stepped back and motioned for them to enter the back room. Bejral entered and moved around the small table to stand with his back to the far wall.

Behind Bejral, Frichim entered. He was a quiet man with piercing eyes above a hawk nose. He ran his gang with ruthless efficiency and was rumored to be one of the deadliest knife fighters in the entire city.

Karrel came next, her long black hair pulled back from her face into a braid that hung halfway down her back. Her perpetual frown landed on Koral as she entered the room, as if she was judging him and found him wanting. He had never seen her with a different expression on her face in the dozen years he had known her.

Last in line was Gaitu. A tall man but skeletally thin, he was no friend of Bejral—the two gangs had been at odds for a long time—and the fact he was here with Bejral told Koral that this was no social call.

"Take a seat," Koral said. The small table in the center of the room had only four chairs. Bejral noticed and, while the others sat, motioned for Koral to take the last chair.

"No, I'll stand," Koral replied, looking the gang leader in the eyes. Bejral hesitated, and Koral could see him clench his jaw. He wanted Koral seated so that he wouldn't have to look up while he talked, but Koral had no intention of playing the other man's game. He gave Bejral an even look and waited.

Finally, Bejral grabbed the chair and sat down, his mouth twisted into a grimace.

"What brings you here, away from your gangs tonight?"

Bejral made to stand, but Koral motioned for him to stay seated.

"We want to talk to you about the woman," he said. Koral noted Karrel's eyes shift toward Bejral for an instant.

"Which woman is that?" he asked.

"Phana," and Bejral's mouth twisted as he said her name.

Koral hadn't expected this, but he hid his surprise.

"What about her?"

"We want to know why she's still working for the Wolf. She killed a bunch of the Wolf's people, *our* people, and used some kind of sorcery to do it. Why is she still alive?"

Koral looked at each of his visitors, his thoughts racing. He had heard the rumors, knew some people were now uncomfortable around Phana, but he hadn't expected this. Qudovo had been a madman. He had brought his fate upon himself by choosing to go against the Wolf. From that point, he had been a dead man, regardless of whether he had gone after Phana or not.

But he couldn't say that to Bejral and the others.

"You came all the way over here to talk to me about *this*?" he asked, letting just a hint of disbelief into his voice. "I didn't know you believed every rumor that made its way into your corner of the city."

"It's not just a rumor," Gaitu said in his low voice.

"Of course it is!" Koral snapped.

"Look, I know you and her … well, you got to stand up for her. But she killed a bunch of people from her last gang. That's not rumor, and you know it. Someone saw her, saw it happen. And it wasn't any normal fight. She's a sorcerer or a witch, or something like it."

"Except no one *did* see it," Koral argued. "It's always a friend of a friend who heard it from someone who was supposedly there. But you never hear from someone who saw the fight happen."

"We got a witness," Bejral said, his mouth now twisting into a smug grin. "Someone who saw it with their own eyes. No rumors, no stories. We know what she did."

Koral hesitated. Phana had never told him exactly what had happened that night. To his knowledge, there had been no witnesses, and he assumed she had killed Qudovo in a straight-up fight.

"You didn't know, did you?" Gaitu said.

"This is ridiculous," Koral replied. "Who is this witness of yours? Where is he? Why didn't you bring him here?"

The other four gang leaders all glanced at each other before Bejral spoke up.

"He's somewhere safe, where she can't get to him. You—"

"We came here first," Gaitu interrupted, "Out of respect for you. We don't always agree with what you decide, but you always play straight with us. So, we're playing straight with you. We have a guy who saw the whole thing. We want to bring this guy to the Wolf, but we know the Wolf had Phana under his protection. We weren't sure he would listen, or maybe something bad would happen to our guy."

Koral wanted to tell them that their fears were unfounded, but he knew it wasn't true. The Wolf would do what he felt necessary to ensure his plans were not disrupted. And if Phana was part of those plans, he wouldn't let anything happen to her.

Gaitu continued, "But now we hear the Wolf don't want her near him, won't let her into Nid's place. Now I think maybe he already knows what she did. And maybe he needs to hear that it don't sit right with the rest of us and he needs to do something about it."

"You man enough to do what needs to be done?" Bejral sneered at him.

Koral saw Gaitu and the others frown at Bejral, but he was facing Koral and didn't see their looks. They weren't here to provoke Koral—Gaitu was being honest when he said they respected him.

But Bejral respected no one. Some months back, Koral had ordered both Bejral and Gaitu to put their feud behind them. Bejral didn't like what he had been forced to do to make amends.

But the others were good leaders, and Koral understood that he couldn't just dismiss their concerns.

"Okay," Koral said. "You feel this witness is reliable?"

He met their eyes one by one in a silent challenge, and each of them nodded. Bejral snorted and said, "Fucking right, he is."

"Then I will take your request to the Wolf. I'll tell him there's a witness to what happened, and that there is concern among the gangs about Phana. If he agrees to hear the full story, I'll set up a meeting with all of you."

"And what if he doesn't?" asked Bejral.

"Then that's the end of it. Like it or not, you'll drop it and move on," Koral answered.

Bejral's face twisted in outrage and he took a deep breath, but Gaitu cut him off.

"That don't sit right with me, but I'm gonna to go against the Wolf. That would be stupid. But I've worked for the man for years now because he treats us with respect. You make it clear to him that it's not just us four. A lot of other gangs are unhappy, too. He's too smart to ignore us, or just order us to forget it."

Bejral was shaking his head.

"This was nothing! Koral won't just hand over his woman, and the Wolf won't listen to us. I told you!"

He stood up and faced Gaitu, who also pushed himself to his feet. The other two gang leaders started to rise, and Koral knew he had to head off what could turn into a fight.

"Enough!" he said, not loud but with all the authority he could muster. The others paused and looked at him, though Bejral was still ready to start fighting, his fists clenched and his shoulders hunched.

"I said I would take your concerns to the Wolf and do what I could to help you. My ... relationship ... with Phana isn't part of this. But you need to be realistic. The Wolf may kick Phana out of the guild, or he may not. Qudovo refused to cooperate with the Wolf, turned his back on the guild in order to pursue a vendetta against Phana. So, while I understand your concern, this isn't as simple as you thought."

Bejral turned to face Koral, his eyes wide.

"Yes, I'm telling you things you didn't need to know," Koral said to him. "It's none of your business. But this whole thing has grown too big to ignore. I will speak with the Wolf, and you will go back to your gangs. I will send a message to each of you once I have a decision from him. You can either accept that, or you can choose to go against the Wolf."

He looked Bejral in the eyes.

"But I think you know what that means."

Bejral opened his mouth to speak, but Koral stepped past him and opened the door into the main tavern. The four gang leaders stood there for a moment, and then Gaitu nodded and walked out, followed by Karrel and Frichim.

Bejral stared at Koral, his eyes narrowed. Koral knew the man was debating with himself if he wanted to push a confrontation. But he knew what would happen to him if he set himself against the Wolf.

His mouth twisting into a grimace once more, Bejral walked out.

Koral pulled the door closed and let out the breath he had been holding. He leaned against the wall and pressed his palms to his temples.

The timing of this could not possibly have been worse.

Chapter Seven

CEDARO POURED A SHOT OF WHISKEY INTO EACH OF THE brown ceramic cups, stoppered the bottle, and set it down on the top of the wooden crate. Laita took one and he took the other.

"To absent friends," he said with a sad smile. Laita knew he was referring to her parents, but it was also a common toast in the military, and she had more than enough absent friends to echo the sentiment.

Laita took a sip of the whiskey, rolling it around in her mouth to pick up the flavors. She swallowed and leaned back against the wall. The two of them stood in one corner of the cellar, outside the hidden room where Namal and the others waited, poring over rough maps of the city that Cedaro had brought them.

"I've put out some feelers," the innkeeper told her. "I've heard the very occasional rumor that a group of Ythis citizens have banded together against the Emperor. But nothing concrete. Of course, I never bothered pursuing the matter any further before now, so don't even know if the rumors are true."

"One can hope," Laita replied, picking up the bottle to pour them each another shot.

"I trust the person I've asked to look into it. If there's a way to make contact, he'll find it for me. He also knows better than to ask why I'm suddenly interested."

Laita had to suppress her urge to tell Cedaro to be careful. She trusted him, and had to trust his judgement when it came to talking to those people in Ythis that he knew, and she didn't.

He took a sip of his own whiskey and slowly placed the cup back down on the crate. Then his eyes met hers.

"When I received your message, I wasn't sure what to make of it. The young man who had brought it … I didn't know who he was—"

"One of my runners," Laita explained. "I sent him ahead because he's practiced at moving through enemy territory without drawing attention to himself. I knew he wouldn't get caught and he'd travel much faster than any of the squads."

Cedaro nodded.

"I understand that now. But I admit that I doubted what was in the letter. It was … I couldn't believe that you were a traitor."

"I'm not," she whispered.

"Not to the Empire, but to the Legion? Laita, you have turned on the Legion, and that makes you one, regardless of what is in your heart. You have good reasons for what you are doing, no doubt. That I believe with all my heart. But you must accept the fact that you have abandoned your oaths …."

Laita opened her mouth to protest, but Cedaro held up one hand to forestall her.

"… Or at least some of them. You have *chosen* to be an oathbreaker, though, and that is no small thing. The world is not kind to people who make such decisions. And it makes me worry for you even more."

Laita wanted to argue, to explain that she had no choice in her decision, but she forced herself to consider Cedaro's words. He wasn't judging her for choosing to desert the Legion. But he was reminding her that actions have consequences. She *was* an oathbreaker. And there were a hundred different superstitions about what happened to those who broke their oaths. Sure, some of them were nonsense. But many superstitions had started with a grain of truth somewhere.

"I was ready to help arrange passage for you on a ship," Cedaro said after a moment. "But you aren't planning to leave Ythis. Instead, you are here to do something. Something big, something dangerous."

She wanted to tell this man everything, but still she held back. It was her responsibility, and she wasn't ready to share it. If Kied had been here ….

No, she wouldn't go down that path. It led to nothing but sadness.

"When two oaths conflict with each other," she said softly, thinking through how much she was prepared to reveal to this man, "one of them must take precedence. If you must break one oath to keep another, then you must choose which is more important. And not just important to you, but to everyone you serve."

"And that is what you have done here," Cedaro said, understanding what she was trying to tell him. She nodded.

"I'm doing what *has* to be done. I have a chance to make a difference, to correct a wrong that is so big, I wouldn't be able to live with myself if I let it continue."

"And those who follow you feel the same way?"

Laita hesitated. She wanted to say, "yes, they all believe it as much as I do," but she knew that wasn't true. They wanted justice, sure. They wanted a better world than the one they had. But they followed her because it was *her*. She knew she commanded respect and loyalty through her own actions, and people followed her because they believed in her. They believed that she knew her purpose, and by following her it meant that maybe they knew their own purpose as well.

"They're too young," she murmured, not realizing she was saying it out loud.

"And so you have yet another oath, and another conflict."

Laita looked up at him, not understanding where he was going with this.

"You had an oath to the Legion, and if I'm understanding you correctly, it was in conflict with your oath to the people of the empire. It forced you to choose one over the other. But you also have an oath to the people who serve under you. Those people in that room, and the others scattered across the city, and the ones who are still coming here."

Cedaro took another drink, draining his cup, giving Laita a chance to digest his words. She understood his point, and waited for him to swallow the alcohol before she spoke.

"Are you suggesting that I should put the soldiers who chose to follow me above the entirety of the empire?"

Cedaro gave her a warm smile.

"I'm not suggesting anything. What I fear is that you are heading into an impossible situation in an attempt to justify to yourself your choice to leave the Legion. I understand that you couldn't follow orders that you knew to be wrong. That's the Laita I remember. But to leave the Legion, you had to break an oath. And now you have a decision. You could take these young people who follow you, and you could lead them away from the Empire. You could take them from the Legion and go somewhere else. That would also fulfill the need to only break an oath in order to keep a greater one."

"It's not an either/or decision, Cedaro. I'm not doing what I'm doing just to justify my desertion from the Legion. My desertion from the Legion is a *result* of my choice to do the right thing here in Ythis."

"Why do I feel that the cost of what you are going to do here in Ythis will be much greater than the breaking of an oath to the Legion, Laita? All those soldiers, all those *people*, who follow you—what will be the cost to them?"

Laita could feel anger welling up inside of her. Cedaro was supposed to understand her. He was supposed to support her choice. He was supposed to realize the sacrifice she was making for the people of the Empire.

"You think I should take my 'followers' and flee, don't you?"

She couldn't keep the accusatory tone from her voice. She worried that she was burning a bridge with this man. What would they do if he decided he couldn't support her choice to stay in Ythis? She didn't want to even consider her options here, the choices she might be forced to make to keep her mission and her people safe.

But Cedaro didn't seem to take offense. He picked up the bottle and poured another shot into his cup—Laita realized that she hadn't even finished her first—and continued to speak quietly and calmly to her.

"I can't say if you should flee the empire, Laita. I can't say, because I don't know what you're going to do in Ythis. Nor do I *want* to know. But as much as I support you, you know that I've always challenged you. I'm not in your Legion, and you're not my commander. You're the little girl I loved like you were my own daughter. And I fear for your safety. I've always worried about you, when you were out being a soldier. And now you're here, and I want nothing more than for you to become a part of my life again. If I had my way, you would stay here in Ythis and come to work right here in my inn."

Laita couldn't imagine working as a serving wench or—horror upon horrors—in the inn's kitchen.

"But I know that is not going to happen, and so my heart breaks for you. I look into your eyes and I see pain, my dear. And it kills me to see it, because you don't deserve pain."

Laita felt tears running down her cheeks, and she couldn't stop them. She had done so well avoiding thoughts of Kied, and the ache in her heart at his loss. And now she couldn't push it away any longer.

Cedaro reached out and Laita wrapped her arms around him. He brushed his hand down her hair and held her, and she wept quietly.

She wasn't sure how long they stood like that, but eventually she felt well enough to let go. She took a deep, unsteady breath and drained the whiskey in her cup, swallowing it without taking the time to taste it.

"You must be tired," she said to Cedaro.

"As long as you want to talk, I'm here to listen."

She tried to smile at him but knew she probably just looked sad, and reached for the bottle.

"Then I want to tell you about a man I knew named Kied."

*　　　　*　　　　*

THE RED FLAG WAS MOSTLY EMPTY WHEN NAMAL STEPPED THROUGH the door. A couple of drunks were sprawled face-down at one of the tables, and four thugs played cards at another. The bartender was an older man, lean and wiry, dark hair going gray.

Namal was dressed in his farmer clothes, and he weaved among the tables to the bar. Pulling up a stool, he sat down and leaned wearily on the top of the bar.

"New face," said the bartender, pausing in his cleaning of some cups behind the bar.

Namal didn't look directly at the man, keeping his eyes on the bar, pretending to be exhausted.

"Ale," he said, pulling out a small coin.

The bartender stepped over directly in front of Namal and said nothing. Namal raised his eyes and met the other man's gaze.

"I said, 'new face,'" the bartender repeated.

"My face is pretty fuckin' old," Namal answered back. "You servin' or not?"

"I don't know you."

"You know everyone in Ythis?" Namal asked.

The bartender leaned forward and sneered into Namal's face.

"This bar ain't *for* everyone in Ythis."

"Are you Danz?" Namal asked in a low voice.

"Are you stupid?" the bartender shot back. "I'm Lassadar."

He rested his fists on the top of the bar, making his elbows stand out to either side.

"Schurk," he said, waiting for Namal's reaction.

"That supposed to mean somethin' to me?"

Schurk blinked at him a couple of times, as if he couldn't believe Namal didn't recognize the name. Namal heard a couple of the chairs at the table near the door scape against the floor. He figured the four thugs were now watching what was happening at the bar. He didn't turn from looking at Schurk.

"Fine," Namal said, cutting off Schurk just as he opened his mouth. "You don't want my coin, I'll take it elsewhere."

He stood and turned to find the gang standing and blocking the way to the door.

Namal sighed and prepared for a fight. He had a knife in his boot, but wore no sword and no armor. He was no stranger to bar brawls, of course, and wasn't too worried if no one pulled a weapon. But if it got deadly, he knew he was in trouble.

"Who wants to go first?" he asked the thugs.

The biggest of the four, a bald man with skin like oak stepped forward.

"Who the fuck are you?" he asked in a deep baritone.

Namal hesitated. There was no bluster here. He had been told to see Danz at the Red Flag about getting their contingent's equipment smuggled into the city, and had assumed the bartender was the man he was looking for. But he realized he might be mistaken.

"I've made arrangements," he said in a low voice. "I'm here to see Danz."

"You didn't answer my question," the large man answered back. "Who. The fuck. Are you?"

Namal figured these four must work for the criminal guild in the city, and realized one of these was his contact, probably the big man. He wasn't going to tell anyone his name, and had preferred to do this quietly, but the situation had gone sideways and now he had to set it back in the right direction.

"I'm the guy who's payin' you to bring a shipment in off the *Emerald Elephant*. Now which one of you dumb fucks is Danz?"

The other man, smaller and perhaps younger than his large companion laughed out loud. Namal saw he had a friendly face, despite the scowl that he had been wearing a moment ago. The two women seemed surprised at Namal's tone. Perhaps they were used to people showing deference.

But Namal only gave respect to those who earned it.

One of the women spoke up.

"You don't get to call us names just 'cause you're paying. I'm about ready to slit your throat and let you bleed out in the alley, old man."

Namal almost let out a sigh of relief. Now he knew he was talking to the right people. He grinned at the four, and there was no humor in his expression.

"And I'm about ready to teach you all what happens when you mess with a professional. I don't have time to stand around with my dick in my hand, waiting for one of you to get wet. Where the fuck is my shipment? If you can't deliver it, maybe I should go talk to your boss."

Namal knew the head of the crime ring in the city was based out of a bar called the Wolf's Den, but he had no intention of going anywhere near there. The last thing they needed was a confrontation with the local thieves' guild. But it was usually an effective threat against the street-level goons.

He half expected one of the thugs to come at him, but the big one just nodded and looked at the others.

"He's okay."

The three others visibly relaxed and returned to their table.

"I'm Danz," the big man said to Namal. He gestured for Namal to sit down on the stool again, and he came over and leaned on the bar. Namal watched him warily, but the other man was relaxed and gave off no indication he was looking for a fight. Namal leaned on the stool, but didn't fully sit, just in case.

"The *Emerald Elephant* ain't here yet," Danz explained. "Not expected for another few days. We know about your shipment, and we'll put it in a nearby warehouse when it gets here."

"How will I know when it arrives?"

"I can send a message to wherever you're staying," Danz offered. Seeing the look on Namal's face, he nodded and said, "Okay, then you come back here in … give it three days just to be sure. We'll have your stuff."

"Do I have to go through all this bullshit again?"

Danz snorted, but Namal couldn't tell if it was a laugh or not—the man didn't seem capable of smiling.

"You think we just talk business with everyone who walks in that door? This is Ythis. You don't trust anybody until you know who they are. And then you still don't turn your back on them."

"I'll have to keep that in mind," Namal said pointedly. Danz gave him a look and Namal realized the big man was sizing him up.

"It's different when you're doing business. The Wolf never cheats his customers—it would be bad for his profits. But don't ever think about crossing him."

Danz looked Namal in the eyes and spoke very clearly.

"I mean that. Don't ever fuck with the Wolf. He's not just some local criminal who's managed to stab his way to the top. The Wolf is beyond any petty bullshit. He's the smartest guy you'll never meet, and he'll see you coming a week before you reach him. And by then you'll already be dead."

Namal could see Danz was not blustering—the man clearly feared this Wolf character. And this was Ythis, after all. If this guy had managed to take control of crime in the Empire's largest and most important city, where he had to be careful not just of the Watch, but of the Church and bunch of powerful sorcerers, then he wasn't just some tough thug.

"I'll remember that. But I don't intend to cross anyone. I'm payin' for a service, and if you hold up your end of the deal, I'll hold up mine."

"Then there won't be any problems," Danz confirmed. "Three or four days. Don't hang around here, either."

Namal gave him a nod and pushed himself upright.

"You got balls, old man, I'll give you that," Danz offered as Namal turned to leave. "You weren't intimidated at all."

Namal couldn't help but grin.

"I'll bet you're a beast in a fight," he offered to the large man. "But I've been slayin' beasts for a long, long time."

Danz just looked at him, and then turned back to his table where the others had restarted their card game.

Namal walked out into the street and turned into the first alley. It took him nearly an hour to make it back to the inn. By the time he got there, he had managed to control the trembling in his hands.

Eleventh day of Highsummer,
8 days to the Arrival

Chapter Eight

PHANA STOOD ON THE ROOF OF ONE OF THE STONE buildings that lined the vast, open square where the daily market sprawled each day from dawn to dusk. The merchants were long gone, having collapsed their simple stalls and packed up their merchandise as soon as the sun touched the horizon. Phana was always amazed at how quickly the market square emptied out, hundreds of merchants disappearing like ghosts, leaving nothing but dust and small bits of debris in their wake.

On the far side of the square was Slaves' Row, the street where the slave merchants plied their trade. The last of the day's slaves were being led away by Church soldiers, the final step in each day's trade of flesh.

The noble estates made their purchases at the opening of the markets each morning, picking out the best slaves—those with actual skills, or great muscle or endurance. Then came the merchant houses, buying up those not quite fit for the nobility but still able to work.

By midday, the best slaves were all gone, and the prices began to drop. The afternoon was much slower, as a few wealthy families, neither noble nor part of the merchant houses, picked out a few slaves to add to their households.

Perhaps an hour before dusk, the masters of the arena appeared, their servants carrying heavy chains and manacles. They picked out those last slaves who might be able to put up a fight when their lives were on the line, and paid only a fraction of what the best slaves had gone for earlier in the day.

When the arena masters left, the wailing began. For the final remaining slaves knew the fate that awaited them, and they cried out against it. Their pleas were all for naught, however. As the sun touched the horizon, the priests arrived with the Church soldiers. Those last few pitiful slaves were gathered by the soldiers and led away to the great temple in the heart of the city, to be given to Iathephos, the god who dwelt in its depths.

When Phana's mood was dark, she came to the market square and listened to the cries of the slaves echoing across the open space as the last merchants scurried off. She believed someone should bear witness to the voices of those doomed souls, and so she heard them and felt their anguish in her heart.

She hadn't seen Koral since he had left her apartment the day before due to his work for the Wolf, and her mood had sunk again shortly after departing his company. Her circle of friends was fast shrinking, and she had no idea what to do about it. She needed to spend time with other people who wanted to have her around, but she couldn't think of anyone who might be available.

Phana rolled her shoulders and took one long, last look over the empty market square. It seemed so lonely out there, the open space bereft of purpose through the long night.

She considered her options. If she wanted to be around people, the Warren should be her destination. On the other hand, the Nobles' District held more opportunities for mischief.

Someone is watching me.

Phana didn't know how she knew, but she didn't question the feeling. She dropped into a crouch and moved into the shadow of a chimney near the edge of the rooftop. Someone was out there, not on this roof, but definitely nearby.

An assassin? Possibly. Iadan Eorallo wouldn't have had time to hire anyone yet—she had only stolen his wine three nights ago. It would likely take a few more days before he could set anyone on her trail, and no one could have caught up to her so fast.

She thought about the other thefts she had done recently from noble houses. No, she had remained undetected and unseen in every other case.

Perhaps the watcher was another thief, using the rooftops to get from one section of the city to another while remaining hidden. But she knew that wasn't it—the watcher had been focused on her with an intensity that brought her to full awareness. Whoever it was, they had been looking specifically for Phana.

The sensation was strange, almost familiar somehow, though she couldn't remember ever feeling it before. It set her on edge. She didn't like being reminded of how much she didn't know about her own history.

She looked out across the other rooftops, her eyes piercing the darkness, hoping to spot the watcher. The darkest shadows dissolved under her gaze and she scanned the buildings around her.

There was no sign of anyone else.

Fine, she thought. *You want to watch me? Let's see if you can keep up with me.*

She took off running across the roof and launched herself across a wide alley to land on her feet on the opposite side. Without slowing, she sprinted over this rooftop as well and leaped down to a lower building.

She changed direction and ran to the left, jumping from rooftop to rooftop before changing direction again. She continued this zigzag course across the tops of multiple buildings for the next few minutes.

And just as suddenly as she had started running, she stopped and ducked into a deep shadow where a four-story tenement abutted a shorter building housing a merchant's business. She waited a few seconds and ….

The watcher was still there, still focused on her. And Phana was still unable to see who it was, or even where the person was hiding.

A cold shudder ran through her body. Whoever was tracking her was skilled beyond anything she had ever encountered before. But more than that, there was something … powerful … about the person's presence. Again, the familiarity tickled her mind, but there was a blank space where the knowledge should be.

Phana had no idea how she did what she did. It wasn't sorcery, as far as she knew—she had never bargained with dark entities to gain her abilities. At least, she didn't believe she had, though for the first time she began to wonder how she could be so confident of that fact.

The great gaps in her memory could hide just about anything.

Regardless, she had never met someone who had abilities like hers. But now … whoever was out there watching her could completely hide from her, even though she could see in the darkness. And they were able to follow her without becoming visible.

What if the person out there was just like Phana? What if they already knew her? What if they had the answers to her missing memories?

For a moment, she considered standing up and revealing herself. Calling out to the person and telling them to come out and speak to her. But then her doubts closed in. What if it *was* an assassin? Even if they were not hired to kill her, the person might still be a threat to her. She could be putting her life in jeopardy if she revealed herself.

Then again, if this person could follow her so well, what would it matter? If they were out to harm her, their attack would most likely come when she was distracted or otherwise unable to mount an effective defense. Right now, she was alert and aware of the person's presence. This truly was the best option available to her.

She stood up and stepped away from her place of concealment.

"I know you're out there," she said aloud, not yelling but projecting her voice so that the person would be able to hear her. "I know you're watching me. I'm not looking for a fight. I just want to know who you are. Why don't you come out and speak to me?"

She waited, feeling the attention of the hidden person like a light shining on her from somewhere out in the darkness.

"You don't need to be afraid of me. I'm not going to attack you. I just want to talk."

But shortly after she finished speaking, she felt the presence fade away, as if the person had withdrawn. She almost called out again, but swallowed the impulse. The fact that the pursuer didn't answer her was not a good sign. It didn't indicate someone with friendly intentions.

The feeling of being watched was now completely gone. Phana believed they had left and were no longer close enough to see her. She backed into the shadows and leaned against the wall.

She didn't need this right now. There was enough going on with

Koral and the Wolf, and she wasn't sure she could handle yet more trouble. But the world really didn't care what she preferred. Trouble would come when it came, and her only option was to face it and deal with it.

Fine, she thought to herself. *Whoever you are, you're good. But I've got abilities you haven't seen yet. If you do want a fight, then that's exactly what I'll give you.*

*   *   *

THE OFFICE WAS NEAT AND TIDY, THE LARGE DESK MADE OF SOLID wood and the chair behind it looking expensive and thoroughly comfortable. Though he had been instructed to sit in the smaller chair facing that desk, Koral paced back and forth while he waited for the Wolf to appear. He didn't feel ready to have this discussion, but knew he had no choice.

He couldn't deny that he loved Phana—he had never met a woman like her and knew he never would. There was something about her, more than her intelligence, her humor, her beauty. She carried a power within her that made Koral's blood sing when he was near her. She was more *alive* than anyone else he knew except, perhaps, for the Wolf.

As if summoned by the thought, the door in the far wall of the office opened and the man himself stepped through. Koral felt his heart lurch as he saw his employer. The Wolf's long, dark hair was tied back with a leather cord, and he wore short, dark whiskers around his mouth. And his face ….

Koral hadn't seen this face in quite some time. This was the face of the man who had first caught Koral in the kitchen of that inn more than ten years ago.

He was one of the few people who understood that each person who saw the Wolf saw a completely different man—some short, some tall, some young or old, different skin tones and hair colors—and they always saw him the same way ever after. There were rumors that he was under some kind of curse, or that he was a sorcerer or shapeshifter of some kind.

To Koral, the Wolf had first appeared as he did today, and that was how Koral had seen the man for the first two years he had worked for him. And then one day, the Wolf had suddenly worn a completely different face. Koral had somehow known it was the same man—there was something about the Wolf that he could recognize no matter he looked like.

And since that day, his appearance had never changed again.

Until today.

What did it mean? The Wolf's face only heightened Koral's uneasiness, as if his employer's appearance was a reminder of how they had started their relationship so many years ago. Was it intentional on the Wolf's part?

Then again, Koral wondered—as he used to when younger—if the Wolf's appearance was based on the observer rather than the observed. Was it Koral who supplied the Wolf's face in his own mind? If so, was his brain trying to tell himself something today?

He realized he was just standing there, gaping at the Wolf as the other man walked across the room and sat in the chair behind that dark wood desk. The Wolf waited for Koral to come to his senses, his face relaxed, no hint of either a smile or a frown.

Koral forced himself to close his mouth and take the chair facing his employer.

"Something has happened, I take it?" the Wolf asked, his voice harsh and guttural compared to the one he had when wearing the previous face. Koral knew his own expression had given him away, and it was pointless to try to hide it.

"We have a problem," he answered, choosing his next words carefully. "It's those rumors about Phana."

He saw the Wolf's eyes narrow slightly but the man said nothing, waiting for Koral to explain.

"Apparently, some believe they are no longer just rumors. I was visited a short while ago by some of the gang leaders who wanted to discuss their concerns."

"They demanded that I do something about her," the Wolf summarized, seeing where this was going.

He nodded.

"They told me they had a witness to the fight between Phana and Qudovo. That witness is apparently the source of the rumors about Phana, that she's a witch or something and used her powers to kill the men who attacked her."

The Wolf waved off Koral's words and leaned forward in his chair.

"We don't have time for this. I have something more important for you to deal with. Chaject has disappeared. And I ... suspect ... the explanation isn't not going to be something simple."

Koral knew Chaject, knew the gang leader as a serious, reliable man who wouldn't simply go off on a drunken bender or otherwise shirk his duties to the gang.

"When did he disappear?"

"He was seen the night before last. No sign of him yesterday or today. Look into it and find out what happened. Report back to me as soon as you know anything."

The Wolf stood up as if to leave.

"Sir, the other gang leaders are demanding an answer about Phana. They know you've banned her from the Den. They want you to hear the words of this witness."

The Wolf's brows gathered into a deep frown, and Koral could almost *feel* his displeasure, as of waves rolling onto a beach from a stormy sea.

"Demanding? Who are they to demand anything from me? Your job is to handle the leaders of the gangs and give them their marching orders. Did you give in to them when they came crying to you?"

Koral knew he had made a mistake. The Wolf had been running things so smoothly for so long, everyone had forgotten how he had achieved his current position. He was not a man to give into *anyone's* demands. He gave orders, he didn't take them.

"I listened to their concerns and agreed to talk to you and let you know they have a witness. This thing with Qudovo unsettled them, and everyone in this city is on edge. But it was nothing but rumors and some unhappy muttering until you banned Phana—"

"Enough about Phana!" the Wolf snapped. "Your relationship with her is clouding your judgment, and that makes you useless to me. My decisions about that woman are orders, and you will obey them, or you can go work for someone else."

"I'm not questioning your orders, sir. I'm concerned about the gangs."

The Wolf opened his mouth and Koral half-expected that he was about to lose his job entirely. But then the Wolf stopped and took a deep breath.

"As I said, we don't have time for this. Not now. When it comes to Phana, I can't trust you to see clearly."

Before Koral could say anything else, the Wolf stepped around the desk and sat on the corner. He no longer looked angry, but there was a tension around his eyes that Koral couldn't remember ever having seen before.

"You have the position I've given you because I know I can trust you. But on this subject, your judgment is compromised, whether you know it or not. So I'm not going to waste time with explanations or reasoning. You have a choice to follow my orders, or leave my service. I know you're smart enough to make the right decision."

The Wolf stood up and moved to the door that led into his private rooms.

"Your only priority is to find Chaject or find out what happened to him. I'll deal with the gang leaders myself."

The Wolf left the office and Koral remained in his chair for another minute, thinking about his options. Was the Wolf right, was his judgment compromised when it came to Phana? He had tried to put his feelings for her aside when making decisions about the gangs, but the Wolf obviously didn't see it that way.

So the Wolf had simplified the decision for him. Either obey the man's orders, or leave the guild. Choose Phana or choose the Wolf.

But he knew it wasn't as simple as picking sides. The Wolf may had banned Phana from his property, but he hadn't kicked her out of the guild or declared open season on her. He also wasn't going to share his reasoning with Koral, and there was nothing to be done about that.

He stood and left the office. He had a mission to complete and he would focus on that for now while he tried to decide what he would—or even could—ultimately do.

*   *   *

THE TIPPED BUCKET WAS A SAILORS' BAR, TUCKED DOWN A NARROW alley between two large warehouses just north of the docks. From the street, only a stout wooden door was visible, the painted bucket having long ago worn away, leaving only the barest outline on the pitted wood. A steep staircase led to a cellar under the warehouse on the western side of the alley, where a space had been built for the patrons to sit and drink away their money and their memories.

The tavern was dingy and cramped, and the air carried a heady mixture of cheap ale, sweaty, unwashed bodies, and stale piss. Those who frequented the Tipped Bucket rarely came in groups of more than two or three—this was a place for solitary drinking and moody introspection until enough quantities of alcohol were consumed to bring about dreamless unconsciousness.

The whores who worked the dock area did not bother to come into the Bucket looking for customers. They had long ago learned that their efforts were better spent at other, livelier, establishments.

Laita hunched over the table, staring down into her mug of ale, seeing her reflection in the dark water, a stranger staring back at her. Her scalp itched from the wig of long hair that hung down around her face, a too-warm shawl draped around her head and over her shoulders, and she was sure she felt many small *somethings* crawling under the ratty shipmate's clothing she wore. But she kept herself still and focused on waiting.

Namal sat beside her, his head cradled in his arms on the table. He snored gently, giving off the impression of a man who had just completed a long day of hard labor followed by too much ale and not enough food. His outfit matched hers—minus the shawl—and she wondered if his clothes were also infested.

She'd have time to ask him later where he had gotten these outfits, although she wasn't entirely sure she wanted to know.

They had come here shortly after her speech to the squad, the sun now long set, the darkness bringing with it that feeling of doom hanging over the city. They'd been here for two hours, and were now on their fifth round of ale, though Laita envied Namal's decision to avoid having to deal with any further drinks by feigning uncon-sciousness. She wished she had thought of it first.

The door at the top of the staircase opened and someone came inside. The heavy thump of boots reverberated in the narrow space as the new arrival clomped down the stairs and entered the main room. Laita kept her head down—the man they were meeting would figure out who they were soon enough, and she didn't want to make things obvious.

She heard the boots thud over to the bar and a low baritone mut-tered something to the bartender, who also happened to be the proud owner of the Tipped Bucket. Then the boots came over to Laita's table and the visitor pulled out a chair and sank into it with a weary sigh.

Laita paused for a moment, and then raised her head just enough to peer out under the wig at the newcomer.

He was a young man, just out of his teens, solidly built and dressed as a dockworker. He was filthy, like any dockworker at the end of a long day, but she could see that he was handsome under the dirt, with piercing blue eyes and light brown hair cropped close to his scalp.

She gave him a low grunt of acknowledgement and led her head drop back down to stare into the mug once again.

He took a long pull from his own mug and then crossed his arms and leaned them on the table, which wobbled and groaned slightly from the additional weight—the furniture in the Tipped Bucket not exactly being solid.

"I'm Irako," he muttered in a low voice, pitched to carry only to those at the table.

"You're late," Laita whispered back. "You were supposed to be here an hour ago."

Irako shrugged his wide shoulders.

"Can't always get away whenever I want."

They sat in silence for another minute before Irako spoke up again.

"Listen," he murmured. "I got the message and I'm here. Being careful is more important than being on time. If that's a problem for you, then I can walk out right now, and you'll never see me again."

But Laita knew she couldn't let that happen. This was her first real lead and she needed to play it out as far as she could.

"Fine, let's move on. Word is that you're part of a … movement. One that wants to see a certain change come about. Is that correct?"

Irako took another pull from his mug.

"Where did you hear that?"

"From our mutual friend, the one who arranged this meeting. We've been looking for any signs of a local resistance, but it's been very dry so far. Of course, we can't just go from tavern to tavern, asking out loud if anyone is plotting against … well, you get the idea."

"You've been discreet, I'll give you that," Irako replied. "But how do I know you're not agents of the Imperial Guard? I'm just a common dockworker, with no knowledge of any plot against anyone. Why shouldn't I just report the both of you for suspicious activity or something?"

Namal's gentle snores ceased abruptly, and when he spoke, it was apparent that he had been fully awake the entire time.

"Listen, boy," he said in a low growl. "If you can't trust us, and we can't trust you, then why did you come?"

Laita raised her head just enough to look Irako in the eye. He looked back at her, and it was obvious he was worried.

"Ythis is a dangerous city," he said. "You never know when your words will be taken the wrong way and you'll end up in the dungeons under the Fortress, even if you haven't done anything wrong. Maybe …."

Laita could see the fear in his eyes. He had come because gaining an ally for the resistance was important. But this resistance, whoever they were, had sent him because he was expendable. And he knew it.

And if, in truth, he was an Imperial agent himself, then he was the best actor she had ever seen. And they could dance around this subject all day and get nowhere. Everything was a gamble. Laita could have taken her force and left the Undying Empire altogether. That would have been the safe move. But she still believed they could make a difference.

She was putting everything on the line—her own life, the lives of those who followed her, the very meaning of Kied's sacrifice. And without local help, there was no way they would succeed in their mission.

But for some reason, she believed this young man. There was an honesty about him that came through when she looked into his eyes. And he needed a reason to believe in her.

"I'm Laita Naschect," she whispered to him. "And I've got a force in Ythis that can accomplish what everyone else thinks is unachievable."

Namal sat up, his eyes wide, and she saw he was suddenly ready to fight or run, depending on Irako's reaction.

Irako looked at her blankly. He still didn't know who she was.

"I'm a commander … *was* a commander in the Imperial Legion. I led the Second Contingent, Chimera Regiment. We're the group that has left the Legion."

She the realization on his face as he put the pieces together.

"By the Abyss!" he whispered under his breath, his eyes going wide. "I heard rumors that Chimera Regiment had turned traitor and that the rest of the Legion was hunting it down. Are you telling me that's true?"

"Not the whole Regiment," she told him. "Not even the entire contingent. I've got just over two detachments' worth—about two hundred soldiers."

"You're a wanted criminal," Irako told her. "It's said you slaughtered villagers, put towns to the torch, killed a bunch of your own soldiers."

Laita closed her eyes for a moment. Of course that's how they would play it. By now, the rest of the Regiment had probably taken over the mountain passes and valleys, and anyone who had been living there, anyone who hadn't fled when Laita sent out the messages to the villagers to abandon their homes, would be dead.

The Emperor wanted no witnesses to what he had done. He wanted no one to find the gate, even if it was now destroyed. He wanted to erase what had happened.

"I saved the lives of countless innocent villagers, Irako. I had orders to murder them all, and I turned away from my oath and saved as many as I could. That's why I'm a criminal. I refused to obey the

Emperor and kill Imperial citizens. He needs to be stopped. And I have a force that can do it."

Irako stared at her.

"Two hundred soldiers …?"

"Not all of them are in the city right now. But they're coming into Ythis, a few at a time. I don't know if I can bring them all in safely, and I want to be ready to move on any opportunity that comes up."

Laita glanced sideways at Namal. He was watching Irako intently. She noticed that one of his hands was below the table, and she knew he had a knife in his fist and was prepared to use it if Irako turned on them.

But the young man stared into Laita's eyes and she saw something blossoming there. Hope, perhaps? He took a deep breath, gave her a small smile, and then seemed to relax slightly.

"Yes, there's a resistance in Ythis, and I can introduce you to the leaders. We're not large, but we have a lot of resources. And your presence here is a dream come true."

Twelfth day of Highsummer,
7 days to the Arrival

Chapter Nine

I T WAS THE SAME TAVERN AS LAST TIME, THE SAME TABLE, AND perhaps even the same tankard. A different fly was crawling across the surface, though.

Phana hadn't gone to her spot on the roof near the market tonight. After the strange encounter the previous evening, she wasn't sure if it was a good idea. She was trying not to call herself a coward, and not entirely succeeding.

The door to the tavern opened and a man walked in. He was alone, and Phana noted he moved with the easy grace of a skilled fighter. His dark hair was cropped short and his tanned skin contrasted with the white tunic he wore beneath a thin grey cloak.

She noted the pair of daggers at his waist, and knew there would be others on his person, hidden but easily accessible. This was someone who was no stranger to violence.

The man walked a few paces into the tavern and looked around. When he saw Phana, his gaze stopped. Then he turned to the bartender, ordered a drink, and turned back to her table.

She watched him approach. Nothing about his demeanor indicated he was here for a fight. He reached her table, looked down at her, and smiled.

Not bad, she thought. *If I was single …*

"Excuse me, are you Phana?" he asked in a friendly tone.

The fact that he asked for her by name caused her to tense up. She thought he might have just been looking for an attractive woman to seduce. But he was here for her specifically.

"Who I am is none of anyone's business," she said without malice.

It was a simple statement of fact. But his smile didn't falter.

"My name is Borolt. I was hoping I could buy you a drink and we could chat for a bit."

"Why would I want to do that?" she asked him, raising her eyebrows.

"Because it's a free drink, or maybe a few. And hopefully some interesting conversation. I'm just looking to talk, nothing more."

Is this who was following me last night?

But the feeling of familiarity wasn't there when she looked at him. But what were the odds that someone had been chasing her just last night, and now here was a man she didn't know wanting to talk to her?

She shoved the chair on the other side of the table out with her boot. He took the invitation and sat down. The serving wench came by with a tankard for him and another for Phana, and he paid her.

When she was gone, he rested his hands on the top of the table. Phana said nothing, waiting.

"As I said, I'm Borolt. Borolt Zale. And you are Phana?"

She gave him a nod.

"Well, it's nice to meet you Phana. I've been hoping for a chance to talk to you."

"You could have just spoken up last night," she said.

The look of confusion on his face told her that he wasn't her unseen watcher.

"I'm sorry, I wasn't here last night."

She waved it off with her hand and drained her own tankard before setting it back on the table.

"So you want to talk to me? Then talk."

Borolt chuckled.

"Okay, you're suspicious, with good reason. But you've got nothing to worry about from me. I don't work for the Watch, or the Guard, and I'm certainly not a priest. I'm just here because I'm curious about some rumors that I've heard."

Phana could feel a flush of excitement rush through her body. She had to stop herself from visibly reacting. Someone was looking into the rumors about her, which meant that someone was taking them seriously. And this man wasn't part of the Wolf's guild, of that she was sure.

But then who was he?

"Rumors are rumors, Borolt. You can't believe everything you hear on the street."

"Very true. But I'm quite good at separating out the exaggerations from the truths. And I believe there's something … interesting … at the heart of the rumors about you."

"Then you're braver than most."

He smiled at her again and leaned back in his chair. Nothing about him gave any indication he was a threat to her. That didn't mean she could trust him. But she was getting tired of all the secrets, the manipulations, and the mysteries. Her patience for playing games was well and truly exhausted.

"What do you want, exactly?"

"As I said, I'm just here to talk. I'm very interested in what I've heard. One would think that in a city with the Church and the Six and the Emperor himself, anyone special would be working for one of them, or perhaps dead at their hands. But you'd be surprised at how often people with extraordinary abilities end up in Ythis."

"You don't know the half of it," she replied, unable to keep the smile from her face.

She couldn't help but like this man, whoever he was. He seemed … decent. Which meant he was probably some kind of creature from the Abyss or something, and was hoping to consume her soul. She wasn't sure she could trust her judgement these days.

Or ever.

He leaned forward and crossed his arms, resting his elbows on the table. When he spoke, it was in a low voice.

"A lot of people are talking about you. Many of them are afraid of you. They think you can turn into some kind of ice creature and freeze people where they stand. Now I know people exaggerate, but someone did see you do something extraordinary. And I'd like to talk to you about that."

Phana almost stood up and walked out. But she was so tired of it all.

"And why should I trust you? Everyone seems to want me for something, but no one seems to just want *me*."

She felt a pang of guilt as she said it. Koral certainly wanted her. She couldn't believe that he was just following the Wolf's orders. She'd felt his passion, and she had to admit to herself that she felt his love for her.

But Koral was conflicted, and as much as she wanted to believe he would put her first, she didn't really *know* if it was true.

"I don't believe that no one wants you," Borolt said. She looked at his face and saw that he probably didn't mean it as anything more than a simple compliment.

Good, I don't need the complication.

"Okay, yes, I have someone," she answered. "But even that is ... I can't seem to just reach a place where things are normal. Everyone has ulterior motives for everything they do. I can't really trust anyone."

"We're in Ythis," Borolt said in response, and he was right. No one in Ythis was totally honest. You couldn't survive in this city without having secrets, without lying, without manipulations.

Maybe Phana was just tired of Ythis altogether.

"You didn't answer my question," she said to him.

"Which question was that?"

"Why should I trust you? I just met you. You came here looking for me based on some rumors you heard. What's *your* ulterior motive?"

Borolt nodded thoughtfully and took a deep breath.

"My job is to know what's going on in Ythis. I protect the interests of someone, and so I need to know when something is a potential threat. The information I gather is not used against anyone. But I need to know what areas of the city need to be avoided, what factions will cause my employer trouble, that kind of thing."

He stopped and shrugged.

"I'm not here for any reason other than to know what's going on. And there are a great many people who are talking about you. So I'm curious about what is true, and what is talk borne of fear and those ulterior motives you mentioned."

Phana surprised herself by shrugging back at him.

"Okay, then," she said. "What do you want to know?"

*   *   *

THE LEATHER STRAPS CREAKED AS CHAJECT TRIED TO TWIST HIS
wrists out of the restraints. He lay on a heavy stone slab in the center
of the room, his wrists and ankles stretched out to the four corners
and bound in place.

Relael smiled as he entered the room through the door near the
"head" of the slab, where his prisoner couldn't see him. He pushed
the heavy door closed behind him but did not drop the bar.

The room was dim, lit only by a single candle on a small table in
one corner. Two of Relael's assistants, dressed in plain brown robes,
stood to one side. They had done an excellent job quietly capturing
this man. Chaject was more reserved than many of his fellow gang
members, and it had taken some effort to get him alone. But Relael's
people were well-trained and good at their jobs.

They had used the Church soldiers to conduct the capture, but
none of the soldiers had been told who this man was, nor why the
Church wanted him. And the soldiers knew not to ask questions.

"My apologies," Relael said to his prisoner. "I had hoped to come
speak with you yesterday, but there are always so many things to do,
and never enough time. I trust you've been kept as comfortable as
possible?"

"Let me go now or you're a dead man," Chaject spat back at him.
"You think you can cross the Wolf? It's the last mistake you'll ever
make."

Relael looked down at Chaject and slowly moved around to the
side as he spoke, so that his prisoner could see him clearly.

"There are two things you need to realize about me. First, I'm far
too careful to leave a trail leading back to me. Such things can cause
distractions, and I do so hate distractions. Second, the Wolf is nothing to me. He lives because we choose to let him live. He knows better than to pit himself against us."

Chaject looked at Relael and then his eyes widened as he noticed
what his captor was wearing.

Priest robes.

The realization came crashing into his head and Chaject's mouth opened, though no sound came out. He yanked at the straps, and the leather chafed at his wrists and ankles, but there was no escape.

"Yes, my friend. You are inside the Temple. I see you understand your predicament now, and I expect that you'll decide to be more cooperative."

"Wha—" Chaject's voice came out as a croak and he stopped and then tried again. "What do you want from me?"

"I only want you to answer a few questions. From what I hear, you're all talking about it anyway. I just want you to tell me the truth of the matter."

"Why me?"

Relael shrugged.

"We needed to grab someone, and you made it easy for us. You like your privacy, apparently. We did not want any witnesses. So here you are.

"If I answer your questions, will you let me go?"

"That depends. What exactly will you do if I let you go? I believe you threatened me with the Wolf just a moment ago."

Chaject shook his head, his eyes still wide.

"I was just … just trying to scare you to let me go. I don't need to tell the Wolf anything. I mean it—he doesn't need to know."

Relael turned to his assistants and nodded to one of them. The young man pulled a long wooden box out from a cabinet built into the frame that held up the slab of stone. He placed it on the edge of the table and opened it. Relael looked over the metal implements inside the box and then turned back to Chaject.

The gang leader couldn't see what was in the box, but he could guess. He started panting, and he met Relael's gaze and began to plead.

"You don't have to do anything to me. Just ask your questions. Please."

Relael motioned for the two assistants to leave the room. Relael didn't need help to interrogate this man, and he had no intention of sharing any details with them that they didn't need to know.

When they had stepped out of the room, Relael closed the door again, but this time he lowered the bar. He most certainly did not want to be interrupted this evening. He turned and moved to stand near Chaject's head.

"You are familiar with a man, a former gang leader, named Qudovo."

"Yeah, I knew him. But he's dead." Chaject explained.

"I'm aware of that. He's dead, and so are his closest companions. Killed on the same night, in fact. By, so the stories go, the same person."

He leaned down closer to Chaject's face.

"It's not Qudovo's death that interests me. It's the *manner* in which he died."

"The witch," Chaject whispered.

Relael tried not to wince at that word. He'd had quite enough of witches lately, and no interest in encountering any more. He hoped that Chaject's descriptive term was inaccurate.

"What witch?"

"She ... she killed Qudovo and the others. Used some kind of witchcraft. Froze them from the inside."

"And you witnessed this?"

"No. But I spoke to someone who did."

"And where is this witness?"

Chaject blinked up at him.

"I—I don't know. Some of the gang leaders have him hidden away. They're worried that he might be killed."

"By the witch?"

"No, by the Wolf."

Relael stepped back away from the table, once more out of Chaject's sight. The gang leader tried to twist his head to see him, and began to moan when he couldn't find him.

"Please," the gang leader pleaded. "I'm telling you everything I know."

Relael ignored the man on the table and considered the implications. Someone had witnessed the woman kill the gang leader using witchcraft, or sorcery, or something else, perhaps. Some of the gang leaders were hiding this witness because they were worried the Wolf would have the man killed.

What was the connection between the Wolf and the woman?

Relael stepped around to the side and rested his hand on the wooden box. Chaject stopped pleading and watched him with wide eyes.

"What is the woman's name?"

"Phana. Don't think she has a family name."

"And this Phana … she's the Wolf's lover?"

Chaject shook his head.

"No, her lover is the Wolf's right-hand man. Koral Creyss."

"And why would the Wolf kill the witness to her murder of the gang leader? To protect this Koral Creyss?"

"I don't know," Chaject whined. "The Wolf doesn't tell us why he does things. But he's had her under his protection for about a year. No one is allowed to lay on a finger on her."

Relael paused, watching his prisoner. The gang leader lay there, chest heaving as he gasped in fear for his life and his soul.

"I'm telling you the truth!" he shouted. "I've answered all your questions. Please, no one will know I spoke to you. I promise."

Relael wasn't happy to discover this Phana was tied up in the Wolf's business. It was an unnecessary complication, especially that the Wolf was protecting her for some reason.

As much as he had told Chaject that he wasn't afraid of the Wolf, the truth was that the Hidden had orders not to go directly against the crime lord without Assirra Untoleu's direct permission. What kind of power did the man have, to get that kind of consideration from the High Counselor of the Hidden?

He had to consider going directly to Assirra and telling her about the Wolf's involvement. The sooner she knew, the better. She'd be angry with Relael if he kept it from her and it ended up causing difficulties later.

But of course, Relael had no desire to put himself in front of that woman unless it was absolutely necessary. His control was getting worse, and a slip up would mean his death. If he was forced to go back to her again and again, he would inevitably be found out.

His only hope was to find this Phana, tell Assirra where she was, and then let the High Counselor deal with her directly. And if the Wolf decided to get involved, let them fight it out amongst themselves. He held no illusions that he would play a major role in that kind of confrontation.

"Okay, my friend," he said to Chaject in a reassuring voice. "Just two more questions for you. First, what does Phana look like."

"She … she has straight dark hair to her shoulders. She's tall but not big. She's … pretty. Not pretty like a proper lady, but she looks good, and there's something about her…."

"Go on," Relael urged.

"She's just … you have to pay attention to her when she's around. It's like she's more *real* than most people."

He paused again, but with Relael's further urging provided a detailed description.

Relael had one last question.

"Where do I this Phana?"

The gang leader licked his lips.

"She doesn't come around very often anymore. But sometimes she goes to the Wolf's Den to meet up with Koral Creyss when he's not working. And he usually works out of the Crown and Coin, so she probably goes there sometimes, too."

Relael smiled.

"You see? That wasn't so bad. You probably even told me the truth."

"I did! I told you everything I know!"

"Yes, well, you have to say that, don't you? You certainly would not admit that you had lied to me about anything. Or left anything out. And all I have is your word."

Chaject's eyes had gone wide again, so wide that Relael thought they might pop right out. Which gave him an idea or two.

"Please … please … I've told you everything. You don't have to torture me, or kill me."

"You're absolutely right, my friend. I do not *have* to do anything like that."

Chaject started howling as Relael reached into the box and pulled out a thin metal rod, pointed at one end, and a serrated knife.

"But one can't be too careful, can one?" he asked his victim.

Chapter Ten

L AITA STOOD IN THE ALLEY, WAITING FOR IRAKO TO ARRIVE. Namal was nearby, watching for any signs of an ambush or other dangers.

After their initial meeting with Irako the previous evening, he had told Laita exactly what he thought of her decision to admit who she was to the unknown man.

"Just because he didn't call down the Guard on us at the tavern, that don't make him trustworthy. He could have gone off to plan an ambush, and you intend to walk right into it."

She understood his concern, but it she hadn't felt there was much of a choice.

"At some point, we have to trust someone, and it's better to seize the initiative and act rather than sit back and react," she told him. "Something about Irako—my gut tells me he's at least honest. And we need help. None of us have ever lived in Ythis. None of us are familiar enough with the layout of the city, we have only the barest contact with the criminal underworld, and we're seriously lacking in resources, including money.

"But just because I believe that Irako isn't going to betray us, it doesn't mean I trust the people we will meet tonight. I need your eyes, your ears, and your gut. I'm going to be talking to these leaders of the Resistance, and I need you to watch their faces and their movements. I'll say things that will shock some of them, and you need to tell me afterward which of them reacted and what they did."

She wasn't sure she had fully convinced him, but she was also his commander and he understood when it was necessary to follow orders.

Now, Irako stepped around the corner and stood at the mouth of the alley, the lamps from the street illuminating his face for a moment. Laita stepped out of the shadows and nodded at him in greeting. He looked at her and then back at the darkness of the alley.

"Is your friend not with you?" he asked in a low voice.

"He's nearby."

"Where? The leaders have agreed to meet with you tonight, but we have to go now."

"He'll follow along," she told him.

Irako hesitated.

"What if we lose him? It would be better if we all went together."

Laita smiled.

"We won't lose him. Let's go."

The tone of command in her voice was enough to get Irako moving. He looked out at the street in both directions, and then led her out of the alley, heading north. She walked beside him, not speaking. After some minutes had passed, he glanced sideways at her.

"You're not what I expected."

"And what were you expecting?"

"I don't know—I never thought you'd come to Ythis at all, so I never imagined I would meet you. I just … I guess I'm surprised you're not some big, muscled soldier. You know, someone who couldn't possibly blend in and look like anything other than a soldier."

"You haven't known many soldiers, have you?"

He chuckled and shrugged his shoulders.

"The only ones I see are the members of the Imperial Guard."

"Yes, that would color your perception, I think."

"I honestly don't know the difference between the Imperial Guard and the Legion. Why does the Empire have two armies?"

This was not the first time Laita had fielded this question, sometimes from the soldiers under her own command.

"The Legion is the official army of the Empire. We defend the borders—we *expand* the borders by invading neighboring regions. We also operate within the borders of the Empire, in the rural areas outside the big cities. We are pretty much the definition of the word 'soldier.'"

Irako glanced at her and nodded.

"The Imperial Guard, however, is the Emperor's personal force. An even more elite group within the Guard protects the Emperor himself, and the rest of the Guard protects his palace and the city in which he resides."

"You mean Ythis."

"In this case, yes. There was a time, however, when he spent part of the year here and lived part of each year in one of the other cities. So the Guard maintains a garrison in all those major cities across the Empire, tasked with protecting the local administrators who run the regions, as well as the noble families."

She looked around as they walked, taking in the slow transition from the poorer section of the city to the slightly more affluent.

"If a force from outside the Empire managed to breach our borders—and they'd have to fight and defeat the Legion to do so—and made their way to Ythis, the Guard would lead the defense of the city."

Irako considered her words.

"Okay, that's what they do. But why do they look so different from soldiers of the Legion?"

"That's because the Legion is out there," she said, waving her hand to indicate somewhere beyond the walls of Ythis. "We're out where there are no nobles and other 'important' people of the Empire. It's a functional army, practical, with no time or energy to deal with appearances. But the Guard deals with regional administrators, noble families, and the Emperor himself. In that context, appearance matters. They are usually big and muscled, with gleaming breastplates and clean uniforms."

She shrugged.

"They're just as dangerous as us, though. The elites are most definitely *more* dangerous. The Imperial Guard goes through rigorous training, just like we do. In some cases, their training is better, because they have lots of money and there are fewer of them to spend it on."

Her mind drifted toward the fight she knew she would have to lead against the Guard when they assaulted the palace. There would be no avoiding that fight, and it wouldn't be easy. After a couple of minutes, she realized that Irako had also fallen silent.

For the next while, he led her north into the Merchants' District of Ythis, where the wealthiest families that held no noble titles had their estates. Eventually, they neared the area where a chest-high wall—more decorative than protective—marked the beginning of the Nobles' District.

Irako slowed down and glanced back.

"If your friend is near, he should join us now. Once we go inside, he won't be able to follow. This place is for members only."

"And what is 'this place'?"

"It's a private club called The Forest. You must have merchant holdings to join, and only members are allowed inside, with a few special exceptions. Most members have no idea our resistance even exists, but the leadership uses this place to meet and discuss our plans. They're waiting for us inside."

Laita held up her left arm and whistled twice. Within a dozen heartbeats, Namal emerged from the shadows of an alley a short distance away and approached.

Irako gave him a short nod, but Namal merely eyed the young man and said nothing.

The Forest was housed in a three-story building of carved stone blocks that occupied a large block at the very north end of the Merchants' District. There were no decorations or identifying marks, other than a small metal plaque sporting an engraved tree mounted on the wall beside a pair of what appeared to be large bronze double doors facing the street.

Irako led them around to a remarkably garbage-free alley that ran along the rear of the building, where a single stout wooden door stood closed against the night. He rapped on it three times, pausing, and then twice more. The door opened and lamplight spilled out into the alley.

A beefy, bald man with a truncheon in his huge fist stood blocking the doorway. Irako stepped into the light spilling from the doorway.

"It's me, and these are my guests," he said to the man, gesturing at

Laita and Namal. The doorman looked them over carefully, his eyes expressionless.

"Lotta knives," he grunted in a deep, rumbling voice. Laita was impressed—both she and Namal had gone to considerable lengths to conceal their blades from prying eyes. Irako turned and looked at them with a slight frown.

"Knives?" he asked.

"Is that a problem?" Laita asked the doorman.

"Dunno. You tell me," he rumbled back at her.

"We're here to talk to some people. Not to cause trouble."

Irako looked from the guard to Laita and back again.

"I will vouch for them," he said to the big man. "They won't be any bother."

The doorman looked down at Irako, and his expression said it all—Irako's word wasn't worth anything to him. The young man turned back to Laita.

"Can you leave your weapons here? They'll be safe—"

"Not a chance," Namal growled at him.

"But—"

"It doesn't matter if our weapons are safe. It matters that *we're* safe. We're not going into an unknown building without any way of defending ourselves if there's a threat."

Laita agreed with Namal and simply gave Irako a look that told him this was non-negotiable.

"One knife each," the doorman said. "But if you cause any trouble, I will put you both down."

Laita considered both the offer and the threat, and nodded. She had no intention of getting into any confrontation with anyone. And if this turned into a situation where they needed more than one knife, then it was an ambush and they were probably not fighting their way out no matter what.

She divested herself of her backup daggers, and kept only a long knife. Namal hesitated, but she nodded to him and he also handed over his extra weapons. The doorman placed their blades on a shelf just inside the door and then moved aside to let them pass.

They entered a short hallway with doors on either side and a wooden door bound in iron at the far end. Irako moved to the end of the hallway and knocked on the door. A small plate in the door slid back, and a pair of eyes regarded the trio. The plate slid closed and they could hear bolts being drawn back.

As the door was pulled open, a waft of air blew out into the corridor, heavy with moisture and the smell of earth and grass. They stepped through the door into a thoroughly unexpected environment.

The interior of the building seemed to be mostly one large, open space. The entire floor was covered by growing grass, and a half-dozen fully-grown trees were scattered across the open area, ornate lanterns hung from their branches providing the only illumination. A long bar of dark wood stretched across one wall, and small tables were nestled under the trees and in nooks created by flowering shrubbery.

Laita looked up to see that the roof was of stone, just like the rest of the outer walls. She turned to Irako.

"This is incredible. How do they get the trees and plants to grow in here without sunlight?"

Irako shrugged.

"No one knows. The woman who owns The Forest won't tell anyone how she does it."

Laita turned back to the room, noting that it was not crowded. Pairs and small clusters of people sat conversing in the nooks or at the tables under the trees. She counted perhaps a couple dozen people visible in the open space.

"Who are we meeting," she asked Irako.

"They are waiting for us in one of the private rooms." He gestured to one side where Laita now saw a few doors inset into the wall opposite the bar. He led them across the forested space, and Laita noted that the ground was soft and had the slightly springy feel of a well-tended garden.

Irako stopped outside one of the doors and turned to Laita and Namal.

"I want you to understand, these people are taking a great risk meeting with you directly. Some of them are powerful and important people in this city, and they have a great deal to lose if you turn out not to be who you say you are. Please keep that in mind when you meet them."

Namal grunted in what Laita knew to be amusement but Irako would probably take for acceptance. She wasn't entirely sure what to expect, but Irako's tone gave her the feeling that these "leaders" likely had an overly inflated sense of their own importance. She prepared to engage her diplomacy skills and hoped this was not entirely a waste of her time.

Irako rapped twice on the door, and it was pulled open by someone on the other side. Laita saw a woman perhaps a dozen years older than herself, pretty, with long black hair hanging loose around her shoulders. She was dressed in simple tunic and leggings, with a vest that poorly concealed the dagger hanging at her belt.

The woman looked at Irako and their eyes met for a moment, and then she turned her gaze on Laita and Namal. Laita gave her a quick nod, but the woman didn't acknowledge the greeting as her eyes traveled over Laita's face and down her body. She did the same with Namal and then stepped back and motioned for them to enter.

Irako led the way into the room and Laita saw it was narrow and long with a table running down the middle and a sideboard holding bottles and a platter of food. Five other individuals were gathered around the table, and a single lamp hung from the ceiling at the center, leaving the corners of the room in shadow.

The woman closed the door behind Namal and moved to step in front of it, but Namal put his back to the door and rested his hand on the hilt of his own knife. The woman eyed him for a moment, but then gave a small sniff and stepped back to lean against the wall just out of his immediate reach.

One of the men had stood as they entered and was moving around the table toward Laita. Irako began to introduce the man, but he spoke over him with a deep, cultured voice.

"Ennius Nasiri," he said extending his hand. He was a handsome man, tall and well-groomed, with olive skin and deep, brown eyes. She noted that his clothing was expensive and tailored as he took her hand and lifted it to his lips.

"Commander Laita Naschect," she said, her voice all business. "My companion is Sergeant Namal."

Ennius gave her a broad smile and slowly let go of her hand. She swallowed her sigh and turned to the other man who was standing on the other side of the table, but Ennius wasn't finished yet.

"You have no idea how glad we are you managed to make contact with Irako here. I think a partnership between us could be greatly beneficial."

Laita turned back to him and gave him a small smile.

"Perhaps, once we sit down and talk through the matter, we can find ways to work together."

Ennius began to speak again, but Laita turned back to the other man and gave him a Legion salute. His eyes widened, and he returned the salute, but reluctantly.

"Tasius Bhandar," Irako said by way of introduction.

Laita moved around the table to take the man's hand. He was older, well past retirement age for a soldier, but his bearing was still that of a military man. And Laita knew that he, out of everyone in this room, would likely be the most hesitant to work with her. To a career soldier, Laita's decision to leave the Legion could only be treason. This man would need convincing that she had made the right decision.

Irako motioned to the woman seated beside Tasius. The top half of her face was hidden behind a mask that one might wear to an exclusive masquerade party for the extremely wealthy. It was black, with glittering sequins stitched into the lace edges. Red-tinged horns curved up from either side of the mask, looking more like something to hang a coat on than anything threatening.

"This is—"

"Don't you dare, Irako," the woman interrupted sharply. "She doesn't need to know my real name."

"Oh, Zita," Ennius said, grinning at her.

"Stop it!" she nearly shouted at him. "You threaten all our lives by telling complete strangers who we really are. How do we know she's not a spy for the Imperial Guard?"

"You don't," Laita answered. "Any more than I know that none of you are spies. Namal and I could have been walking into a trap tonight. But we came anyway, because we have a goal, and its chance of success would be greatly improved by having local help. I don't need to know your real name to do what I came here to do, madam."

An old woman, seated at the very end of the table, spoke up.

"Well said, though Zita also has a point. We all endanger our lives by doing this, and we've been lucky so far. But there's nothing wrong with her wanting to protect her identity. You know what'll happen if any of us get caught."

"My dear Galla," Ennius said smoothly. "I would die before giving you up to the Imperial Guard."

The old woman snorted.

"That's a load of shit, Ennius. If they get their hands on you, you'll tell them everything they want to know. By the time an Inquisitor is done with you, you'll be volunteering information. We all would. Don't fool yourself into thinking you'd be able to stand the kind of torture they can bring to bear."

She turned to Laita.

"Welcome, Commander Naschect. My name is Galla Javadi, and I'm too old to care if they come for me. If you can really help us get rid of the Emperor, it's worth the risk as far as I'm concerned."

Laita bowed to Galla, taking an instant liking to the small woman. She radiated a strength that belied her age and size.

"This is …." Irako said, and hesitated, not knowing if he should continue volunteering names.

"Xuthos," said the thin, middle-aged man seated at Galla's left hand. He didn't stand or make any attempt to physically greet Laita. He lounged in his chair as if his spine was liquid, and his mouth was twisted in a permanent sneer.

As much as Laita like Galla, this man immediately annoyed her.

"And this is Oriuna," Irako finished, motioning to the woman who had opened the door for them. Laita turned and gave a bow of her head to the woman once more, but again it was not returned. Oriuna simply looked her over again and said nothing.

Interesting group, Laita thought to her herself. It was obvious that not all of them agreed with the decision to meet with Laita and

Namal. She wasn't sure if it was because of the stories about her that had been spread by the Legion, or for some other reason. She would have to tread carefully—the last thing she wanted was a schism in the resistance leadership over her presence.

"Thank you all for meeting with us," she said to the room, turning back to the table. "I understand the need for caution, and the uncertainty about dealing with me. You have no doubt heard some terrible things about me—probably some things that I'm not even aware of yet, as my travel has prevented me from gathering intelligence about what's going on back in the mountains."

"Irako tells us you deny the charges against you," said Tasius, who had returned to his seat but still gave the impression of standing at attention. "Assuming you are telling the truth and you didn't slaughter those people, it's still true that you *have* deserted from the Legion."

Laita pulled out a chair and sat down. Ennius returned to his own seat at Galla's right hand.

"Yes, I did give the order to desert from the Legion. The Emperor put me in a situation where I had to betray the Legion, or betray the Empire. It was not an easy decision, by any means. But, as a Legionnaire, I have a duty to protect the Empire. And the *people* are the Empire, not the man who sits on the throne in the Imperial Palace."

She looked from face to face around the table, but focused on Tasius. If anyone was going to refuse to deal with her, it would be him, and she had the feeling he might be the most valuable member of this group.

"I don't want to fight the Legion, sir. I couldn't ask that of the soldiers under me. And I don't feel that the Legion created this problem. The problem is the Emperor himself. That's why we came to Ythis, to remove the problem."

Tasius gave her a short nod, but didn't comment. She couldn't tell if he agreed with her or not.

"We've all had to make decisions in our past that we wish were otherwise," Ennius said smoothly into the silence. "I know there have been a few investments that I wish I could take back."

The masked woman, Zita, turned to Laita.

"So what happens after?"

Laita waited for her to elaborate, but the woman just glared at her. "After?"

"Yes, after the Emperor is gone. Are you planning for the Legion to take over? Make this a military dictatorship? The noble families won't stand for that, you know. We expect things to settle down with a new Emperor as quickly as possible."

Laita blinked at her, amazed at how the woman just assumed the removal of the Undying Emperor would be so easy.

"My dear Zita is correct," Ennius chimed in. "We'd like to minimize disruption to our businesses. A smooth transition is best."

"Aren't we getting a bit ahead of ourselves?" Laita asked them.

"Zita and Ennius already agree on a candidate," Xuthos said, his sneer never leaving his face. "They assume the rest of us will just fall into line."

"You know my husband is the most qualified—"

"Everyone, please!" Laita interrupted before their argument could build momentum. "I'm sure this is an important discussion, but right now I was hoping to find out what resources you have. My soldiers are coming into the city, and the longer we're here, the higher the chance that someone will be recognized, or some kind of mistake will happen, and we'll draw attention to ourselves."

"The sooner we get rid of that tyrant, the better," said Galla. "Even if I don't agree on who his replacement should be."

"I'm more concerned about getting past the Fortress and into the palace. I was hoping that you might have gathered some intel, perhaps plans of the Fortress or information from someone who has been inside. Any information about their numbers, patrols, and so forth. What is security like in the palace itself? Anything that will help us complete our mission."

Tasius leaned forward in his seat and rested his forearms on the table.

"You think like a soldier, commander. You're concerned with tactics and logistics. With the success of your mission. But these people are concerned with the city, with their own interests, and with the opportunities for personal power you represent."

Ennius puffed up like a bird.

"Now that's not fair, Tasius. I've spent many years building up my businesses and they've suffered under the Emperor's rule as much as anybody. I've given my support to the resistance from the beginning. I pay for this room, and for the runners who take our messages back and forth."

Laita couldn't believe what she was hearing. This was not what she had in mind when she heard there was a resistance inside Ythis.

"So what resources do you all have?"

"My resources are considerable," Zita answered while adjusting her mask. "We're one of the most important noble families in the empire."

Ennius nodded at Zita, smiling, and turned to Laita.

"While I am not a noble, I do have extensive wealth through my businesses."

He gestured to Xuthos.

"Xuthos here is very popular among the younger nobles, those who do not stand to inherit the bulk of their family's wealth. They would make excellent leaders of your people."

"I'm just an old woman with too much money and time on my hands," said Galla.

Ennius turned to her.

"You, my dear, are the heart of this rebellion, and your advice and guidance are priceless."

Galla waved off his compliment, and he turned back to Laita, gesturing at Tasius.

"And Tasius, as you no doubt realize, has the military experience."

Laita stood up and looked around the table.

"But how many people do you have? How do you manage their safety and coordination among the cells?"

She saw Tasius look down at the table's surface, his mouth twisted in a grimace. The others all looked confused.

"How many people?" Ennius asked. "I'm not sure what you mean. We're all here. This *is* the resistance."

Chapter Eleven

THE SOUND OF TWO OR MORE PEOPLE HAVING VIGOROUS—and apparently rather enjoyable—sex was loud through the thin wooden wall. Esurap glanced over at the closed door and shrugged at Koral.

"Not much trade this past week," he said by way of explanation. "That thing hanging over the city—no one was thinking of fucking."

Koral was curious despite himself.

"So what changed tonight?"

"You can only go so long," Esurap said, grinning. "After a while, it don't matter what's happening to Ythis, you just got to do it."

Koral nodded. He understood. If you lived in Ythis, eventually you got used to anything. That feeling of dread that hung about the city as soon as the sun went down kept growing, but no actual threat had revealed itself yet. People could only take so much before they just pushed through it and went back to their normal business.

"Okay," Koral said, changing the subject back to the reason he was here. "Chaject said nothing unusual to anyone?"

Esurap shook his head.

"It was a regular night. We was downstairs, usual stream of customers, everything the same as it always is. Chaject left late—was already first light. Said he'd see us later."

"And he went back to his own place?"

Koral knew that Chaject had a small apartment in a tenement just down the street. He was a private man, and chose to maintain a separate residence from the rest of the gang, who all lived in this decrepit building that doubled as a brothel and drug den.

Esurap shrugged again.

"Don't know."

"He had someone, right?"

"Yeah, Olourin. He's downstairs. He don't stay at Chaject's place, though. Only goes there when they want some alone time."

Koral swore under his breath. If Chaject had been like most of the gang leaders, there would be witnesses. In a building like this—part gang residence, part brothel, part drug den—someone was always awake, always moving around. There was little to no privacy. It meant that if something happened, someone else would be aware of it.

But Chaject was the exception. And that made Koral's job a lot more difficult. His privacy was the main obstacle to finding out what had happened to him.

If anything *had* happened to him. They still didn't know why he had disappeared. Perhaps he decided to run away, and there were many possibilities there. Maybe he had met someone new. Maybe he was stealing from the Wolf and decided it was time to get away before he was found out. It was even possible that he had overdosed on some drug somewhere that he couldn't get through his own gang, and his dealer didn't know who he was.

And if his disappearance was due to some outside force, the options became almost limitless. The simplest was that he was grabbed off the street by the Church looking for people to sacrifice to Iathephos. From there it only became ever more complicated.

It was even possible his disappearance was related to the growing sense of dread that hung over the city.

Koral asked Esurap to come downstairs and point out Olourin, and Koral introduced himself to the man. Olourin was thin and showed signs of drug addiction—too skinny, pale skin, sunken eyes, and hands that trembled ever so slightly.

"I'm here to look into Chaject's disappearance," Koral explained.

Olourin sighed and nodded wearily.

"I knew he'd leave sooner or later," the man explained.

Koral sat forward, thinking this might be the answer.

"Why do you say that?"

"He was getting tired of me. Stopped inviting me over to his place. I knew it was over, but we kept on as if we were still together, you know?"

"You think he found someone else?"

Olourin gave a barely perceptible shrug.

"Maybe. He didn't say nothing, though."

"Did he say anything the last night he was here? Something that might have sounded like a goodbye to you?"

"No, he barely spoke to me. Not like he was angry or anything. Just like—he acted as if I was just one of the guys."

Koral gave Olourin a look of sympathy, and then put on his serious face.

"Olourin, I have to know. Was he skimming?"

"No … I don't think so—wouldn't be like him to do that. He never talked about anything like that."

"I *will* find out if he was skimming and ran off with the money. And if you knew about it, I'll eventually find that out, too. So if you're not being honest with me …."

Olourin barely reacted. He just gave another weary nod.

"I know what will happen. But if he was skimming, he never told me. Maybe he already found someone else and then ran off with them and the money."

Koral could see Olourin was speculating at this point, and he would get nothing else useful from the man.

"Okay. Look, if you remember anything he said that might seem unusual or might be related, even if it's probably nothing, you tell Esurap and he'll let me know. Is that clear?"

Olourin nodded.

"Is he the new leader of the gang, then?"

"For now," Koral answered. "He'll keep things running as they were until I name an actual successor. First I need to find Chaject and determine his whereabouts."

Koral went back up to speak to Esurap.

"Keep things steady until I find Chaject. If there are any problems, come to me."

"Sure," the other man replied. "You really think you'll find him?"

"One way or another."

Koral turned and walked back down the stairs and out into the night, mentally reviewing what he knew. He had already ransacked Chaject's apartment, but there was barely anything there, and nothing that pointed to the man's whereabouts. If he'd been killed there, his murder had left no blood or signs of a struggle.

Chaject had been reliable for a long time. He didn't cause trouble, didn't demand special treatment or more money, and didn't abuse the gang members under him. There was nothing to make Koral believe he had been skimming, and he just didn't believe Chaject had run away.

And that meant that someone had taken him out.

Koral knew that Chaject was probably already dead—this was Ythis, after all. The more important question was who had done it, and if it was the beginning of something bigger. Could it be the opening move against the Wolf and his grip on crime in the city?

But unless someone else disappeared, there was no pattern to follow. It was a single incident with no leads.

Koral's thoughts were running in circles. He needed to take a break and relax. If there was something he was missing, a distraction might just prove beneficial by letting his mind come at it from a different angle.

And he wanted to see Phana. Though they had been together only the day before last, he already missed her. The question was where she might be. It was still early in the evening, so she wouldn't be out on one of her adventures in the wine cellar of a nobleman. And she certainly wouldn't be at the Wolf's Den.

He considered that she might show up the Coin and Crown looking for him. Though if he wasn't there when she arrived, she wouldn't wait around. She'd go somewhere where she could relax.

Koral decided that he'd start at the bar where he'd found her the other day after their argument. If she wasn't there, he'd head over to the Coin and Crown and see if she had come looking for him.

The thought of spending the rest of the evening with her quickened his step. He hoped she'd be happy to see him.

*　　　　*　　　　*

BOROLT PAUSED, TAKEN ABACK BY PHANA'S WILLINGNESS TO TALK. He recovered quickly.

"Okay, did you really kill that gang leader and his men?"

She gave him a smile that didn't reach her eyes.

"Of course I did. He betrayed me and people I care about. He tried to hunt me down. That was a mistake."

Borolt nodded.

"So how did you kill him and his men?"

"Qudovo was easy. He was already afraid of me. I pissed him off once and he tried to beat me. I gave him two black eyes and nearly broke his arm, and walked away without a bruise on me. So he knew he wasn't going to kill me himself."

"That's why he brought others with him," Borolt mused.

"Yeah, when he decided to turn away from the Wolf, a few idiots followed him. He had one of them on a rooftop with a crossbow. Even poisoned the crossbow bolt in case the shot didn't kill me. I spotted the guy before the fight started. Qudovo was obvious—he tried to maneuver me so that my back was to the guy on the roof, and I knew what he was doing. So I let him do it."

"You knew the crossbow bolt wouldn't kill you."

Phana laughed out loud.

"Are you kidding? If I'd been hit, I would have died for sure. But like I said, Qudovo was easy. He got me into position and then took a breath like he was going to lunge at me. I knew that was the moment. So I leaped at him instead and grabbed him. I'm fast—not faster than a crossbow bolt, of course, but I knew my sudden movement would give me a second or two before the other guy shot at me."

She paused and Borolt, caught up in her story, urged her on.

"That's when you used your … abilities."

"No, that's when I kicked Qudovo in the balls. He wasn't expecting it, and as I said, I'm fast. I grabbed his shoulders as he bent over, spun around behind him and yanked him upright. The crossbow bolt took him in the chest."

Borolt couldn't hide his disappointment, and she laughed again.

"He got caught by his own trap. I wanted to stand there and watch him die, but there were others nearby and the guy with the crossbow was probably reloading as fast as he could. I ran for a nearby alley and was going flat out when I disappeared from their view."

"The guys on the street chased me. They thought I would try to outdistance them. When they came into the alley I was waiting in the shadows. The first guy dropped when I stabbed him in the eye. The second guy was still moving and tumbled over the body of his friend. I stabbed him in the back of the neck as he was trying to get up."

Borolt held up a hand.

"You're going to tell me that you took them all out with knives and skill? I know something special happened that night."

"Oh, it did," Phana agreed. "But it wasn't me who did it. If you've been asking around, then you know why Qudovo turned on me."

Borolt tried to pretend he was confused by her statement, but Phana looked him in the eyes and smiled grimly.

"You don't get to lie to me, Borolt Zale. You know about Jadir and his sister. Jadir was my friend before his sister became … what she became. After I killed Qudovo, Jadir hunted them down for me. He was the one who filled their lungs with ice."

"Then why does everyone believe it was you?"

"Jadir is dead," Phana told him with a straight face. "A bunch of priests were there to see it and make sure he didn't survive the fall. But people need someone to blame. Koral holds a position of responsibility, he's fucking me, and jealousy makes people believe some stupid shit."

Borolt sat back in his chair. He frowned at her as he digested everything she had told him.

"I admit, these rumors are a pain, but they're also useful. People are afraid to get on my bad side, and it makes life easier at times. And it doesn't matter if I deny it or not, people will believe what they believe."

Borolt sighed and nodded.

"Yes, I know about the young man and his sister."

He paused.

"What ended up happening to her?" he asked casually, and had

Phana not been on her guard, she might have answered without thinking.

"I don't know," she told him. "She disappeared right after Jadir fell off the roof."

It wasn't a lie. Marilsa *had* disappeared, right out from under the eyes of the priests who were there to capture her. But Phana wasn't about to share the rest of the story with this stranger.

She looked up and saw Koral come through the door. He spotted her almost instantly, and then his eyes went to the back of Borolt's head and he frowned.

Oh, great, she thought to herself. *I'd better not have to deal with a jealous boyfriend now, too.*

Borolt followed her gaze and turned his head as Koral approached their table. Their eyes met, and Koral's face flushed red.

Borolt stood up and held his hands out in front of his chest, stepping backward away from the table.

"What the *fuck* are you doing here?" Koral said to him, jaw clenched and his hand on the hilt of the dagger on his belt.

"Just talking," Borolt answered, his hands still out. "Just having a friendly conversation."

Phana also stood as the other handful of patrons in the bar turned to watch.

"Koral, what in the Abyss are you doing?"

Koral looked at her, confused by her reaction.

"I'm trying to figure out why you're having a friendly drink with Borolt Zale."

Phana was shocked to hear that Koral already knew the other man.

"Do you have any idea who this is?" Koral asked her.

"Yes," she answered. "He already told me his name."

"But do you know who this *is*?"

"Koral," said Borolt before Phana could respond. "Your employer and I are on good terms. There is nothing wrong with me talking to people in his guild. That's what I do, talk to people."

"That's a load of shit and you know it! You're nothing but a lackey for—"

"Careful, boy," Borolt shot back, his hands dropping to his own belt. "You should know better than to throw around insults when you're nothing more than a cheap imitation of me. The Wolf wanted his own Borolt Zale, and since he couldn't get *me*, he settled for *you*."

Phana grabbed the edge of the table and yanked it up, tipping it over and sending the tankards crashing to the floor. Both men had to leap backward to avoid getting hit. They turned to her, their argument momentarily paused.

In the corner of her eye, she saw the bartender open his mouth to speak up about the flipped table, but he thought better of it and closed his mouth again, watching.

"I'm done with this shit," she said in an even voice. "One of you is going to explain what's going on, or I promise you'll both regret it."

She was highly satisfied when both men realized she meant it, and neither had any interest in getting into a fight with her.

"My employer and the Wolf have an ... understanding," Borolt explained. "What I told you earlier was totally true. I gather information to ensure that my employer is aware of potential threats to his own activities in the city."

Phana realized that in her enjoyment toying with Borolt and making up stories to satisfy his curiosity, she hadn't continued to press him about who, exactly, his employer was.

"So just who do you work for, Borolt? If I recall correctly, you told me it wasn't the Watch, or the Imperial Guard, or the Church."

Borolt paused, and Koral answered for him.

"Your friend here works directly for the sorcerer Veylar Dust. You know, one of the Six."

Chapter Twelve

THE BAR WAS SILENT. NO ONE MOVED. IT WAS ALMOST AS IF everyone held their breath.

Phana turned slowly to face Borolt.

"You need to leave," she told him. "*Now*."

Borolt looked from Phana to Koral and back. She saw him think about trying to talk his way out of this, but then realized that it would only make things worse. So he turned and walked out the front door.

Everyone in the bar watched him leave, and then all eyes turned back to Phana.

Without another word, she followed.

"Phana," Koral called after her, but she kept walking, not trusting herself to speak to anyone at that moment.

She stepped through the door and saw Borolt heading east, so she turned in the opposite direction, not having any particular destination in mind. She heard Koral come jogging up behind her.

He matched his pace to hers when he reached her side.

"Phana—"

"Not right now," she said, interrupting whatever he had been about to say.

"I need—"

"Not. Right. Now."

He heard the note in her voice and took the hint. He continued to walk along beside her, and she wasn't sure if she wanted to tell him to get lost or not. She knew he had done nothing wrong. It didn't make her any less angry—at him, at Borolt Zale, at the world.

They were nearing the market square, and she had an urge to go into the middle of that vast open space, let the cold flow through her veins and just … explode. She wanted to see what kind of destruction she could cause if she could just let it all loose.

But as they reached the edge of the square, she realized that she was just exhausted. It was too much. At some point, she'd been having fun. She was in a gang, she had a place where she belonged, she took lovers when she felt like it—there were no shortage of offers—and she just didn't have any real concerns.

And then Jadir had come to her that night, worried about his sister. And though her relationship with Koral had also started at that time, everything else had been horror and pain. And since Marilsa and her protector had left Ythis, she had been restless. The young girl's words—perhaps the words of the old witch herself—had echoed in her thoughts ever since that night she used her power.

She stopped a few strides into the square and stood staring at the big empty space. The last of the slaves were long gone with no one to witness their cries of despair.

She was tired of waiting.

She was tired of not knowing what she was waiting *for*.

Phana turned to look at Koral, and he stood there, a few paces away, watching her but saying nothing.

"Thank you," she told him.

"For what?"

"For shutting up when I needed you to."

"I … you're welcome."

She wanted his arms around her, but she also knew she'd scream at the feeling of being trapped. She looked at him and gritted her teeth.

"A fucking sorcerer?"

"Yeah."

"How did you know who he was?"

"The Wolf knows him. They've had … dealings … in the past. They're okay now, but there was a time when the Wolf wanted him dead. Only the fact that he was Veylar Dust's pet kept him alive."

Phana raised her eyebrows.

"So even the Wolf is afraid of a sorcerer?"

"I wouldn't say 'afraid' so much as the Wolf isn't going to start a war with a sorcerer unless the fight is worth it. He didn't feel Borolt was worth it."

They stood there in silence for another minute.

"He was asking about the rumors, wasn't he?"

Koral's voice was mild, but Phana knew he was being very careful not to show how much he wanted to know why Borolt was at the bar talking to her.

She sighed and nodded.

"Yeah, I guess the Six are interested in me now, too. Just what I need."

"Did you … what was he asking?"

She looked at Koral and had the suspicion, once again, that he was playing a role with her. His clumsy attempt to get her to reveal what she had said to Borolt wasn't like him at all. Was he trying to be endearing? Get her to see him as harmless so she'd tell him everything?

He had never asked her directly if any of the stories about that night were true. Did he have complete confidence that she was normal, and the stories were all exaggerations? Or did he know what had really happened and didn't need confirmation from her?

Why couldn't she just trust him?

"I told him I killed Qudovo by tricking him into taking the crossbow bolt meant for me. And that Jadir killed everyone else."

Koral frowned.

"But that night, Jadir was in the Warrens when—"

"I know! I lied to him, Koral. Did you think I'd tell him the truth?"

He gave her an even look.

"I don't know what the truth really is."

"You've never asked."

He sighed.

"I often don't know how to talk to you, Phana. I didn't want to ask, because I figured if you wanted to tell me, you would. But then it seemed that if I didn't ask, you weren't going to volunteer anything. But once the rumors started spreading about you, I didn't know what to say. Do I ask you if you're some kind of sorcerer? Should I even give the rumors any thought? They're just stories made up by people who weren't there, right?"

He stopped and waited for her to respond. But Phana didn't want to answer him. Once again, she was wondering if she should trust him. Would anything she told him immediately make its way to the Wolf?

Was Koral just another version of Borolt Zale, working for a man of power who had his own agenda, to use people and discard them when they no longer served any purpose?

Or was Phana being completely unfair to Koral? Was he simply trying to do his best in a difficult situation, trying to keep his feelings for her separate from his duty to his employer?

"Are you asking me now?" she said, terrified of the answer she knew was coming, but needing to know, one way or the other.

Koral stood there for a moment, staring at her.

"You want me to force the issue, is that it? You want me to demand answers. And it either absolves you of your own choice to tell me, or it proves to you that I can't be trusted. Is that what you want?"

Phana knew he was right. If he did demand answers, then she would be able to make the decision she felt she probably needed to make. She could end it, and walk away knowing that she had done the right thing. It would be one less complication in her life.

But was it what she truly wanted?

"I want you to do what's right for you."

"By the Abyss!" he shouted. "I can't keep doing this dance!"

He spun as if to walk away, but then turned back.

"The fact that you don't trust me isn't my problem—it's yours. I've been nothing but honest with you, but apparently that isn't enough. Fine. As far as I'm concerned, you killed Qudovo in a fight, and then fought and killed the men who followed him, one-by-one. And unless someone proves to me otherwise, that is what happened."

He gave her a long, searching look, and then shrugged.

"Take care of yourself Phana. I'm going home."

And then he turned and walked away.

She stood in the empty square, watching Koral walk into the night. Opening her mouth, she almost called out to him, and then stopped.

Clenching her fists, she growled out loud. What was stopping her? What part of her couldn't just let go and tell him everything?

This wasn't her. She wasn't helpless. She didn't *do* this. When Phana wanted something, she went out and got it. She made decisions and accepted the consequences. She didn't let anyone else rule her life.

Lately, however, it seemed as if everyone else knew what was going on and she was left alone in the dark. She was letting herself get buffeted back and forth by whatever winds blew her way.

Maybe it was time she took back control of her life.

"Koral, wait!" she yelled, jogging out of the square in the direction he had gone. She couldn't see him and increased her pace, looking into each alley as she passed.

"KORAL!"

And then she turned a corner saw him up ahead. He had stopped and was looking back at her.

In her mind's eye, she saw the darkness behind him come alive and lunge forward, swallowing him up without a sound. She almost screamed out at the thought, and only the fact that she could still see him standing there allowed her to keep her calm.

She slowed and held back a sob. Koral walked toward her and she clenched her fists again, this time to stop the trembling. The image in her mind had been so vivid, almost as if it was a memory of something she had just seen.

The feeling of being watched was suddenly back, like a bucket of cold water thrown into her face. She grabbed Koral's arm and pulled him to her, looking around for the source of the feeling.

Something tugged at her perception from above and to the right. She looked, and saw a slightly darker patch of shadow in the corner where a building abutted another taller structure. The watcher was *there*.

Dread hit her in the gut as she realized it might be a demon sent by the sorcerer Veylar Dust to watch her—or perhaps even eliminate her.

"What do you want?" she whispered to the watcher, sure that it could hear her even though it was over a hundred paces away.

"Phana, what's wrong?" Koral asked her. Her eyes flickered to his face, and then back to that spot where the darkness—

It was gone.

The feeling of being watched drained away and she knew she was alone with Koral once more.

"Phana—"

"I'm sorry," she said, turning to face him. "I want to talk to you. I want to tell you everything. I've just … I was afraid that what I'm going to tell you will push you away."

She let go of his arm but kept her eyes on his.

"And I don't *want* to push you away."

Koral tried to slide his arms around her waist, but she stopped him.

"Not here."

"Phana, I—"

"For the moment, you have to trust me," she said to him. "We have to go somewhere quiet, somewhere you know is safe. Not your apartment, or mine. Not here."

She scanned the tops of the buildings lining the street.

"And not somewhere I've been before."

Koral took her hand and, without further questions, led her down a side street. They walked for almost forty minutes in silence before coming to a small building with apartments above a bakery. He pulled out a key and led Phana around the back to a wooden staircase. They ascended the stairs and he let them into a small one-room apartment.

As he lit a candle, Phana looked around at the small wooden table, the pair of simple chairs, and the cot tucked against the back wall. She sat in one of the chairs and, when he was done, he sat in the other chair and leaned forward, his hands on his thighs.

"We're safe here," he said, and she suppressed the urge to argue with him. No matter where they went, she knew that her mysterious pursuer would be able to find her. But there was nothing she could do to stop it.

"I need to tell you what happened that night," she said to him. He nodded but remained silent.

"I … I've been worried that whatever I told you would … that you'd tell the Wolf."

She could see the hurt in his eyes at her words.

"I know, and I *am* sorry for that."

"Phana, what happened out there when you caught up to me? What were you looking at?"

She took a deep breath and then shrugged.

"I can't answer that. I don't know. Something has been following me, and it was there tonight, watching me when I ran after you."

"Some*thing*? Not some*one*?"

"I don't know what—or who—it is. But when it watches me, I can feel it. The first time it happened, I didn't know exactly where it was coming from. This time, I could see where it was hiding."

"What did it look like?"

"It was hidden in the shadows. And not just regular shadows. It was like it was cloaked in darkness."

Koral sat back in his chair, his eyes wide.

"Yes," Phana said, acknowledging his worry. "I know. And there's more."

"I'm starting to get the feeling that you're going to tell me things that are well outside of my experience."

"Yes, that's exactly what I'm going to do. And then you're going to go to the Wolf and arrange for me to meet him."

He shifted uncomfortably in his seat.

"Phana, he's trying to distance himself—"

"It doesn't matter. I need to meet him and talk to him. I need answers. You're going to tell him everything I tell you. And then you're going to convince him to meet with me."

Koral was shaking his head.

"I'll do what I can, but I can't predict how he will react. Shit, he might already be aware of all of this and that's the reason he's keeping you at arm's length."

Phana had already considered that. She had kept it from Koral, but that didn't mean that the Wolf didn't have other means of finding out what she was capable of doing. He probably already knew everything.

She hated the idea that, once again, everyone else was one step ahead of her. But her feelings on the matter wouldn't change reality.

"I can't just put my life on hold and sit around, waiting for others to act. I think the Wolf does know quite a bit about me. More than I know about myself, in fact. I want to talk to him. I have questions and he's going to give me some answers."

She leaned forward and took Koral's hands in hers.

"Koral, I will never willingly hurt you, do you understand?"

"What—?"

"I need you to understand that. No matter what, I will never hurt you."

He looked into her eyes, still confused, but he agreed.

"Okay, I know you won't hurt me. But what does that have to do with anything?"

"Because I did kill Qudovo and the others who followed him. And I didn't use my knives. I used … something else."

Koral went very still, as if he had turned to stone. She could feel his hands in hers, and there wasn't the slightest tremble. He was waiting to hear what she had to say, and he had locked himself down in preparation.

"I have something inside me. A power of some sort. And I can summon it when I will it. I can do things that … well, Qudovo died from the poisoned crossbow bolt meant for me. But the others … I … I froze them. I filled up their lungs with ice and watched them suffocate, one by one."

Koral opened his mouth and paused. And then he spoke in a tight, controlled voice.

"It's all true, then."

"Some of the rumors are exaggerations, but yes, it's true."

Koral gently pulled his hands from hers and stood up slowly.

"Stay here for a couple of nights," he said. "Lay low. I will go speak to the Wolf."

He turned toward the door and Phana rose from her chair.

"Koral, I—"

He turned back to look at her, and something in his eyes stopped her.

"Come to the Crown and Coin the night after next. I'll see you then."

Koral opened the door and walked out, pulling it gently shut behind him.

Phana stood staring at the closed door for a long, long time.

Chapter Thirteen

LAITA FORCED HER FISTS TO UNCLENCH AND SHE LAY HER palms flat on the table. She slowly sat back down, keeping her eyes on the table's surface.

The others seated around her watched as she forced herself to remain calm, and no one said anything. They could obviously tell that their news was not what she had been expecting to hear.

This was it. These six people—seven if she counted Irako—made up the entire rebellion in Ythis.

They were playing a game, one that allowed them to imagine a world where the Emperor didn't exist and one of them was in charge of it all. A game where they talked and imagined and wished, but that was it.

A game, nothing more.

She wanted to scream. She wanted to scream *at them*, one by one, and tell them exactly how little they mattered. How little they were doing. She wanted to shatter their illusions and lay bare the reality that they were nothing but frauds.

This was no resistance.

She had revealed herself to these people. There were now seven witnesses who knew who she was, knew she was here in Ythis. Seven people who didn't understand how dangerous their game could be for each of them. Seven people who could let slip the wrong word in the wrong place and doom Laita and all her soldiers.

Seven people she might now have to kill?

No, that would bring even more attention down on her. The Imperial Guard would get involved in the murder of a noblewoman, at the least.

Laita heard Namal shift behind her and knew he was thinking the same thing. If she drew her knife, he'd be right there to start slitting throats an instant later.

But there was no way to kill seven people before one of them screamed. And that would quickly bring others, and there was only one way out of this room. And if even one of the seven survived, they would turn on Laita and reveal ....

She stopped herself. She wasn't going to murder anyone. She didn't do things like that.

Besides, she knew it was her own fault. She had let herself fall for the idea of an underground resistance against the Emperor. One with people who could support her. One with foot soldiers, and contacts, and money, and information.

One that could supply the necessary diversion to draw away soldiers from the Fortress when she was ready to launch her attack on the palace.

And she had massively misjudged the circumstances here in Ythis.

This was supposed to be a turning point, and perhaps it was. But the turn was in the wrong direction. She had told Namal that she was willing to risk her life on the chance that she could get help. Namal had disagreed with her, and he had been right all along.

But she had remained stubborn in her belief that it was the right thing to do. And now she had led them into what might be a disaster for them all.

What mistake might she make next? Ythis was well outside of her area of expertise. She was a military commander, not a spy. She wasn't trained to operate in hiding and lead a rebellion to topple a ruler. She had assumed that she could infiltrate the city, get what information she needed, and launch a surgical strike at her target. But that wasn't how the Legion operated, and she was asking her people to do things for which they hadn't been prepared.

And she wasn't prepared to lead them.

Maybe this was the signal that she was on the wrong path. Maybe it was time to reevaluate what she was doing, and change her course.

Maybe it was time to admit defeat.

Such a thought galled her, though. They had barely tried, and she was thinking of retreating. Could she still face her soldiers if she gave up so easily? Would they still respect her, still follow her, if she admitted that this entire mission was doomed to failure from the start?

Had she led them into a dead-end? What if there *was* no good way out?

She had to consider the fact the lack of a real resistance movement was an indication that her mission was beyond her or her army's capabilities. Perhaps a sizable resistance couldn't exist here in Ythis. Perhaps it was simply too dangerous. Perhaps any real resistance would be found out.

Wiped out.

She had hoped for help, but all she had were a handful of dilletantes.

It changed everything.

She raised her head and looked at them, still sitting around the table, watching her.

Waiting for her to speak.

Waiting for her to tell them what would happen next.

Waiting for her to …

To lead them.

To lead seven people who didn't have the first clue what they were really up against.

That's what she was, though, wasn't she? A leader?

At least, she was the leader they had. She was in over her head, but sometimes you make do because you have no other choice.

And no army ever had all the resources it needed. It was up to the commander to make sure the mission was a success by using what resources they *did* have in the best, most efficient way.

But what did they really have here?

A noblewoman?

A *rich* noblewoman.

A wealthy merchant.

Laita needed money. Without money, there was no food for her soldiers, especially in a city. Her army couldn't forage, and couldn't simply take what they needed from local farms as they marched to their destination. She had to buy what she needed.

So Galla, Ennius and Zita could be sources of money.

Irako seemed to know the city quite well.

Tasius might be able to share some insights into the Imperial Guard's forces.

Xuthos was likely useless to her. The idea that a bunch of young, restless noblemen would command her soldiers was ridiculous. Though perhaps she could use them to cause the diversion she had been considering.

And then there was Oriuna. The woman did not appear to be pleased by Laita's arrival in the city. Ennius had neglected to mention her when he was bragging about their various accomplishments. So what was her role?

Regardless, perhaps it wasn't as dire as she initially thought. Managing these people, especially those with the larger egos, would be a chore. But if she could get access to their money, at least that one problem could be solved.

And then it would be a matter of extracting what useful information each one might have.

Laita had spent time with ambassadors and 'special observers' before on missions for the Legion. They were usually a drag on her time and required far too much handholding. The worst ones tried to get involved in her decisions on how best to use her forces. But she had learned how to handle them.

It was a pain, but she could do it.

She couldn't trust them. Any of them. But she was already committed—they knew who she was and why she was here. If any of them talked, it was all over.

But that was always the danger. She could either run away, or push through.

Legionnaires pushed through.

It was time for her to be commander for these people just as she was for her own soldiers.

She took a breath and considered her words carefully before she spoke.

"I admit that I was hoping you'd have more personnel in your insurgency. My force has the fighting aspect covered, but people who know the city to act as messengers and transportation of goods would be helpful. However, Legionnaires are experienced at using the resources available to their utmost, and we'll make do with what we have."

Ennius opened his mouth to speak, but Laita spoke over him. She wasn't going to let her planning get derailed by someone going off on a tangent.

"The first thing we need to ensure is that the soldiers have places to stay, and that they can be fed. I have people working on the first problem, and some of my soldiers have already gotten jobs in the city. However, there is no way for us to be able to purchase enough food for everyone on the meager salaries of those who have found work. We need food, or we need money to *buy* food."

She turned to Ennius.

"Are you able to ship food to a few locations around the city where it won't arouse suspicion? Any properties that you own, that we could use as central distribution points?"

Ennius considered it, frowning.

"Not really. I do own a couple of warehouses down near the docks, but they are always busy and full of workers shipping goods in and out of Ythis."

No one else was in any better of a position to provide such nondescript methods of distributing food.

"Okay, then. That means our people will need to buy food at the markets. And for that we need money."

Ennius and Zita exchanged glances, and Laita could tell that neither was willing to just throw coins at her without some control over how it was spent.

"I'm sure we can come to some … arrangement regarding the purchase of food," Ennius offered. "Perhaps we buy it directly and send it to wherever you're staying."

Laita suppressed a laugh at his ridiculous suggestion.

"I'm sorry, but that wouldn't work. Having deliveries to every location where my soldiers are hiding means giving out those locations to your employees. There's already a reward for my head, and all we need is one person to get greedy, or just be indiscreet. No, this has to be done quietly."

"You want us to just give you our money," Zita said in a peevish tone. "We don't know you, and I don't give money away to just anybody. You could be doing some kind of … what's the word? Oh, a *con*. How would we know until it was too late?"

It was difficult for Laita maintain her composure. This woman was going to be useless, and Laita would have preferred to just order her to leave the room and let the adults talk. But she couldn't do that without offending the others.

And she couldn't afford to make any enemies at this point.

"You're right, Zita," she said instead. "You don't know me. And I don't really know any of you. Anyone in this room could be a spy for the Imperial Guard, keeping tabs on your group to make sure you never get any farther in your plans than you have so far. So there's very little reason for us to trust each other."

The rest mostly looked down at the table, not wanting to meet each other's eyes. They all had secrets, and none of them wanted to be the one to reveal too much to the others.

"If you cannot help me, then I will find another way. This seems to me to be the easiest, and the one with the smallest chance of exposure. Any other plan I've considered increases the chance that we will be discovered, and then the full might of the Imperial Guard and the Legion will come down on Ythis until they root out me and every single one of my soldiers. But if I must do it alone, then I will find a way to do so."

Galla snorted and leaned forward, looking Laita in the eyes.

"This is just silly. If you need money, then I will give you money. It's not like I'm spending it on anything else anyway. And if you turn out to be running some kind of con—to use Zita's word—then this foolish old woman deserves what she gets."

Laita smiled and thanked her. As she did so, Zita and Ennius both began to bluster.

"I never said I wouldn't—"

"I was just about to offer—"

"Hush!" Galla said and the table fell quiet. "My estate, such as it is, is quite small and I have only a handful of servants. While I trust them to a point, I cannot guarantee their loyalty to me. Otherwise I would offer my home to hide as many of your soldiers as we could fit in there. But money is something that I can freely give. Tell me how much you need, and it's yours."

"I appreciate any help you can give us," Laita told her.

She looked around the table.

"The other major resource we lack is information. I need to know whatever can be discovered about the Fortress and the Imperial Palace. Is there somewhere I might be able to find plans from when they were constructed? Do you have any contacts in either place—servants who are sympathetic to your resistance, for example—who could talk to me about the layout, the patrols, and so forth?"

She saw Irako look over at Oriuna, and she looked back at him, expressionless. Laita waited, but the woman said nothing.

"I might know someone," Tasius admitted. "He's a retired Guardsman. He was loyal to the Guard, and probably still is. But I could talk to him, see if he might share some stories with me."

Tasius shrugged.

"It's not much, but it's all I've got."

"We'll need to set up meetings with my people," Xuthos said to Laita, his eyes roaming over her face and body. She suppressed a shudder and tried to figure out what he meant.

"Your people?"

"The nobles who will command your soldiers," he clarified. "They'll need to meet, so that we can establish the pecking order."

"No."

Xuthos raised his eyebrows.

"What does that mean?"

"Your people—and I assume you mean the young nobles that Ennius mentioned—will never meet any of my soldiers. They will not lead them. They will not command them."

"You said you've got two hundred people following you. Who's going to command them all, then? You?"

"I already *do* command them. And there is an established *chain* of command that ensures the right people are making decisions based on the orders I give them. We will not introduce inexperienced people who have never been soldiers into that chain of command."

Xuthos turned to Ennius and gestured at Laita as if to say, "you try to make her see reason."

Ennius put on a serious expression like he would slip on a pair of expensive gloves. She was sure this was his 'negotiation' face.

"My dear, I believe—"

"I am Commander Laita Naschect. You may call me Laita or you can call me commander."

Ennius stopped and stared at her for a moment before nodding.

"Very well, Laita. I think you're dismissing the value that Xuthos' friends can bring to this mission. They are excited by the prospect of doing something of value for the Empire, even if they don't know exactly what it might be. That kind of enthusiasm—"

"Gets people killed," Laita interrupted.

"And then they are already accustomed to command," Ennius said loudly and quickly.

"Command? What forces have they commanded?"

"Well, they're *nobility*. They have servants, underlings, and many of them oversee some business interests ...."

He trailed off, and Laita could see he was aware of how silly he sounded. She managed to keep the scorn out of her voice when she spoke, but it wasn't easy.

"Soldiers aren't servants, Ennius. Soldiers are trained to fight, to kill, and to die serving the Empire. And they are commanded by people who are trained to fight, to kill, to die, and to *lead*."

Ennius kept his expression neutral, but Laita could see he was embarrassed by her words.

Xuthos snorted and crawled up from his chair.

"I think we've talked about this enough tonight. I have other things to do."

Without another word, he walked toward the door, gesturing for Namal to move out of the way. The sergeant didn't budge.

"Commander?" Namal asked her.

Laita turned to look at him and saw the anger in his eyes. She knew he wanted to teach Xuthos a lesson in manners. But she didn't want to have a confrontation tonight. She nodded at him, and he stepped out of the way.

Xuthos yanked the door open and walked out, leaving it open behind him. Namal stepped up and closed it, and Laita glanced back to see the cold fury on his face.

Ennius and Zita also stood.

"Yes, this was a good start," Ennius said to the others. "Let's think about what was said here today, and we'll meet again next week at our usual time."

Zita nodded once and turned to Namal.

"May I also leave?" she said in a condescending tone.

Again, Namal stepped to the side of the door and Zita waited for him to open it for her. When she realized he wasn't going to do so, she narrowed her eyes at him. Ennius scurried forward and pulled it open, gesturing for her to lead, and she swept out.

"Good evening, everyone," Ennius said before pulling the door closed behind him.

Laita stood up as well, but Galla motioned for her to sit back down.

"My apologies, Laita. We don't always get to choose our allies. But now that those three are gone, let's really get to work."

Laita returned to her seat as Oriuna came over and sat in the chair recently vacated by Ennius. Galla did not seem surprised at the woman's sudden participation.

Irako sat down in Zita's chair and Galla gave him a smile.

"I'm sorry, Oriuna," Laita said to her. "When Irako was making introductions, I didn't catch your area of expertise."

For the first time, a slight smile turned up the corners of Oriuna's mouth. She glanced from Laita to Namal and back.

"I know all the secrets," she said.

"Secrets?"

Galla barked a laugh and waved her hand at Oriuna.

"Ythis is little more than a pot full of secrets, Laita. The city runs— no, it *thrives*—on all those things no one is supposed to know. Oriuna seems to have access to a surprising number of them."

"How do you manage that?" Laita asked the woman

Oriuna chuckled.

"That's exactly the kind of secret that powers Ythis," she said. "And one shouldn't spend power like that freely. I'm sure I'll answer that question at some point, but we haven't yet reached that point."

She looked over at Namal.

"Shouldn't your sergeant join us?"

Laita nodded at Namal, and he reluctantly came over to sit in the last vacant chair beside Oriuna, where Xuthos had slouched before he left.

"Tell us what you need," Galla said to Laita. "Let's see how we can help."

Thirteenth day of Highsummer,
6 days to the Arrival

Chapter Fifteen

HIS NERVES WERE ON EDGE AS KORAL WAITED FOR THE summons to see the Wolf. What face would his employer be wearing today? And was it the Wolf who choose how he looked or was it in the mind of the viewer? If the latter, what did that say about Koral's mental state?

If the former, what message had the Wolf been trying to give him?

Koral looked around the main room of the Wolf's Den. The bar was crowded again tonight. With the dark cloud hanging over the city, people were nervous and trying to drown their fears in alcohol and companionship. For some it appeared to be working. For others, it just made them feel worse.

Despite the crowd that gathered here, everyone seemed to be behaving. This was the Wolf's personal tavern, after all, and causing trouble was never a good idea. If you started something in the Wolf's Den, the bouncers were the least of your worries.

Koral leaned against the bar, the patrons giving him his own space. He was known as the right hand of the Wolf, and afforded a certain amount of respect because of it. He generally didn't take advantage of it. He didn't want to be that kind of person.

But sometimes he accepted the benefits that came with it.

A young man came through the door from the back area of the building and whispered in Nid's ear. The bartender and nominal owner of the Wolf's Den moved over to Koral and reached across the bar to touch his shoulder.

"He'll see you in the training room."

Koral turned and went through that same door, guarded on the other side by four large men with long daggers at their belts and chain vests over their broad chests. He nodded at them and they stepped aside to let him pass.

Beyond the main room of the Wolf's Den was a maze of passageways, staircases, and heavy doors—many locked or barred—that took up not only the building that housed the tavern but also filled the interior of the connected buildings on either side and behind. This was the home of the Wolf, and there were still areas that Koral had never seen despite his years of serving the crime lord.

He was familiar with the training area, though.

As he descended the stairs into the short hallway that led to the training room, he saw another two large guards standing on either side of the door. The sounds of swordplay came ringing down the hallway.

One of the guards turned and hammered his huge fist into the door three times. The room beyond went silent. The guard pulled the door open and motioned Koral to step through.

He had never seen the Wolf engage in any kind of physical training, combat or otherwise. He didn't know if the Wolf was skilled with a blade or simply watched his bodyguards training against each other.

There were two people in the room with the Wolf. Though Koral had seen them many times in the company of his employer, he did not know their names. But he knew they were two of his most deadly bodyguards.

The man was huge and seemed made of pure muscle. Despite his size and bulk, Koral knew how fast the man could move and had heard rumors that he was able to take an opponent apart not just through strength but through speed and precise strikes that could target nerve clusters and other vital spots.

The woman was much smaller, but no less deadly. A thin sword was strapped to her back, and she was almost inhuman when she moved. At rest she appeared to be a very lifelike statue—she was so still it was impossible to tell she was even breathing. Yet when she moved, she was like flowing liquid, with a smoothness that seemed impossible in a human body.

The two of them stood facing the door as Koral entered. The Wolf was between them, facing away and wiping his hands on a cloth. He turned and looked at Koral as the door was closed behind him. He was still wearing the same face that Koral had seen a few days ago.

The face from the past.

"Have you found Chaject?"

"No, sir. I've been searching, and I have my people out, but nothing yet."

The Wolf frowned at him.

"When you asked to meet, I was expecting news."

"I do have news, sir, but it's something else. Phana—"

The Wolf held up his hand, cutting Koral off.

"Do you remember what I told you three nights ago?"

"Yes, sir. I—"

"Your judgement is compromised, and I don't have time to coddle you, Koral. I ordered you to spend your time finding Chaject. If you cannot do that, I will replace you with someone who can."

The Wolf eyes were locked on his, and Koral didn't know what to do. He honestly felt that the Wolf would want to know about the … thing … that was following Phana. And he wasn't sure how to broach the subject without jeopardizing his position in the Wolf's guild.

He took a deep breath.

"If you don't trust me to come to you with something important … maybe you *should* replace me."

There was no anger in his voice, only resignation. For the first time in a long time, he was lost. Torn between the woman he loved and the man who had changed—probably saved—his life, he didn't know which way to turn.

Perhaps there *was* no good solution and his time with the Wolf was over.

When the Wolf spoke, his voice was mild and even more frightening for the lack of anger.

"Is that a threat, Koral?"

"Sir, I honestly wouldn't know *how* to be a threat to you. All I can do is come to you when I feel you need to know something important, or when a decision needs to be made that I can't make myself.

You feel that I can't be objective when it comes to Phana, and I'm not going to argue that. But if that means you'll dismiss anything I have to say on that subject, then I can't do my job anymore. It will pain me to leave your service, but if you don't trust me, then I don't know what else to do."

The Wolf continued to look him in the eyes, saying nothing. He swallowed, knowing it was over. He would be escorted out of the Wolf's Den and then he'd be on his own for the first time in many years.

"Okay," the Wolf said. "Tell me why you're here."

Koral opened his mouth but couldn't get the words out. He was being given a chance—and he knew it was his *only* chance—to prove that he still had value to the Wolf.

"I think Phana is related to the dark cloud hanging over Ythis. Not directly—I don't believe she's causing it herself—but something has come into the city looking for her. She ... she admitted to me that the rumors about her are true. She does have some kind of power or something. And now something is following her, watching her. She saw it the night before last, or at least saw where it was hiding. But she is sure it is here for her."

The Wolf slowly sighed disapprovingly.

"Koral, I already know all of this."

"You do?" he blurted without thinking. "How?"

"I think your proximity to me has made you forget who I am. You're not my only source of information, Koral, nor do you understand the resources I have at my fingertips. And this is what I mean when I say that your judgement is compromised."

The Wolf walked over to stand right in front of him and he realized how much taller the other man was. The Wolf looked down into his face, and there was no warmth there.

"I told you I wanted distance from Phana. I didn't want us linked together. And then you discover what must have certainly been a revelation for you. And instead of reasoning it out, putting together the timing and coming to understand *why* I don't want to be connected to that woman right now, you came here at her bidding to tell me something I already know."

The Wolf raised one finger and pushed it into Koral's chest.

"And you didn't just come here to tell me this news. If Phana admitted to you that she has this power, then she also demanded you come here and get me to agree to meet with her. And here you are."

The Wolf lowered his finger, but didn't step back.

"Let me make myself absolutely clear to you. You are a nothing more than a child wandering in the dark. You cannot see what's going on around you, and even if you could see it, you are helpless to affect it in any way. Keep getting involved in these matters and you will *die*. Furthermore, what's more important to me is that you are an ongoing connection between Phana and me, and that's precisely what I do not want."

Koral was speechless. He felt as if the ground was sliding away under his feet and he was going to fall, endlessly.

The Wolf took a step back.

"In recognition of your service to me over these past years, I will not, despite my better judgement, throw you out of my life entirely. But listen carefully, for I will not give you another chance after this. You will throw every moment you have into finding out what happened to Chaject. Find him, or find his body. Discover where he was, and who he was with. That is your only job now, Koral. Someone else will take over dealing with the gang leaders—you no longer have that responsibility. You will also stay away from the Wolf's Den for the foreseeable future. When you have something to report on Chaject, tell Elmther at the Crown and Coin, and he will get a message to me."

Koral slowly opened his mouth, but the Wolf cut him off.

"If the next—and only—words out of your mouth are not 'yes, sir,' then we are done for good. Is that clear?"

Koral was numb inside. He couldn't believe what had just happened. He was going to lose everything unless he did exactly what the Wolf demanded.

"Yes, sir," he said in a low voice. He turned and left the room and made his way back through the passages to the main bar area, and passed through the Wolf's Den without a word to anyone else.

He simply didn't know what else to do.

*   *   *

ACROSS A CITY AS LARGE AS Y THIS, THERE WERE COUNTLESS TAVERNS scattered among the endless streets and alleyways. Some were large and well-known. Others managed to remain open only through the patronage of a handful of regulars. The Wandering Horse appeared to be one of the latter, little more than a room tucked into the basement of a row of buildings on the eastern side of Low Town, just north of the Warren.

The small sign hanging above the steps leading down from the side of the road was long faded and acted as little more than a marker for those who knew what it represented.

Namal had been given clear directions, though, and found the tavern without too much difficulty. He descended the dozen stairs and stepped through door. The main room was just large enough to contain five small tables and a short bar on the back wall. A bartender sat on a stool behind the bar, leaning back against the wooden shelves behind him with his eyes closed, his head resting against the dark bottles of liquor.

The place was otherwise empty except for a single figure sitting at the table in the corner.

Namal closed the door behind him and walked to the table. Oriuna looked up at him and motioned for him to take a seat.

He pulled out a chair and sat down. The soft snores of the bartender came to him in the silence of the room.

"I'm supposed to get my own ale?" he said in a low voice.

Oriuna's mouth quirked up at the corners, not quite a smile but certainly more than he had seen at the meeting the previous night.

"You might want to remain sober for this."

Namal shrugged.

"It's been a very long time since a mug of ale was able to get me drunk."

She stood up and walked behind the bar, grabbing a mug and drawing from the sole cask stored there. The bartender didn't even twitch as she returned to the table and set down the drink.

"What do I owe him?"

Oriuna waved off his question as unimportant. Namal wondered if she owned the tavern and the barkeep was her employee.

"We have more important things to discuss," she said, as if reading his mind.

"You didn't have much to say last night."

It was Oriuna's turn to shrug.

"I'm always concerned about the … reliability … of my fellow conspirators. I don't say much in that room unless I have to."

Namal shifted uncomfortably in his chair.

"You saying you don't trust the others?"

Oriuna chuckled quietly and shook her head.

"Of course not. And you shouldn't, either. No one in that room is there for altruistic motives. Every single one of them has their own agenda."

"Not you, though?"

"Of course I do," she said, and her tone was sharp. "You'd be a fool to believe otherwise."

Namal considered her words. They didn't surprise him—he didn't trust anyone in this city, with the possible exception of Laita's friend Cedaro. And it was obvious that some of those in the room last night were there to take advantage of the opportunity to grab power if the Emperor fell.

"So what are we doing here?" he asked her. "From your own words, I shouldn't trust you either."

She leaned back and crossed her arms over her chest. She said nothing for a moment, just looking into his eyes.

"We don't need trust to work to the same ends. Our goals align, and that's good enough."

"For now," he replied. "But what happens when we get near to accomplishing our goal? Is that when you betray us to get whatever it is you want?"

Oriuna uncrossed her arms and leaned forward over the table.

"I won't need to betray anyone to get what I want. Once the Emperor is dead, what happens afterward doesn't require me to sacrifice anyone or anything to achieve my goals. It'll happen eventually, regardless of what I do."

There was something in her eyes, her voice, that gave Namal the impression she was being honest with him. If she was faking it, she was very, very good. He realized he was staring at her, and suddenly felt self-conscious and keenly aware of his age.

Though she wasn't exactly young herself. Perhaps ten or fifteen years his junior, but no more than that.

He forced his mind away from those thoughts that would inevitably lead to places he didn't want to go.

"So what's the point of this meeting, then?"

She nodded once, as if approving of his question.

"The others believe they are the entirety of the resistance. They are not. Irako knows others—young people like him who are committed to doing something. They lack real leadership, but they believe in the cause, know the city very well, and are willing to do whatever it takes to help."

"Why doesn't the so-called leadership of the resistance know about 'em?"

"Irako doesn't fully trust them. He's concerned that his people will be thrown away on some meaningless gesture that will accomplish nothing. He knows no one at the top would care one whit for those he represents."

"But you know about 'em," Namal pointed out. "That means Irako trusts *you*?"

She couldn't hide the smile on her face.

"Irako knows I'm not an idiot. He understands that I want our resistance to succeed and I'm not going to waste lives needlessly. Plus, he's an idealistic young man. One who thinks he feels something for an older woman."

Namal could feel his face flushing.

"You and he …?"

Oriuna chuckled again.

"Why not? He's an attractive young man."

She watched Namal, her grin widening as he tried to keep his own face neutral. He didn't want to think about why he was disappointed by this news. It was none of his business. If she and Irako were a couple ….

No, he wasn't going to let himself go down that road.

"Irako trusts my judgement. I told him that I was going to reveal everything to you, and he agreed."

"Everything?" Namal asked. "There's more?"

"Yes, there's more. But you don't get it all tonight. Tonight, we talk, and I get to know more about you. You've put yourself at risk coming here, but it's not just dangerous for *you*. We're all in danger. And I like to know who my allies are."

"Why me?"

Oriuna blinked at him, not understanding his question.

"Why are you talking to me instead of … my commander?" he said, almost saying Laita's name out loud. As much as the bartender appeared to be asleep, Namal didn't know him and wouldn't take the risk. And it was always possible this conversation was being heard by hidden ears.

Oriuna raised her chin and gave Namal and open and appraising look. It was different than how she had looked him over last night. Then, she had been sizing him up as a potential threat. This time, there was a slight grin playing at the corners of her mouth, and something in her direct gaze caused his stomach muscles to tighten up.

"I'm not the kind of person who deals directly with those at the top," she said finally. "I prefer to work in the background. I find I can accomplish more that way."

She didn't try to hide her smile as she continued.

"And I wanted to meet with you, specifically."

"Why—" Namal coughed as something caught in his throat. He tried again.

"Why was that?"

"I thought you'd be interesting. You follow your commander without hesitation and obviously trust her judgement. And you're extremely protective of her. And you look at her with something in your eyes … not romantic, but familial. She's like a daughter to you, isn't she?"

"I have nothing but respect for—"

"Obviously," Oriuna said, interrupting him and waving her hand to forestall his protests. "But that's only part of it. You care about her more than just as a soldier following orders. You chose to abandon the Legion to come here. You know the chances of success are very, very slim. You know that you're more likely to die than accomplish your goal. And yet you came here, anyway. You followed her, despite what it might cost."

"If you think we're gonna die without accomplishing anything, then you really don't know her at all. Lai—uh, my commander is like no one else I've ever served under. She won't fail. If she has to pull down this whole city, stone by stone, in order to succeed, she'll do it. And somehow she'll protect all the innocent people who live here while she does it."

Namal couldn't hide the pride in his voice as he talked about Laita. He had been terrified that she was going to throw her own life away in her grief over Kied, but at the same time, he knew nothing could possibly stop her.

And he knew that he had just admitted to Oriuna that he felt more for Laita than respect. He did love Laita and wanted only the best for her. She deserved a good, happy life, and he was willing to sacrifice himself to save her, if such an act became necessary.

He wasn't her father, but he was just as proud of her as her real father could ever have been.

Oriuna continued to smile at him. She had gotten the answer she wanted out of him after all. Though her victory wasn't in her eyes. Her smile wasn't one of someone who had just scored a hit on an opponent.

"I also wanted to talk to you because I could see how much your commander trusts you. And she doesn't seem like someone lacking in good judgement. Which means you're also extraordinary. You ... intrigue me."

Oriuna got up and grabbed Namal's mug. She went behind the bar, took a second mug from a shelf and filled them both. The bartender continued to snore as she returned to the table.

"So let's have a friendly drink and talk. I want to know you. Tell me your story. We're going to be working very closely together, after all."

Namal raised his mug in a toast and took a long pull. The mug helped to hide the blush that he felt rising to his face again.

Fourteenth day of Highsummer,
5 days to the Arrival

Chapter Sixteen

S HE DIDN'T STAY IN THE ROOM, OF COURSE.

Feeling angry and wanting to confront her pursuer made her stand up and grab the door latch at least three times during that first night.

But each time, she forced herself to stop and think about what might happen. Koral had made a promise to her to convince the Wolf to finally meet her. He was putting himself in a precarious position with his employer for her, and she needed to trust him.

The truth was that the Wolf might already know what was hunting—no, she didn't want to think like that—what was *following* and watching her.

So, she stayed in the room and eventually fell into a restless sleep.

However, by mid-morning, when the sun was well into the sky, she was ready to grab some food and water. Her watcher had so far only appeared at night. Phana considered her options and decided that she would go out and get food during the daytime, and be back in the room well before dusk.

Her trip out was uneventful—she didn't even bump into anyone she knew—and she was back in the room shortly after noon. More than once, she found herself pacing back and forth in the small space, itching to get out and move.

By the time the sun was setting, she felt as if she had worn a groove in the floor between the chair and the door.

One more night, she told herself. *I just need to wait through the night and then tomorrow I can get outside again.*

But, between her desire to confront her problems head-on and her growing boredom, she found it difficult just to sit in the room, hour after hour. She wasn't tired, and knew she wouldn't get much sleep again tonight. The monotony of sitting in a small room, alone, with nothing to do but watch the walls was torture.

She kept looking at the door, struggling with her desire to take action.

It was just past midnight—or so she figured—when it returned. The feeling came over her once more. Her watcher was back.

And then it faded away, as if it had not found her and had moved on.

She sat there, her fists clenched, wanting to yank the door open and go chasing after it. Instead, she took a deep breath and tried to relax.

It hadn't found her. She hoped.

When dawn came and the sounds of people moving about on the streets filtered through the door, Phana was more than ready to get out. She had slept little all night, and yet was not feeling tired.

She went out and broke her fast at a small shop that sold bread and cheese. And then she realized she had nowhere to go all day. She didn't want to spend the entire day at the Crown and Coin. She'd end up drunk by the time Koral arrived this evening.

There was no one for her to visit. Right now, she didn't really feel that she had many friends, and she wasn't in the mood to go searching for someone who wanted to have her around. She'd end up in a fight and that would only make things worse.

Instead, she wandered the streets, walking all the way up from the bay to the square outside the Fortress. The imposing walls rose up from the flagstones and towered over her. On a hill beyond the Fortress she could see the spires of the Imperial Palace. One of the towers caught her eye and she felt … something. A slight pull, or a … familiarity?

And then it faded, and she sighed heavily. Of course, the palace was familiar. She had been through this square before, had probably stood in this very spot and looked up at those towers, rising behind the blocking walls of the Fortress.

She wondered what the palace building itself looked like, under those slender towers. Few people in Ythis ever got beyond the Fortress walls to see the entire palace with an unobstructed view.

She felt like visiting her usual haunts, and then realized that she couldn't do that now. The darkness of nighttime allowed her to travel the rooftops unseen. To stand at the edge of the market square and listen to the mournful wails of the slaves on the auction block.

But the square wouldn't be empty at this time of day. It was too early, and the entire market would be full of hundreds of people, buying and selling, shouting and arguing.

And the slaves would still have what little hope remained to them. Some might even pray to Ythis' god to find them an owner who would simply have them do back-breaking work instead of spending their meagre lives for entertainment. Or sacrifice.

She moved on from the Fortress. Soon enough she came to the outer wall of the Forgotten City. The endless dead rested here in their thousands. Lives spent in luxury or poverty, pampered or in pain, the beautiful and the ugly, the hale and the sickly, the brilliant and the stupid. All eventually came to the same place in Ythis.

The noble families and the wealthiest merchants spent great sums of coin on the most elaborate mausoleums in which they interred their dead. The destitute got mass graves, buried under dirt and heavy stones to prevent scavenger animals from getting to the corpse-flesh. Everyone pretended there was a difference between those final resting places, but Phana thought it was ridiculous.

The end was the end. Once you left the flesh behind, it no longer mattered what happened to the body. All that mattered was whether your soul got free to flee this world, or got sucked into the Abyss, or captured by demons, or consumed by a god.

Phana stood looking at the heavy iron gates that led into the Forgotten City. They stood open during the day so that mourners and grave tenders could come and go. At dusk they were closed and locked, for everyone knew that ghouls roamed the pathways after the sun went down and they would kill and eat anyone they found inside the walls.

As she moved on toward the West River Road, she caught a glimpse of the tower that stood near the western edge of the Forgotten City. It belonged to one of the Six, the legendary sorcerers of Ythis. Phana knew there was an open space around the tower where no one was brave enough to erect any buildings. She followed the road that curved around that disturbing landmark, not having any desire to get close to a sorcerer.

Once on the West River Road and heading back down in the direction of the Bay of Ythis, Phana stopped for a mid-afternoon meal at one of the small shops that lined one of the major thoroughfares.

And then she felt it again.

She was disoriented for a moment, for the sun was still high in the sky and she was surrounded by people. She looked around in confusion until she realized what the feeling represented.

The watcher was back, and it was nearby. She could tell it was close by the intensity of the feeling, but not where it was.

Phana looked around at the nearby rooftops, but there was no patch of darkness and no figure she could see.

She backed up against the wall of the shop where she had just purchased a pastry with pieces of sausage baked into it. She faced the street and looked around at the people passing by, searching for someone who might be watching her.

And then the feeling faded once more. Phana growled under her breath and realized she was crushing the pastry in her fist. She pushed herself from the wall and strode out into the street, continuing to look around.

The watcher was gone, and she knew she wouldn't be able to find whoever it was.

"By the Abyss, I've had enough of this."

A passerby frowned at her and she realized she had spoken aloud.

With a few more hours to kill, Phana turned in the direction of the Crown and Coin. Perhaps she needed a few drinks, after all.

*   *   *

DESPITE THE NARROW, TWISTING STREETS OF THE WARREN AND THE rapidly fading light as dusk swept over the city, Laita had no difficulties following the directions she had been given. Even in this heat, she wore the hood of her cloak up and noted that she was not alone in doing so. Her knives hung visible on her belt, a warning to anyone who might see her as a potential victim.

She reached the building she had been told to find, a three-story tenement that appeared to be in some disrepair but was in better shape than many she had passed in this part of Ythis. She strode through the front door and up the rickety stairs to the top, where she was faced with the doors to four apartments.

The second room on her right was the one she sought. Resting her right hand on the hilt of her knife, she knocked softly with her left. The door opened immediately to reveal Irako, who motioned her inside and closed the door behind her.

Laita looked around the small apartment and took in the single room with a narrow cot, a small chest of drawers, a table with only one chair, and the closed shutters over the only window. She turned to Irako and spoke in a low voice.

"Are we going to the Forest?"

He looked down at his feet and shuffled in place.

"They … no one else is available tonight."

Laita grabbed the single chair and sat down.

"I'll be honest with you, Irako. I haven't been impressed with your friends and their efforts so far."

He paced over to the cot and sat down on the edge. It nearly tipped, and he adjusted his position so that he wouldn't fall over.

"I'm sorry. I know things aren't as good as you were hoping. We do believe in the cause. All of us do. It's just … they get caught up in all the politics and keep forgetting that we still have so much to do before any of that matters."

"If any of them had any real idea of how much danger we are all in, they wouldn't forget. One mistake, and it's all over. You seem to understand that, but the rest …."

Irako considered her words before responding.

"It's not everyone. Oriuna understands—she's even more careful than I am. And Tasius knows exactly what we are risking. The others are all … well, they're rich. They are used to being able to buy their way out of trouble."

"Their wealth won't help them if we get caught."

"I know. And I think they know it, too. But it's hard for them to change their habits. And they all see this as an opportunity. You heard what they said. They're already plotting to become nobles, or more."

Laita nodded, unable to hide her grimace. If she didn't need these people's help, she would cut all ties from them, disappear out of their lives and let them wonder where she had gone. But she couldn't do it all herself, and they had resources that were necessary.

"Tell me more about Galla."

Irako looked up and smiled.

"She's the smartest person in the whole group. Her husband died almost twenty years ago, and she's run the business and the family since. Their fortunes have gone up, and their enemies …."

Laita waited for him to go on, but he just shrugged.

"What enemies does she have?"

Irako chuckled.

"None, anymore. There were rivals, back when her husband ran things. People he had done business with and ended up on the opposite sides of some nasty disagreements. But he died and Galla took over. And those people who had been out to take the Javadi family down suddenly had other problems to deal with."

"What kind of problems?"

"Business problems, health problems, marriage problems, you name it. At least one merchant fled the city with his two remaining sons while he still had something left. The others ended up destitute, some in the hands of slavers. Others fell into the clutches of the Church. Galla doesn't have any enemies anymore. People stay on her good side."

If Laita hadn't been impressed by Galla before, she certainly was now. There seemed to be more to the old woman than Laita had first assumed.

"Can she be trusted?"

"She has no love of the Emperor, that's for sure. She talks about how the Emperor, the Church, and the Six keep all the power to themselves, and the citizens are the ones who suffer. She wants to see him fall, and the sorcerers and priests along with him."

Irako frowned at Laita.

"That's the thing that no one seems to talk about. Everyone wants the Emperor gone, but he's only part of the problem. The balance of power in the Empire is held between all three groups. If one starts to become too powerful, the others temporarily align to knock them down a peg. And if the Emperor falls, then there could be a war between the Church and the sorcerers, not just in Ythis, but in all the cities of the Empire."

Laita had already considered the possibility of open fighting between the remaining factions. Such a war had the potential to take down civilization as they knew it. Countless innocent people would die in that war.

As a military commander, Laita had also considered the alternatives. If the balance of power was close enough, they might avoid a direct conflict. There was no guarantee the outcome wouldn't be mutually assured destruction. That was, at least, until one or the other side gathered enough power to ensure a victory.

But should they go to war, the people of the Empire would be caught in the middle. And yet, they were already caught under the bootheel of three factions that cared nothing for them. Laita had considered the potential positive that might result from such a conflict. Whoever won—assuming there was a winner—would be severely weakened.

And in such a weakened state, could the people take back control of their lives? Could they band together to overcome whichever side remained and be free to choose their own rulers?

It was a gamble, to be sure. But if she did nothing, then nothing would change. And the Empire needed to change. It couldn't go on like this. Too many already suffered.

"I cannot guarantee you that things won't get much worse before they get better. But I can assure you of two things. One, I have no desire to rule the Empire myself, which means you can trust me to do what is best for the people I am sworn to protect. And two, I have no plans to leave as soon as this mission is completed. I will still be here to do whatever I can to ensure that the people have a chance to come out of this better than they were before."

She realized Irako was staring her in the eyes. His face was serious, but he was no longer frowning. There was something in his look that seemed different to her. And then she understood. She was seeing the beginnings of his faith in a better future.

She hadn't expected that. But she hadn't shared her doubts and fears with this young man. All he saw was a commander who was dedicated to the common people of the Empire. Someone who was willing to fight for people like him and ask little in return.

She was used to some soldiers looking at her like that when she was giving commands in the heat of battle. She had seen it on the faces of the soldiers who had watched her kill the priest outside of that cursed cave in the mountains. Irako wasn't a soldier, no matter what he had done in service to this little rebellion of theirs.

"Those are important things to think about," she said to him. "But I think it's something we need to discuss with the rest of the group. For now, I have pressing concerns that I must address. My soldiers are still coming into Ythis, and I need to find them places to stay and the means to keep them fed and hidden. Galla said she'd give me money, but that's only a part of the problem."

Irako understood.

"There is a criminal guild in Ythis. I wouldn't call those people trustworthy, exactly. But they keep their distance from the Church and the Six. For the right price, they will provide services, ask no questions, and keep silent about it afterwards. The only problem I see is one of scale. A local gang isn't going to be of much help."

From Laita's experience in taking control of cities, she was familiar with how criminals operated.

"Is there a group—a council or something—where the local crime lords discuss their business, resolve disputes, set territories, that kind of thing? We might be able to make contact with one of these crime lords and negotiate something."

Irako looked at her, surprised. Then he chuckled as he answered.

"Ythis doesn't have a council. Crime in this city is controlled by a single man."

Laita raised her eyebrows.

"One man? I find that hard to believe. How does he maintain control?"

Irako leaned back on the cot.

"Ah, you haven't yet heard about the Wolf. It's quite a story …."

*   *   *

THE WARM AIR WAS THICK WITH MOISTURE AND IT FELT TO NAMAL as if the entire city had been submerged underneath the Bay of Ythis. Oriuna walked beside him in companionable silence. They had spent a few hours talking in the bar the previous evening, and Namal had found himself telling her much of his life story, despite his usual reluctance to talk about himself.

He had also found her to be an intelligent, funny, and intriguing woman. What he had learned about her had only whetted his appetite to know more.

As they had parted, she had told him she wanted to show him something, and so tonight they had met up in Midtown near the Watch House, and were slowly walking northwards.

"It's really not safe for me to be out here," he muttered to her in a low voice.

"Weren't you out earlier looking for your weapons?" she asked him. "Besides, it's safer than you think," she replied. "The Watch doesn't care about catching criminals, mostly because they're all crooked, and partly just to spite the Imperial Guard. And the Guard has more important things to do unless they get confirmation that you're here in the city."

"I had to meet with the man who is holding them," he replied. "And convince him to hold onto them for another week until we find a way to distribute them to our people. This is different."

Oriuna laughed and hooked her left arm in Namal's right, as if they were just a couple out for a walk. But this was Ythis, a city far too dangerous for couples to head out for an evening stroll just to get some air. Even north of Low Town, in this area called the Rows, where the tenements had gotten smaller and less decrepit, and some streets were lined with narrow row houses, there was still little wealth in this part of the city.

It was, perhaps, less dangerous to be out on the street, but Ythis was notorious for its countless gangs that controlled the neighborhoods across the city. Not that he was worried about a fight—both he and Oriuna looked like they could handle trouble and most gangs would likely bypass them in favor of more vulnerable targets.

"Tonight is as much about the success of your mission as your earlier meeting was," she replied. "Besides, how often do you get to stroll along in the evening with an attractive woman on your arm?"

"Well, as much as I appreciate your … company, I'd feel more comfortable if my sword arm was free."

Oriuna looked sideways at him as she let her arm drop.

"You don't ever stop being a soldier, do you?"

The question took him by surprise.

"Have you forgotten *why* I'm in Ythis?" he asked.

"Not at all. I'm not talking about that. I'm asking about you in a general sense. Do you ever stop being a soldier?"

Namal considered her question for a moment before answering.

"Not really, not anymore. When I was younger, being a soldier was something I did when I was working, but it wasn't who I *was*. I'm not sure when that changed. But I guess I spent so much time in uniform, that eventually the soldier became the real me and that other guy just … faded away."

Oriuna walked beside him in silence for a few moments. Finally, she held up a hand and he stopped. They were on a street lined with apartments over small shops of various types. The mouth of a narrow alley was just ahead.

"This way," she said in a low voice, and ducked into the darkness of the alley.

Namal stepped around the corner, his hand on the hilt of his knife. The darkness was impenetrable, and he hesitated, not wanting to stumble over whatever might be concealed by the shadows.

Oriuna reached out and grabbed his forearm, pulling him into the alley and out of sight of the street.

"Wait here," she whispered, her lips nearly touching his ear. Her breath was warm, and he felt a shiver run down his spine, though he tried to suppress it so that she wouldn't feel it through her hand on his arm.

Just then, several figures passed the mouth of the alley. In the dim light from the lanterns hung at each intersection Namal could see the ruffians—a gang on their way to some illegal business, no doubt.

Once they were past, he turned to where he thought Oriuna's face would be.

"How did you know?"

When she spoke, he realized she hadn't turned her head, and they were nearly nose-to-nose. He could almost her feel her lips just in front of his own.

"I know this city, Namal. It's why you need me."

Without wanting it to happen, he felt his body begin to respond to her closeness. Embarrassed, he stepped back from her.

"We should go," he grunted.

But she hadn't let go of his arm and she stopped his retreat.

"Not that way."

She turned and led him further into the alley. He looked up and could see stars hovering in the narrow gap between the walls. Then they turned a corner and the alley grew brighter. Ahead, the passage-way opened onto a wider street and he realized that they had come far enough north to reach the Fortress.

He stopped.

Oriuna's hand slipped off his arm as she took a couple of steps before stopping and turning back. He couldn't make out her face, but her silhouette was clear with the light coming into the mouth of the alley.

"What are you up to?" he asked her, his hand back on the hilt of his knife.

"I'm showing you the Fortress," she replied warily.

"I've seen the Fortress already."

She paused and then chuckled softly to herself.

"You're taking my advice to heart. That's good. But I didn't bring you here to be captured. If I was going to do that, I'd have had a few dozen soldiers surrounding the bar while we were having that drink last night."

He had to admit she was right. Still, he wasn't ready to trust her completely.

"Why are we here? You're not going to walk in and take me on a tour, are you?"

"That would be wonderful, and very useful, but I'm afraid it's a bit out of my ability to get us out of that building if we go walking into it. But I do want to point out a few things to you."

"I know how to evaluate a Fortress."

"Yes, but I know some of the secrets of this particular one. Secrets that might interest you."

"First, I'm interested in hearing how you know of these secrets."

She did not immediately answer. He could tell she was looking at him, evaluating how much she should tell him. He gave her time to consider her response. She had said she wanted Laita to complete her mission successfully, and it was time for Oriuna to commit something.

When she spoke, there was no longer any playfulness in her voice.

"I have access to … assets that none of the others know about. I know other people who would like nothing more than to see the Emperor fall, no matter what happens after. But those people will not join this resistance movement, nor will they let anyone other than me know who they are."

"That sounds like little more than well wishes, to be honest," he replied candidly.

"They can provide you with a lot more than well wishes. For starters, they can provide you with information you need to get into—and through—the Fortress without having to fight your way in step-by-step. They can provide plans of the Palace, so you know where you're going once you get inside. They can provide the right distraction at the right time, to draw off as many of the Imperial Guard as necessary so you might even manage to get out alive after you've accomplished your mission."

Namal considered her offer. To have access to information about the interior of the Fortress, along with information about the Palace, it meant there must be some highly placed traitors in the servants or administrators who worked there, or perhaps even in the Imperial

Guard itself.

The Guard was supposed to be incorruptible, but there were always those who were willing to enrich themselves by betraying others.

"And what do they get out of it, after the Emperor is gone?"

She shrugged.

"That's not for me to say, to you or anyone. One thing you must realize about Ythis is that there are a dozen or more factions, always working with and against each other. On any given day, half of them want to see the Emperor gone, and the other half want him on the throne. And it's not always the same halves."

She glanced over her shoulder at the Fortress and then back to Namal.

"You can either accept my assistance or you can reject it. But these are the answers you're getting tonight. Shall I start explaining the Fortress to you or do you want to leave?"

Namal stood there, considering her words and his options. Finally, he stepped up beside her and looked out at the imposing building facing them across the open square.

"Tell me everything you can."

Chapter Seventeen

S HE HAD BEEN WORRIED ABOUT GETTING DRUNK BEFORE KORAL showed up. That didn't seem possible tonight.

Phana's tankard had been refilled at least four times, but it didn't seem to be making any difference. Her thoughts were still clear, still focused on the matter at hand. She was counting the minutes, watching the sunlight through the small windows on either side of the door change as it slowly sank toward the horizon, the shadows creeping across the floor and the tabletops, reaching out toward her to eventually envelope her in its darkness.

When the light through the windows had disappeared completely, the door opened and Koral stepped through. He strode into the Crown and Coin with a purpose, heading immediately in the direction of the back room.

His eyes scanned the tavern's common room, and before he had taken five steps across the wooden floor, he saw her. His stride faltered, and she saw it in his eyes.

He'd failed.

No, she thought to herself. *It's not his failure.*

But Phana couldn't deny that her first urge was to blame him. He had been her one chance to see the Wolf, and he'd failed to convince his boss of the urgency of her need.

Koral slowly walked over to the table where Phana sat. He looked down at her tankard, still half-full.

"We need to talk," he said in a low voice.

She stood and motioned for him to lead the way. She could feel the eyes of the other patrons on her as she followed him toward the back room. They had no idea what this was about, but they had all heard the news that Phana was no longer allowed at the Wolf's Den. They knew who she was, that she was in a relationship with Koral.

Only Elmther, the owner of the Crown and Coin, had welcomed her as he always did. She liked him, though now she knew his eyes were on her as well.

She wanted to turn and scream at them to get out of the tavern. That this was none of their business. She could feel it stir in her blood, the chill creeping down her arms and legs, and she stopped and squeezed her eyes shut, trying to crush it down inside her, refusing to let herself lose control.

When she opened her eyes, Koral was standing at the door to the back room, staring at her with wide eyes. His body was tense, as if he was ready to run.

He's afraid of me.

The realization was like a physical blow. She knew then that something had changed between them the moment she told him the truth about herself. He still loved her, of that she had no doubt.

But she also frightened him.

She forced herself to take a deep breath and then nodded at him and gestured for him to go into the back room. She followed him in and closed the door behind her.

He turned and looked at her but didn't say anything.

"He won't meet with me," she said into the silence. She tried to keep her voice neutral, not wanting to sound like she was accusing Koral of anything.

"He knows," Koral replied. "He knows ... everything. He knew the truth about you. He knew about the ... thing ... that's following you. Or at least he knew something like that would probably happen. He knows that you're the reason—"

Phana waited for Koral to finish the sentence, but he snapped his mouth shut and just looked at her.

"I'm the reason for what, Koral?"

His eyes went to the surface of the small table in the center of the room, and his face went very still.

"You can't just start a sentence like that and leave it hanging," she told him. "You owe it to me to finish what you were about to say."

Koral looked back up at her and opened his mouth. Nothing came out, and he cleared his throat.

"You're related, somehow, to the feeling of doom hanging over the city."

Phana wasn't afraid very often. Fear was an uncommon emotion for her—she had confidence that she would find a way to win out against most obstacles. She had been in some pretty tight spots before and managed to come through nearly unscathed. And she knew what she had inside her.

She was afraid now.

She grabbed a chair and slid herself into it, her legs going weak.

"He said that?" she asked Koral. "That I was causing it?"

Koral shook his head.

"No, I … I said I thought it might have something to do with the shadow that is chasing you. He confirmed it."

She felt cold, but not like the chill that lived in her blood. Rather, she felt like she was shivering inside, as if her heart, lungs, and organs had turned to jelly and only heat could keep them intact.

"What else did he say about it? The shadow, I mean?"

"It's the reason you were barred from the Wolf's Den. This is why he wants distance from you. Whatever is following you, the Wolf doesn't want to be anywhere near it."

Phana tried to process what Koral was telling her. If the shadow was that powerful—to bring down the sense of doom over the entire city—what chance did Phana have against it? Even if she let loose the ice in her blood, it couldn't possibly be enough to save her from something that was able to blanket the entire city in fear and despair.

The Wolf knew it was after her, and he wouldn't help. In fact, he was obviously afraid of whatever it was. And he also apparently believed that if he didn't interfere, it would leave him alone once it had done ….

What was it going to do? It had found Phana multiple times, and yet it kept retreating. It watched her, and then when she became aware of it, the shadow disappeared.

It was waiting for something. Did that mean something else was coming to Ythis? Something bigger or more powerful, coming here for her?

"I don't know what to do, Koral. I was hoping for something, some information that I could use. Maybe even help."

Koral cleared his throat again. She could tell he had more news, none of it good.

"What else?"

"He was … angry that I came to see him on your behalf. He stripped me of all my responsibilities. I'm no longer in charge of the gang leaders."

Anger replaced fear in Phana's heart. She imagined marching into the Wolf's Den and bringing down the walls until she found the Wolf. She could do it, if she really let loose. Find the man and *make* him reveal what he knew.

But she also knew it wouldn't work. She didn't even know what the Wolf looked like, and Koral had explained to her about his changing appearance. She might walk right past him and never know it, and Koral's description of the man would be useless to her.

Not to mention the lives that would be lost as his people tried to defend him from her. She wasn't ready to start slaughtering otherwise innocent people yet.

Yet?

That was not a pleasant thought. Phana was a killer, but she liked to believe it was only to protect herself or others who were in danger.

Koral was looking at her, waiting for her reaction.

"Are you out?"

He gave a small shake of his head.

"He said he would give me one last job, and that was only because I had served him for so long. But if I mess it up, I'm gone."

"What do you have to do?" Phana asked, and a small part of her mind imagined Koral pulling a knife and lunging at her. She pushed the idea away, horrified at her thoughts tonight.

"One of the gang leaders went missing a few nights ago. I need to find him, or find out what happened to him. But I'm not allowed to return to the Wolf's Den. I'm a connection between you and the Wolf, and so now I can't go anywhere near him either."

"Son of a dog! He expects you to remain loyal, but he damned sure doesn't return that loyalty when you need it."

"He didn't throw me out. That's a lot more than most would get."

"Koral, listen to yourself. This isn't reasonable!"

Koral's hand clenched and he shouted—actually *shouted* at her.

"What in the Abyss do you expect me to do, Phana? Just walk away from everything? I've got nothing else, nowhere else to go! The Wolf's guild has been my life for years now, and anything I could do in Ythis would end up crossing the Wolf eventually. How long do you think I'd last if that happened?"

She raised her hands and motioned for him to calm down, or at least lower his voice. She didn't want anyone in the common room of the tavern to hear his words.

"And let's be honest, here. If he kicks me out, he'll probably have someone kill me. I know far too much about his guild, about his habits, about the private areas of the Wolf's Den. If I'm not with him, then I'm a threat and he doesn't just let threats hang around."

Phana opened her mouth and almost suggested that they both leave Ythis together. Abandon this city, the Wolf, and everything else.

But she stopped. She wasn't ready to leave Ythis. As much as she feared what the shadow represented, Phana knew she wasn't going to run. She was going to find out what it was, and she was going to confront it. Even if it meant her death.

"So what now?" she asked Koral instead.

"Now, I find Chaject. One way or another, I do what the Wolf ordered me to do. And then we see what happens next."

"And where does that leave me?"

Koral looked at her and shrugged.

"Do you really think I have anything to offer you here? You can fill a man's lungs with ice. You're being hunted by a shadow that's hung this cloud of doom over the entire city. The last time I got involved with people who were … special … I came within a hair's breadth of bleeding to death. What in the Abyss could I possibly do to help you now, and are you really willing to gamble my life on it?"

Phana had never seen Koral so angry before, and his words stung her. She wanted to tell him that all she wanted was for him to listen,

to be a friend, to help her work out her own plan of action.

But that wasn't completely true. She wanted more than that. She had demanded that he go to the Wolf for her, and he had been punished for it. And now she wanted him to ignore the Wolf's orders and help her with … whatever was coming for her.

She tried to keep her own anger out of her voice, but she couldn't help but feel like Koral was abandoning her.

"Then do your mission for the Wolf, Koral. I've always taken care of myself before, and I can certainly keep doing it now."

She walked out of the room and didn't look back.

*   *   *

THE ALLEY WAS DARK, AS EXPECTED, BUT IRAKO LED THE WAY confidently. Laita followed, her hand on the hilt of her knife. Just because she was going to meet the Wolf tonight, it didn't mean some thug might not try to mug her in the dark.

She nearly collided with Irako as he suddenly stopped. Glancing over his shoulder, she saw the silhouette of a figure standing in the middle of the alley.

"Drulo?" asked Irako in a voice that Laita thought sounded a bit shaky.

"Who's asking?" the figure replied slowly in a deep voice.

"I … I'm Irako. I'm here to meet Drulo."

The figure stepped forward into the dim lantern light that reached into the mouth of the alley. Irako took an unexpected step backward and bumped into Laita.

The man gave a grunt of what Laita figured might be laughter.

"I'm Drulo. I'll take you to see the Wolf."

Irako let out an obvious sigh of relief.

"Are we going to the Wolf's Den?" she asked the large man. Drulo shrugged.

"Sort of. Follow me."

He turned and marched off along the alley and Irako followed without a word. Laita glanced back over her shoulder to check that they were not being tailed, and then matched step with the men in

front of her.

It didn't take long to reach a cross-street to the main avenue where the infamous Wolf's Den crouched among the simpler storefronts and two-story apartment buildings. Drulo led them into an alley to an iron-bound wooden door apparently leading into the back of a small tailor's shop. He knocked twice and the door was pushed open to reveal a lit hallway and two other large men armed with truncheons.

The men stepped aside and Drulo entered the building, leading the way to the left. Laita followed, looking around. They passed other side passages, down short staircases and up others, and took several twists and turns before stopping at another nondescript wooden door.

Despite the meandering course, Laita's sense of direction had not been fooled. She knew they were only one level below the ground and at the back of what would have been the Wolf's Den tavern itself. If it came to it, she was sure she could find a more direct route back to the alley.

Of course, if it became necessary to suddenly leave by herself, then she would have bigger problems than just becoming lost.

Once again, Drulo knocked twice and someone on the other side pulled the door open. The man on the other side was of a thickness to Drulo, taller but similarly broad-shouldered. But while Drulo carried some extra weight on his body to smooth out his proportions, this man was chiseled, the huge slabs of muscle protruding from his frame.

He wore a sleeveless tunic and loose pants with black leather boots. His muscles moved under the skin of his arms like living creatures as he let go of the door and stepped back.

Drulo didn't enter the room, but moved aside in the hallway and gestured for Laita to enter.

"The Wolf will come soon," he told them.

Laita suddenly realized that she hadn't been relieved of her long knives when they had entered this place. She wondered if this man would demand that she hand over any weapons before meeting with the Wolf. She didn't like the look of him—his physique was almost

unnatural, and he stared at her with dead eyes that didn't seem to fully register her as a living person.

She stepped through the doorway and saw the room wasn't very large. A wooden table sat in the center, two chairs on one side facing a lone chair on the other. Another closed door pierced the wall on the opposite side of the room.

Irako followed her in and the muscular man closed the door. There was no visible lock or bar, Laita noticed, which meant they weren't trapped in here. She kept her distance from the Wolf's thug, though, just in case.

He motioned to the two chairs on the same side of the table, but didn't say anything. Irako immediately took one of the seats. Laita looked at the man and then the door.

"What if I prefer to stand?"

"The Wolf will come when you sit," the man answered in a voice that growled with menace.

Laita didn't like it, but she lowered herself into the other chair, tensed and ready to leap up and draw her knife at the first sign of a threatening move.

A moment later, the other door opened, and she got her first look at the Wolf.

He was younger than she had expected. Tall and thin, with long white-blonde hair hanging past his shoulders, his pale face was completely shaven. Cold, piercing blue eyes sat above a hawk nose and a mouth that turned down at the corners. The Wolf was dressed in an immaculate silken robe dyed blood red, a simple pair of sandals on his feet.

He moved around the table and stopped behind the other chair.

"I am the Wolf," he said in a voice tinged with what Laita felt was a certain amount of scorn. She already didn't like this man, and found it impossible to trust him.

A woman came through the doorway and pulled the door shut behind her. Laita nearly leaped out of her chair as this woman moved into view. She carried a long, slender sword at her waist and the way she moved was like liquid come to life.

Laita would not want to fight either of the Wolf's companions un-

der any circumstances. She hoped it wouldn't come to that.

The Wolf pulled out the other seat and lowered himself into it, before resting his arms on the table.

"I have been told—in broad terms—what you need," he said. "I don't need to know the details. Drulo can take care of that."

Laita looked into his eyes and had to suppress a shiver. There was something … off … about this man, but she couldn't put her finger on what exactly it was.

"I see," she replied. "You understand that secrecy is paramount."

He smiled slightly, though it seemed more like a sneer to Laita's eyes.

"Of course. Much of my business dealings require discretion."

She forced herself not to sigh in his face.

"This goes beyond mere discretion. There may be those who offer threats or rewards for information about the locations you will provide to us. Should the Imperial Guard come to you and make demands, how secure are you in denying them what they want to know?"

The Wolf frowned at her, his eyes narrowing.

"I am the Wolf. *No one* makes demands of me."

"And if they offer rewards, instead?"

"I do not have time or inclination to play word games with you, commander. Are you asking me if I will accept a bribe in order to turn on you?"

He paused for only an instant, not long enough for her to respond.

"If so, you need to reconsider that question. I did not get where I am by betraying those with whom I do business. I will keep my end of any agreement we come to, as long as you do the same. This city understands how I operate, including the Imperial Guard, the Watch, and anyone else who may want to know your whereabouts, or those of your people."

Laita nodded at him.

"Thank you. It was not my intent to give any offense, but not everyone lives up your code."

He waved off her apology.

"It is not a code, merely good business. It is how I operate, because

I have more important things on which to concentrate."

"So, all that's left for us to know is the cost of your services."

He named a sum that was high, but not surprising. Laita knew she would have to make some special arrangements to meet it.

But as she opened her mouth to agree, her vision went cloudy, though the Wolf's face remained clear to her. And then his visage twisted and mutated, his features shifting as she watched.

She heard herself gasp as the Wolf's hair melted away and his face rearranged itself into that of a wizened old man, skin covered in brown age spots, bright green eyes protruding above sunken cheeks. Laita shoved herself backward in the chair, slamming back against the wall behind her.

With a lurch, everything snapped back into place. Her vision cleared and the young, blonde man still sat across from her, a shocked look on his face.

There was a flash and the tip of a long blade appeared, stopping just under her chin, held in perfect stillness by the woman who had entered after the Wolf.

Irako gave a yelp as the muscular man yanked his head back and held a knife at his throat.

"Wait!" Laita blurted. She held her arms out, away from her own weapons.

Neither the knife nor sword moved. Irako's eyes bulged as he looked at Laita, certain he was about to die in this room under the Wolf's Den.

The Wolf rose to his feet and narrowed his eyes at her.

"What just happened?" he asked her, and his voice was deadly calm.

"I ... I ... it's something that happens to me sometimes," she told him, trying to come up with a believable excuse for her behavior. She didn't know what had just occurred, but she felt that telling him the truth was the wrong idea.

"A few years ago I was in a battle that was ... bad. Afterwards, sometimes I ... see things that aren't there. Arrows falling toward my face. Men in armor with axes coming at me. Things that I saw back then ... it's like it's happening over again."

Laita had never experienced this herself, but she had spoken to soldiers who had. They described it as if they were back there in that battle, about to be killed. And their bodies reacted as if they were in danger without thinking.

"When I am tense, it sometimes comes back," she finished, looking the Wolf in those cold, blue eyes.

"I'm very tense these days."

The Wolf continued to stare at her, and she was afraid he could tell she was lying to him. With a single word, both she and Irako would be dead and her soldiers would all be on their own.

The Wolf leaned forward slightly.

"And is that *all* you saw?"

Laita almost nodded, but the blade at her throat reminded her that was not a good idea.

"Yes," she whispered. "It was all so real. I'm so sorry."

The Wolf paused, his gaze locked onto hers. Then he turned and stepped to the door, pushing it open. He looked back at Laita one more time.

"You have your price. Drulo will take the payment. We will not meet again."

He left the room and the woman held Laita at the point of that sword for a few seconds more. Laita met her eyes and saw no emotion there—just deadly focus. And then the woman drew back the sword and flowed out of the room through the same doorway, shutting it behind her.

Laita turned to the muscular man, who released Irako and sheathed his knife. He pulled open the other door and Laita saw Drulo waiting in the hallway beyond.

Moving carefully so as not to alarm anyone, Laita rose and proceeded out of the room. Irako followed on unsteady legs.

As the door closed behind them, Drulo looked them over and grimaced at their appearance.

"Looks like you two had one bastard of a meeting. Let's go."

Fifteenth day of Highsummer,
4 days to the Arrival

Chapter Eighteen

U NLIKE THE PREVIOUS OCCUPANT OF THE TABLE, THE woman didn't look afraid. She stared at the ceiling and ignored Relael and his two assistants.

He was impressed with her bravery. She knew she wasn't going to leave this room alive, and had apparently already come to terms with it. It was a shame he couldn't find some way to turn her to his own cause—he figured she would be a valuable asset.

But of course, it was a risk he couldn't take. She worked for the Wolf, and there was no way to know what hold the man had on her. If she left this room alive, Relael couldn't know for sure that she wouldn't report everything back to the crime lord.

It was such a waste.

He stepped up to the table and waited for her to acknowledge him. Her eyes glanced in his direction and then returned to the ceiling.

"What do you want from me?" she asked. Her voice trembled ever so slightly, and she tried to cover it by clearing her throat.

Relael smiled down at her.

"I just want answers to a few questions. Nothing more."

"And then you'll kill me."

This time, her voice was flat, emotionless. She understood her predicament and was trying to ignore her fear. To accept what was coming.

"I'm afraid it would be too much of a risk to let you go. Your employer wouldn't take it well if you reported back to him about our encounter here."

"Fuck him," she said, her mouth twisting. "Fuck the both of you."

"I understand your anger, Neysi. I would be angry, too, in your place. You've done nothing to deserve this, after all. You were simply in the wrong place at the wrong time."

He leaned over her and looked down into her eyes.

"And you had the misfortune to be acquainted with the wrong person."

She closed her eyes and took a deep breath, letting it out slowly.

"Her," she said through gritted teeth. "This is about *her*, isn't it? I'm gonna die because of that bitch."

Relael blinked and straightened up. How did this woman know about Phana? No, it couldn't be that. Neysi must be thinking of someone else.

"Who do you think is the cause of this?"

"Phana," she spat. "I knew she'd bring this down on all of us. I warned them to stay away from her, but it don't matter. She already cursed us."

Relael felt his hands trembling. This was better than he could have hoped. Neysi already hated Phana, and obviously knew a lot about the other woman. His spies were gathering information on Phana—though he hadn't told them why, of course—and had reported that she was friends with some of the gang members at the Red Flag tavern. Relael had ordered them to kidnap whoever presented the best opportunity, hoping they would get someone who could provide more information.

Neysi was the first to leave the Red Flag by herself.

Once again, Relael motioned for his assistants to leave the room. When the door was barred, he turned back to Neysi.

"You're right, of course," he told her. "This is all about Phana."

Neysi cursed loudly and called Phana a series of creative and insulting names. Relael smiled through her tirade.

"Phana is certainly a threat," he continued when Neysi's rage had played itself out. "And I'm going to do something about that. You can rest assured that whatever you tell me tonight will help end that threat."

Neysi turned her head to look into his eyes.

"Gimme a knife and tell me where she is. I'll kill her myself."

Relael tried to hide his disappointment. He was hoping Neysi knew where Phana lived. The woman was acquainted with a great many people, but apparently had not shared much information about herself with others. His spies hadn't managed to ferret out any details about where she stayed or how to find her. He had ordered someone to watch the Crown and Coin, but so far, she hadn't shown up there.

"We'll get to that," he said out loud. "But at the moment, I don't know where she is. What I want from you is everything you know about Phana. You've spent time with her. I want to know about her habits, her opinions, her likes and dislikes. I know she's involved with Koral Creyss, but who else does she spend time with?"

"Phana don't give a shit about anyone but herself. She's using Koral just like she used Qudovo. I'm not surprised the Wolf ordered her to stay away. He knows she's trying to work her way up to him. She probably figures if she fucks the Wolf, he'll let her run the guild or something."

"And Koral? Would he know where she is?"

Neysi snorted, her sneer telling him her opinion of Koral Creyss.

"She regularly disappears on him and he has no idea where she goes. She's probably got a bunch of lovers around the city and goes from one to the other, keeping them all under her spell. She's a witch, no doubt, and she knows how to make all the men want her. Even the ones who don't like her would still fuck her if given the chance."

Relael suppressed a smile. There was more than a hint of jealousy there, coloring Neysi's opinion of Phana. From what he had heard so far, she was physically attractive but no great beauty. But apparently there was something about her that caught the attention of any man in her vicinity.

Could it be witchcraft or some other supernatural phenomenon? Or was it just charisma and force of personality?

"Tell me what you know about that night she killed Qudovo and the others. Has Phana ever said anything about what happened? About what she did?"

Neysi turned her eyes back to the ceiling.

"You're really going to kill her?" she asked in a low voice. "You're

Andrew J. Luther

not just going to recruit her to the Church or turn her into your assistant or something like that?"

A single tear leaked out of one eye and ran down the side of Neysi's head.

"I promise you, I fully intend to kill her. But I've heard that it's not so easy a task, and I need to know about what she can do. How she can defend herself."

"You're a priest. Can't the Church just crush her? Don't you have a god on your side?"

"We do not invoke our god unless we must," he told her in a soft voice. "To do otherwise would result in the deaths of so many other innocent people. Our god is not a precise instrument that we can use to eliminate a single person. His power is vast … and rather indiscriminate."

Neysi's control finally broke and she let out a sob. She had been prepared to face death when Relael entered the room, but it hadn't come yet and the waiting was the worst part. Even the bravest can hold on only so long before it becomes too much to bear.

"It's okay," he said in a calm voice. "You don't need to be afraid. I will make another promise to you that should help. Your soul will not be given to our god who dwells in the temple below us. You will be freed."

Neysi shook her head and he realized that his words had not been comforting after all.

Well, he'd tried to be gentle, and that was no longer working.

"Neysi!" he snapped, his voice hard.

Her eyes sprang open and she looked at him.

"You've whimpered and complained long enough. Now you will tell me everything you know about Phana. You'll dredge your memories of every scrap, every detail. I need to know how to find her. I need to know what I'll face when I take her. I've been more than patient with you, but it's time to get to work."

She looked up at him and he expected her burst out in a fresh bout of sobbing. He was surprised when she spat in his face.

"I already said 'fuck you.' You're a fool if you think I trust you. You want Phana for yourself. I want her dead! So, either let me go and I'll do it myself, or just kill me and you and her can fight it out. Maybe you'll both kill each other and Ythis will finally be better off."

Relael sighed and wiped the spittle off his face with a soft cloth. He reached under the table and retrieved the wooden box, placing it at Neysi's side. She kept her eyes on the ceiling, not wanting to see what he was going to do to her.

"One way or another, young woman, you'll tell me exactly what I want to know. And I'll tell you something, too."

He smiled.

"I was hoping it would eventually go this way."

*   *   *

THE ALLEY WAS NARROW AND SMELLED LIKE ROTTEN GARBAGE. Jiska stood at the entrance, his hand on his sword, peering into the narrow passage between the buildings. The sound of the water lapping against the quay a few blocks away was faint but unmistakable.

The first couple of days in this city had proven unproductive. The Guard, while cooperative to an extent, had not been particularly eager to help. Hinara's demand to have members of the Guard wait around the gates undercover had been met with a 'perhaps' and a lack of action. He had outlined his plan to capture Laita Naschect, and Sergeant Danashy had been unimpressed.

Danashy had explained that he didn't have spare soldiers to cover the gates and the docks all day and night "until someone suspicious shows up," as he had put it.

But then last night, Quaest had returned from his mission to blend into the dock area and see what he could find out from the lower classes in the city, with news that Hinara had needed to hear.

"Sir, there is a resistance in Ythis," Quaest had explained. "A group that wants to overthrow the Emperor. None of the dockworkers know anything more about them—who they are, how to contact them, anything."

"Then what does it matter? That is something for the Imperial Guard to deal with."

"Sir, there is very little information about them, and no one really talks about them. But over the last few days, someone has been looking to make contact. They've been asking around, and though they've been pretty discreet about it, it reached the right ears and that person told me."

That was it, the break they needed. Hinara could *feel* it. Laita Naschect—or her people—were in Ythis and they were trying to contact locals who wanted to overthrow the Emperor. And whether or not such people existed, it didn't matter.

His next step, of course, was to make direct contact with the criminal element in the city. If the commander was here, she would mostly be in hiding in the slums of Ythis, and who would know those areas better than the parasites who thrived in such surroundings?

But now, Hinara's patience was wearing thin—he didn't feel like waiting on the road while his aid stood there, afraid to move forward.

"Proceed," he snapped, and Jiska glanced back over his shoulder guiltily.

"Are you sure, sir? This could be an ambush."

Hinara narrowed his eyes at the other man and drew in a slow breath. No doubt Jiska heard that intake of air and understood what it meant. Without another word, he stepped into the alley and moved toward the single doorway they could see. As they got closer, Hinara saw that it was open just a crack.

He followed a few steps behind Jiska, confident that he was entirely safe. These people wouldn't be so stupid as to harm a Legion officer—it would be a swift end to their petty and pointless lives.

No matter where he went, no matter how large the city or small the village, there were those who refused to follow the laws, who decided that they would put themselves above the Empire itself. Hinara had no use for such people. As far as he was concerned, they should all be rounded up and executed for crimes against the state. Cull them until people learned they couldn't consider breaking the Empire's laws without consequences.

His mission this afternoon was the result of the laxness of the Ythis Watch and all other such organizations across the breadth of the Empire. If there had been no criminal underworld, Laita Naschect and her fellow traitors would have had no one with whom they would have been able to buy support. These criminals would take anyone's coin, and so presented the traitors with options they should not have had.

And now he was in a position of having to deal with them on their terms.

Jiska reached the open door and knocked softly. Hinara stepped up beside him and hammered his fist into the wood, effectively shoving the door farther open. The light from the alley revealed a small room with a fireplace in one corner and an assortment of cooking utensils on a scarred wooden table. Another door led into what he assumed was the tavern proper.

That door now opened, and a man stepped through. Hinara heard Jiska mutter "shit" under his breath at the size of the man. But the huge figure made no threatening move, just looked Hinara and Jiska over.

"You both are new at this," he said. It wasn't a question.

"I do not *intend* to become experienced with this," Hinara snapped back. It was bad enough he had to deal with these people, he certainly wasn't going to let them show him disrespect.

The other man didn't visibly react to his jab.

"I'm Danz," he said. "Let's step back outside."

Jiska nervously backed up as Danz approached. Hinara didn't move, however.

"Where are we going?"

Danz stopped a pace away from Hinara.

"Outside. We can't talk in here."

"You want me to meet with you in an alley?"

"This won't take long."

Hinara sneered at him.

"I—not you—will decide how long this takes. I am not one of your common thug friends. I expect—"

To his astonishment, Danz merely put one of his large hands on Hinara's chest and pushed him backwards as he walked forward. Hinara was forced to back up, or fall on his rear in the muck of the alleyway. Danz pulled the door closed with his other hand.

Hinara backed away an extra couple of paces and put his hand on the hilt of his sword.

"I should drop you for putting your hand on an Imperial officer," he snarled. The big man just looked at him evenly and shrugged, as if he was ready for whatever Hinara wanted to try.

"You wouldn't get what you want if you did that," was the reply. "I'm not looking for a fight, guys, but you won't order me around like one of your soldiers. You deal with me like this or not at all."

Hinara ground his teeth. This man obviously thought the criminals ran Ythis. He didn't understand the power the Legion wielded.

"You forget yourself," he snapped back at the man. "You have been *permitted* to conduct your illegal activities at the mercy of the Imperial Guard and the Legion. We have bigger targets to deal with. But push us, and we will come down here in force and round up the entire lot of you. We will see what your 'terms' mean when you are swinging from the gallows."

But Danz snorted, as if he found Hinara's threats amusing.

"Ah, you both are new to Ythis. You're lucky you were directed to me. Some guys wouldn't have patience for your bullshit."

Hinara had to resist a nearly overwhelming urge to draw his sword and cut this man down where he stood. But Danz continued.

"You want to meet with the Wolf. I can make that happen. But you need to understand something important, here. The Wolf won't put up with your threats. If you go in there and start insulting him, giving him orders, or telling him you'll have him arrested …."

He snorted again.

"If you're lucky, he'll merely end the meeting and you'll be tossed out on your arses. If you're unlucky, one of his Wardens will put both of you down before you can blink."

Hinara wanted to ask how a common criminal had managed to get a Warden—as far as he knew, those protectors were reserved exclusively for nobility—but then he realized that any bodyguard can claim to be a Warden. It was all just bluff and bluster. What else could one expect from liars and cheats?

"I am an Imperial officer, and I will be treated with respect," Hinara said to him, trying to keep his voice cold and even. As much as he hated to admit it, he needed this man. At least, for now he did. After Laita Naschect was in chains, however, Hinara could decide whether Danz was worth his further time and attention.

"But I understand," he continued, "that the Wolf has also earned a measure of respect in Ythis. I can deal with him as an equal when we meet, as long as he does the same."

Danz heaved a sigh. He didn't seem convinced by Hinara's concession.

"And I can certainly make it worth the Wolf's while to meet with me. I have enough money to keep his interest."

This time Danz had the audacity to chuckle out loud.

"The Wolf may be a businessman, but if you think he'll do anything for a coin, then you've got the wrong idea. The Wolf decides his reasons for making agreements—sometimes it's money, often it's some other reason that none of us know or understand. The Wolf doesn't need you. Can you understand that? And can you behave if he agrees to meet with you?"

Hinara did understand now. These people didn't have any respect for the Legion, or the Imperial Guard, or even the Emperor. They didn't understand the power that could be brought against them, and so they played their little games secure in their ignorance.

But if Hinara wanted to explore this option for finding Laita, his only choice was to play the game as well. He quickly ran though the other possibilities. Every other method would take time and resources. The Wolf might be the faster shortcut to finding out where she was hiding with her people.

"You are right," he said finally. "I am new to Ythis. I realize now that things are done differently here. It is an adjustment, but one I can make. I will treat the Wolf with all due respect."

Danz remained silent, considering Hinara's request. Then he gave a slow nod.

"I'll send a message to you in an hour or two with an answer from the Wolf and instructions on where to go to meet him."

Hinara turned and began to march back toward the main street. He could hear Jiska scurrying to catch up. This was a temporary inconvenience, but Hinara now resolved to make a case to his superiors once this business with Latia Naschect was over. Someone needed to clean up the streets of Ythis, and Hinara Angumu was the man to do it.

Chapter Nineteen

PHANA STOOD ON THE ROOFTOP NEAR THE EDGE OF THE market, listening to the wailing of the slaves as they were led away toward the Temple. Tonight, she felt no sympathy for those literal lost souls. They were no different than the chickens or pigs or other food animals that the merchants slaughtered each morning so that the citizens of Ythis could eat.

It was how Ythis ground on and on, consuming lives for the benefit of others. No malice, no mercy. Yes, there was a great deal of malice in the hearts of individuals who lived in the city, but taken as a whole, Ythis cared nothing for the suffering or the pleasure of any one person. It simply existed, grinding lives under its wheels, endlessly spitting out new lives to keep it going, only to consume them eventually as well.

Phana's anger at Koral had not cooled any since the previous night when she had walked out of the Crown and Coin, and likely out of his life for good. And then a fresh wave of anger—at herself this time—as she realized she was still qualifying her decision as 'likely' instead of 'finally.'

She knew she was afraid to let him go completely, and that fear only added fuel to her rage.

Once again, she considered her choices. To leave Ythis wouldn't necessarily solve any of her problems. If whatever was hanging over the city had come here for her, it would only follow in her wake if she went somewhere else. And she didn't see how leaving Ythis would provide any opportunities to learn more about herself, to unlock those memories hidden behind that black veil in her mind.

Ythis was all she knew, no matter how hard she tried to think back past the last few years.

Phana took a deep breath and tried to relax. She realized she had been clenching and unclenching her fists, and so she forced her hands to go slack and let her shoulders drop.

A moment later, she was all tensed up again. The restless energy was back, and she felt the need to *do* something. She could no longer force the issue with the Wolf—she had no way to reach the man now that Koral was cut off. If she went to the Wolf's Den, she would end up in a fight, one that still wouldn't get her a meeting with the crime lord.

And that dark cloud still hung over the city. She had become essentially immune to its constant oppressive feeling of dread, but the rest of the populace was still reeling under the fear that gripped the city each time the sun went down. And it was only growing stronger.

She turned away from the square and moved to the rear of the building, where she quickly climbed to the floor of the alley. Turning northeast, she moved in the shadows between the merchant shops and tenements on either side, heading in the direction where she could cause the most mischief.

It was time to pay another visit to one of the noble estates.

The streets were nearly deserted of regular citizens, though a large patrol of Imperial Guard marched down the street near the Fortress as she crossed from the west side of the city to the east. Phana kept to the alleys to avoid catching the attention of the soldiers—the last thing she needed was to be tossed into a cell just on the suspicion of a terrified sergeant.

She moved past the Fortress and headed into High Town, where the tightly packed streets gave way to the homes of the wealthier merchants and storefronts of more specialized and expensive offerings. Near the south end of the district, she passed a stone building that was the home of Ziarithllo Ilisti, the famed historian and collector of ancient books and scrolls that held the long history of not just the Empire, but of the time before the coming of the new gods and the rise of the Undying Emperor.

This area was near enough to the Fortress—and in a direct route between the Imperial Guard headquarters and the northern district where the nobles had their estates—that Phana expected to run into more patrols. The noble families would be demanding a heightened presence of soldiers to help ease their fears of whatever doom was growing over the city.

More than once, she had to wait for a patrol to pass her by before continuing her journey. Still, it wasn't long before she passed into the Nobles' District, where the sprawling estates of the noble families lined the wide avenues.

As she moved along the high stone walls that lined the outer boundary of each estate, she mentally ran through the list of noble families and what she knew of their particular interests. Unlike her recent theft from Iadan Eorallo, she had no goal in mind tonight. She was doing this to keep herself busy and calm her overwhelming restlessness.

She heard the sound of marching boots on the cobblestones, and quickly ascended one of the stone walls. Once at the top, she peered over to make sure there were no estate guards nearby. The mansion of the noble family was some distance away, well-lit by many hanging lanterns as the sky continued to darken with the coming night, and she could see the guards clustered together around the main entrance. There was no threat of them seeing her in the shadows of the wall.

She slipped over the top and let herself down into the grounds of the estate as the sounds of the patrol on the street outside drew nearer. She waited while the group of what she guessed were a dozen or so Imperial Guard soldiers passed by and continued on their way down the avenue.

And then she felt it. Her watcher was back.

In an instant, she knew it was there. She also believed it was the same being that had started following her—was it only four nights ago? It seemed like a lifetime had happened in those four days and nights, and she was surprised at how short a time it really was.

She looked around at the scattered trees that decorated the grounds of the estate, but couldn't tell where her watcher was hiding.

"By the Abyss, I'm tired of this shit," she muttered to herself.

At the guard post in front of the mansion, a pair of dogs started barking. She glanced across to see the guards grabbing spears and shields and forming up in front of the doors to the mansion.

The dogs were in a frenzy now, barking and trying to break free from their leashes. Phana wondered if the presence that was watching her was the cause of their distress.

And just like that, the feeling of being watched faded away. An instant later, the dogs' barking faded into whines and yips. With a suddenness that took the guards by surprise, the dogs turned and, instead of trying to get out at whatever they had heard or smelled in the gathering darkness beyond the lantern light, the animals retreated back behind the guards and attempted to return inside the building.

The sudden change from aggression to terror had an immediate effect on the men and women stationed at the doors. Phana could hear them shouting at one another, their commander ordering them to 'hold' while their line wavered. One of them grabbed a horn and blew three short blasts, pausing before repeating the signal.

At the third such trio of blasts, Phana heard the running of booted feet from the other side of the wall. The guards had summoned the patrol to come to their aid.

She could feel the eyes of her watcher on her once more. Whatever had caused the dogs' sudden reversal was likely something the shadow had done. And now the estate was soon going to be crawling with guards and Imperial soldiers.

She leaped up and grabbed the top of the wall, pulling herself up and over. The Imperial Guard patrol was at the gates of the estate about a hundred strides further down the wall. She dropped into the shadows at the base of the wall and slowly retreated from the cluster of soldiers.

Once again, the feeling of being watched faded away.

Was her pursuer waiting on the grounds of the estate? Was it now planning to do something to the soldiers coming to reinforce the nobles' guards? Would she hear tomorrow about the slaughter of a noble family?

It wouldn't be the first such family to be exterminated in Ythis in the past year. Apparently, a trained Warden had murdered the Ida-phos and Najare families some months ago before fleeing the city. The woman was still wanted by the Imperial Guard, and Phana had heard about the significant price on her head.

The noble families, of course, were still skittish and the current darkness hanging over the city each night hadn't done anything to calm their fears.

The patrol entered the grounds, and Phana could hear the shouting as they raced to reinforce the noble family guards.

Phana considered leaving the area completely. The noise would likely have alerted the guards on other nearby estates, ruining her chances of successfully stealing something of value.

And then her watcher was back again. She looked up at a tree that rose on the other side of the stone wall and could see the deeper blackness among the branches.

She wanted nothing more than to confront her pursuer, but this wasn't the place. Phana was still angry, but she felt a smile spread across her face.

"Fine, then," she said to the figure in a low voice. "You want to watch me? Let's see how long you can keep up."

And she turned her back on the shadow and began to run.

*   *   *

KORAL STEPPED THROUGH THE SMALL KITCHEN OF THE CROWN AND Coin, pulled open the rear door that led into the narrow alley behind the tavern and stepped out. Shoving the door closed behind him, he turned to regard the small figure in the shadows.

"What have you got for me?" he asked.

A boy stepped into view, no more than ten years old. He was filthy and dressed in tattered rags, his dark hair hacked short with what must have been a dull knife. He cocked his head at Koral and whispered back.

"Someone saw your man. They'll talk to you tonight, if you come now."

A flush of relief flooded through Koral's body.

"What's the price?"

"Food. Something good … meat … and bread … and cheese."

Koral pulled the door back open and stepped into the kitchen. He grabbed a full loaf of bread from a shelf and tossed it out to the boy. He then grabbed a small pot and carved a thick chunk of roast pig from the spit, dropping it into the pot, followed by a second bread loaf. Finally, Koral tucked a sizeable round of cheese under one arm and stepped back out into the alley.

The boy had already taken a couple of bites from the loaf in his hands. Koral kicked the kitchen door closed and gestured for the boy to lead the way.

The diminutive figure rushed down the alley and turned toward West River Road, one of the two main thoroughfares that cut through the city, running parallel to the river that wound down toward the Bay of Ythis. Koral followed, jogging to keep up with the boy. He didn't want to lose his only lead.

The boy didn't go all the way to the main road, but instead stuck to the narrower streets and back alleys, working his way south and east toward Low Town. However, when they reached the Bridge of Fleeting Shadows, the last bridge that spanned the West River before it joined with the East River just north of the Dock Ward, the boy turned and headed to the stone barrier at the side of the bridge, climbing up on top.

Koral caught up to him and grabbed his shoulder.

"Where are you going?"

The boy held his perch on the stone railing and looked down at the flowing river some twenty feet below.

"There's a path here. Hold on, it's slippery."

He shrugged off Koral's hand and lowered himself down to a narrow strip of dirt at the top of the steep slope that led down to the river. Keeping a grip on the stone barrier, the boy moved along the hidden path toward the underside of the bridge.

Koral climbed over the stone barrier and carefully lowered himself to the dirt ledge on the other side. He moved slowly along the path, never letting go of his grip on the top of the stone.

The path dipped down to run below the bridge, where stone supports anchored it to the side of the ravine that held the rushing river. Koral could see a faint light coming from among the huge stone pillars, and as he reached the first of the pillars saw that the ground widened out here, leaving a clear space where a half-dozen children had gathered.

A small fire burned in a brazier, casting dim light around the area, and some blankets and other bedding was tucked against the stone pillars well away from the edge that led down into the water below. Koral realized that some of the street urchins apparently lived here beneath the bridge and he was sure that very few adults were aware of this space right under their feet.

The boy handed the bread to a girl of about ten or eleven years. She took a large bite and then passed it on to the other children, who were all at least a year or two younger. Koral set the pot down and put the cheese beside it.

"Your friend here says that one of you saw what happened to the man I'm looking for."

The girl nodded as she chewed and swallowed the bread.

"I did lookout work for Chaject sometimes. He was nice."

"Where did he go?"

The girl looked at the boy who had led Koral here, and Koral saw the fear in her face.

"You can't let anyone know I told you. I don't want them to come for me."

"No one will know about you. I just need to know where Chaject is."

"The men took him."

Koral had expected this, but it still pained him to hear it confirmed.

"Did you get a good look at the men?"

She nodded.

"Chaject was at the gang's building, the one they use as a whorehouse. He didn't have jobs for me for a week, so I went to ask him if he would have any work soon. He paid better for lookouts than most. Gave us food, too."

This she said looking down at the meat in the pot, as if suddenly remembering the rest of the food I had brought. Koral was surprised that the other children hadn't attacked the meat and cheese as soon as he had set it down, but they all watched the girl, waiting for her.

"I was waiting outside—not all of his gangers are nice, and two of them keep telling me I could make more money whoring. Chaject wouldn't let me, but some of the others are creepy."

Koral made a note to go back to the gang's home and make sure that, in Chaject's absence, they hadn't considering recruiting anyone too young. It was not something he would permit, either.

"I was outside when I saw a couple of men come down one of the side alleys. They waited in the dark. A couple more came up the cross-street and waited, too. I saw a whole bunch of men gather around."

She paused and glanced around at the other kids.

"I wanted to warn the gang, but there was no way to get in there without them seeing me. I was hiding in a nook across the street, and they didn't see me in the shadows. But if I crawled out of my hiding space, they would see me and probably grab me."

"Did you get a good look at the men? Where they Watchmen?"

The girl shook her head.

"I saw them when Chaject came out of the building. He was alone, and the men ran out from all sides. The ones behind Chaject pulled a sack down over his head, and they just piled on him."

"Were they wearing anything recognizable? Were they from another gang?"

The girl looked Koral in the eyes as she spoke, and her words caused chills to run up his spine.

"They were Church soldiers."

"Are you absolutely sure?" he asked her, his mouth suddenly very dry.

"Yes. Chaject stopped struggling soon after they pulled the sack over his head. He didn't cry out or anything. When he stopped fighting, they picked up his body and ran off down the side street. I heard a carriage and horses."

He let out a low breath. The Church had abducted a gang leader who served the Wolf. This was worse than anything he had imagined. If the Church had decided to target the Wolf's guild, Koral was not sure if the criminals could possibly survive.

It seems Chaject might have been targeted directly. Perhaps he had crossed paths with a priest and caused his own trouble at some point. But that was a *best*-case scenario at this point.

Koral would have to get back to the Crown and Coin and get word to the Wolf as quickly as possible.

"I promise that no one will know you told me about Chaject. But stay away from the Crown and Coin for a while. I'll get the word out when things clear up. Be careful and stay safe."

The girl looked at him, and then at the children clustered around her.

"Ythis is never safe," she said to him, and he was unable to disagree.

Chapter Twenty

THE CARRIAGE WAS EXPENSIVE BUT NOT ORNATE. THE driver remained on his bench, but the footman stepped off the back and opened the door for Hinara. The pair of Imperial Guardsmen at the main gate of the Fortress eyed the carriage but kept to their posts. They obviously felt no need to get involved in Hinara's business.

Jiska stepped forward and spoke to the footman.

"Are you taking us to see the Wolf?"

"Our employer is waiting to meet you. Please step inside."

Jiska looked back at Hinara, unsure what to do. Once they were inside the carriage, they would be at the mercy of the Wolf's men. They might disappear, and he knew the Imperial Guard wouldn't put much effort into finding him.

But this was the opportunity they had, and Hinara wasn't about to let it slip through his fingers.

"Get in," he ordered his subordinate.

Jiska looked at the footman, who remained expressionless. Frowning, he entered the carriage.

Hinara stepped up and took a seat, ignoring the footman. The door closed and a moment later the carriage lurched into motion.

"I wouldn't have thought a crime boss would have a carriage like this," Jiska commented. "Seems a bit … wealthy."

Hinara didn't respond. He was watching the streets carefully, noting the route. He had been informed where the Wolf's Den could be found. The carriage wasn't heading in that direction. Instead, it turned east, heading for High Town.

Jiska made no further attempts to engage him in conversation and nervously watched from the windows, fidgeting with the hilt of his sword.

The ride was short and soon enough the carriage pulled onto a street lined with small yet tidy and well-kept homes. It rolled to a stop halfway down the block and Hinara looked out at a two-story nondescript house. The windows were dark, though he expected the draperies were simply closed against prying eyes.

The footman opened the carriage door and Hinara climbed out, Jiska following him. The front door of the house opened, and an extremely large man stood silhouetted in the light from inside.

Without waiting for an invitation, Hinara strode up the short walk to the front steps and proceeded through the door. He noted the great musculature of the doorman, but was unimpressed. Big brutes were often too slow to be much of a threat and were easily defeated by good martial training.

The man turned and led them into a well-appointed dining room. Seated at the head of the table was another man dressed in the clothes of a wealthy merchant. He was an older man, probably just past his sixtieth year, with a neatly trimmed grey moustache and beard, and piercing green eyes. His suit was well-tailored to fit the bulk of his barrel chest and large belly.

"Please, join me," he said in a heavy wheeze. "You'll forgive me if I don't stand, it will delay our discussion somewhat."

Hinara nodded at the man.

"I take it you are the Wolf."

"That I am."

Hinara moved down the table and pulled out a chair at the right-hand place. He motioned Jiska to sit at the far end of the table.

"Can I offer you any refreshments?"

Hinara waved away the offer.

"I prefer to get to the point."

The man gave a wheezy chuckle.

"I understand. This isn't exactly a social call."

Hinara looked around the room, noting the door to what he expected was the kitchen. He saw a staircase leading up to the second floor through another open doorway that led into a hall.

"You weren't expecting to meet me in such a setting, were you?"

Hinara narrowed his eyes at the Wolf. Was the man taunting him? Did he think he could throw Hinara off balance by holding a meeting in a house in a quiet part of Ythis instead of in an alley or the common room of a brothel?

"The setting is irrelevant. I am more concerned with who else might be in this house to overhear our discussion."

The Wolf grinned at him.

"Other than the three of us, the only people in this house are my two bodyguards. And they are always at my side, no matter what I'm discussing."

Hinara glanced at the doorway to the hall again.

"Where is your second bodyguard?"

The Wolf gestured to Hinara's right and he turned and nearly jumped out of his chair. A woman stood in the corner, watching him. A thin sword hung at her side, and she was dressed in dark leather armor.

So still was she that, for an instant, Hinara thought she might be a statue.

Jiska let out a muffled grunt of surprise as he registered her presence.

"Nice trick," Hinara snarled as he turned back to the Wolf. "You are certainly putting great effort into getting the upper hand. I would almost think you do not intend to deal honestly with me."

The Wolf's eyes lost their glint of good humor.

"I don't need to deal in tricks. She's been there since you entered. I would think a soldier would be better at evaluating his surroundings. Then again, I supposed it's not every day that someone encounters a Warden, let alone two."

Despite himself, Hinara glanced back at the woman. He hadn't believed the Wolf's bodyguards would be real Wardens, but now that he saw her in the flesh, he found his skepticism draining away. There was far more to this man that he had expected.

He would have to take more care and not underestimate the Wolf again.

"Interesting," he said, turning back to his host. "I imagine the school does not know she works for a criminal."

"You may imagine what you wish. But I am sure we are both busy men. Why don't you tell me why you reached out to my people and requested this meeting?"

Hinara wanted to correct him—it hadn't been a request, but a demand. He remembered what the thug in the alley had told him, though. He decided to remain as polite as was possible under the circumstances.

"I am aware that you are a fundamental part of Ythis. Your people operate across the city, from the docks to the nobles' estates. Perhaps in the very heart of the palace itself. I believe you are well aware of what goes on in this city, what persons of interest have entered and left, and perhaps where such persons can be found."

He smiled grimly.

"Am I correct in my assessment?"

"There is little that happens in Ythis that I do not hear about, this is true. I hardly have a list of every person in the city along with their location, however. I can only assume you are looking for someone specific."

"I am looking for many specific individuals. Most of them are of little note, however. Former soldiers, now deserters. The Legion would, of course, prefer to round them up and punish them as they deserve. I, however, am after more important prey."

He pulled out the bulletins with the sketches of Laita Naschect and her command squad, and placed them on the table in front of the Wolf.

"These people are also deserters, but more importantly, they are traitors to the Empire. No effort is being spared to find them. I have certain indications that they have come to Ythis. To find this former commander and her inner circle and hand them over to the Legion … well, anyone who did that would be highly regarded and well re-warded."

The Wolf looked down at the papers and Hinara watched him carefully for any signs that the man recognized the faces. But he revealed nothing as he gave a small shrug and looked back up at Hinara.

"The regard of the Legion and some coins. Seems like a lot of effort to gain things I either do not care about or already have in abundance."

Hinara had to fight the urge to pull his knife and stab this man in the face. Who did he think he was, casually dismissing the Legion like that? Only the woman in the corner stayed his hand. If she really was a Warden, Hinara would be dead before his knife could clear the sheath.

He clenched his jaw but kept his hands on the table. He silently counted to ten, taking the time to get control of himself before he responded.

"Does that mean you have no interest in helping us?"

The Wolf looked down at the sheets again.

"I'm not prepared to immediately commit any resources to this. That doesn't mean I will not help you. It also doesn't mean I *will*."

"Those are a lot of words wasted on not saying anything."

The Wolf gave that wheezy chuckle again.

"You're not wrong. I'll tell you this. I'm *interested* in your search for these people. I'm going to fully consider the benefits of helping you, and will let you know what I decide."

"When?"

"I understand you want absolutes. You're not going to get any from me tonight. You've given me something to think about, and that's exactly what I will do."

He reached out and gently pushed the papers back over to Hinara.

"Thank you for a most interesting meeting. The carriage will return you to the Fortress or wherever else in the city you wish to go."

Hinara opened his mouth to speak, but the large man stepped into the doorway at that moment and he realized that nothing he said now would change the Wolf's mind in any positive way.

Without a word, he stood and motioned for Jiska to proceed him out the door. The carriage waited on the street exactly where they had left it.

"Where would you like us to take you, sir?" asked the footman.

"The Fortress," Hinara ordered him as he climbed inside. If he had the full cooperation of the Imperial Guard, he'd have ordered them to kill the Wardens, take the Wolf, and then tell the man's people that they would find Laita Naschect for him if they didn't want to swing from the gallows.

But he didn't have the Imperial Guard. He would simply have to out-think Laita and her people.

He would deal with the Wolf afterward.

*   *   *

A SHEEN OF SWEAT COVERED PHANA'S FACE AND ARMS AS SHE ducked behind a stone wall and brought herself to a halt deep in the shadows. She put her back to the wall and calmed her breathing with a single thought.

For the first time, she was aware of her physical stamina. She had always been more physically fit than almost anyone else around her. She could exert herself for long periods without ever really getting tired out. She had never given it much thought, assuming that her body was just good at physical activity.

But now, she realized that she had been running flat out, leaping up and climbing buildings, diving through shadows and otherwise moving at maximum speed for at least half a bell. And yet, though she should be gasping for breath, she simply brought it all under control almost by reflex.

Something else that separated her from other people.

However, she figured her efforts had not been for nothing. She couldn't feel the watcher, and hadn't felt any sign of it for some time now. For the first time, she began to believe that she could leave it behind if she really tried.

It was still early in the evening, though the sun had fully set, and it was now easier to hide in the darkness.

Phana stayed still, waiting. The last thing she wanted to do was step out into the open and reveal herself if the being was nearby. She didn't want to waste all that effort.

And then it was back.

She almost cursed aloud, but held her breath at the last second.

She wasn't being watched. Not yet.

It was *searching* for her.

She couldn't have explained how she knew, just that it *felt* different. The watcher was sweeping, probing, sending out its senses in order to locate her.

Phana would have drawn further into the shadows, but she was worried that any movement would alert her pursuer. As the thought flickered through her mind, the cold darkness of the creature's senses swung in her direction.

With a start, Phana wondered if even thinking about the being of shadow alerted it to her presence. She closed her eyes and pictured Koral's face, as she had seen him the last time they had made love. His eyes focused on her face. His mouth open, as he gasped for breath. His hair, short, dark, drops of sweat forming on the ends. More beads of sweat on his forehead ....

The searching feeling swung away from her, and a moment later it was gone.

It was gone.

She had done it. She had managed to escape her pursuer, to hide from it, to fool it into thinking she wasn't here.

Phana continued to wait. She had no idea how close it might still be. Perhaps it was hiding its own presence to trick her into revealing herself.

And then the full weight of its gaze came down on her and she gasped out loud. The being was here, and it had found her once again.

Phana clenched her fists and stood up, stepping away from the wall and into the open. The shadow was perched on the edge of the wall no more than fifty paces away, a darker patch in the night.

"You son of a bitch," she whispered, sure that whatever hid in that darkness could hear her. "I'm done running away from you."

She could feel the cold in her veins, pushing to be let out. But she wasn't ready yet to unleash what lived inside her.

But that didn't mean she had to be the prey.

"I think it's time I see what's hidden in that shadow of yours."

Without thinking, she gave into her anger and frustration and flung herself forward, charging at the shadows on the wall.

She had closed half the distance when the darkness withdrew, like a silk scarf yanked away into the night.

Phana slowed her pace and yelled "Shit!" into the night.

And then she stopped and took a deep breath.

At the very edge of her perception, Phana could still feel its presence. Faint, but still there.

She had assumed that she was aware of it watching her because of the power of its gaze. But perhaps she was aware because she could sense it herself.

Maybe she could hunt for it the same way it hunted her.

She closed her eyes and focused on the night around her. The sounds, the smells, the feel of the warm air, and weight of the doom hanging over the city. She relaxed her hands and sent her own perception out, searching for the patch of darkness in the night.

There!

In the same instant she felt its location, she was already moving full out. With a leap, her hands found the top of the stone wall and she heaved herself over, landing in the grass on the other side. Another manor house sprawled in the distance, but she wasn't interested in that.

Her target was in the trees further back on the grounds of the estate.

She didn't pause but threw herself forward, sprinting toward the trees.

Dogs started barking in the direction of the manor house, but she ignored them, her every sense focused on her target.

Once again, the shadow withdrew. But this time she was aware of the direction in which it went. She changed direction, angling across the grounds toward the wall at the back of the estate as pursuer now fled from *her.*

She had been afraid of the watcher, afraid of what it might be, what it might do to her or those around her. She had run, she had hidden, and it had all been for naught. The fact it was now fleeing from her gave her no satisfaction—if anything her anger had only grown more intense.

A part of Phana's mind registered that the barking sounds were now behind her. The dogs had been let off their leash and were chasing her. She was nearing the wall, but she didn't know if she could reach it before the animals caught her. If she stopped to deal with them, her prey would escape.

With grim determination, Phana forced herself to increase her speed. Her legs pumped even faster as she drove herself across the tended lawns of the estate toward the wall where the shadow was now fleeing.

She could feel the dogs at her heels as she neared the wall. With a supreme effort, she pushed off from the ground and leaped toward the stones, putting every ounce of strength into her jump.

The top of the wall hit her in the waist and she nearly toppled over to the ground on the other side. But she managed to grab hold of the edge and swing her body around so that she dropped to land on her feet.

She didn't have time to consider what she had just done, leaping at least twice as high as she had ever done before. She was already running along the street after her target, which was still trying to flee into the night.

They were reaching the edge of the Nobles' District, and the streets began to narrow into High Town, where there were many more buildings.

The shadow flitted between a pair of large houses and suddenly disappeared.

Like a candle being blown out by a gust of wind, there was a sudden void where its presence had sat in her mind.

She stumbled to a halt and calmed her breathing again. Closing her eyes, she pushed her perception out among the buildings on all sides of her.

Nothing.

It was gone.

No, it was *hiding*. If it could move fast enough to escape her like that, it would have done so when the chase began.

Just as she had done when it was searching for her, the being in that shadow had pulled its thoughts, its *presence*, into itself so that she could no longer feel it.

She felt a grim satisfaction through her anger. Hunter and hunted had switched roles. And Phana felt she was better suited to doing the chasing instead of the fleeing.

"You're still here," she muttered out loud. "And I *will* find you. This ends tonight."

The faintest whisper of ... something ... flitted across her mind. It was too tenuous to grab, so she forced herself to relax and open herself up. And a moment later, there it was again.

She didn't focus on it, but instead just noted the general direction.

And then Phana stopped concentrating, stopped pushing her senses out around her. Once again, she focused on Koral's face as she slowly moved in the direction she had sensed.

She walked past the pair of houses and their waist-high stone walls and reached a second pair of homes. These were obviously the manor houses of wealthy merchants. One had a large tree growing in the center of the yard behind the building.

As Phana saw the patch of shadows once again, she focused all her attention on it, hitting the being inside with the full force of her own gaze.

"*My turn.*"

*   *   *

SOLDIERS HAD GRABBED CHAJECT.

Church soldiers had grabbed Chaject.

If the man wasn't dead yet, he soon would be. And Koral didn't want to imagine the manner of that death. Chaject had been a good man, a good leader. And now his soul was likely going to be fed to the God of Ythis.

He shuddered but kept walking, mulling over the possibilities in his mind. The biggest question was why Chaject had been taken.

It wasn't unknown for a gang member to be rounded up by the Church when they were getting low on sacrifices and needed to feed their god. It didn't happen very often—there were usually plenty of slaves too weak or unskilled to work for the wealthier citizens of Ythis or to perform in the arena.

But even when it did happen, it was always a case of mistaken identity. The Church took the homeless and the defenseless for their god. The occasional gang member who spent too much time on the streets or who passed out in a gutter from too much drugs or drink could wake up in the Temple.

But the Church didn't go after gang leaders in the Wolf's guild. The Wolf himself had insinuated to Koral once before that as long as the Wolf's people stayed out of their way, the Church would leave them be.

And this wasn't a random kidnapping. They had waited for Chaject and had operated professionally and with speed to get him off the street as quickly as possible.

What did Chaject know that the Church needed to silence?

Or what did he know that the Church also wanted to find out?

Koral's thoughts inevitably went to the Witch Hunter.

The young witch, Marilsa, had escaped from Ythis, but before she left, she and her brother Jadir had been bound up with one of the gangs. Almost everyone from that gang was now dead, either from Marilsa's actions under the influence of the spirit that had corrupted her, or from Qudovo's decision to go against the Wolf.

Chaject had been a member of Qudovo's gang, before he was promoted to gang leader himself … shortly before the matter with Marilsa and Jadir had begun.

If the Church was still searching for Marilsa—and Koral had no reason to believe they would give that up—might they have discovered Chaject's connection to those who had fallen under her sway? Had he been taken on the orders of a Witch Hunter?

Koral didn't know, but it seemed like it might be a connection. Right now, it was the only possibility he had.

He pulled open the door of the Crown and Coin and stepped inside. When Elmther saw Koral, he stepped out from behind the bar and led the way into the back room. Koral tried not to let himself feel anything about the fact that the back room was no longer his. He tried not to think about the fall from his previous position.

He was still working for the Wolf, and that was better than nothing.

Or it would be, if it hadn't cost him his relationship with Phana.

Elmther closed the door behind Koral but didn't sit down.

"Look," the older man said, obviously uncomfortable. "I know this isn't, uh, right. But I—"

Koral held up his hands to stop the owner of the Crown and Coin.

"You didn't cause this to happen. That's all on me. Besides, this is *your* tavern. You shouldn't feel bad about using your own back room."

Elmther gave Koral a nod, but didn't seem to be any happier about it.

"I found out what happened to Chaject," Koral reported. "He was taken by Church soldiers, and it looks like he was targeted. They were waiting for him, they ambushed him, and they made no effort to take anyone else."

Elmther frowned as he mulled that over.

"What would the Church want with Chaject?"

"I doubt we'll ever know for sure. But I think it may be related to what happened with … the girl Marilsa and her brother."

Elmther made the sign to ward off evil. It was reflective, and Koral tried not to let himself be irritated by that. What had happened to Marilsa hadn't been her fault, but all people remembered was that she was a witch.

Someone knocked on the door.

Elmther opened it to reveal Danz. The big man was rarely seen at the Crown and Coin, as he spent most nights at the Red Flag. Danz was a dependable gang member. He would most likely be promoted to gang leader the next time a position opened up.

Tonight, however, he just looked worried.

He looked from Elmther to Koral and back.

"I... I need to talk to you," he said, not sure who he should be asking.

Elmther met Koral's eyes and they silently agreed to put their own discussion on hold. The barkeep motioned for Danz to come into the room, closing the door behind him.

"What's up?" Koral asked him, immediately falling into old habits. He looked at Elmther, but the other man subtly waved a hand to indicate it wasn't a problem.

"It's Neysi. She's disappeared."

Again, Koral and Elmther exchanged glances.

"When?" Koral asked.

"Last night. She left the Red Flag to go to her apartment, but she never got there. She didn't turn up today, either."

Koral understood the big man's concern, but it wasn't unusual for gang members to occasionally disappear for a couple of days. Usually, it was a particularly nasty bender or perhaps a one-night or two-night encounter with someone else.

But before Koral could open his mouth to say anything, Danz continued.

"I know what you're thinking. That's not it. Neysi and I are together. I had to stay behind at the Red Flag to take care of some business, but I was supposed to go meet her at her apartment afterward. Only, when I got there, I could tell she hadn't been there since she left in the early afternoon."

Danz shifted nervously.

"This isn't like her. She don't just disappear like that. And not when I was supposed to meet her. No one's seen her since she left the Red Flag. Word is that one of the gang leaders also disappeared. I don't like it."

Koral didn't like it either. If Neysi had been supposed to meet Danz at her own apartment, then it was unlikely she had gone off with someone else.

He turned to Elmther and gave him a nod. Koral couldn't give anyone orders anymore—it had to come from the owner of the Crown and Coin.

"Put the word out," the older man told Danz. "No one travels alone. In fact, it's best if you stick to three or more until the Wolf hears about this and sends out his own orders. I'll get some runners to alert the other gang members."

Danz nodded and turned to leave.

"Did you come with anyone?" Koral asked him.

"I don't need an escort," the big man answered over his shoulder. "If someone did something to Neysi, I *hope* they come after me."

"No, you don't," Koral told him.

Danz turned back, his eyes narrowed.

"You know who did this?"

Koral shook his head.

"I have some suspicions about Chaject, but that's it. And there's no connection between him and Neysi—they didn't know each other, and I doubt they ever even met."

Danz moved so fast that Koral had no time to react. The larger man grabbed him by the throat and drove him into the wall, pinning his arms with his body. His face was inches from Koral's.

"Who took Neysi?" he growled.

"Danz, back down!" yelled Elmther. But Danz ignored him.

Koral could still breathe, but barely. He had no doubt that if Danz wanted to, he could crush Koral's throat without too much effort.

"I don't know!" he snarled back at his attacker.

And then Elmther's arm snaked around Danz's throat, holding a large blade in his fist.

"Let him go," the barkeep said in a calm voice. The threat was greater for his lack of emotion.

Danz released Koral's throat and stepped back. Elmther let him go.

"Word is out, Koral," Danz said to him in a low voice. "You're not the Wolf's favorite anymore. If I find out you knew something about Neysi and you didn't tell me in time to help her, nobody will stop me from ripping to you into very small pieces."

Koral said nothing, just stared back at Danz and tried not to gasp for breath.

"Get out," Elmther ordered the big man. "Take two of our regulars and go back to the Red Flag. I'll send word when we know anything."

Danz looked from Koral to Elmther and back again. Without another word, he turned and walked out of the room, slamming the door shut behind himself.

"Don't get careless," Elmther said to Koral. "You shouldn't have said anything, and you know it. I don't know exactly what happened between you and the Wolf, but I do know you've served him and this guild well for years. Don't throw it all away just because you've had a setback."

Koral nodded. Elmther was right.

But it didn't make things any better.

Chapter Twenty-One

WHEN LAITA RETURNED TO THE ROOM UNDER THE White Eagle Inn, Namal was sitting at the table. He made as if to stand up as she entered, but relaxed when she waved him off.

Closing the door, she noticed that he was alone.

"Where are the others?"

"Helping the gangs get our equipment to the tenements the Wolf gave us. Making sure none of it goes missing."

Laita gave a nod, removing her wig and grabbing a cloth to wipe her face clean of the dirt that helped disguise her identity. She noticed that Namal was watching her patiently.

"You were waiting for me," she guessed.

"We gotta talk about Oriuna."

He had told her about the evening two nights ago in the bar, but they hadn't had an opportunity to discuss his meeting with the woman that took place last night. She sat down at the table and pulled off her ill-fitting boots.

"What did you learn?" she asked him.

"How we can get into the Fortress without going through the front gate. Even better, I learned that we might not need to."

Laita raised her eyebrows. This could be good news, indeed.

"Why do I have the feeling the city sewers are going to be involved?"

Namal chuckled.

"Good guess, but thankfully not. The Fortress has got many tunnels under the building itself. They've got a prison down there, storage … all the usual stuff. But those tunnels are extensive. They run beside the sewers, but don't connect directly. And they're old, *really* old, and some of 'em were there before the Fortress was even built. Oriuna says the Guard only uses a small fraction of the space down there. They've blocked up some of the tunnels, but there are ways past the barriers."

"If they don't connect to the sewers anywhere, where is the entry point besides in the Fortress?"

Namal hesitated, frowning.

"She didn't tell me. Said she was holding onto that in case something went wrong."

Laita considered it and knew what was coming.

"She's going to ask us for something."

Namal shrugged.

"Probably. Said the tunnels run under the hill and connect with the palace itself. They were bricked up at some point for security, but there's enough moisture down there that a determined group could get through those walls in minutes, if necessary."

"Seems like that would be pretty noisy," Laita replied. "Not exactly a covert operation."

Namal nodded.

"Once we breach the wall below the palace, it'll be a race to reach the Emperor before the alarm can be raised."

Laita leaned back in her chair, considering the possibilities.

"Not ideal, but still better than fighting our way past the Fortress. You trust her?"

"No," Namal grunted. "At least, not enough to commit to anything. She won't say who she works for, and that's troubling. If her information is right, it means she has sources far better than what I would expect from that group."

Laita agreed.

"So, what's next?"

"I've got Bor looking into her. She don't know him, and he's good at blending in. He's been tailing her since early this morning. Maybe he can ferret out some information about her."

Laita watched Namal's face as he talked. There was something in his expression, something in his voice ….

"What do you suspect?" she asked him.

"What d'you mean?"

"There's something about the way you're talking about her. You're thinking something specific."

A slow flush crept up his face as he turned away from Laita.

"No, I've got nothing …."

"What?" she asked again, smiling. "Did you two get intimate or something?"

She had said it as a joke, but the look on his face as he turned back in surprise told her everything.

"You did!"

"No! I … we … nothing happened. We just talked, and we went out to look at the Fortress."

Laita stared into his eyes, trying to tell if he was lying or not. She had never really thought of him as anything other than the gruff sergeant she had known for years. But despite her seeing him as kind of a father figure to her in certain ways, he wasn't really that old.

She looked at his face and tried to see him as a stranger might see him. As a woman might see him. He wasn't an unattractive man. And Oriuna was closer to his age than Laita was.

"I'm sorry, Namal. I don't want to tease you. It's just …."

"Commander—"

"Laita," she insisted.

"Okay, Laita. Look, I'm no good at this. The Legion has been my whole life for a long time. And Oriuna is … an interesting woman. And, yeah, we spent a bit of time in each others' arms last night after we left the Fortress, though we didn't…well…you know. But, let's be serious, she's probably trying to manipulate me. Or maybe there is something there. Either way, that don't really matter right now. We've got a job to do. And I'm not going to cause problems by doing something I shouldn't."

He took a breath and gave a long sigh.

"I can't trust her. Even if I wanted to trust her, I can't."

He shrugged, and snorted in laughter.

"Fuck, she even told me straight out not to trust her. But if she was trying to play me, that's exactly what she would say. Helps me see her as honest and looking out for me."

"When will you meet with her again?"

"Not for another couple of days. We've got to get the equipment stowed, and then put together our plan. Then we'll meet up—plus you and whoever from that so-called Resistance group needs to be involved—and go over what we need to do. By then, Bor should have a good handle on her."

"Then there's not much we can do about her before then. We have a possible way into, or even past, the Fortress. If it pans out, then we're that much farther ahead of where we were at this time yesterday. If it doesn't, then we must consider alternatives. I'm meeting with Galla tomorrow morning. She said she might be able to provide information about how supplies are delivered to the Fortress. It's another possible way in if this doesn't work out."

Namal nodded and stood up.

"I'm going to go check how the equipment is moving. I hate sitting here while others do all the work."

He grabbed the dirty, moth-eaten coat that he wore around the city and pulled up the hood.

"Be careful out there," Laita said to him softly. "I can't afford to lose you."

He put his hand on her shoulder and gave it a reassuring squeeze before he left the room.

Laita sat at the table, considering what he had told her. She didn't like what she knew of Oriuna so far. The very idea that the woman was trying to manipulate Namal got her blood hot. She wouldn't let that woman hurt her closest friend and confidant.

Then she realized where her line of thought was going and tried to calm herself. It was just as possible that Oriuna was attracted to Namal, and was enjoying their time together while they planned out this mission. She wouldn't be doing any of the fighting, wouldn't be putting her own life on the line. She might be just like the others in the Resistance—people for whom the actual mission was less important than what came after.

Perhaps Oriuna just assumed success. That was just as dangerous, as far as Laita was concerned. There were still too many things that could go wrong.

But then, she had to remind herself that hope for what came after was what kept most of them going. Without hope, none of them would even be here in Ythis, trying to change things. And Laita fervently hoped that Namal would come through this mission alive and unharmed. He deserved some happiness.

A tiny part of her mind, however, kept telling her that people rarely got what they deserved.

*   *   *

THE AIR WAS WARM AND CLOYING, AND NAMAL FOUND HIMSELF unable to draw a deep breath as he walked down the street toward the docks area. He slowed his pace, and tried to let himself relax. His chest was tight and the oppressive weight that hung over the city wasn't helping. But he knew he would be no use to the soldiers under him if he let himself get too wound up to make good decisions.

Turning onto the street where the Red Flag was located, he nearly bumped into another man who was coming the other way. Namal quickly sidestepped the man, who raised his head with a wary look before moving around Namal and proceeding down the street.

Namal turned back in the direction of the Red Flag when a voice froze him in his tracks.

"Sergeant?"

He wanted to keep walking, but it was obvious that he had hesitated when the other man called out to him. Namal glanced back over his shoulder.

"Ain't no sergeant," he growled back. He took another step when the other man spoke again.

"But ... aren't you Sergeant Namal?"

The man was speaking loud enough to be heard by the few other people on the street. It was still early evening, and sailors were moving from tavern to tavern looking to make the most of their shore leave. Namal couldn't afford to let this man keep calling out his name.

He cursed under his breath as he turned around. He knew his

disguise—such as it was—would most likely fool anyone who had only seen sketches of his face. But if he was spotted by someone who knew him, then the clothing and dirt would only go so far.

He took a good look at the other man, who was staring at his face. The man looked vaguely familiar, but no name came to him and he couldn't recall where he might have seen him before.

"Lower your voice," he told the man. "Who are you and what do you want?"

The man looked surprised by his response, but complied with his order. When he spoke, it was pitched just loud enough for Namal to hear.

"Um, you're Sergeant Namal, right? Of the Tenth? Dragon Regiment?"

Namal said nothing, only waited for the man to identify himself.

"I'm Sergeant Illilo. Or, well, I was."

He held up his right arm and Namal saw that it ended at the elbow.

"Got wounded in a skirmish and was discharged from the Legion. But I served under you in the Tenth. Well, I was just a soldier then, when I …."

He drifted off as Namal just stood there, watching him. Perhaps he was starting to think he had the wrong man.

"You *are* Sergeant Namal, right?"

Namal didn't know what to do. This man obviously recognized him. If he denied who he was, it would stick in the man's mind. Illilo might get curious enough to reach out to others from the Legion, asking about his former sergeant. And those questions could reach the wrong ears.

"Yeah," he said slowly. "I'm Namal. I'm not a sergeant anymore, either."

The look of relief on Illilo's face was a knife in Namal's heart. He had seen too many expressions like this over the years. Young soldiers, about to go into a battle where they were likely to die, but grabbing at whatever inspiration their sergeant or commander could give them.

Or, as they lay there dying, bleeding out in the churned mud of a battlefield, believing the empty platitudes of their superior officers, who kept telling them they were going to be fine.

Illilo took a step forward.

"You, um, you were the best superior officer I ever had, sir. After you transferred, I swore that if I ever had the chance, I would buy you a drink if I ran into you again."

Namal's mind was racing. What was he going to do? He couldn't just brush the man off and walk away. This one chance encounter could ruin everything, had put everyone in danger. He was now stuck in a situation where he was damned no matter what course of action he took.

Illilo took Namal's silence to indicate interest.

"I was on my way home just now. Are you in a hurry? Let me buy you a drink. Toast to old times, eh?"

Namal gave him a nod.

"Someplace quiet. Out of the way."

He could see the slight confusion on Illilo's face. The other man wasn't sure why Namal was acting this way. But it was most likely only heightening his curiosity. He had to do something to reassure the other man.

"Yeah," he grunted. "Old times were better than these. You can tell me about the arm, and I'll tell how I ended up here."

Illilo's face broke into a big smile.

"Yes, sir! There's a tavern I know of not far from here. Nice place, and very quiet. Sailors don't find it lively enough, and so it's only locals."

Illilo led the way down the block and then turned off onto a side street. Namal walked beside him, watching the streets around them. Trying to think of a way out that wouldn't compromise everything they were trying to do.

You know the only way out.

He shut that line of thought down hard. There had to be another way to salvage this.

All those lives hang in the balance—your soldiers, Laita, the rest of the command squad, the innocent citizens of the Empire ….

There was a dark alley up ahead, and Illilo was going to lead them right past it. No one else was visible on the street. It was a chance for

Namal to take action and remove the threat.

Illilo continued to speak in a low voice, unable to wait until they were seated at a table together.

"After you transferred, another sergeant was brought in from a different squad. He was a tyrant, and we soon figured out he was so tough on us to hide his own incompetence. You were always tough, but we *learned* so much from you. You made us better soldiers. This guy only wanted to punish us."

Namal had always been able to reconcile the need for the few to sacrifice themselves for the good of the many. This mission they were on in Ythis was just such a need. Sometimes you had to send soldiers into situations when you knew they weren't going to come back out.

He had very rarely had to make that decision himself, though. The benefit of never letting the Legion raise him above the rank of sergeant. Let the lieutenants and commanders make the hard choices. He simply had to make the most of what he was given to work with.

They were almost at the alley, and Namal couldn't decide what to do. One life against how many? But Illilo hadn't done anything wrong. He wasn't even a soldier anymore.

Would he tell anyone about his encounter with his old sergeant? Could Namal make it clear to him how necessary it was to keep his identity a secret? Would that not simply make Illilo more curious? It was too easy for this man to start something that would bring down the entire mission.

They stepped in front of the alley mouth, Illilo continuing his story.

"So, we quietly agreed to have him removed. The entire squad pulled together and we became the most incompetent group of soldiers you've ever seen. After our performance under you, it didn't take long for the lieutenant to figure out what the problem was."

Namal clenched his fists in frustration.

Act or not?

With a low growl of frustration, Namal grabbed Illilo's arm and yanked him sideways into the darkness of the alley. He clamped his hand over the other man's mouth as Illilo realized what was happening.

The man tried to put up a fight. He was a trained soldier, and missing arm or not, he knew how to use what resources he had to defend himself. But Namal had been teaching soldiers for years.

As he pushed his knife into Illilo's chest, he felt as if his own heart was being cut in half. Even in the darkness of the alley, he was close enough to see Illilo's eyes go wide, feel the man's breath on his face.

"I'm sorry," Namal whispered to him. "I'm so sorry."

Illilo's legs gave out and he slid down the wall to the filthy floor of the alley. Namal pulled out his knife and gently pulled his hand away from Illilo's mouth.

"Wh … why?" Illilo managed to whisper.

"I'm trying to save the Empire," Namal whispered back to him. But Illilo's eyes had already gone blank, and he knew the man hadn't heard him before he died.

Namal carefully wiped Illilo's blood off his knife using the man's own clothing. He put the weapon back in its sheath and then closed Illilo's eyes.

Standing up, Namal wanted to scream until his voice gave out.

But he couldn't. The soldiers needed him. Laita needed him.

He stepped out of the alley back onto the side street. It was still empty of people. He moved to the next cross street and began to make his way back toward the Red Flag.

He would tell no one what happened tonight. Laita had enough on her shoulders.

Namal would continue to carry whatever burden he could for her.

Chapter Twenty-Two

N
O MATTER HOW MUCH SHE TRIED, NO MATTER HOW MUCH
effort she put into it, her opponent always stayed just out
of reach.

Phana had nearly caught up to the shadow multiple times over the last hour, but somehow it kept twisting away at the last instant, widening the gap for a while before she could manage to catch up again.

She could no longer ignore the fact it was playing with her.

They had worked their way through High Town, across to the eastern edge of the city where the great stone wall rose like a mountain above the homes huddled in its shadow. And then back north into the Nobles' District once more.

Phana had been led in a great circle and realized that they would soon near the very spot where this chase had begun. All that effort, and she was right back where she had started.

She slowed her run to a jog, and then a walk. Finally, she stopped and looked around herself. She was currently standing in middle of one of the main roads that cut through the district. Far in the distance she could see the torchlight of another patrol, this one heading away from her.

The shadow had raced off ahead. Phana waited in the street, no longer pursuing it. This was the chance for whatever it was to escape, if that's what it had really been trying to do.

She knew she was taking a gamble. If it really was desperate to get away from her, she had just let it go. But she no longer believed that to be the case. She expected it to return to watch her once more.

And then it was back. It stopped farther away from her than it had previously. But its presence was still enough to call her attention to it.

"Fine," she whispered to it. "You're faster than I am. And if you ever get up the guts to fight, you know where to find me."

Turning away from the shadow, she tried to figure out what to do next. She had been feeling restless, and the night's events had certainly given her a distraction. She knew her body should be exhausted, and while she did feel tired, she wasn't anywhere close to being ready to sleep.

The noble estates stretched out on either side of the road and she looked left and right at the homes of the wealthy and powerful. People she didn't know and who had such influence over life in the Undying Empire.

Her anger had burned itself out. But she wasn't ready to go home just yet. She had come out here to do mischief tonight. She had been distracted, all right. But there was no reason she couldn't have some fun while she was here.

She turned back to the shadow.

"If you won't face me," she whispered, "then stay out of my way."

Phana turned and moved to the stone wall on one side of the road. She didn't know the names of all the noble families and wasn't familiar with this estate. But that didn't matter to her. She climbed the wall and slid over and into the shadows on the other side.

Like most of the other estates, there was a small group of guards and dogs around the well-lit entrance to the mansion. And like the others, the guards were too afraid to go out and patrol the grounds. So she moved along the wall and toward the rear of the estate.

A large terrace stretched out along the back of the mansion. A beautiful garden with manicured trees and flowerbeds surrounded the terrace and stretched out across the grounds. A second group of guards were stationed here, with another pair of dogs.

Phana knew she could reach one of the side windows without alerting the dogs, as long as the shadow didn't follow her. She moved across the grass toward the side of the mansion, where the lantern light didn't quite reach. In a few moments, she had reached the wall and was looking up at the first set of windows that appeared to look into a large dining room.

These windows were glazed and had no way to open. Of the set of windows on the next level above, however, all had shutters that were closed, and likely locked. But locks didn't stop Phana, and if the shutters were closed, then the windows would not be glazed.

She ran her hands over the outer wall and felt its roughness. There were more than enough handholds for her to climb up to the second story. She began to ascend, keeping nearly silent as she slowly moved up the wall.

The shutters, while ornate and thick, still used only a simple latch on the inside. Her thin dagger was able to slip though the small crack and lift the latch. She pulled the shutter open just enough to peer inside.

The room was small, four beds crammed in together, each with a small dresser at the foot of the bed. All four beds were occupied, the soft breathing audible to Phana as she hung on the side of the wall. The door on the far side of the room was closed.

This was obviously a servants' bedroom. Phana knew she could easily slip past the sleeping figures without disturbing them, but her ability to get through into the rest of the house undetected would depend on that door. If it squeaked or groaned when opened, it could wake up one of the room's inhabitants.

Still, Phana knew she could easily escape back out the window before anyone was awake enough to put up any kind of resistance. And a little bit of risk added some fun to the proceedings.

She pulled herself up and through the window, gently lowering herself to the floor. She pulled the shutter closed but left it unlatched in case she needed to retreat quickly. Gliding across the floor, Phana watched the sleeping figures, all women of middle years. None of them moved or otherwise gave any indication that they might wake up.

The door was thin and had a simple latch to keep it closed. She grabbed the latch and pulled it up and then began to ease the door open. It made the faintest squeak as she moved it, and Phana froze. There was no change in the sounds of the breathing behind her, however.

A small lamp on a table in the hallway behind gave off dim light.

She continued to ease the door open, the sound faint enough not to disturb the sleepers behind her. It made no noise as she pulled it closed. If she needed to come back this way in a hurry, however, she knew that opening the door quickly would likely cause it to emit a much louder squeak.

Of course, if that happened, it would be because she was being chased by guards and it wouldn't matter who she woke up.

She moved into the hallway and looked around. The bedrooms of the noble family would be on the third floor above, along with sitting rooms and their personal offices. While some of their best possessions would be up there, Phana expected that guards would be stationed on that floor to ensure that nothing nasty came for their employers while they slept.

The ground floor was the next best place to find something of value. Nobles loved to impress each other, and so the dining room and lounge would likely have some treasures to show off. Considering that the guards were stationed right outside the front and rear doors, Phana didn't expect there to be anyone moving about inside on the ground floor.

She proceeded down the servants' stairs and entered the dining room. Her eyes were immediately drawn to the chair at the head of the table. Made of dark wood with expensive silk cushions, the back of the chair was quite high. The wood was carved with ornate patterns, and a large ruby was inset into the top of the chair, surrounded by lesser jewels.

Phana smiled. This was designed to impress visitors and make any who sat in the chair seem like royalty. Its purpose was to remind everyone of the power of the person who sat here.

Phana immediately hated the chair, and knew she would have to take the jewels.

She pulled out her knife and moved to the chair, preparing to pry the ruby from the dark wood. But as the point of the knife touched the edge of the ruby, the night outside exploded into a cacophony of barking, followed immediately by the shouting of the guards.

In moments, the entire house would be awake.

*   *   *

TO RELAEL'S SURPRISE, THE NARROW, TWISTING STREETS OF THE Warren were mostly deserted. Though it was well past midnight, the Warren only really came alive after the sun went down and remained so until the break of dawn. But a handful of figures furtively skulking in the shadows were all that were out tonight.

The sense of doom suffocating the city each night was likely the cause of the empty streets. Relael smiled grimly to himself as he walked. At the least, it made his current task easier.

Or perhaps not.

Two figures stepped out of a narrow alley on his left and stopped in his path. The lack of hanging lanterns in this part of the city meant the only light came from the occasional candle near a window in the worn and broken tenements that lined this street, and a guttering torch mounted on a metal pole at the intersection of three streets up ahead.

Relael sighed. He regretted not bringing his own lantern, now. He had decided against it due to the attention it would have brought to him. But at least everyone would have seen his priest's robes and known to leave him alone.

"This is a private road," said one of the figures in a gravelly voice. His companion stepped around Relael, trying to move behind him. Relael took a deep breath and spoke in a resounding voice.

"I welcome your souls, my friends! Our god Iathephos is ever hungry."

He slowly spread his arms, his hands facing up, as the night suddenly seemed to press down more heavily while a faint slithering sound echoed through the darkness.

There was a time when Relael would not have said that name aloud. To speak the name of Iathephos was to invite his attention, and no sane person would ever do that. The god that dwelt in the cavern beneath the Temple sent only madness, curses, and doom to those who caught his notice.

Only the priests, who were already touched by madness, could channel his energies to accomplish miracles. And it immediately and inevitably destroyed them, body and soul.

The figures paused and the one in front of Relael drew a long knife, but he seemed hesitant to approach any closer.

"I am on a pilgrimage, my friends," Relael said confidently. "I bring the presence of Iathephos into the deepest corners of Ythis this night. Join me in reveling in our god's majesty."

"Shit," said the man on Relael's left, backing away. "He's a priest."

"No," the other sneered. "No priest would come around here alone. He's just some crazy."

Neither approached any closer to Relael, though.

"You think me mad? Perhaps the light of Iathephos can open your perceptions."

Relael raised his arms, hoping the thugs wouldn't call his bluff. Unlike a real priest, Relael had no ability to call on the power of his god.

Not yet, anyway.

The second, smaller cutthroat continued to back away, but the one in front of Relael drew himself up and took a step forward.

This was not good. The heavy feeling of the night passed while the sound faded away. The sight of the god had passed over Relael and found nothing of interest here, and calling its name further would only bring him trouble in the future.

The man took a second step and then froze. Relael felt a light touch at his hip. He looked down to see a young girl standing at his side, her small hand on his robe.

"She waits for you," the girl whispered.

The two men spun and ran off down the narrow alley from which they had emerged. Relael smiled down at the girl.

"It seems you and I together were too much for them."

The girl smiled back at him.

"I will take you to her."

Relael lowered his arms, and the girl took his hand, leading him through a long, winding path to stand in front of an old tenement that looked abandoned. A single candle glowed in the window on the third floor.

The girl led him inside and up the staircase. He was glad for her help, for the inside was nearly pitch black. The girl moved with confidence, as though she could see her way up the stairs and along the passage.

She opened the door and the light of the candle nearly blinded him. He squinted his eyes and entered the room.

A small, wooden table sat in the center, a rickety chair on either side. The candle stood in the middle of the table. An old woman sat on one side, her head turned slightly toward the door. Relael could see by the light of the candle that both of her eyes were milky white.

"Please come sit down," she said in her cracked and ancient voice.

Relael moved to the other chair and sat carefully, worried that it might crumble under his weight. But it seemed sturdier than it appeared.

He glanced over at the door to find it closed and no sign of the girl.

"Thank you for the escort," he said to the witch.

"The streets are always full of predators. But they still remember the old ways and know better than to get involved in my business. Though I'm surprised you didn't bring your own escort into the Warren. Even one such as yourself can find danger here."

Relael shrugged and then realized the old witch couldn't see his gesture.

"I prefer to conduct certain business without extra witnesses."

The old woman nodded solemnly.

"I had expected this visit before now," she said with a tremble in her voice. "I have not had the opportunity to express my thanks for your help those months ago."

"Oh, you're welcome, though I know you understand it was by no means an altruistic act on my part. When my brethren came for you, I recognized that there was no value in your death. You are no threat to the Church. On the other hand, you *can* provide me with assistance when I need it."

The woman nodded her head once, slowly.

"I understand what you did you for me, and the price of your act. I will help you as much as I can, though you must understand the limits of my abilities."

Relael chuckled.

"Of course. I will ask of you nothing you cannot easily provide. Which brings me to my visit tonight."

The old woman gestured for him to continue.

"There is a woman named Phana. She was involved in that matter with the young witch. I want to locate her."

The old woman's shoulders slumped slightly at Relael's words.

"I thought everyone who served the girl is dead," she said softly.

"That's nonsense. I know that Phana is still alive. So is her lover, Koral Creyss."

"And the Church wants vengeance on those who helped the girl? They do not know where the girl is now. Can't you let them be?"

"I understand your concern, though you are in no position to argue," Relael replied, not unkindly. "So, I will tell you this. As far as anyone in Ythis is concerned, the Church considers the matter closed. A Witch Hunter is on the trail of the girl, and he *will* eventually find her. Those left behind in Ythis are of no consequence in this matter."

"Then why do you look for Phana?" the witch asked.

"That is not the only matter in which she was involved. That is all you need to know."

"I suppose it was only a matter of time," the old woman replied. "She was careless. Someone would notice, eventually."

Relael leaned forward in his chair. The witch knew about Phana's fight with the gang leader, about what she had done that night. He considered that he might have to eliminate the witch once he had what he needed from her. High Counselor Untoleu had told him to keep this mission secret, but he had been forced to use his servants and spies, and now the witch.

The others didn't know his reasons for wanting to find Phana. The witch knew too much. At what point would she become a liability?

"Tell me what you know of this woman," he demanded.

"She has power in her, *that* I can confirm. She is no witch, nor a sorcerer either. It's in her blood."

"What is it?"

"I do not know. Though I suspect it is very old. Older than the Empire."

"Older than the coming of the gods?"

The old woman hesitated before answering.

"I believe so."

Relael sat back and heard the chair creak. He tensed, but it continued to hold.

"Why do you believe this?" he asked her.

"When she used her power, it called to me. It was like a great beacon that lit up the sky above Ythis, and I could see it with my third eye. There was something about that light, something ancient. I have felt it before, very faintly, very far away from Ythis. She is not the only one with this source of power."

"How do I find her?"

The witch raised her thin, bony shoulders slightly.

"If she uses her power again, I will know where she is. But the beacon fades away after a time. I could not find her now unless you have something that belongs to her. And even then … she may be able to hide from my sight, regardless. I do not know."

Relael clenched his fists. He needed to find this woman. And the only direct connection to her seemed to be Koral Creyss, the Wolf's right hand. Having the Church soldiers capture some random gang members was one thing. To grab Creyss would escalate the matter dramatically.

"How do I suppress her powers?" he asked.

The old woman smiled.

"Perhaps your god?"

"Don't be flippant, witch!"

"I wasn't," she snapped back at him. "You're a Churchman, though. You've got access to more power in Ythis than any other group, even the sorcerers. But as I said, what Phana has comes from inside her. It's not something she knows, or a connection to something from outside this world. Connections can be severed. Knowledge can be countered. But blood is part of you."

Relael stood up and brushed his hands down the front of his robes.

"Thank you for the information. If you discover anything else, send a message to me and I will return."

The old woman nodded silently and Relael felt a small hand grip his palm. He looked down to see the young girl at his side. The door to the hallway stood open once more.

Relael let the girl lead him back down to the street. They said nothing to one another as she escorted him to the edge of the Warren. More than once, Relael saw cutthroats and thugs move out of their way and let them pass in peace. He wondered what the witch had done to earn such fear and respect. Or maybe it was all just superstition doing her work for her.

No one wanted to cross a witch.

He considered again that he might need to eliminate the old woman. But she still had her uses, and for now he decided to let her live.

They reached the point at which the crumbling tenements gave way to warehouses and shipwrights' offices. The girl slipped her hand from his, and Relael looked down to thank her for her help. She was no longer there.

Relael grimaced and began to walk back toward the Temple.

*   *   *

SWEAT COLLECTED IN THE SMALL OF HER BACK, UNDER HIS PALM resting lightly on her skin. She didn't want to move, but the spot began to itch, and she was forced to shift his hand away so she could scratch.

"We should get back," Kied said in a sleepy voice. He made no attempt to move, however.

Laita sat up and reached for her tunic.

"Don't fall asleep. If you're still here at dawn, you know what'll happen."

Kied nodded slowly and rolled onto his back. She looked down at him, at his relaxed body, lean and firm and ….

She forcibly suppressed that line of thought. No matter how much passion they had already spent tonight, she could feel herself wanting him again. But there wasn't time for more lovemaking.

Sex. It's just sex. Nothing more.

She knew she was lying to herself, but she needed the lie. It had certainly been just sex when they started. He was a good-looking man, a decently skilled lover, and he took instruction well.

The problem was that after the sex, they had begun to talk. And, against all her hopes, he turned out to be a good person. He was intelligent, and witty, and genuinely cared about others.

He was the very last thing she needed right now.

This was all temporary. They were here for a year at most before they would get the opportunity to take assignments elsewhere in the Legion. That was how it worked. Once you were identified as a good candidate for a command, you were sent here to this training camp. You trained the soldiers under you, and you received training from those above you.

The Legion got you to work with new soldiers while they evaluated your ability to command and taught you everything you needed to know to take over a detachment.

It hadn't taken Laita and Kied long to find themselves alone together. She had met him only two months ago. They had been doing this for half that time.

And her feelings for him were growing.

Sex. It's just sex. Nothing more.

It was a mantra she had to repeat to herself. What if they were both here for the full year assignment? Could she keep doing this with him for another ten months?

Easily.

That wasn't the question, though. Could she keep doing this with him for another ten months and not fall in love with him?

You're not falling in love with him. Sex. It's just sex. Nothing more.

After this, they might never see each other again. They were part of the Legion. They would be given their own commands. Even if they happened to end up in the same Regiment, they might operate in different parts of the Empire and never cross paths.

There was no future here. The Legion was her future.

But ten months could be both a lifetime and an instant. Long enough to form feelings that were dangerous to her personal goals. Short enough to make her feel she hadn't had enough time with him, after all.

She didn't need this. Then again, sometimes this was exactly what she needed.

Kied sat up and began to gather his own clothes. He looked at her in the dim moonlight and gave her a grin.

"I'm going to be so tired tomorrow."

"It's already today," she told him. "And yeah, you are."

He raised one eyebrow.

"And you're not?"

"No. I'm far tougher than you."

He laughed.

"That you are."

She wanted to kiss him. She wanted to ….

Laita forced herself to stand up. She belted on her short sword and looked down at him.

"I don't know if this is such a good idea."

He looked up at her, a slight furrow on his brow.

"We're professionals," he said in serious tone. "We won't let it affect anything."

"I know, but …."

She should end it. It had been nice—

It was wonderful.

But she knew it was going to end badly. She didn't want to have to deal with the difficulties because she couldn't control herself.

Kied stood and pulled on his own clothing. He tightened his belt and adjusted his own sword.

"Look, we both know this can only go so far. That's the life we're choosing, because of who we are. And I've thought about this a fair bit over the last month. We can keep ourselves closed off to this, and go about our own ways. But that's not us being fair to ourselves. There's nothing wrong with us forming a connection, even if it's temporary. Because the alternative is to not form any connections at all."

He stepped forward and looked into her eyes.

"I don't think that's healthy, and I don't think it's right. We're human beings. We need these connections. And, I admit, it's going to be difficult to say goodbye to you, when that time comes. Because I'm not going to want to say goodbye. But I'll do it, and I'll remember what we had here, and I'll value our time together. And I don't want to end it before that time comes."

She put her hand on the back of his neck and pulled him close and kissed him. It was some time before they parted again.

"Have a good sleep," he said to her with a smile.

She nodded, not wanting to speak, and turned and left the empty barracks building at the end of the row. Only about two-thirds of the buildings were currently occupied, which gave them a perfect place to meet up each night.

As she walked back to her own quarters, she thought about his smile. And then she thought about that kiss. Her heart felt as if it was being squeezed, but it was a good feeling.

You're definitely falling in love with him.

"Fuck," she whispered to herself.

Now, sitting alone in the hidden room under the Crown and Coin, Laita wiped her tears away with the back of her hand and tried to bring her thoughts back to the present.

By the time their duties had forced them to part, she had fallen truly and deeply in love with him. But she had taken the moment to say goodbye before she had moved off to her own command. And when she had heard about his imprisonment, she had understood that she had lost him for good. But then he came back into her life, if only for a moment.

And then she had lost him again. And this time, there would be no miraculous escape, no sudden appearance to throw her life into chaos. He was gone forever.

She hadn't stopped loving him, and she still couldn't stop. For a while, after his death, when she was traveling south toward Ythis with Namal, Pilayni, Addiru, and Keynter, she had let herself be angry with him.

He had died, just when she really needed him. He had left her to do this by herself. He had started this rebellion with his refusal to obey orders, but he wasn't around to help her finish what ultimately had to be done.

But when the anger had faded, the grief came back. She wanted to let him go, to cherish the memories of their time together, to accept that he was dead and move on.

Why *couldn't* she let go? It was like she was still connected to him. It was like loving someone who had left you, but still having to see them around. The pain was still there, because you couldn't get any distance from them.

Laita *had* distance, though. Kied was buried in a valley in the northern mountains. She wasn't seeing his face, except in her memories.

And yet, she still couldn't accept that he was dead.

She grabbed her boots and began to pull them on. She couldn't spend time wallowing in her grief. There were people counting on her. And they needed a commander who could lead them, with a broken heart or not.

But as she donned her disguise, she knew that when she eventually fell asleep tonight, Kied's face would fill her dreams.

Chapter Twenty-Three

PHANA JAMMED THE POINT OF HER DAGGER INTO THE WOOD at the edge of the ruby and shoved. A large sliver tore free from the chair with a crack.

The dogs outside were in a frenzy. Shouts began to sound from inside the house, and Phana figured she had only a moment or two before someone would find her.

She knew she should get moving, get out of the house before she was caught. But she gritted her teeth and jammed her dagger deeper into the crack in the wood and kept prying. There was no way she was going to let the figure in the shadow continue to wreck her life. She had come here to steal something, and that's exactly what she was going to do.

Over the barking of the dogs, the guards were shouting at each other, searching for whatever was causing the animals to lose control. Phana could hear booted footsteps coming down the stairs—another group of guards was already inside the house. If they were going to reinforce those outside, then she had another minute or two.

But if they were searching the inside of the house ....

She snarled as another piece of wood broke off the back of the chair. The ruby was still stuck in the wood, though a good third of the gem was now exposed. Phana forced the dagger deep into the space she had broken open and yanked.

The crack of the wood as the ruby came free may not have been as loud as the barking dogs, but it *was* loud enough to be heard by the guards inside the house. Phana heard one of them shout "The dining room!" as they changed direction toward her location.

Phana tucked the ruby into a pocket sewn on the inside of her tunic and grabbed the chair. There was no time to find another way out of the house, and the windows here were fully glazed and could not be opened.

Not without causing some damage, anyway.

But since the guards already knew where she was, there was no longer any value in remaining quiet. She picked up the chair and moved to the windows. With all her strength, she flung the chair at a large window, which immediately shattered into hundreds of pieces.

The smash of the glass was enough to even give the dogs pause in their barking. The double doors leading from the main hallway into the dining room were shoved open by the guards. Phana took two steps and dove through the window, avoiding the jagged shards of glass still stuck around the edges of the frame. She hit the ground outside in a roll and was on her feet an instant later, running flat out toward the stone wall at the edge of the estate.

For the second time tonight, a horn was sounded by the guards to summon the Imperial soldiers patrolling the Nobles' District. An instant later, a crossbow bolt buried itself beside her foot as she ran. Phana began to zigzag, though she was soon out of range and deep enough in the darkness to make further shots impossible.

By the time the guards released the dogs to give chase, Phana had enough of a head start that she was easily up the wall and over before the animals could catch up to her. She saw the light of the patrol rapidly approaching from the east, so she took off westwards and was long gone before anyone could mount an effective chase.

The feeling of the shadow watching her stayed with her as she left the Nobles' District and made her way across the city. The sky had changed hue with the eventual coming of morning when Phana reached the Market District and ended up on the roof of the same building she been standing on the first time she had felt the presence of that shadow.

She stood in the middle of the roof and looked around her. She couldn't spot the shadow, though she knew it was close.

"Fuck you!" she shouted, her rage at the constant presence of the watcher filling her up with a blood-red haze. "You're nothing but a coward! You want me? Then come and get me!"

And then she saw him.

One moment there was nothing, and then he was there, striding toward her across the rooftop.

He was tall, and thin, dressed all in black, a silver belt buckle at his waist. He had no visible weapons, and his hands were covered in gloves.

She raised her eyes to his face and gasped. It was a bucket of cold water over her rage. She didn't know this man, but something clicked in the back of her mind, and …

She stands on a stone platform above a crowd of men and woman kneeling on the ground, their arms stretched out as they bow over and over, chanting in a tongue she does not understand. To her left, the most beautiful woman she has ever seen stands beside her, a golden goblet in her right hand. The woman's long blond hair stirs in the cool breeze coming across the clearing as she takes a sip from the goblet.

Phana turns to look out over the heads of the worshippers and sees a thick forest ringing the clearing. Torches mounted on spears are stuck in the ground around the outer edge of the kneeling supplicants.

The woman hands the goblet to Phana, and she takes a sip of the dark liquid, the copper taste filling her mouth. She swallows and the liquid burns pleasantly as it slides down her throat. The blond woman knows the secret of this heady mixture, and she makes it only on special occasions such as this.

Phana hands the goblet back to the woman and wipes her hands on her long white gown. She grips the sides and lifts it over her head, tossing it aside as she stands naked before the worshippers.

"Shall we begin?" the other woman asks.

Phana nods.

"It's time to reap," she replies with a smile.

Phana snapped back to herself as the man took another step toward her. She met his gaze, their eyes locking, and …

She moves through the trees, smoke curling around her. The sounds of battle—the clash of metal swords on wooden shields, the screams of the dying, the shouts of the commanders trying to impose some semblance of order on the great chaos around them, the crackle of flames as the fire spreads from tree to tree—are a minor distraction.

Phana is looking for someone, and she knows he is near. The ice flows through her veins as she moves along, stepping over a broken shield and the broken body beneath it. The symbol on the shield seems familiar, but she cannot place it.

And then she feels him, hiding in a gully just ahead. She breaks into a run, flinging herself over fallen logs and scattered corpses. Reaching the gully, she leaps down to find the man huddled under an overhang.

He is old, his skin wrinkled and covered in brown spots. Faint whisps of hair float around his head as he turns to see her, his green eyes filled with tears.

"You cannot hide from me forever," she says to him.

"Please," he begs. "Don't do this. Those lives out there don't matter. We can make peace. We can find a way to coexist."

Phana shakes her head.

"You are a snake, just like your lover and her brother. You've turned the others, but we will never submit to you. This is our world."

There is a growing roar behind Phana, like a wave rushing through the forest, sweeping away everything in its path.

The old man stands and wipes the tears from his eyes.

"We are alone here now. They have taken our mothers and fathers from us. We cannot fight them and win."

Phana laughs in his face as the roar grows louder behind her.

"I bow to no one. You may desire to roll over and become their dog, but I will fight to my last breath. We could have stood together and won, but you and that bitch wanted it all for yourselves. And now you die."

The noise is now too loud to ignore and Phana turns to see a vast horde of naked, slavering humans rushing through the forest toward her. Their eyes are dead, their mouths distended, and their fingers have been stretched into long, wicked claws.

She glances over her shoulder to see the old man fleeing up the side of the gully. She ignores him and lets the cold flow up and out, covering her skin with frost.

She laughs as the first of the dead creatures reaches her.

Phana gasped for breath as the man stopped a few paces away. Her legs were weak, and she knew she was going to fall. As the world tilted, her eyes began to close ....

She stands at the top of a tower, looking out over an endless sea of stars below her. No, she realizes, those are campfires stretching out across the plain, a vast army camped in the night. They are here for her, for her companions. She turns to see a huge man standing beside her, his great hands resting on the stone railing. His long hair is grey though his beard is dark. He looks down at Phana and his expression is grim.

"They will attack tomorrow," he says in a deep voice that rumbles in Phana's chest. "I count fifty thousand, maybe more."

"Let them come," Phana hears herself say and she revels in the idea of these men throwing themselves at the tower. The cold in her blood surges and Phana feels more alive than ever before.

"We could leave tonight," says a voice at her shoulder. She turns to see the man from the rooftop. His eyes are dark, and his long black hair hangs down his back in a long braid. No hair covers his face, and the angular bones of his cheeks and chin appear carved from marble.

"I'm tired of running," Phana says. "Tomorrow we will go out and meet them."

She reaches out, one hand on the arm of each of her companions.

"Tomorrow we reap what they sow."

Phana felt her back hit the rooftop, the man standing over her. She tried to summon forth the ice in her veins, but she couldn't fight the shadows that surrounded her as the world went dark.

*   *   *

THE SMELL OF BURNT WOOD HUNG IN THE AIR AS LAITA MOVED down the alley toward the back of the tenement. She had been told the building was near one of the sorcerers' towers, on the edge of the lawless maze of streets and alleys they called the Warren.

The Tower of Ash, Cedaro had called it. She understood why the Wolf found it easy to keep this tenement empty for his own use. No one wanted to live too close to a sorcerer.

As she stepped around the corner, she caught movement in the shadows to her left. An instant later her knife was in her hand and she put her back against the wall facing the alley in case anyone was following from behind.

"Fuck off," said a man's voice. "This place ain't for you."

She paused a moment, not sure if this was one of the lookouts. She didn't want to say the pass phrase if this was just some homeless man who had moved into the small space behind the building.

"Hsssssst!"

A new voice came from the shuttered window one story above her, pitched just loud enough for her to hear. Her and the man in the shadows.

"It's her," the voice whispered down to them.

"The oath abides," the man whispered to her.

"To protect us all," she whispered back.

"Over here," he said in a low voice and reached into a dark doorway and pulled aside a large, heavy drapery. The light of a single candle illuminated his face, and Laita could see he was one of the soldiers who had chosen to follow her here to Ythis.

She stepped up and placed her hand on his shoulder, looking him in the eyes. Then she stepped into the room and he let the drapery fall to cover the door.

On the other side of the room, a bare wooden staircase let up to the next floor. She moved over to it and Bor stepped into view, holding another candle. He motioned her to come up.

She ascended and then followed him up another set of stairs to the third floor. He opened a door and she squinted against the light of multiple lamps scattered across a large room. She stepped in behind him, and he closed the door.

The walls, door and windows were covered with more heavy draperies, held in place by wooden planks nailed across the windows and along the walls.

"It helps muffle sounds in here so anyone on the street won't be able to hear us," he explained. "You don't have to whisper, but don't shout. It only does so much."

She nodded at him and looked around the room.

Two cots were tucked into a corner of the room, a small table and a pair of chairs against the opposite wall. Three crates were placed in the empty space in the center. They had been pried open, and she could see the glint of steel.

"Our armor and weapons," he said.

"Tell me this isn't everything."

"No, the rest of the crates are in other rooms on this floor. We open only a few at a time, just to make it easier to keep track."

She moved over to him and clasped his forearm. He gave her a satisfied smile as he returned the grip.

"Nice work."

"Thank you, commander. It feels good to have our stuff back. Like we're real soldiers again."

She heard a soft knock on the door and Bor opened it to reveal another of her soldiers.

"Sergeant Namal is here," the man said and left.

"I'll be right back," Bor told her and left the room.

She moved over to one of the crates and pulled out a short sword. It had already been oiled and sharpened, ready to be given out to the next soldiers to arrive.

A minute later the door opened and Namal entered, followed by Bor. As she saw Namal's face, she instantly knew something terrible had happened. He was trying to hide it, but she knew the man too well.

"What is it?" she asked him. "What happened?"

He frowned at her and shook his head.

"Nothing."

"Sergeant?"

"Commander, it's been a long day and I'm very tired. That's all."

She knew he was lying. But if it was something urgent, he wouldn't play games and keep it to himself. Still, if something bad had happened, it could affect them all.

"Are we in some kind of danger?"

In response, he lifted his hands and gestured to the room around them.

"Yes we are, commander. But no, there is no new danger that we weren't already in when we got here."

He met her look with one of his own that said he wasn't going to talk about whatever had happened, and she knew she was simply going to have to trust him. She turned to Bor and saw that his satisfied smile was now gone.

"I have a report to make to both of you," he said. "It concerns the woman, Oriuna."

She glanced over at Namal, but he was still wearing that stone expression that he used when he was hearing bad news or trying to deal with a fresh tragedy.

"That was exceedingly fast," she said. "Please proceed."

Bor gestured to the two chairs, but neither Laita nor Namal were in a mood to sit.

"After speaking with Sergeant Namal early this morning, I attempted to find out what I could about Oriuna. I went to the tavern where she had met Namal the previous two nights. It was closed when I arrived, as it was still quite early. However, I didn't have to wait too long before she arrived on foot.

"She had a key to the front door, and she used it to enter, but she locked the door behind her. I had no good way to get inside until it opened, so I kept watch from down the street. About an hour after she arrived, a man showed up on foot and knocked on the front door. I saw her open it, and the man handed her a message and then left without saying a word.

"She returned back inside for another hour and then left the tavern, locking the door behind her. She then went on foot north toward High Town. When she arrived at one of the main thoroughfares, the East River Road, she stopped and waited at the intersection.

"A few minutes later, a carriage pulled to stop in front of her. She entered, but I couldn't see if anyone else was inside. The carriage began to pull away, and I had no choice but to chase on foot."

"Can you describe the carriage?" Laita asked him.

"Black, single driver, no doorman. Fairly standard type you see in the city for hire. Some of the wealthier merchant houses use them, and …."

"Go on," she urged him.

"I was able to keep up with them because it was mid-morning and the streets were crowded with people. Also, they were in no hurry as they weren't going anywhere in particular. The carriage merely wound its way through the streets for a while before returning to the same intersection where she had been picked up."

"That's one way to have a clandestine meeting," Laita murmured.

Bor nodded.

"When the carriage stopped and I realized where we were, I figured she would be getting out. But I guess their discussion wasn't quite done, as she remained in the carriage for several minutes before the door opened. It gave me time to get into a position to see into the carriage when she emerged."

Bor looked from Namal to Laita and back.

"There were two priests in the carriage."

"What?" Laita almost shouted before remembering Bor's earlier warning.

"You must be mistaken," Namal said gruffly.

"No, sir. There were two priests in the carriage. I can't imagine anyone would choose to wear priest robes if they weren't part of the Church, sir."

"Where did she go after that?" Laita asked him.

"She returned to the same tavern. I waited another hour, and then one of the soldiers relieved me. He said that she was still at the tavern as of an hour ago, sir."

Laita turned to look at Namal, but he kept his gaze straight ahead, as if he didn't want to meet her eyes.

Oriuna knew everything about the Resistance in Ythis.

And she was working with the Church.

Sixteenth day of Highsummer,
3 days to the Arrival

Chapter Twenty-Four

PHANA WAS SWIMMING IN DARK WATERS, THE SKY ABOVE HER a navy-blue fading to orange and red near the horizon. The sun was low behind the line of pine trees that ringed the lake in which she floated. The water was cool on her skin and it caressed her pleasantly as she rolled onto her stomach and looked out across the expanse of water to the single point of light on the shore.

A campfire, bright in the growing shadows of dusk, was tended by a lone figure, his back to her as she kicked out and began to swim toward it. The splash and ripple of the water as she moved was the only sound—no birds or animals could be heard.

The band of color on the horizon was fading quickly, and she looked up but could not see any stars in the darkening sky. She continued to swim, pushing her arms into the water, kicking her legs, aiming for the distant fire.

She soon realized that, no matter how fast she swam, the shore came no closer. So she stopped and just floated, watching the fire and the lone figure seated beside it. She considered calling out, but she didn't want to break the quiet.

Finally, she saw the figure stand. Slowly and deliberately, the figure turned toward her. Though backlit by the fire, and across the distance of the water, she could see his eyes clearly.

The eyes of the man on the rooftop.

She gasped as the water turned to ice around her.

And gasped again as she sat up, her eyes snapping open to see a plaster wall in front of her.

She looked around and saw that she had been stretched out on a small bed, the only furnishing in the room. A single wooden door—currently closed—pierced the wall in front of her. The floor and ceiling were of unpainted wood, and there were no windows.

She calmed her breathing and looked down to find that she was still fully dressed, even to her boots, as she had been on the rooftop … was it minutes ago? Hours? Days?

She had no sense of time, though the pressure in her bladder told her it must have been at least a couple of hours, or more.

The sounds of movement came from the other side of the door, the distinctive clatter of a wooden bowl or plate being set down on table. She thought about climbing out of bed but wasn't entirely sure her legs would hold her up.

The images were vivid in her mind and she couldn't ignore them. The faces of those she had seen kept coming back to her—the beautiful woman at her side while the people worshipped at their feet, the old man she had wanted to kill, the bear-like man at the top of the tower.

And the man she had met last night on the rooftop. He had been in her dream and he was now here.

She saw her hands were trembling and she clenched them into fists. Was she going mad? Were they dreams, or visions, or memories? She was terrified of that last possibility. She couldn't remember her past and that had been something that frustrated her before. Now, for the first time, she wasn't entirely sure she wanted to know who she was.

She had killed before, more than once. Life on the streets of Ythis wasn't safe. And gangs inevitably got into conflict with each other or with the few criminals who were not part of the Wolf's guild. But killing didn't bring her pleasure—it was something to be avoided when possible.

But now, she could feel that thrill of pleasure she had experienced in each of those visions. It wasn't just fighting, or killing, but *slaughter* that excited her. Was that who she had been in the past?

No, it was impossible. They had to be just dreams. She had never been to those places. She had lived in Ythis for her entire life. The man must have planted them in her head as part of some manipulation. And she wasn't going to fall for it.

She swung her legs over the side of the bed and leaned forward, but a wave of dizziness caught her.

What had he done to her? She had never fainted before that she could remember. He must have used some kind of power on her, to take away her consciousness. To give her these visions. He was trying to confuse her so that he could get her to ….

What *did* he want?

She forced herself to take a deep breath, and as she did so, her mind took her once again to that tower. She saw the vast army spread out below her. She saw the large man at her side. Seeing his face brought a stab of sorrow to her heart. She loved him as if he was family, and she knew that was the last time they had been together.

Phana jammed the heels of her palms into her eyes and rubbed them, trying to think of something else. It was too much. They weren't memories.

They *couldn't* be memories.

The woman's face came to her and Phana heard herself snarl. They were close, so very close that they shared everything.

Phana stands in the clearing among the shattered bodies of the worshippers. She is covered in their blood, the warmth of it comforting her. The woman still stands on the platform. She smiles at Phana and Phana smiles back ….

"No!" she shouted, pushing herself to her feet. She staggered and had to lean down over the bed to steady herself. That last vision was not one she had seen before. The man was still doing it to her. Still trying to push himself into her mind.

He wasn't going to kill her. He was going to *use* her. He was going to feed her lies and then get her to do whatever it was that he wanted.

She remembered the warning she had received in the voice of a young girl in the alley ….

"If you are who I think you are, Ythis is the most dangerous place for you to be. The forces arrayed against Marilsa are nothing

compared to what will come after you should certain parties learn of your existence."

Was this man the person the girl had meant by her warning?

"There is more to your life than you remember, Phana, that much I know. Your power called to me, and it calls to others. Be careful what attention you bring on yourself. Be careful what you bring to Ythis ...."

Had Phana called him to Ythis by using the power in her blood? And if so, what would she be able to do against him?

If only the Wolf had been willing to talk to her, she would have an idea of who the man might be. And then she remembered what the girl had said about the Wolf ....

"If I am right, the Wolf will only give you stories and lies."

Did that mean this unknown man might give her the truth, after all? Did it mean the visions in her head were real? She knew she wasn't a normal person. There was no point in pretending anymore. And the great darkness that occupied the space in her mind where her memories should be was impenetrable and had been for ... how long?

How many years had she really been in Ythis?

And, not for the first time, she wondered who the young girl had been. How did Phana know she could trust her? Maybe the Wolf was the only person who did know the truth.

She turned toward the door and steeled herself for what was about to happen. Perhaps she had kept her power under control for too long. Perhaps it was the only thing that would keep her from being controlled by others.

She reached deep inside herself and felt that cold center. She touched it and felt it flare to life inside her. If the man tried to do anything else to her, she would let it loose.

"You must be hungry," the man said from the room beyond. His voice caused a twinge in her memories, both completely new to her and yet so familiar. "Please come join me. You're safe here ... Phana."

He said her name hesitantly, as if unsure about being so familiar with her.

Phana stepped to the door and grabbed the latch. Taking a deep breath, she pulled it open.

The room on the other side was not large. She realized she was in a small, single-story house. A fireplace occupied one corner, a single chair set to one side. A wooden table took up a good amount of the rest of the room, food set out on a counter mounted to the wall near one end.

The shutters on the single window were open, and she saw it was morning, likely still early by the quality of the light. She had been unconscious for at least a few hours, though she had no way of knowing if it was more like days.

He sat on one side the table, facing her. His hands rested on the table's surface, on either side of a bowl and a wooden spoon. A matching pair sat on Phana's side of the table.

"Please," he said to her. His voice was low, smooth like silk, and there was a pleading note to his words. "We need to talk. You no doubt have some questions, and I believe I can give you answers."

The cold pulsed within her body, and she held tight to its power.

"Who in the Abyss are you?" she asked him.

"My name is Yarrian."

The sound of his name caused her heart to beat even faster. The ice surged in her veins, as if seeking release.

"That doesn't tell me anything."

He gave her a small, sad smile.

"Not yet, perhaps. Your memories are ... fragmented. I'm afraid to go too fast, though. I don't know exactly what was done to you ... I'm worried it might harm you if I reveal it all at once."

He gestured to the other bowl.

"Please join me. As I said, you are safe here. I am the last person to want to see you come to harm."

"You have a pretty creepy way of showing it," she snapped back at him. "Whoever you are ... *whatever* you are, I've had more than enough of you following me. Watching me. Causing me difficulties wherever I go. I don't like games."

He looked at her and she could see his eyes glistening as if he was fighting back tears.

"I'm sorry, Phana. I wanted to just reveal myself to you. But I was afraid of what it might do to you. You've lost so much, and I thought if I just showed you my face it would all come crashing back and drive you mad, or worse."

"So what you did was for my benefit, of course. How noble."

"I let you sense my presence. I knew it might be familiar, but not overwhelming. And … I tried to make you angry."

"You succeeded."

"Your anger protects you. Last night, I saw that you had reached the limit of your patience. I could feel your anger. So I pushed you. And I kept pushing until I was sure showing myself wouldn't kill you. It was still almost too much."

"The visions you put in my head were certainly a bit much. Try to get inside my skull again and I promise you it'll be the last thing you do."

Yarrian opened his mouth as if to protest, and then stopped to consider his words before speaking.

"Like you, I possess … abilities … that normal people do not have. Implanting false memories into a person's mind is not one of them. I want to talk to you, tell you about your life that you cannot remember. Your memories are in there, Phana. They've been blocked from you, and I want you to have them back."

"As I said, how noble of you."

"You and I are … family. In a manner of speaking. We traveled the world together, you and I and …."

She pictured the big man at the top of the tower. It was becoming more difficult to control the cold and she could feel it trying to leak out, to blanket the room around her with frost. She closed her eyes and pushed it back down, wrapping it up in her will once more until it was nothing but a tiny cold spot deep in her chest.

Yarrian let out a breath and relaxed slightly. She realized he had been aware of her power the entire time.

She still felt the need to empty her bladder. It was distracting and her anger was fading quickly in the face of his … passiveness. She didn't trust this man by any stretch. But her curiosity was aroused, and she had been searching for answers for a long time now.

She couldn't just ignore the opportunity, even if it was probably all lies.

"Where can I relieve myself?"

He gestured to a narrow door on the back wall.

"There is a shared outhouse in the yard."

She opened the door to see a small yard surrounded by houses like the one in which she had woken. To one side sat a shack that was the outhouse.

When she had finished, she returned to the room and closed the door. Yarrian still sat in the same place, his own meal not yet touched. She moved to the chair opposite him and sat down. The smell of the stew in the wooden bowl triggered her hunger and she heard her stomach growl.

"I have plenty of food," he said. "Eat as much as you wish."

She took a bite and watched his face. He was handsome, she'd give him that. His eyes never left her, as if he was hungry only for the sight of her. It wasn't a sexual look, but rather it was as if he couldn't quite believe she was here at his table, and he wanted to get his fill before she disappeared.

"If you're not going to eat," she said to him around a mouthful of food, "then talk. Your name is Yarrian, but I still don't know who you are. What are you doing in Ythis? How do you know me? Why do I feel that I should know you? And why have you brought this doom to hang over the city?"

Yarrian blinked at her.

"Doom? You mean the dark weight that hangs in the night air?"

She nodded, continuing to chew.

"I am not the cause of that. It is … something else."

She waited, but he did not elaborate.

"Do you know what it is?"

He gave a small shrug.

"It is familiar to me, in a way. If you had all your memories, it would be familiar to you as well. But I know it's impossible, what I feel, and so there is no point speculating."

She stopped chewing and glared at him. He seemed to understand that he wouldn't be able to evade the question entirely.

"We had a companion, and there is something in that feeling that reminds me of him. But as I said, that's impossible. I know nothing further about it."

He looked down at the table and she saw a great sorrow in his face. He cleared his throat and looked back up at her.

"I hope to be long gone by the time it reaches the city. You'll have to trust me to tell you more when you're ready."

"So you're not planning on taking up residence in Ythis?" she asked him, looking around the small home.

"No!" he said, his eyes wide. "I'm taking a great chance just coming here. How you've survived so long …."

He paused.

"Spit it out!" she demanded. "You can't keep drifting off in the middle of a sentence. Either you're going to tell me what's happening or you're not. But I'm not going to waste my time with you if you don't have anything to say."

He looked down at the table again and took a deep breath.

"I felt you from very far away. When you opened yourself up and let the power inside you come out, I knew it was you. It took me some time to get here, as I didn't want to believe at first that this was where you had ended up. And I had to move slowly. But this growing weight on the city gave me the opportunity to enter without them realizing I was here."

"Who?"

"The same people who are now hunting for you. I do not know what roles they play in Ythis—perhaps they are hidden and act only behind the scenes. They are like us, only they want us dead. You are lucky that they have not found you yet."

"You say they are like us. So what is it about us? Who are we? How can we do … the things we do?"

Yarrian gazed at her levelly.

"I will explain it all to you, Phana. But it must be slowly. They took your memories from you. They did something to your mind. And I don't know what traps they might have left behind."

Chapter Twenty-Five

A S THE SUN ROSE, LAITA HAD STILL GOTTEN NO CLOSER TO a decision.

When Bor had told them the news a few hours earlier, Namal had quietly gone to another room to sit and stare at the wall, speaking to no one. She had let him go, understanding his need for distance.

She had wanted to say something to him, but she was at a loss. She didn't know if it was better to be his commander or his friend at that moment, and then the chance to say anything had passed and he was gone.

Bor had arranged for runners to stand by, ready to head out as soon as she gave word. But she had not had an answer to his question.

"What do we do?"

Laita understood what he was asking. If the Church was aware of their presence here in Ythis, had they failed before they had even begun? Was the Resistance nothing more than an elaborate trap for her and those who followed her?

The Empire was ruled by a triumvirate of powers, and the Church was perhaps the most dangerous of the three. The sorcerers—the Six—mostly kept to themselves and their own intrigues and plans. The Emperor had to be the balance between the Church and the Six, which provided a limit on his own ambitions.

But the Church? They had their own soldiers, their own informants, and the power of a god. They served a being from another reality that lived in a great chamber below the Temple, fed a constant meal of souls and wielding power that drove its priests insane just from proximity.

If there was one thing Laita had learned about those in power, it was that they would do anything to maintain that power. There was no way the Church would support an insurrection.

Which meant that their enemy knew about their intent, about their resources, and perhaps even knew where some of her people were hiding in the city. The mission was compromised, and she could see no way to save it.

And now she had to make a decision on what to do next.

Should she order her soldiers to flee the city? They couldn't hide in Ythis if the Church decided to come after them in force. But where could they go? Should she do what everyone had expected her to do in the first place—leave the Undying Empire and head for another land where she would be safe?

But if she gave the order to leave, would that trigger the Church to take action? Perhaps the Church was waiting until Laita was ready to order the attack on the Palace, and then they planned to round up the soldiers and "break" the Resistance, saving the Emperor from the traitor Legionnaires.

They would have a major bargaining chip with the Emperor, not to mention demonstrating their superior knowledge and power compared to the Six.

All they needed to do was continue to feed Laita information, help her prepare for her assault on the Imperial Palace. And then, when she was ready to act, they would sweep in and take everyone at once.

She didn't want to think about how her soldiers would feel. So much work, so much preparation, all for nothing. Some would no doubt desert her contingent. Perhaps one or more might contact the Legion or the Imperial Guard and give up their fellow soldiers in an attempt to save themselves.

And even if she led them out of the Empire, could she provide a direction for the entire contingent? They had been trained to be Legionnaires. And most of those who followed Laita were idealists. Becoming mercenaries was about as far from their self-image as it was possible to get.

How many would she lose?

Now, the sun was climbing steadily into the sky and she heard Bor come back into the room. She remained at the small table, turning the problem over and over in her mind, like she had been doing all morning.

"Commander?" Bor said hesitantly, and she knew what he was asking.

I don't fucking know what to do!

She wanted to shout it, but knew she couldn't. They needed her. She had gotten them into this situation, and it was her responsibility to get them out.

"Bor … I …."

She needed her command squad. Ellend was still out there somewhere, creating a false trail that showed Laita and her soldiers heading for another city on the coast. But she could still talk to the others, see what they thought of the matter.

"Please send a message to Saeda and the rest of the squad. We need to meet. Bring them here, but tell them to make sure they are not followed and to scatter their arrival."

Bor saluted her and left the room.

Now she had perhaps two hours before she'd need to tell them that it had all been for nothing. To see the realization on their faces that they'd given up everything, and had failed anyway.

Fuck the Church! Bunch of betrayers.

Except the Church was betraying a bunch of people who were, by any definition, traitors to the Empire. It wasn't the *Church* who were traitors.

Unless they are.

That thought stopped her cold.

Those in power want to maintain that power.

Of course they would want things to stay the same.

Unless they don't.

But why would the Church want to throw the Empire into chaos? They had been instrumental in establishing order in the early days of the Empire, helping the Emperor unite the fledgling city-states under his sole rule. Laita had read about that time, about the power of the Church and how they took whoever they wanted for their god, how they controlled Ythis and the other cities, backed by the power of the terrible beings from another world.

But the Emperor had grown in strength, had formed alliances with the first sorcerers, only three of them in Ythis at the time. Their number had eventually grown to five and had stayed that way for decades. And now there were six.

The Church is slowly losing power.

She scoffed at the thought. The Church still had vast power over the people of Ythis and other major cities of the Undying Empire.

Then again, there is an infinite difference between *vast* power, and *all* power.

A shiver ran up her spine. She was assuming the Church intended to stop their killing of the Emperor. What if they *wanted* him dead?

She slowly stood up from her chair as the idea ran through her mind. The Church did not have the strength to challenge both the Emperor and the Six. But if one of those pieces was removed from the board, then it would entirely change the game.

But if the Church was secretly backing the Resistance, that meant the end result of the Emperor's death would be an overall increase in their power. And if they were supporting the objective of killing the Emperor, then it meant they were ready to capitalize on the event as soon as it happened.

There was no easy answer to that problem, but she had time to consider possible strategies. And her command squad would be able to help her see the opportunities and threats.

But now Laita knew what she had to do. She would meet with Oriuna directly. As much as she wanted to rely on Namal, she knew he wouldn't be able to see the woman without his anger overcoming his better judgement.

She needed to play this delicately. Simply confronting Oriuna would not accomplish anything useful, and might force the Church's hand. But if she could let Oriuna know that she was open to an unexpected alliance ….

It wasn't going to be easy. She was walking a tightrope with a very deep pit below her. But, perhaps, all was not lost.

At least, not yet.

Bor returned to the room and saluted.

"The messages have gone out, commander."

"Thank you, Bor. You did an excellent job yesterday. Not many people would be able to keep their head when confronted with the reality of the Church.

He smiled at her.

"I may have invented a few new swear words on my way back here. But I did manage to control my bladder, which wasn't a sure thing at that moment."

She chuckled with him, somewhat amazed that they could make a joke about having to deal with the *Church*. Once again, she was reminded how much she needed her command squad.

"I'm gonna kill her."

Namal's voice was a low growl. He was standing in the doorway glaring into the room. For an instant, Laita thought he was talking about *her*.

Then she realized who he meant. He was going to try to kill Oriuna.

"No," she told him.

He turned to face her.

"With all due respect, commander, you will *not* order me to stand by while she betrays us all to the Church. The things we've done to get this far, the sacrifices we've made—"

He stopped short, his mouth hanging open. She could see the pain on his face. What had happened to him last night? She hadn't had the chance to push the discussion with him, and now certainly wasn't the right time.

"If you go after her, then the Church will know we're aware of them. Then there's no reason for them not to bring down their full might on us *today*."

"They don't know where the soldiers are hiding—"

"That's an assumption, sergeant. One that could get everyone killed."

Namal took a step into the room and nearly shouted.

"She's gonna get everyone killed anyway!"

Laita paused, giving him the cold look that she used when soldiers were on the verge of panicking. It worked well to remind them that she was in charge, and they should be more concerned with her judgement than whatever else was facing them.

It didn't work nearly as well on Namal—he had been around too long to be completely affected by it—but it did cause him to pause. He understood the reason for the look even if he wasn't intimidated by it.

He took a deep breath and let it out.

"Laita," he said, but she cut him off. This wasn't a discussion to be had between friends. He needed to listen to her, and there was no room for him to second guess her.

"I have a plan for Oriuna. One that will be derailed by her death. The mission is more important than the insult to your pride."

Laita noted Bor quietly stepping toward the door, but that wasn't going to help her maintain the proper tone that she needed for this confrontation.

"Bor, remain here."

He stopped and tried to look anywhere but at the two of them. She didn't care where his eyes were. What mattered at the moment was his presence.

"The mission is over, Lai—commander. It's done. The Church knows we're here, and they know why. There's no way we can do what we came here to do."

"Then killing Oriuna won't change that. It's petty vengeance, and I forbid it. That's an *order*, sergeant."

He blinked at her, and then looked at Bor and then at the floor. When he spoke, there was a catch in his voice, as if he was having difficulty keeping himself together.

"I'm sorry, commander. No, I'm sorry, *Laita*, but I don't know if I can keep obeying orders. I'm not really a soldier anymore. None of us are. To the Empire we're just traitors, to the Legion we're traitors and deserters, and the so-called Resistance sees us as convenient tools. But soldiers? I think we need to give up on that. It's a lie."

Laita's heart was pounding in her chest. She could see Namal's pain and how it was tearing him up inside. She had hoped he would respond to her as his commander, but instead it had only pushed him closer to the edge.

"Namal, don't do this."

She could hear the pleading in her voice, and she hated it. Now she regretted asking Bor to stay in the room. But to dismiss him now would only send him away with a head full of his own doubts.

"Laita, you gotta leave Ythis. Take anyone who will follow you and get out of the city. Get out of the Empire. It's over. We lost."

"You once told me that you'd follow me into the heart of the Abyss. That you believed in me. Were those lies?"

She saw a tear run down his cheek as he looked at her.

"I'm here, Laita. I did follow you. And I do believe in you—"

"Then you need to listen to me," she said, interrupting him. "You need to do what I ask. It's *not* over. We *haven't* lost. And I need my command squad to accomplish my plan."

"What plan?"

She hesitated, not wanting to spell it out yet. It made sense in her head, but she was worried it would sound crazy if she said it out loud.

It is *crazy.*

But her moment of silence gave him the opportunity to work it out for himself. He knew her too well, and sometimes it worked against her.

"You're gonna meet with her," he said accusingly.

She nodded.

"I'm going to speak with her and find out—"

"The moment you tell her we know about the Church, she'll call in the priests and their soldiers and you'll be in chains, or dead."

"You don't know that!"

She didn't intend to shout, but all her frustration, all her anger, all her fear came out in those four words. It surprised both Namal and Bor, who had never seen her lose her temper before.

"By the Abyss, Namal, you seem to think you're the only one who can figure out how to deal with an obstacle. You say you believe in me, but you don't. Not really. But you seem to forget that Oriuna isn't a soldier, and quite frankly, it's not like you have much experience with people who aren't in the Legion."

"And you're being naïve if you think you can trust her!"

She felt her face flushing as she tried to control her anger, but Namal had just taken a step too far.

"Naïve? Of *course* you'd think so. But maybe, just maybe, others have more experience with people who have never been in the Legion. But that's just too much for your ego to let you accept, isn't it? I would think that someone who was in the Legion as long as you were and never rose above the rank of sergeant would accept that he isn't a master of politics."

That's the way to kick a man when he's down, she thought. His mouth hung open, as if he couldn't believe she had said those words. She knew he had turned down promotions to stay in her command squad, and she had just thrown it back in his face.

And just like that, her anger was gone, and she wanted to claw back her words, but it was too late. His stubbornness had contributed to her anger, but she had chosen to be vicious.

"I ... I'm sorry, Namal. That wasn't fair."

He stood up straight and saluted her.

"You don't have to worry about me, commander. I understand my orders."

He was trying to make a point, but the roughness of his voice betrayed him. She could tell he was struggling to keep himself together.

"If you'll excuse me, I have duties to attend to."

"Namal ...."

"Yes, commander?"

He was rapidly gaining control of his emotions, and his voice was growing colder with each word. He was cutting himself off from her. And it was her own fault.

"Namal, I shouldn't have said that. I'm sorry. Please ...."

"Nothing to forgive, commander. Permission to leave?"

She wanted to grab him, make him understand, but she knew if she moved or said anything else, she'd lose control in front of Bor. And she had a responsibility to the rest of her people, no matter how much she wanted to make things right with Namal.

She gave him a nod, and he turned and left the room. She managed to wave Bor off and he also left, nearly running out the door.

She wasn't sure how she was going to repair things with Namal. She wasn't sure if it was even possible anymore.

Chapter Twenty-Six

J EYRRA FROWNED AT KORAL AND CROSSED HER ARMS OVER HER chest.

"What else do we need to do?"

They were standing in Jeyrra's room in one of the three-story tenements on the edge of the Warren. Jeyrra's gang oversaw a portion of the Dock Ward that ran along the southern shore of the city, those streets that surrounded the western edge of the Warren. She had been a gang leader for years and Koral knew her to be competent and deadly.

"For now, nothing," he told her. He had helped spread the word among the gangs to make sure no one ever traveled alone, at least until they figured out what was happening. With Chaject captured by the Church soldiers and Neysi now missing, there was a serious risk that the Church itself was moving against the Wolf's people.

Jeyrra clenched her fists, as if she wanted to hit someone.

"We can't just sit here. If someone is picking us off, we need to do something."

"I know, Jeyrra. But we don't know yet exactly what is going on. The Wolf has been informed and will make a decision soon. Just be ready to move if he gives an order."

Jeyrra uncrossed her arms and stepped close to Koral, speaking in a low voice.

"Is it true what we heard? Are you out of the Wolf's inner circle?"

He hesitated, not sure what to say. Word had no doubt been passed around that he no longer had the authority to give orders directly. The gang leaders would need to know that as soon as possible.

But the Wolf would not have shared any other information unless he deemed it necessary.

"Yes, it's true," he told her. "I'm no longer operating as the street boss. I'm here purely as a messenger. For now, if you need an answer or quick instructions about something, talk to Elmther at the Crown and Coin."

"What happened?" she asked and then raised her hands. "Sorry, you don't have to tell me. It's none of my business."

"It's okay, Jeyrra. My … my judgement was compromised about something, and the Wolf decided that I needed to step down until I could get my priorities in order."

"Love can do that," Jeyrra said knowingly, and Koral wasn't sure what to think about the fact she automatically assumed it had something to do with Phana.

It only made it worse that her assumption was right.

"So just make sure none of your people go off by themselves right now. If we're being hunted by someone, let's make sure we don't make it easy for them."

"What about you?"

He shrugged.

"I'm careful and I know these streets better than just about anyone."

She snorted and shook her head at him.

"You're being silly. I'll send a couple of my guys to escort you back up to the Crown and Coin."

"Jeyrra, I have to move fast, and I'll be going all day. Besides, it's daytime. No one is going to snatch me off the street in broad daylight. And your people just worked all night. They need their rest, too. I'll be fine."

Jeyrra narrowed her eyes at him but she knew she wouldn't be able to persuade him.

He left the tenement, stepping out into the morning streets already filled with people. Activity on the docks started before dawn and the clatter of wagons, the shouts of dockworkers, the cry of gulls and more filled the air.

He glanced up and down the street and a flash of movement caught his eye. He looked at the mouth of a nearby alley and saw a young girl dressed in a simple shift standing in the shadows.

He knew that girl. She served Undilsa, the witch.

As soon as his eyes focused on her, the girl motioned for him to follow and she backed into the alley. As he crossed the busy street, he couldn't help but wonder if he was heading into an ambush. Who else might be waiting for him in those shadows?

But no, the witch would never work with the Church. They would destroy her if they knew of her existence in the city and her very survival depended on keeping as far away from the priests as possible.

He reached the entrance to the alley and saw the girl standing about twenty paces back. He glanced around, looking for any potential hiding spots where assailants might be waiting—it paid to be cautious, after all—and then entered the alley and approached the girl.

When he was close enough, she looked up and down the passage and then began to whisper to him.

"You need to find her, Koral. You need to warn her."

A chill ran up his spine.

"Warn who?"

"Phana," the girl said with wide eyes. "She's in great danger."

"I haven't seen her since the night before last. Do you know where she is?"

The girl shook her head, her long hair fluttering around her.

"She is hidden right now. That presents its own dangers, but she must deal with that herself. But once he leaves, she will be revealed again."

Koral immediately wanted to ask who "he" was. He couldn't stop the thought of Phana being with someone else from filling his mind. But he knew that wouldn't help. If Phana was in danger, he had to get the details and find her.

"What's the danger?"

"A priest who is not a priest has been searching for her. The Church has become aware of her, and she is being hunted."

"Is that the darkness that keeps following her?"

"No, he is keeping her safe for now, but you know Phana. She won't stay with him. You must warn her."

"How do I find her if she's hidden? Does the Church know where she lives?"

"Phana has kept that a secret. But the priest will do anything to find her. You must warn her, Koral."

"Why are you helping Phana? How do you know her?"

The girl smiled, and she no longer looked like a child. There was something in her expression that spoke of greater years of experience behind those eyes.

"If I am right, a fight between Phana and the Church would be bad for Ythis. For the innocent people who would die in such a conflict."

"Okay, I'll go to her apartment and wait there. I can't get the Wolf to lend me any help—"

"No!" the girl said out loud, and then hunched her shoulders and looked back up and down the alley once more before returning to her whisper. "Phana should stay away from the Wolf as well. He is just as much a danger to her as the Church."

Koral's mind reeled. The Wolf was a danger to Phana? She had been trying to meet with him, demanding that Koral help her reach him. And he had done his best to make it happen. And now he was hearing that his failure had saved Phana.

From the Wolf.

The man that he was sworn to serve.

"What danger does the Wolf pose to Phana?" he demanded. But the girl gave another shake of her head.

"You must go and find Phana quickly. Warn her that the Church is hunting her. Tell her to stay away from the Wolf. Ythis is not safe for her. If they find her, the Phana you know will die."

A shadow dimmed the alley, and Koral glanced over his shoulder at the alley's mouth to see a large wagon passing by. He turned back to the girl, but she was gone.

Koral snarled clenched his fists. He wanted to punch something. Phana was in danger. Phana was with another man—apparently related to the darkness that had been following her. The Wolf was as much a danger to her as was the Church.

And he had no idea how to find her.

Spinning on his heel, he strode back out of the alley and turned to the north. He'd go to her apartment and wait there for a few hours. Perhaps she would return home and he could speak to her.

Otherwise, he had no idea how to reach her.

*　　　　*　　　　*

IT WAS TIME FOR HER TO LEAVE.

Yarrian had been gone no more than ten minutes when Phana leaped up from her chair and strode to the door. She paused, her hand on the latch. If she left, she was walking away from someone who might be able to give her answers.

Not that he had given her very much so far. Aside from a few veiled references to the people in her visions and some intimations that she was much older than she had thought, he had said nothing concrete. He kept saying that he'd have to go slowly with her.

He thought there might be traps in her head. Revealing the wrong memories too quickly could kill her.

Was it true, or was it just a way for him to manipulate her? Would he just trickle out hints and vague intimations to keep her with him? Did he have any actual intention to tell her what she needed to know about herself?

The truth was, as familiar as his face was to her, she didn't trust him. *Couldn't* trust him. She had only the one memory—if that's what it was—of standing at the top of that tower with him and the other giant of a man. Who was Yarrian, really?

He claimed to be like her, a part of her extended family. But he wouldn't say any more about that family, no matter how hard she had pressed.

And then he had said he had to leave. That there were things he had to do to ensure she was safe. He promised to be back before dusk. He had warned her not to leave this small house.

But Phana was not one to let anyone tell her what to do. His warnings only mattered if he was telling the truth, and she still had no way to know if that was the case. Besides, she was not about to give up her independence for anyone, regardless of who he was.

She yanked the door open and stepped outside, the sun high in the sky above. She estimated it was perhaps another hour until midday. Closing the door behind her, she looked around to get her bearings. She was on the far eastern side of the city where the individual homes of successful merchants gave way to the clustered dwellings of the middle classes.

For the first time, she realized that this house must belong to someone. It hadn't been empty and didn't seem abandoned. Where was the family who lived here? Had Yarrian done something to them? Driven them away? Killed them?

Wanting to be as far away from the house as possible, Phana turned west and started walking. She could be back at her apartment well before the sun reached its zenith. But what would be the point of going back there? She wanted to keep moving. Not only did it help her think, but she needed to see other people, to feel she was a part of this city now that she had been excluded from the Wolf's guild almost completely.

As usual, she found herself wandering in the direction of the Market District. She was drawn to that part of the city, where the crowds were thickest, where the bustle of the city was at its greatest. The market was the heart of the city, and its beat kept the blood flowing.

It took her almost an hour to travel across the breadth of Ythis. Out of habit, she avoided Watch patrols and didn't go into the high-class districts where the Imperial Guard patrolled the streets. And she constantly scanned the crowds for signs of anyone following her.

Her trip across the city was uneventful, and she spent the afternoon wandering the market. There was no sign of Yarrian's presence, and she didn't see anyone she knew. Her thoughts were in turmoil and kept spinning back around and around to the memories that had been revealed to her last night.

If they were real memories, then Yarrian was the only person she knew who might be able to help her recover the rest of them. But then, if the memories *were* real, did she absolutely want to know what kind of things she had done in the past? And, of course, the visions could have been created by Yarrian in order to manipulate her. She had no way knowing if he could be trusted at all.

So she walked through the market, buying some food from a vendor and eating while moving through the crowds. The hawkers shouted to her about the fine quality of their wares. The servants of the noble houses wandered in small groups through the alleys between the endless stalls, all dressed in the livery of their employers' houses. Watch patrols marched in fours through the crowds, waiting for the shouts of "thief!" to call them to action.

Phana reached an intersection where a small clearing in the middle of the stalls opened up to let people pass. She turned to find herself face-to-face with a man who stopped and looked at her, his eyes slowly widening. There was something vaguely familiar about his surprised expression.

"You!" he shouted, raising an arm and pointing it at her.

And then Phana placed him. He was in his nightclothes as he opened the door between his sleeping chamber and his office. Phana crouched on the windowsill and waved at him.

"Thanks for the wine!" she had said to him as she dropped to the ground outside the Eorallo estate.

"THIEF!" he shouted at the top of his lungs, and every person nearby spun to see who was being accused. "THIEF! GRAB HER!"

He lunged forward, hands grabbing at her arm. But Phana was too fast for him. She spun and elbowed him in the face, knocking him sideways. And then, as his retinue behind him started forward, Phana took off sprinting into the crowds.

Those nearby—seeing her strike her accuser in the face—flung themselves out of her way as she raced past. But soon enough the crowds thickened with people who had not heard nor seen the altercation and were busy upon their own errands. She glanced back to see a quartet of Watch guards rushing after her.

Knowing that it would do no good to attempt to push through the tightly packed bodies in front of her, Phana turned sideways and leaped over a small table into the middle of a stall selling tapestries. The owner of the stall leaped up from his camp chair as she raced past. A couple of tapestries were strung up on a wooden frame at the back of his stall, and she tore them down and plunged into the stall on the next row over.

And nearly collided with a large, black iron cauldron hanging over a fire. She twisted out of the way and barely avoided contact with the hot metal, the smell of lamb stew filling her head. An instant later she was out of the stall, across the alleyway, and into another stall selling dyed fabrics.

Once more she tore through the back of the stall into the next row over as shouts of outrage followed behind her. Breaking through past a merchant selling wooden protective carvings, Phana emerged onto a row that was half empty of people.

She turned and raced down the row toward the edge of the market. The Watch was now far behind and struggling to catch up. By the time she reached the streets of the Market District that surrounded the great market square, her lead was long enough that she was no longer in any danger of being caught.

Slowing to a steady walk, Phana cut down multiple side streets and had soon lost any pursuit. She found herself grinning at the unlikely odds of running into the one man from the Eorallo estate who had seen her the night she had stolen the amphora of wine. Then again, he *was* the procurer, and probably spent about half his time at the market.

It was still early in the afternoon when Phana decided that she might want to get off the streets for a while. She didn't want to go back to the house where she had woken up that morning. Yarrian would no doubt come searching for her when he found her gone, and she needed some time away from him to process the visions in her mind.

She returned home and walked into her one-room apartment before suddenly stopping.

Someone had been in here.

Her belongings, sparse as they were, were mostly left as she had last seen them. But someone had been sitting at her small table. There were crumbs left from a meal of what looked like bread and cheese, and a couple of small dates sat to one side—dates that had not been there when she left the apartment yesterday.

There was nowhere for anyone to hide in the single room and Phana knew she was alone. Who had come here looking for her? Only one person besides herself knew she lived here.

Koral.

She wasn't sure how she felt about him being in her apartment while she was gone. On the one hand, she was still angry with him. On the other hand, she wouldn't have minded seeing his face waiting for her. The truth was, she wanted to talk to him, tell him what had happened to her, feel his arms around her.

But he wasn't here now. And she had no idea where in the city his duties might have taken him. Tonight he would likely be at the Crown and Coin. But going out after dusk meant that Yarrian would almost certainly find her.

So she stretched out on her small bed and stared at the ceiling, turning over the visions again and again in her mind.

Chapter Twenty-Seven

THE LARGE ROOM WAS MOSTLY EMPTY, A HANDFUL OF YTHIS citizens talking to members of the Watch, the day sergeant seated at the desk on the raised platform near the center of the room.

Hinara marched across the floor toward the desk, his fists clenched. He silently cursed the waste of an entire morning.

He had arrived at the Watch House early, barely an hour after dawn. If there was any group who would know about the Wolf, the Watch would be it. They were the eyes and ears on the streets of Ythis.

He knew there was a chance that the head of the Watch wouldn't be in yet, but he wanted to get started as soon as possible, and he figured he would wait in the main room and assess how the Ythis Watch conducted their affairs.

It had been an exercise in frustration.

The sergeant on duty at the time was lazy and indifferent. He had greeted Hinara's request to see the captain with a grunt and a shrug of his shoulders.

"Not in yet."

"When is he expected?" Hinara had asked.

"Dunno."

Hinara had waited for him to offer anything further, but the man had gone back to staring off in the distance.

"What time does he usually come in?" Hinara had demanded.

The man shrugged again.

"Midday?" he guessed.

It was not the answer Hinara wanted to hear. He had expected the captain of the Watch to be punctual and efficient, but it seemed he was overestimating the man. It did not bode well for Hinara's expectations for the rest of the Watch.

He had left a message for the captain, fully expecting it to be misplaced by the sergeant long before the head of the organization arrived. He wasn't going to let it stop him.

He reached the raised desk and confirmed that a different sergeant was now seated there. This man was also overweight, the buttons on his Watch uniform struggling to contain his expanding stomach. He seemed more alert than the previous sergeant, spotting Hinara's approach and frowning.

"Investigator Hinara Angumu, here to see the captain. I left a message earlier—"

"Yeah, I got it," the man snapped, cutting him off. "Lieutenant Yithare will see you in a minute."

The sergeant motioned to one of the younger members of the Watch, who immediately turned and began to ascend the stairs to the upper level.

"Wait a minute. I'm here to see the captain," Hinara argued, finding himself once again on his back foot in his dealing with the Watch, and not liking the feeling one bit.

"And the captain handed it down to the lieutenant."

He shrugged.

"Orders are orders."

"This is a matter of Imperial security," Hinara snapped at him. "I do not care—"

"Neither do I," the sergeant snapped back. "Take it up with the lieutenant."

"Investigator Hinara?"

Hinara turned to see the young Watchman had returned. His eyes widened as he saw the look on Hinara's face.

"Sir, uh, the lieutenant will see you now. This way, please."

Hinara turned back to the sergeant, but the man had turned away and was talking to two other members of the Watch, giving them instructions for their next patrol. He wanted to give the man a dressing down, especially in front of his subordinates, but he had wasted enough time.

For a moment, his desire to confront the sergeant warred with his need to see the captain. Finally, he took a deep breath and turned back to the messenger, motioning with his hand for the young man to lead the way.

The Watchman went back up the stairs, Hinara on his heels. They reached the landing on the second floor, and he was led to a plain wooden door in a long hallway pierced by at least a half-dozen others just like it.

The Watchman knocked twice and opened the door. Hinara stepped through to see a man in his middle years, his sandy brown hair speckled with gray. The man's uniform fit well, and he stood and offered his hand.

"Lieutenant Yithare."

Hinara stepped into the small office and took the man's hand, giving it a perfunctory shake.

"Investigator Angumu."

The lieutenant gestured for Hinara to take a seat, and he did so, looking around at the office. There were no decorations on the walls, and the man's desk was neat and tidy. Hinara felt a small glimmer of hope rise within him. Perhaps the leadership was not so lax, after all.

"I had expected to see the captain," he began, and the lieutenant nodded.

"I understand. But the captain is extremely busy right now. She gives her regrets, though, and asked that I report directly to her on whatever it is you need from us."

Hinara wanted to argue, to demand he be given due respect, but the lieutenant was obviously trying to be helpful. Perhaps he could forego the need to speak to the captain directly.

"We have some fugitives in the city, lieutenant. We believe they are planning to do something violent and harmful to Ythis and perhaps to the Emperor himself."

The lieutenant's reaction was not what Hinara was expecting. The Watchman frowned and rubbed the side of his face with his hand.

"Investigator, protection of the Emperor falls under the remit of the Imperial Guard."

Hinara heard something in his voice, a strange note and a twist to his lips as he mentioned the Guard.

"The Imperial Guard is fully aware of the threat. If these traitors come anywhere near the Emperor's palace, or the noble family estates, the Guard will respond appropriately. That's not why I am here."

The lieutenant sat back in his chair and crossed his arms. The frown hadn't left his face.

"Lieutenant, my job is to find these traitors before it comes to that. They are here in Ythis. They are making plans. They are gathering resources. They cannot do that and stay hidden. They need to eat, they need somewhere to stay. Your people know the city like no one else, I expect. Someone must have noticed something … unusual. This is potentially a large group."

"How large?"

"It could be as many as two hundred."

The lieutenant blinked at him.

"Two hundred? That's more than a few traitors. That's larger than the entire Watch. Tell me they don't have much in the way of weapons."

"They most likely have their swords," Hinara answered. "And armor, mostly leather. Crossbows, too."

"Where did they get … wait, are we talking about soldiers?"

"Yes, lieutenant. About a half a contingent of former Legionnaires."

He could see a look of panic in the lieutenant's eyes, so he held up his hands.

"I am not asking for anyone to fight them. In fact, taking them down is the Legion's job, and we would like nothing better than to do it ourselves. These people are deserters and traitors, and their very existence is a challenge to the reputation of the Legion itself."

He lowered his hands to his lap.

"The problem is not fighting them. The problem is *finding* them. This is a large city, and they are hiding among the populace. We cannot just march a contingent or two into the city and start going block-by-block."

"Are you absolutely sure they're here in Ythis? There's no place to hide two hundred people. They'd have to be scattered across the city. How are they being fed? How are they communicating?"

"That, lieutenant, is how I am hoping the Watch can help me. You have people across the city. They walk the streets and see what is going on. I am sure you have informants who give you tips for money. There is a large reward for these traitors, at least for their commander and her closest subordinates. Surely, someone will have seen something and be willing to trade that information for ready coin?"

But, to Hinara's surprise, the lieutenant seemed like he wasn't sure.

"Well, that depends."

"On what?"

"On what arrangements they've made with whom."

Hinara narrowed his eyes at the lieutenant.

"I met with the Wolf last night."

He caught just the smallest look of guilt pass over the lieutenant's face, but the man covered it by frowning again.

"Is he … is he hiding these traitors?"

Hinara considered lying to see what the lieutenant would do. But then again, word would no doubt get back to the Wolf, and he didn't want to make an enemy of the criminal just yet. The man might yet prove useful if he decided to play it safe and help the authorities apprehend Laita Naschect and her people.

"He did not say either way. But I have made him an offer that he is considering. To be honest, if the Wolf decides to help us, I will not need the Watch to do anything at all. But, of course, I would prefer to deal with the law in Ythis."

"Well, Investigator, I'll have to discuss this with the captain before I can make any commitments."

"I would think your captain would be eager to stop what could end up being an attack on the city itself from the inside. Who knows how many will die if these traitors get the opportunity to move forward with their plans? I would think that if you passed the word to your Watch members, you would probably have a solid lead by dawn tomorrow. Why wait?"

The lieutenant looked uncomfortable, and that was when Hinara knew. The Watch was in the pocket of the Wolf, and would need to check in with him before they committed to helping the Legion.

Once again, he was being delayed by corruption. The Imperial Guard didn't want to help because they were too lazy and unimaginative to understand the danger posed by Laita Naschect. The Wolf didn't want to help unless he could be sure to make the most profit out of his decision. And now the Ythis City Watch was stalling because they were riddled with corruption.

He saw it clearly now. Ythis was a cesspool that needed a good cleansing. It was time for the Legion to come home to the capital of the Undying Empire and take control. To wipe out the criminals and the traitors. And to run the city under the command of the Emperor himself.

"I will speak to the captain this afternoon, Investigator. I will send a message to you as soon as I have the details of what we can do to help you."

Hinara stood and straightened his uniform.

"Of course you will," he said, looking the other man in the eye. He didn't hide his disdain, and he was sure the lieutenant could see that Hinara knew what was happening here.

The lieutenant rose and began to offer his hand, but Hinara turned and marched out of the room.

He needed a reason to convince the Legion to come here in force. One way or another, that was exactly what he was going to get.

*   *   *

THE STREET WAS BUSY ENOUGH IN THE EARLY AFTERNOON THAT Laita's people could blend in and remain close enough to respond quickly if this didn't go well. She stood at the end of the block, looking toward the Wandering Horse Tavern. According to the soldier who had been keeping watch, Oriuna had come here this morning and hadn't left yet.

And now Laita was going to put herself in danger to speak with the other woman directly. Another risk, but one she had to take herself. This entire situation had the potential to spiral out of control, and she couldn't trust anyone else to put aside their personal feelings and deal with Oriuna properly.

She had intended to meet with Galla this morning, to discuss how deliveries were made to the Fortress. Now, she wasn't sure if any of that would soon matter. It all depended on what waited for her inside that tavern.

With Addiru trailing a few paces behind, Laita began to walk down the street toward the tavern entrance, noting the position of her soldiers and their awareness of her. She reached the handful of steps leading down below street level to the door of the tavern and paused for a breath. Then she moved to the door and pushed it open.

The tavern was empty of patrons. Only a single figure sat at a table in the middle of the floor. Laita's eyes adjusted and she saw it was Oriuna.

"Please come in and have a drink with me," the woman said. She had apparently been waiting for Laita. Addiru stepped up behind and peered in.

Laita stepped across the threshold and looked around the room. The single door behind the bar was closed and she could see no other way for anyone to enter the tavern. Addiru stood at the door, holding it open with his foot.

"You're safe here, Laita. I understand you're worried about what you discovered yesterday, but I have no interest in capturing you or harming you in any way."

She knows. She was waiting for me because she knows that we know.

Laita considered turning and running.

"If I wanted to capture you, it would already be too late," Oriuna said seriously. "I could have had people block off the streets as soon as you opened the door. You can leave if you want to, but I think we need to have this conversation. You think so, too, or you wouldn't have come."

Laita turned to Addiru and motioned for him to go back up to the street. He looked at her questioningly and she raised her eyebrows at him. With one last glance around the interior of the tavern, he let the door swing closed as he retreated up the steps.

"He could have stayed for a drink," Oriuna offered.

"I think this should be just between you and I."

"I was hoping that Namal would have come with you. I wanted to
…."

She drifted off and Laita thought she heard a note of resignation
in her voice.

"I thought it best that he didn't come. You might not have survived
the encounter."

Oriuna looked down at the table.

"That's not what I wanted."

"What *do* you want?"

"Me? I want to see Namal again. I like him. There's something
about him that …."

"I'm not here to talk about Namal and what might have been between the two of you. What do you—and your *masters*—want?"

Oriuna visibly flinched at the word.

"You've figured out what they want. That's why you're here. The
question is how they can help you achieve your objective."

Laita shook her head.

"I don't want anything from the Church. I'm not willing to pay the
kinds of prices they demand."

Oriuna stood and moved over to the bar. She grabbed a bottle of
whiskey and two glasses and came back to the table. Laita waved her
off, but she poured a measure into each glass anyway.

Sitting down, Oriuna lifted her glass and hesitated, as if she was
trying to think of a toast. But she gave up and simply took a mouthful of whiskey and swallowed it down.

"The Church agrees with your goal of removing the Emperor. It's
as simple as that. His demands have become more and more … dangerous to the survival of the Undying Empire itself. I don't know exactly what happened in the mountains, what he was trying to achieve
there, and I don't need—or want—to know. But I do know it was
enough to cause you to abandon the Legion and come here. It was
enough to get almost two hundred soldiers to follow you."

"Stop," Laita told her. She looked at the whiskey and almost
grabbed the glass, but she knew she needed to keep her wits about
her.

"I'm going to be blunt with you. I don't know what position you have in the Church. I don't think you're a priest—you're too normal for that—but you obviously work for them. So I'm probably going to be insulting you when I say that I'd like nothing more than to wipe the Church, and everyone connected to them, off the face of this world."

Oriuna didn't react to Laita's remark—only lifted her glass and took another sip of whiskey.

"But I'm smart enough to know that I can't do a damned thing against the Church. You've got those gods of yours, and nothing can stand against that. I'm also not going to ally myself with the sorcerers, either. As far as I'm concerned, you're both equally insane and vicious and a danger to all the regular, innocent people across the Empire."

"Innocent? Now that's a discussion we need to have at some point. I've lived in Ythis my whole life. There's not a single innocent person in this city, not a one who wouldn't kill their own mother—or own child, even—for a shot at some wealth and power."

"Spare me the tales of woe," Laita said, feeling her anger rise at the arrogance of the other woman. "I'm not going to debate the relative merits of normal people against the priests who sacrifice countless lives to an abomination from another world."

"Oh, I'm not going to argue on behalf of the priests, Laita. I know exactly what they are, better than you do by far. Everything comes with a price. They pay theirs willingly."

She leaned forward and crossed her arms, resting her elbows on the table.

"But you have a goal. You could even say it's an impossible dream. You're going to try to kill the Undying Emperor. You think all you're going to face are Imperial Guards in the Palace. You think short swords and crossbow bolts are going to win the day. But they're not. You need help."

She gave Oriuna a skeptical look but the other woman continued.

"You need the kind of help you can't get from the Wolf, or from your Legion training, or from drive, and courage, and perseverance. And the Church is offering you that help."

"Then what's the price? You're right, everything *does* come with a price. Some pay it willingly, some try to cheat the system, and some end up paying the price for others and get nothing in return. Where do I fit in?"

Oriuna shrugged.

"You make your own choices, Laita. No one forced you to come to Ythis. No one forced you to take on the mantle of 'savior of the Empire.' Don't tell me you haven't thought about what it will likely cost you to reach the Emperor and kill him. And you won't be the only one paying that price, will you? You think none of your soldiers are going to die? That none of them will end up paying the price for others and get nothing in return?"

"The Church is offering me help. What do they want in return?"

Oriuna picked up the glass and downed the last of the whiskey. She made to reach for the bottle again, but Laita grabbed her arm.

"What do they want?"

"They want," Oriuna replied, "for you to succeed or die trying."

Chapter Twenty-Eight

THE CARRIAGE CAME TO A STOP AND RELAEL HEARD THE driver jump down to the cobblestones. The door was pulled open and a dirty beggar stepped out of an alley and climbed into the cab to sit across from Relael, beside a small sack on the opposite seat. The driver shut the door again and a moment later, the carriage started moving.

Relael looked over the man seated opposite him. In the close confines of the carriage, with the heavy drapes closed over the windows, the smell of unwashed flesh and other, even less savory, odors thickened the air. The beggar was dressed in a ragged tunic and pants, his calloused feet bare. His dark hair was long and matted.

"Where is she?" Relael asked the man.

The beggar reached into the bag and pulled out one of the pastries. He closed his eyes and inhaled the smell of the food, leaning back against the rear of the seat.

Relael forced himself to wait as the man took a large bite of the pastry, releasing the smell of the hot meat filling. Mixed with his own scent, it made the overall stench in the carriage worse rather than better.

The man opened his eyes and looked at Relael. He could see the exhaustion in the man's face. It was a job that Relael knew he could never do himself, posing as one of the street people to spy on others. This man was a professional, and so Relael gave him a few moments to enjoy a bit of comfort before he made his report.

Finally, he gave a small sigh.

"We can't find her," he said, grimacing.

"Why not?" Relael snapped at him. "It can't be that difficult to find someone when you know her name, you know what she looks like, and you know where she spends her time!"

The man shrugged and took another bite before speaking.

"Sir, we had her at the Crown and Coin two nights ago. But when my man tried to follow her as she left, she just about disappeared. She was up onto the roofs, and by the time he climbed up, she was gone. He said he never saw anyone move that fast before. So we're watching the Crown and Coin in case she comes back. I've got someone at the Red Flag, and I've even got someone at the Wolf's Den, just in case."

"What about Creyss?"

"He hasn't seen her since two nights ago, either. We must be extra careful with him—he's got enough experience to tell when he's being followed. Not only that, but he appears to be looking into certain disappearances."

Relael swore softly.

"Well," he said out loud, "we knew it was only a matter of time before they figured it out. Does he have anything yet?"

"We don't know. Last night he was at the Crown and Coin, and I had two men tasked to follow him if he left. But a couple of hours later, they saw him on the street *returning* to the tavern. He must have left through the back alley, which we can't easily watch and stay hidden ourselves. We weren't expecting it to be an issue, as so far he's always just used the front door of the tavern."

"You think he knows he's being followed?"

The spy shrugged again.

"That was my first thought. But then why didn't he return the same way he left? We'd never have known he was gone. And I can't figure out why he'd want us to know he's aware of our watchers. So maybe there's another reason he left via the back alley."

Relael considered the problem, turning it over in his mind, trying to think what he would do in Koral's place.

"Perhaps he doesn't care if he's followed most of the time. But he was going somewhere he wanted to keep secret and so took the hidden route. It no longer mattered by the time he came back."

Relael swore again.

"He had probably gone to meet with *her.*"

The other man shook his head.

"It still doesn't make sense that he'd walk right back in the front door of the tavern when he returned. It still told us that he sometimes leaves through the back alley. It'll be harder for us to cover it—I'll have to task a couple more men to watch the cross-street so that they won't be seen. But it's not impossible. And now he won't be able to use that route again."

"You're right. But if he didn't know we're watching him, then why leave by the back route?"

The spy considered it for a few moments.

"Maybe someone else came to speak to him, someone who *doesn't* use the front door of the tavern. If Creyss left with them, he'd go out the same way they came in."

"Phana?" Relael asked.

"Possibly but unlikely. She's been seen to use the front door as well, and since she can lose my people so easily …."

Relael didn't like it. There were too many variables, and the search was taking far too long. The High Counselor was going to call Relael in for a report at any time now. He had barely been able to keep himself together during their last meeting six days ago. If he had to go in and tell her he had failed to find the woman so far, the stress would likely cause him to make a mistake—a mistake that could end his life.

"So, where is she?" he asked the spy.

"There was a report of someone breaking into one of the noble estates last night. A thief stole some gems from a dining room."

"Was it her?"

The spy shrugged again.

"I wouldn't rule it out. We know she's a thief, and we know she's gone into at least one other noble estate before. If she had any idea that we were searching for her, I expect she'd go to ground somewhere. Ythis is too large to search effectively if someone doesn't want to be found. What I think is that she's one of those people who never stays in one place for very long. Maybe she doesn't even have a home of her own. But it makes it hard to pin her down."

"I don't suppose you have a solution," Relael said calmly, though he was barely containing his anger at the man's nonchalant attitude.

"I've got a team of soldiers in a building a couple of blocks away from the Crown and Coin. Creyss spends most of his time there, and I expect Phana will return there in a few days at most. As soon as she shows up, one of my watchers will alert the guards and we'll have the place surrounded long before she's ready to leave again."

"And what if she doesn't go back there?"

"Then we keep following Creyss and eventually he leads us to her."

"We cannot wait for another week … or more! This woman needs to be found quickly!"

The spy considered it for a moment and then spread his hands wide.

"There's one person who probably knows where she is. Or at least where she will be. Grab him and get what you need out of him."

Relael sat back in the carriage seat. He had been trying to minimize the damage to the Wolf's guild because he understood that the Church was not supposed to go against the crime lord directly. Grabbing the Wolf's right-hand man would definitely cross that line.

But the spy was right. The only way they might find Phana quickly would be through Koral Creyss. Relael was taking a gamble that no one in the Wolf's guild knew it was the Church who was responsible for the disappearance of the other two gang members.

If he was right, then the disappearance of Creyss wouldn't lead back to Relael and the Church. If he was wrong, Creyss' disappearance could be the spark that ignited a confrontation between the Wolf and the Church. He was sure the Church would come out of that conflict on top. But the fact that the High Counselor had declared the Wolf off-limits made Relael wonder what kind of damage the criminal might inflict.

Still, Relael wouldn't succeed by sitting back and waiting. Time was not on his side. He had to act decisively, or he'd fail in his mission entirely.

"The next time Koral Creyss leaves the Crown and Coin, take him. But I don't want the soldiers in Church uniforms. Make sure there is no direct trail back to us—the area around the tavern is too busy to risk having witnesses."

The spy gave Relael a nod.

"Wait for night, or take him whenever we get the chance?"

Relael paused for only an instant before making his decision.

"First chance you get, do it."

He rapped on the roof of the carriage and the driver brought it to a halt near the mouth of another alleyway. As the spy prepared to depart, Relael thought back to Neysi's words as she lay strapped to the table.

I warned them to stay away from her, but it don't matter. She already cursed us.

It looked like Koral Creyss was now also going to pay for his association with this woman. Perhaps Neysi had been right about her, after all.

*   *   *

NAMAL SLOWLY WALKED BACK TO THE TENEMENT WHERE THE weapons were being distributed. He hadn't seen Laita since their argument in the early hours of the morning, but he knew she had gone to meet with the traitorous bitch, Oriuna. He figured he could go in, help with some of the logistics, and be gone before she was done.

But after he gave the password and walked up the stairs to the large room on the second floor, he found that Laita and the rest of the command squad were assembled. Laita turned to him as he entered.

"Ah, sergeant, I'm glad you're here."

Namal saluted Laita and looked around the room at the others. Not only were Saeda and Bor here, but Addiru, Keynter, and Pilayni were waiting as well. They all gave him a quick salute and turned back to Laita. He could feel the tension rise as he stood there.

Bor must have told the rest about what happened between Laita and I, he thought. *Just great.*

Laita waved him to one of the chairs that had been brought into the room for this meeting. He had expected Laita to be gone most of the afternoon. If she was already back, then her encounter with Oriuna either didn't happen, or it had all gone down quickly.

"First, I want to be clear why Pilayni, Keynter and Addiru have been invited to this meeting. They are not part of the command squad, nor are they squad sergeants. But they have traveled with Namal and me to Ythis and have assisted us in various elements of our mission here. For the purpose of this discussion, I am asking them to respond as representatives of the common soldiers in the force we have here in Ythis."

She looked at each in turn.

"I want to hear about your concerns and what you think of the situation I am about to outline for you."

They nodded their agreement, though Pilayni looked self-conscious and Addiru's eyes constantly flicked from one members of the command squad to another. Only Keynter seemed excited by the prospect of having a say in whatever decision was going to be made here today.

Laita took a deep breath.

"I met with Oriuna right before returning here and summoning all of you. I can confirm that she works for the Church."

Namal felt his blood run cold. As much as he had already known her true loyalties, the confirmation still felt like a blow. The three younger soldiers all gave voice to their surprise and horror at the revelation. Laita held up her hands for quiet before continuing.

"We spoke and clarified a few things. Before meeting with her, I thought about what we learned yesterday and tried to figure out why the Church hadn't already come for us. And I came to the conclusion that the Church would like nothing more than for the Emperor to be removed from his position of power."

This time, there were audible gasps from all the others. Namal felt little surprise at the news. To have the Church betray the Emperor seemed perfectly reasonable to him. No one in this city could be trusted, especially those in power.

"My discussion with Oriuna bears that out. The Church hasn't captured us or turned us in because they want us to succeed."

She paused, and Saeda took that opportunity to speak up.

"Commander, that is not exactly comforting. If the Church wants the Emperor dead, it means that they stand to gain a great deal once

Andrew J. Luther

he's gone."

"Exactly, Saeda," Laita replied. "There is a balance here between the Emperor, the Church, and the Six. The sorcerers and the priests are always at each other's throats. The Church is really the most powerful of the factions, but the Emperor throws his support behind the Six when he wants to reign in the priests, and he withdraws that support if the sorcerers become too demanding."

"But what will happen if the Emperor is removed?" asked Addiru. There was a quaver in his voice as he spoke, and Namal could see the fear in his eyes.

"War," he answered. "War between the sorcerers and the Church. Not just here in Ythis, but everywhere in the Empire. There are sorcerers in Caladur, Esten, Jh'tira, Yintoq ... probably most, if not all, of the provincial capitals."

"The ones in Ythis are just the most powerful," added Keynter.

"But if the Church is more powerful than the sorcerers ...." Bor suggested.

Laita raised one palm and they all stopped talking to listen to her.

"Yes, the Church is more powerful. There is a god in each of the nine major cities, and even the sorcerers can't stand against that kind of power."

"But they'll still fight for their survival," Namal argued. "They'll unleash their demons and people will die ... more people than we tried to save in the north."

Laita rubbed the back her neck with one hand as the rest of the command squad looked from Namal back to her.

"You're right. It won't be a quiet takeover. If the Church goes after the sorcerers—and there's no reason to think they won't—then those cities may end up being laid to waste."

She took a deep breath and let it out slowly.

"That's what we're facing. I knew there would be trouble once the Emperor was killed. But I ... I just didn't realize the Church was ready for this, waiting for this opportunity. They want us to succeed because they know they'll end up in control. But countless innocent people will die, and not just during the transition. As much as the Emperor uses and abuses the common people, he is still a controlling influence on the Church."

"Commander, are you saying that we can't proceed with our mission?" Keynter asked her, disbelief obvious in his voice. "Everything we gave up, everything we've done to get here and now we're quitting?"

"No, that is not what I'm saying," Laita replied. "This is why I've called you all here. We need to discuss this. We need to decide on a course of action, and I want to hear your thoughts on the matter. If we proceed—and we succeed in our mission—then we will be handing the Empire over to the Church. The Emperor is one man, powerful, difficult to reach, but still a single target. The Church is another matter entirely. Two hundred soldiers can't go up against the Church and win."

"We can't just stop now," Keynter argued.

"Bullshit," Namal growled at him. "If we go ahead, then all we do is trade one tyrant for a worse one. Is that what you want?"

"I want my life back!" Keynter shouted.

"It's too late for that," Bor snapped at him. "We're here now, this is the situation we're in, and we have to do what's right."

"Stop!" said Saeda, and they all looked at her. "We don't even know what all our options are yet. I want to hear the commander's plan."

Laita held up her hand again to prevent anyone else from continuing.

"This is what I see as potential outcomes. One is that we go ahead with the mission. We know the Church wants this to happen and we know they will try to assume all authority over the Empire once the Emperor no longer stands in their way.

"Two, we abandon the mission and attempt to withdraw. We will have to leave the Empire, as we'll be hunted down as long as we stay within its borders. Further, we will have to do it all at once, because once the Church realizes that we're not going ahead, there is no reason not to capture us or turn us in to the Imperial Guard and the Legion.

"Three, we find someone else to take the Emperor's place. Someone who the Imperial Guard and the Legion will follow and who will willingly throw the might of the Empire behind the sorcerers in order to balance out the Church's power."

"Unlikely," Namal replied. "Even the members of the Resistance can't agree on what happens after the Emperor is gone. The nobles will fight each other. They won't provide a united front, which is what you'd need to get the Guard to go along with it, never mind the Legion."

"But if we selected a candidate ahead of time, someone powerful enough that he or she will have at least a solid backing from some other noble families, then we can install that person immediately, before anyone even knows the Emperor is dead."

Namal shook his head at her.

"That means we gotta reveal ourselves to one of the heads of the noble families here in Ythis. That's madness. They have no reason to believe we'll succeed, and they can get more benefit out of turning us in. No noble is going to risk their neck on these kinds of odds."

"Then do you have another option?" she challenged him.

"I don't need another option. I already told you it was over. We're done. Your meeting with that woman just confirms it. The Church is going to sacrifice us all. Either we do what they want, and we all die on the mission, or we refuse, and they give us to their god. Our only option is to pass the message to the soldiers to run for their lives. Then at least some will escape."

"By the Abyss, I used to look up to you!" Keynter said to him. "When did you become such a fucking coward?"

Namal was on his feet, his hand on his dagger, before he even realized he was moving. Keynter's eyes were wide, but he also jumped to his feet. Bor and Addiru also surged forward, Bor lunging for Keynter and Addiru trying to step in front of Namal.

"Enough!" Laita shouted, and everyone's training kicked in, freezing them in place for an instant. Just enough time for them to realize what they were doing.

"Keynter, I asked you for your concerns. I will not, however, stand for insubordination," she told him coldly. "You are dismissed for now. We will discuss this later."

He looked at her, and then back at Namal, his eyes narrowed. Then his jaw tightened, and he stood up and saluted her.

"Yes, commander. I request permission to return to my old squad. I know where they are staying, and I think it best that I resume my position with them."

Namal could see Keynter was just as angry at Laita for calling him out as he was at Namal for what he had said about their failed mission.

"Yes, that is for the best. I will send a message when I wish to speak with you."

"Good. At least they know how to be soldiers," he muttered as he walked toward the door, and Namal felt the overwhelming urge to hit him. But Addiru grabbed his arm as he started to follow.

"Sergeant, please," Addiru said to him in a low voice. "The rest of us still need you."

Namal turned to him and saw the fear in his eyes.

We're lost, he thought to himself. *We're all going to die here for nothing.*

Seventeenth day of Highsummer,
2 days to the Arrival

Chapter Twenty-Nine

T HE FENCE AROUND THE ESTATE WAS OF WROUGHT METAL, and rose only slightly above chest height. The gates were ornate, but stood wide open, a flagstone pathway leading up to the double doors at the front of the large stone building. Tall, narrow windows pierced the stone walls at regular intervals, though all were covered by heavy draperies.

Phana stood at the end of the walkway and looked up at the two-story building, suddenly unsure of herself. The place certainly didn't appear welcoming, despite the gate standing open. And it did not resemble any other home in this district, either. But Phana knew that the great historian Ziarithllo Ilisti lived here, and possessed one of the most extensive collections of written histories of anyone in the Empire.

Phana, however, had no reason to believe the historian would help her. This was his private residence, and it wasn't open to the public. She had heard very little about him, other than what he did and the large number of scrolls and books he possessed. She might be turned away at the door and that would be the end of it.

And as much as Phana knew she could easily break into a building such as this, she would need the historian's help to find the information for which she was looking.

Taking a deep breath, she proceeded up the walkway. The dark wood doors, banded in iron, and perched on a landing a dozen stone steps above the flagstones, looked down upon her as she approached. She climbed the stairs and stood before the double doors. There was no knocker or bell pull, and so she reached out and rapped on the door with her knuckles.

After a few moments, when no one came to the door, Phana hammered her fist on the doors a few times in the hope that someone would hear her. She waited, wondering if anyone was in the building at all.

At the sound of a bolt being drawn back, Phana stood up straight and put a friendly smile.

The door was pulled open, and a woman of middling years in the clothes of a servant—though not a slave—looked out at Phana, squinting in the morning sunlight. The woman said nothing, so after a moment Phana spoke up.

"Good morning. My name is Phana. How are you this morning?"

The woman continued to look at her but didn't speak.

"Um, my name is … I mean, I'm hoping you can help me. Is the master of the house in?"

"I don't know you," the woman answered coldly. "And that means the master of the house doesn't know you either. What do you want?"

"If I could just speak to him for a few moments, I promise to not take up too much of his time. I'm looking for some information, and—"

"Who do you represent?" the woman interrupted.

"Represent?"

"On whose behalf have you come? Who wants to consult with Master Ilisti?"

"I do," Phana replied and woman blinked at her.

"No, I'm asking who you work for."

"No one. I'm looking to consult with Master Ilisti myself."

The woman looked Phana up and down.

"The master only performs professional consultations," she said, and began to close the door. Phana stepped forward and stopped the door with an outstretched hand.

"I'm willing to pay him."

"Willing and able are not the same things. You could not afford the master's fees."

Phana was becoming irritated, and she didn't hide it as she replied.

"You're making an awful lot of assumptions about what I can and cannot afford. That's a decision your master should be making."

"The master does important work. My *job* is to keep away any unnecessary interruptions."

"Another assumption on your part. This is about as *necessary* as it gets."

The woman glared at Phana for a moment, but she met the woman's gaze calmly and unflinchingly. Finally, the woman yanked the door open.

"Step inside," she ordered.

Phana stepped through the door into a large foyer. A wide staircase in front of her led up to a second-floor balcony that ran around the outer edge of the room. Many doors led out to side rooms both on this level and from the balcony above. The entire room was dim, the only light from a pair of lamps set on marble tables against the walls to either side.

The woman shut the door and pushed the bolt home.

"You can wait over here," she said and marched off to the first room on the right. Phana followed and found herself in a small lounge with a few chairs arranged against the walls. A small, low table sat in the center of the room, its polished surface reflecting the heavy burgundy drapes that covered the windows.

The woman pulled a drawstring to open the draperies, and the beams of sunlight highlighted the thick dust motes floating in the air. With one last glare at Phana, the woman walked out of the room, pulling the door closed behind her.

Phana sighed and sat down on one of the chairs. She had no doubt the woman would describe Phana as pushy and rude and that might cause the historian to refuse her request for help. But there was nothing more she could do at this point. She was inside the house, and would at least get a chance to plead her case.

She waited quite some time before she heard movement and muttered voices on the other side of the door. She tried to put on an expression that was both friendly and yet serious, and realized her slight smile wasn't remotely genuine. She decided to just look serious as the door opened and she got her first look at the historian, Master Ilisti.

The man was old, with greying hair cut short to his scalp and a neatly trimmed beard. He was thin, though he moved with a confidence that told Phana he was certainly not frail. His dark robes were expensive, the sleeves much shorter than current fashion would dictate, and he wore no jewelry on his fingers or around his neck.

His bright eyes met Phana's as he stepped into the room. She rose and extended a hand, and he took it and bowed over it, though it was a perfunctory movement. He was not here to welcome her, but to discuss business.

"Good morning, my lady," he said, and his voice was deep and full of gravel.

Phana smiled at him.

"Good morning, Master Ilisti. Thank you for taking time out of your busy day to see me."

"Yes, well I must apologize, but I'm afraid you have me at a disadvantage, as your name is not familiar to me. Which noble family do you belong to?"

Phana glanced from the historian to the woman servant—still standing in the doorway of the room—and back.

"I'm sorry. I think there must be a misunderstanding. I don't belong to a noble family."

"You don't?" the historian said, looking confused. "And yet your face is vaguely familiar to me. Do you work for one of the families?"

Phana shook her head.

"No, I have no family. I've come here entirely on my own. I hope you can help me, though of course I understand that you must be paid for your consultations."

Master Ilisti's confusion left his face and he straightened up.

"Young lady, I do not appreciate you lying to my servants in order to see me. My work is important and every interruption costs me money."

"I didn't lie," Phana said evenly. "I said that I could afford your consultant fees, and I meant it. Money is not an issue, Master Ilisti. I need your assistance, and I'm willing and able to pay for it."

The historian frowned at her and opened his mouth to speak, and then stopped. He stood there, his mouth open and his eyes going wide. Phana froze, not sure what was happening.

"It can't be …." he whispered, his eyes glued to her face.

"Are you okay?" she asked him, and his servant stepped into the room and reached out a hand to touch his shoulder.

He blinked at her, as if coming out of a trance, and then reached out and took Phana's hand.

"My lady, I just realized where I've seen your face before. Or at least someone who looks remarkably like you, though her hair is longer. You say you have no family, but do you remember your parents?"

"My parents? No, I don't remember …."

She paused, not sure how much she should tell this man, this stranger. But then, she was here to find out whatever she could about herself. She had these memories, and she wanted to know if there was any truth to them. She had to take a leap of faith.

"I don't have any memories older than a few years. I can't remember my parents, or my childhood, or anything. I don't know who I am, but I recently have learned … a few things. I'm hoping you can help me connect some of these … bits of knowledge."

Master Ilisti gently let go of her hand and turned to the woman at his shoulder.

"I will have to cancel my visit this afternoon. Please prepare an apology and have it sent immediately. But this lady will be staying. The two of us have much to discuss."

Phana let out a breath of relief. He was agreeing to help her.

He turned back to her and smiled for the first time.

"My lady, I have a charcoal sketch of you. Or at least a sketch of a woman who looks exactly like you. Only this sketch is old. Much older than you. And the writings that were found with it … I believe they predate the founding of the Undying Empire."

*   *   *

THE FRONT DOOR OF THE CROWN AND COIN WAS NEVER LOCKED. Though most taverns closed when the owner retired for the night, the Wolf had tasked a pair of gang members to operate the Crown and Coin around the clock. Elmther lived in a small apartment on the second floor of the building, and he was always available if some-one needed to liaison with the Wolf's people during an emergency, no matter what time it was.

Though it was always open, only on rare occasions would there be patrons in the tavern in the small hours of the morning up un-til shortly before midday. It was still early enough for the tavern to be empty now—aside from Haedue and Lyntan—as Koral walked through the front door. Haedue was behind the bar, and Lyntan was reclining on a chair leaned back against the wall, his boots up on a nearby table. When they saw Koral, Lyntan immediately removed his boots from the table and sat up.

Apparently Koral hadn't lost all his power to intimidate the young-er gang members quite yet. He waved off Lyntan as the young man opened his mouth to apologize.

"Has anyone been by?" he asked them. All the gangs knew to re-port any suspicious activity, including the disappearance of any gang members, directly to the Crown and Coin. He didn't mention that he was hoping Phana had come by to look for him.

She hadn't showed up at home yesterday morning, and by midday he had been forced to leave and deal with gang business. He hadn't had time to go looking for her again, and he was getting worried. Every so often, the thought that she had been taken by the Church hit him like a punch to the gut.

If she had been taken, he'd never see her again.

The words of the young girl in the alley—that Phana was with a man who had been the shadow that was stalking her—were, if true, not exactly comforting. And Koral didn't know why the witch Undil-sa would send him a warning about Phana. The witch was on friend-ly terms with the Wolf's people, but she still had her own agenda.

He didn't know who, if anyone, he could trust anymore.

Haedue was shaking his head at Koral's question.

"No one's been here all night. I think most people were off the streets last night, anyway."

Koral grunted in agreement. The feeling of dread had been grow-ing again and last night was the strongest yet. It felt as if a great weight hung above the city, ready to drop and bring doom to every last inhabitant of Ythis.

"Any message from Elmther?"

Haedue shook his head again.

"Okay, I'm going to go make my rounds of the gangs. I'll be back mid-afternoon."

"Is anyone going with you?" Lyntan asked, obviously concerned with Koral's safety.

"No. I don't believe anyone will be abducted right off the streets in broad daylight. Too many witnesses and too many chances for someone to interfere."

Lyntan frowned but didn't argue as Koral pulled the door open, stepping out just as a large carriage rolled to a stop in front of the tavern's door. Koral felt the presence at his side an instant before a pair of hands grabbed at his shoulders.

H   e   was already moving sideways, the man standing beside the   tav-   ern's entrance unable to get a grip on his tunic. The carriage door opened, and two more men leaped out, and Koral saw another three men come rushing around the corner heading straight toward him.

He knew what was happening and he flung himself sideways into a roll. He passed between the legs of the pair of horses secured to the carriage and rose to his feet on the other side, launching into a run. The men who had jumped out of the carriage hadn't expected such a move, and in the few seconds it took them to circle around the carriage, Koral was running flat out down the street.

The three men who had come around the corner weren't blocked by the horses and gave immediate chase. They were fast, but Koral was able to keep his distance ahead of them. He heard the carriage driver yell to get the horses moving.

It would take a moment to get the carriage turned around on the street, and that gave Koral options. The horses would soon overtake him if he stayed on the same street, so he turned at the first cross street, nearly colliding with a pair of laborers carrying large sacks over their shoulders. He spun past them and kept running, turning again at the next street.

The more turns he made, the more the carriage would need to

slow down to follow him.

There was no point in returning to the Crown and Coin. The soldiers—and he had no doubt these were Church soldiers chasing him—would follow him right in. Lyntan and Haedue wouldn't be of any help against a half-dozen trained soldiers, and Koral would be easily captured in the small tavern.

His only hope was to lose his pursuers entirely, or race them to the Wolf's Den. The problem was that he didn't know if more soldiers would be waiting near that location, in case he went in that direction.

He was fairly close to the market square, and if he could make it there the odds would shift in his favor. The crowded market would give him plenty of opportunities to lose his pursuers, and he would be able to blend in with the merchants and shoppers.

But then what?

Koral took another turn, dodging around pedestrians and cutting across the street in front of a wagon loaded with barrels. It gave him the chance to glance back over his shoulder. Of the three men who were close on his heels, one had dropped back and was struggling to keep up. The other two didn't seem to have any difficulty following, though they hadn't managed to close the distance.

Still, any delay and they would catch up to him quickly.

Yet another turn and Koral spotted a pair of City Watch strolling down the street toward him. As the three men followed Koral around the corner, the pair of guards noticed the chase approaching and one put a hand on the truncheon at his belt.

He didn't recognize either of the guards—he mostly knew the sergeants and other higher-ranking members of the Watch, and so these two were as likely to stop Koral as they were to help him escape the soldiers. At least the Churchmen weren't dressed in official uniforms—that would motivate the Watchmen to assist in their pursuit.

He raised his hand to the Watchmen as he approached them at a full run, as if he was asking for their help. That simple gesture changed their perception of what was happening. Suddenly, he was no longer a possible criminal being chased by men he had wronged, but was a victim running from a trio of attackers.

Both Watch guards drew their truncheons as he approached, and they stepped apart to let him through. He had no intention of stopping once he was past them, of course, but perhaps they would delay the other three men just enough to let him get enough distance to escape.

A moment before he reached the Watchmen, however, the one on the left suddenly narrowed his eyes and before Koral could react, the man stepped into his path and lowered his shoulder. He tried to twist away from the Watchman, but he still collided with him and went stumbling over his own feet, hitting the ground hard.

He gasped as his breath was driven out of his lungs. He tried to roll but the Watchman lunged forward and grabbed his tunic at the shoulder. He heard the other one yell "Hold up!" at the pursuing soldiers.

If the soldiers took him, Koral knew he was dead—or worse. There was no coming back from the Temple, and his very soul was in peril. He didn't have time to convince the Watchmen to help him, and a glance told him the soldiers were slowing, their hands out as if they had nothing to hide.

He grabbed the Watchman's hand on his shoulder, pinning it in place. He twisted on his side and drove his foot into the side of the man's knee with all his strength. There was the sound of bones shattering immediately before the man screamed, his grip on Koral going soft.

Koral pushed away from him and came to his feet just as the soldiers reached the remaining Watchman, who spun at the sound of his partner's scream. A knife appeared in the lead soldier's hand and drove into the back of the Watchman's neck. His eyes went wide as the soldier shoved him aside.

But Koral had already thrown himself into a run. He was gasping for breath still, and his body ached from his collision with the cobblestones. The soldiers immediately launched into a chase once more, but this time they began to gain ground on him, as he was no longer able to run quite as fast as he had before.

As he approached a final intersection he was faced with a choice. Turning right would lead him to the market square. Turning left would take him to the Wolf's Den. Despite the Wolf's command not to return there for the time being, Koral knew that he would be allowed in if he arrived with a bunch of men chasing him.

And there was no way the soldiers would attempt to follow him inside that particular establishment.

It was certainly safer than heading for the market square, but there could be other soldiers waiting to cut him off before he reached the Wolf's Den. If that was the case, then he'd never make it.

The corner was approaching rapidly, and he knew he couldn't last much longer. The soldiers were gaining on him with every step and time was running out.

He cut left and headed for the Wolf's Den. Another block and the soldiers were only a few strides behind him. He turned the final corner and saw the building up ahead. Charkel stood outside the entrance, watching the street.

Koral couldn't spare a breath to yell to get the man's attention. He could feel the soldiers right behind him, and so he poured every last ounce of energy into running as fast as he could. His breath was ragged in his throat and tiny sparks began to dance in his vision.

There was no way he was going to make it.

And then, coming down the street from the other direction, he spotted the carriage that had stopped outside the Crown and Coin. They were going to cut him off before he could reach safety.

But he refused to give up and kept running, knowing there was no way to beat the carriage, which began to pick up speed.

And then Charkel glanced in his direction and recognized him immediately. The big doorman spun and yanked open the door to the Wolf's Den, shouting. He turned back and drew two large knives and started running toward Koral.

And a few seconds later, a dozen of the Wolf's people spilled from the building and turned in his direction.

He heard the footsteps of the soldiers at his heels slow and he reached Charkel, who shoved Koral past him and faced the three men who had come to a stop. The other gang members surrounded Koral, facing outward and watching the approaching carriage, knives and truncheons clenched in their fists.

He turned back to see the three Church soldiers start to back away from Charkel. The carriage passed and kept going. Charkel stood still, blocking the walkway at the side of the road, his knives glinting in the sunlight.

And then the soldiers turned and walked away, following the carriage.

Koral felt his legs collapsing, and hands grabbed him and carried him into the Wolf's Den, and sanctuary.

Chapter Thirty

THE NARROW ALLEY WAS FILTHY, STREWN WITH GARBAGE and fetid puddles of unidentifiable liquids. At night, Hinara was sure it would look dark and dangerous. In the morning light, it just looked pathetic. There was nothing to be fearful of in this area of the city.

They were on the northern edge of what the locals called the Warren, and Hinara thought it was an apt name for what he saw. The Watch generally avoided the place, and the local criminals were left to run this part of the city. Hinara expected that entering the Warren was not nearly as perilous as some would like to make it out to be.

Jiska stood at his back, his hand on the hilt of his sword. Hinara silently cursed the other man's cowardly nature. He was an adequate aid—which was about as much a compliment as Hinara could give someone who willingly took such a servile position—but as backup in a dangerous confrontation, he was seriously lacking.

Every so often, Hinara would consider cutting Jiska from his service and recommending the man be transferred to a position in some combat-heavy unit, just to see the look of horror on Jiska's face as he realized his soon-to-be fate. The only thing that stopped Hinara from writing the order was the fact that it would be an inconvenience to find another aid who had the right level of fear and respect that he demanded.

He stopped at a rotting wooden door that led into a tenement that had probably never seen better days, but seemed as if it should have. He shoved the door open and stepped into the narrow hallway. This was the rear of the building, and he could see the rickety staircase further along that lead to the upper floors.

But he wasn't here to take a tour of poverty and desperation. The door he wanted was the second on the left. He moved in front of it and knocked twice.

He heard someone moving inside, and then the door opened a crack. It was dark on the other side, but in the light drifting into the hallway from the exterior door he was able to see a figure peering out at him.

The figure paused, and then pulled the door open and stepped back into the shadows.

"Wait here," he told Jiska and stepped through into a small room that smelled of sweat and must. He pushed the door mostly closed, but left it open just a crack.

The figure stepped away to the far edge of the room. As he eyes adjusted to the darkness, Hinara was able to make out a small cot and a backpack, but no other furnishings. No window pierced the wall, and Hinara figured the room had never had a good airing out, which it obviously and desperately needed.

"Well?" he said to the figure. "I am here. What do you have to tell me?"

Hinara had received the message yesterday in the early evening. It was anonymous, but he had been able to tell right away that it was a genuine lead.

Laita Naschect's soldiers are in the city. I know where each group is staying. I can give them to you, in return for a full pardon.

No mention of the reward money. No grand claims. Only a time and a location to meet listed at the bottom of the message.

This is a soldier who has realized their precarious position, Hinara had thought.

And now the soldier was here in front of him. He had considered asking for some Imperial Guardsmen to accompany him and simply grab the informant. But it was possible there was more than one, and they would have a lookout or two to warn this one if he showed up in force.

"I … I know where Laita Naschect's soldiers are staying."

Hinara smiled grimly. He could hear the fear in the soldier's voice. The man was young, likely a common soldier. Still, his rank wouldn't matter if he had real information.

"So, where are they?"

"I need … I need a guarantee. I want to be pardoned. They lied to us. I'm not a traitor."

"Of course not," he replied, hiding his disdain for this scum. "Laita Naschect is a master at manipulating others, and you were merely following her orders."

He could see the figure nodding eagerly.

"Yes, just following orders! But I don't want … I just … I know I can't go back to the Legion. But I don't want to be executed."

"You will not be punished, if you can help me apprehend Laita and those who willingly follow her. I swear to you, I will sign off on a pardon if you give me information that leads me to her."

Hinara didn't have the power to pardon anyone—he wasn't a magistrate—but this soldier wouldn't know that. Besides, once he had Laita and her command squad in his grasp, he couldn't care less what happened to this man.

"What is she doing here in Ythis? What are her plans, her timetable?"

The figure hesitated before answering.

"I … I don't know. She hasn't told us."

You're lying, he thought. This soldier knew more than he was willing to admit. He probably thought if he feigned ignorance, his innocence would be more convincing.

"I need to know what she is doing so I can protect the innocent people in this city. You do not want to let her harm all those people, do you? You can prove you are not a traitor, right here and now, by helping me stop her."

The figure hesitated again.

"She … I don't think she's doing anything against the city. The soldiers wouldn't do anything to hurt the people … not even the ones who are choosing to follow her."

Hinara found it interesting how the soldier was framing his excuses as if he hadn't chosen to follow Laita Naschect to Ythis himself. It was those *others*, of course.

Still, he wanted to know her plan, and he was convinced this man knew it. He considered drawing his sword and calling for Jiska. There was no other way out of this room, and he stood almost in front of the door. He could take this man into custody and Imperial Inquisitors would simply torture the information out of him.

But he also didn't know how good a combatant this man might be. And desperation might lend him a fury and a frenzy that could put Hinara in serious danger. Jiska would be no help, of course. If blades were bared, that man would be useless.

"Well, you have to give me something useful. Tell me where I can find Laita Naschect and her command squad. Tell me where I can find the soldiers. Traitors do not get treated kindly, and execution comes at the end of quite an ordeal. Spare yourself the torture."

He could hear the soldier breathing heavily.

"I need more than your word that I'll be pardoned. I want it in writing. Then I'll give you everything."

Hinara ground his teeth in frustration.

"You realize I have my own doubts," he told the man. "I do not know if you are lying to me, or trying to draw me into some kind of trap. You are the one who has been branded as a traitor, after all. You have you give me something to show that you are operating in good faith."

Even in the darkness, he could see the soldier clenching his fists. He readied himself to draw his sword quickly if the man came at him. But then he saw the other man's shoulders slump.

"There's a resistance in Ythis. A group that wants to overthrow the Emperor."

Hinara almost laughed at the absurdity of it. The mere thought of the Undying Emperor being taken down was ridiculous.

"And what do these people think they can do?"

"For now, they are providing support to Commander Naschect. That's all I know."

He hesitated again.

"Well, I know one more thing. I know the identity of one member of the Resistance. If you capture him, you can find out the names of the rest of them."

Hinara caught his breath. All he needed was one thread to pull and Laita Naschect's plan would completely unravel. Just one thread.

"The man's name is Irako," the soldier told him. "And I know where you can find him."

*   *   *

LAITA PUSHED OPEN THE DOOR OF THE WANDERING HORSE TAVERN and stepped inside. Oriuna sat in her chair at the same table as yesterday. Only the fact that she was wearing a different tunic told Laita that the other woman had left the tavern since their meeting yesterday.

Oriuna gave her a nod as Laita closed the door behind her and came to sit in the other chair. The tavern was, once again, empty of patrons.

"You look tired," Oriuna told her.

"I have a lot on my mind these days."

"I would think so. Have you come to a decision?"

"I believe so. But I do have a few more questions before I commit to anything."

Oriuna sat back and gestured with one hand.

"Ask away. I'll answer what I can."

"You should certainly expect my first question. What happens after?"

"After he's gone, you mean?"

Laita nodded.

"I imagine that your forces are going to be in control of the Palace, or least a portion of it. By that point, the Imperial Guard will be bringing up their soldiers to recapture the building. The fighting won't immediately end with the death of the Emperor, but the Church will be ready to step in and demand that the Guard pull back, at least temporarily. Long enough for you to withdraw from the Palace, at least."

"And how are we supposed to do that?"

"Getting out of the Palace is easier than getting into it. There's a cliff at the back. Your forces will lower ropes and rappel down."

Laita grimaced at the idea.

"The wall is too far back from the cliff for us to land on it. And there are three guard towers there. We'd be lowering ourselves into a box that will expose us to a crossfire from above."

"The guard towers will be unmanned on the night you infiltrate the palace."

Laita narrowed her eyes at the other woman.

"And how is that going to happen?"

"The Church will make it happen. I don't know the details, but there won't be a living soul in those towers that night. We can guarantee you that."

Laita laughed out loud.

"That's a lot of trust we'll need to give the Church. It's in their best interests to have us all die once the Emperor is dead. If we lower ourselves down into that space behind the walls, a force of Imperial Guards will cut off both exits and the guard towers will lay down flights of arrows on us until we're all dead, or close enough that the Guard soldiers can move in and easily eliminate any stragglers."

Oriuna raised one eyebrow at Laita.

"You're making a big assumption, Laita. What if the Church doesn't want you all dead? What if you're more valuable alive?"

"What value could the Church possibly place on us once we've accomplished the mission?"

Oriuna shrugged.

"The priests seem to feel you can do better for them as a fugitive than as a corpse. You *and* your contingent."

Laita considered Oriuna's words. The priests could simply be lying to Oriuna, in order for her to be more convincing in her meeting with Laita. Once the Emperor was dead, the Church would need to establish control. They would likely bring the Imperial Guard to their side immediately. But the Legion ....

"We're a distraction for the Legion," she said. "If we escape, the Legion is going to want to hunt us down. It'll be a matter of honor for them. As long as we're alive, we represent the worst failure the

Legion has ever had."

Oriuna nodded thoughtfully, as if the idea hadn't occurred to her.

"So then what? What happens after we escape?"

"The Church is making three ships available to you. You'll move down the coast to a rendezvous point and board the ships. You need to leave the Empire, Laita. You accomplish your mission and then you go."

"Where?"

"Wherever you want. You can form a mercenary company in the southern kingdoms, you can go exploring in the east, you can disband for your force, whatever you decide as long as it doesn't bring you back here."

"And once we're gone, what happens here? That's really what I want to know."

Oriuna looked confused.

"What difference does it make? The Emperor will be dead, and you'll be somewhere else."

"It makes a difference to *me*, Oriuna. What is the Church going to do? I can't see them letting the nobles choose another Emperor. And then there are the sorcerers to consider. They're certainly unlikely to throw their support behind the Church."

"Laita, it won't be your responsibility anymore."

Laita looked Oriuna in the eyes, trying to see the woman behind the face. Was she a worshipper of Iathephos? She willingly worked for the Church. Did she truly believe the Church should be in charge of the entire Empire?

"You know what will happen to the people if the Church takes over," she said. "You've heard what the early years of the Empire were like. Do you really want it to be like that again?"

Oriuna looked down at the table.

"You're an idealist, Laita. You think you can change how things are. You can't. This world has only two kinds of people. There are the truly powerful who pull all the strings. And then there are the rest of us. And even the noble families fall into the 'rest of us' category. The Church, the sorcerers, the Emperor, they all have power that we can never wield. Remove one and another takes its place."

She raised her eyes to Laita's.

"That's just the way of things. You want to remove the Emperor, and that's a worthy goal. But you're not going to make things truly better for that 'rest of us' I just mentioned. There's no way that will happen. We're simply trading one power for another. It doesn't really matter if it's the Church or the Sorcerers who step up to fill in the gap, though we both know who is going to win in any conflict there."

Laita looked at the other woman and saw the hopelessness that filled her. Oriuna saw herself as the tool of one of the great powers, and worked for them because she saw her proximity to power as a better option than being entirely powerless.

Laita couldn't accept that. There had to be another way. Everything she was fighting for, everything she had given up getting this far, couldn't just be sacrificed so that one tyrant would replace another.

There *had* to be way to make things better.

"Laita, this is the choice. You need help to accomplish your mission. If you go into the Palace with just your soldiers, you will all die before you ever reach the Emperor. He is a threat to the people of the Empire. You *know* that."

"I also know the Church worships a being that consumes the souls of the people of the Empire."

Oriuna shrugged.

"You can call it worship, and perhaps they call it that as well. But yes, I have heard what the early years of the Empire were like. I've also heard what the years were like immediately before the Emperor and the Church formed their alliance. It was a time of indiscriminate slaughter.

"The ... god ... of Ythis was trapped partway between worlds, but that didn't stop it from using its power to pull anyone within leagues to come and feed themselves to it. And the other gods ... some of them *roamed*, Laita. If the Church hadn't lured them into the temples they built at Jh'tira and Caladur and the rest, there never would have been enough people to make an Empire at all. We'd all have been wiped out.

"The priests don't just worship the gods. They keep them *contained*. I don't want to see what the world would become if the Church were

314

to fall."

"You say they keep them contained, but they *placate* them, Oriuna."

"Fuck, yes!" Oriuna exclaimed. "Do you want the gods to decide they aren't satisfied and need more? Do you think anyone—the Church, the sorcerers, the Emperor, even all three together—could stop the gods if they decided they didn't like the current arrangement and wanted to roam again? I'd rather kill myself if that happened. At least then they couldn't take my soul."

Laita found it difficult to disagree. But where did that leave all those innocent people? Was there nothing she could do?

With a heavy sigh, she turned and looked at the shelves of bottles behind the bar.

"If your offer of whiskey is still on the table," she said, "I think I'll take that drink now."

Chapter Thirty-One

THE PARCHMENTS WERE THIN AND DRY, A WEB OF CRACKS spreading across the delicate sheets. Each was mounted in a shallow box so that they could be moved without touching the surfaces directly. Phana leaned over one, squinting in the lamplight to make out the crabbed writing that scrawled across its surface.

She looked over at the large window covered in heavy draperies.

"Can't we open that up and get some better light in here?"

The historian's eyes widened in horror.

"Sunlight? Oh no, my dear! There's nothing worse for these sheets than sunlight. I'm afraid they would fade beyond legibility if I ever exposed them to full daylight."

Phana leaned back and shrugged.

"Well, I can't read any of this anyway. It's not a language I know."

She didn't tell the man that the letter forms looked vaguely familiar to her. It was as if she had seen them before and was once able to tell what they meant. It was tantalizingly close, but something blocked her memory, preventing the letters from resolving into actual language.

Phana glanced over at the charcoal sketch that Master Ilisti had shown her this morning, the skin on which it had been drawn now brittle with small pieces missing from the image. There was no mistaking who it was in the drawing, though. If it wasn't for the obvious age of the piece, it appeared as if Phana had posed for the artist within the last week or so.

It could only be one of her ancestors, though the resemblance to Phana was uncanny. The only difference was the length of her hair.

The historian had left it propped against a bookcase, and Phana found it somewhat disconcerting to find her own face staring at her as the two of them pored over ancient books and scrolls for some hint as to her identity.

Master Ilisti hadn't said it directly, of course, but Phana thought the old man was starting to believe Phana was the same woman as the one in the painting. She could feel his excitement.

"Tell me again about the tower," he said to her, leaning down and squinting at the writing on the parchment. "Every detail you can remember."

The memory was sharp in her mind. She looked out over the endless sea of campfires, the black stone of the tower cold under her fingers as she rested her hands on the battlements.

The tower was built by the large man at her side. It was to be a home for the three of them, keeping them safe from those who had betrayed them. He had built it beyond the mountain range, on the vast plain of dust where no one would willingly explore. Phana pictured her suite of rooms on one level of the tower, comfortable and familiar. The servants kept to the lower levels when they were not performing services for Phana and her two companions.

With a start, Phana's thoughts snapped back to the present. She gasped and put a hand to her chest, her heart beating so hard she was sure Master Ilisti could hear it battering its way out.

"My dear?" he said, concern in his voice. She couldn't answer, still trying to draw in a breath. "Phana?"

She waved him off and stood up, crossing to the door and stepping out into the hallway. Countless images rushed through her mind of the tower—her own rooms, gatherings in the hall with her companions over meals, arguments over whether they should continue to hide or go after their betrayers, Yarrian's pleadings to go out and travel the world, to leave this continent and visit other lands where their hunters would never find them.

She heard Master Ilisti step to the door to check on her, but he didn't say anything. She was grateful for the silence as the flow of memories slowed to a trickle and then stopped.

With a deep breath, Phana turned to face the historian.

"I'm sorry. That room was just getting to be a bit too much. I prefer open spaces and fresh air."

She could see in the man's eyes that he didn't believe her story. But he nodded and did not challenge her lie. Patting her on the shoulder, he walked off down the hallway to the staircase and called for his serving woman to bring up some refreshments.

Returning to Phana, he stopped in front of her and looked at her kindly.

"Young lady, there is more going on with you than just a lack of memories. You don't have to tell me what it is. But the things you *have* told me … they aren't things one might know unless that person had studied some rare and rather obscure writings. And there's only so much help I can give you without knowing how you've come to this knowledge."

Phana crossed her arms and leaned back against the wall.

"That puts me in a spot, Master Ilisti. The truth is that I don't have any idea how I know what I know. As I said, I don't have all my memories. I could have gotten this information from reading books when I was younger. Or perhaps someone shared these stories with me. I honestly don't know."

"And we live in a dangerous world," he replied. "I must be careful, for my own safety. The way you talk is not as if you are reciting something you've learned. You speak as if you can see it in your mind. Obviously, that is impossible. But then there are things in this world that are beyond what you or I might wish were possible. What if …."

Phana waited for him to continue, but he shook his head.

"What were you going to say?"

"I'm just speculating, and that's not a good way to proceed when dealing with a mystery. It can color what we see."

But Phana was not going to let him put her off.

"Tell me what you were speculating, then."

He hesitated, and then sighed.

"It is obvious that you had an ancestor who lived before the founding of the Empire. You are the exact image of her. Perhaps she was a

… sorcerer. Or someone with supernatural powers. Maybe she did something so that when the right descendant was born, her memories would implant themselves into this descendant. Perhaps her very mind might supplant her descendant's mind, and she would live again. Only something has gone wrong, and it only partially worked."

"That's not a reassuring theory."

"No, my dear, it's not," he replied. "But it's also little more than a guess. After all, it's just as possible that you are the very woman in that sketch, and you've lived all these centuries with your memories missing. At this point, just about anything could be possible."

Phana had to force herself to keep breathing normally. The historian had just verbalized what Phana had tried not to fully acknowledge. Was *she* the woman in that sketch? Were the memories hers, after all?

"The tower," she said through a dry throat. "I can tell you more about it. I can describe it … in detail."

Master Ilisti looked her in the eyes and she saw both excitement and trepidation there. He wanted to know what she knew. But he was also afraid of the consequences. He was worried about what trouble she might bring.

She couldn't blame him.

He led the way back into the room and pulled out a blank parchment and grabbed a quill. Dipping it into the inkwell, he leaned over it and prepared to write.

"Tell me everything, my dear. Every last detail you can remember about the tower."

She stepped back into the room and sat down in the chair. Taking a deep breath, she began to describe the tower and her two companions.

*   *   *

WHILE THE TEMPLE ITSELF WAS THE OFFICIAL SEAT OF THE CHURCH, it was in the buildings immediately surrounding it that most of the actual work of running the vast organization was done. In a huge chamber deep under the Temple, an endless procession of insane supplicants were given over to Iathephos, the god of Ythis, and the waves of madness from that chamber were an almost palpable presence within the giant, black stone building.

All the priests of Iathephos were touched with madness to some degree. To commune with the god, even at a distance, was to open oneself to an alien mind that blasted away any feeble resistance a human might summon within his or her psyche. The higher ranks of the priesthood were filled with the truly damned, their consciousness twisted and warped by the presence of the god below.

Each of the nine major cities of the Empire was built around a single Temple in which dwelt one of the gods who laid claim to the people of this continent. Each deity was a unique being, vastly powerful but completely unnatural to the world it had come to inhabit. When the gods had come forth through their rifts in space, so Relael had been taught, they had destroyed the Old Gods and took their place in this world.

There had been no Empire then, only a series of city-states ruled by powerful warlords or sorcerers. At first, they had tried to resist the new gods, and countless lives had been wiped out. The ruins of a few of these cities remained—blasted, cursed places inimical to human life.

But the founder of the Church, whose name was long lost, had gathered like-minded people to worship and placate these new gods. One by one, great Temples were built, and the gods chose to inhabit these places and accept the souls being offered by their worshippers. It was the Church that had saved humanity and established the places where the gods could reside.

Though each city had its own god, and its own Temple, they were all part of one great organization. The head of the Church resided in the Temple of Ythis, and so the administrative management of the Church was also located in the capitol city of the Undying Empire.

The buildings around the Temple in Ythis were all linked by underground tunnels and passages to allow priests to travel back and forth on their business without having to step outside. Lined with dark red slabs of stone, the tunnels were always lit by hanging lanterns and a constant flow of acolytes and low-level priests—who were still sane enough to handle the bulk of the Church's administrative duties—passed from building to building at all hours of the day and night.

Relael was returning to his office, a small room on the lower level of one of the neighboring buildings, when he spotted Shuyaja approaching from the other direction. He immediately felt one of his hands begin to twitch, and he clenched his fist to stop it as the other man spotted him.

Shuyaja was one of the priests who served High Counselor Assirra Untoleu, a poisonous snake of a man with an unsettling gaze and the air of one who saw through your words to the very thoughts behind them. If he was looking for Relael, then time had now run out.

"Brother Relael," he said in a low voice, his mouth twisted in a sneer.

Relael stopped in front of the man and bowed his head respectfully.

"Brother Shuyaja," he replied, but said nothing else. Shuyaja was the type of man to remain silent and simply stare at someone, waiting for them to fill the void. It worked very well with the younger priests and the acolytes, but Relael was one of the Hidden. Such tricks were wasted on him. He simply waited, his face neutral.

After a moment, Shuyaja gave up the game and continued.

"Proceed to your office. We must speak in private."

He waited for Relael to lead the way, and followed closely behind. Relael had expected a simple summons—High Counselor Untoleu would no doubt want to hear the status of Relael's current mission. The fact that Shuyaja wanted to speak privately meant something else was going on.

They reached Relael's office a few minutes later. Shuyaja followed him inside and closed the door. Relael turned and faced the man, waiting to hear what the priest had to say.

"High Counselor Untoleu wants a status report. It has been one week since you were given your mission, and you have not returned to speak with her since."

Relael paused. If the High Counselor wanted Relael to update her on his progress, why had Shuyaja brought him to Relael's office?

"Should I report to her immediately, or does she have a particular time she wants me to come to her office?"

"Neither. She tasked me with getting an update from you. She is extremely busy, and she will get it from me when she has a moment free."

Relael opened his mouth to speak, and then closed it again. High Counselor Untoleu had given Relael explicit instructions not to tell anyone about the mission, even other members of the Hidden. His spies knew he was trying to find Phana, but not his reasons for wanting her, or even if she was merely a means to reaching someone else.

"I cannot do that," he said. "My orders come directly from the High Counselor. I am not permitted to discuss it with anyone else."

Shuyaja paused only an instant, but it was enough for Relael.

"She is countermanding her previous orders. You are now to report to me."

Relael smiled at him. It was clear to him that Shuyaja was trying to insinuate himself into the mission. Perhaps he had figured out that what Relael was doing was important to the High Counselor and he wanted to be part of it. Regardless, Relael was confident that Assirra Untoleu had not given Shuyaja orders to get an update on the current status.

"When does the High Counselor wish to meet with me?"

Shuyaja was smart enough to know right away that he had failed. He didn't try to argue or add to his lie. His game was over. Relael suspected, however, that the other man would hold a grudge. This was someone to watch. To eliminate, if necessary, no matter how highly placed he might currently be.

"Report to her office first thing tomorrow morning. You had better pray to Iathephos that you have some results."

Relael continued to smile at the other man. He nodded once at the order but said nothing else. Shuyaja glared at him and then turned and left Relael's office, leaving the door hanging open. It was a petty sign of disrespect, though more subtle than slamming the door would have been.

Relael stood there, contemplating the visit. He had no idea how much Shuyaja knew or had figured out. The man might even have his own spies among Relael's people. But Relael's people knew only what they had to know, and that wasn't very much.

Still, tomorrow morning Relael would have to report to the High Counselor directly. And so far, he had little to tell her. He knew Phana was the woman who had used the power that caught his superior's attention. But he still hadn't located her.

She was somewhere in the city, and Relael's people couldn't find her. And the unsuccessful capture of Koral Creyss this morning was yet another failure that would be laid at his feet.

There was little chance he would survive his meeting with High Counselor Assirra Untoleu tomorrow morning. And he had no choice but to walk to his death, regardless.

Someone appeared in his doorway, and at first Relael thought it was Shuyaja coming back. But then he saw it was one of his messengers, the same man who had brought word of Koral's escape this morning. He motioned the man to enter and close the door.

The messenger was out of breath. He had obviously been running, and Koral wondered what bad news he would now deliver.

"What now?" Relael demanded.

"It's the woman, sir," the messenger gasped out.

"Which woman?" Relael asked, a knot of dread in his stomach. He wanted the messenger to be clear. Right now, there was no room for misunderstanding.

"The woman, Phana," the messenger clarified. "We've found her, sir. We know where Phana is right now."

Chapter Thirty-Two

BOR WAS HANDING OUT WEAPONS AND ARMOR TO THREE soldiers as Namal entered the room.

"Bundle them up in those rags and put 'em in the sacks," Bor told them. "Don't let anyone see you've got this equipment—it'll draw interest and make people remember you."

"Yessir," the soldiers replied, and began wrapping the short swords and leather jacks in the rags.

Namal watched them, wondering if he was looking at people who would be dead before their time in Ythis was over. He gritted his teeth, trying to force away the dark thoughts that constantly filled his mind the last couple of days.

"How are things proceeding?" he asked Bor.

"Smoothly, so far, but slowly. We can't risk too many people coming here at once, so we can only supply about thirty people per day. That means another five days before we've got all the equipment distributed."

Namal nodded at him and then watched the three soldiers place their bundles in the sacks. Wrapped in rags, the swords and jacks made odd shapes in the sacks, disguising their true nature. The soldiers saluted both him and Bor and then left the room.

"Where's the commander?"

Bor looked at him and hesitated, as if he didn't want to answer.

"She is, uh, she's meeting with …."

"Oriuna," Namal finished for him. "Of course. Still trying to find a way out of this."

"Sergeant, the commander will figure it out. Even if we end up withdrawing from Ythis, she'll find a way to do it safely and leave no one behind."

Blind faith, Namal thought sourly. *I hope he's not going to pay for it with his life.*

But he had to admit to himself that he felt a small bit of pride at Bor's unwavering belief in Laita. Namal still felt it himself. He was angry with her, sure, but he had chosen to stay with her, to follow her, because he believed she could do almost anything.

He was angry at her, and angry at himself for letting Oriuna play him for a fool.

And he couldn't stop thinking about Illilo, about the expression on the man's face when Namal stabbed him in the chest. A man murdered for being in the wrong place at the wrong time. For wanting to buy his old sergeant a drink to thank him for all he had learned.

Namal had no trouble killing in battle. This was different. And then, to find out the Church already knew all about them, immediately after he had ended the man's life, only added insult to injury. Illilo had died for nothing. Namal had murdered him for *nothing.*

He realized Bor was staring at him, and he rubbed his eyes to cover for his lapse.

"You're probably right, Bor. If anyone can bring any kind of victory out of this mess, it's her. Don't tell her I said that, though. I'm still pissed at her."

Bor smiled and nodded.

"I won't say a word, sergeant."

Namal realized how easy it was to give comfort to the soldiers under him. Bor had obviously been worried about the strained relationship between Namal and Laita since their argument, not even two full days ago. But the members of the command squad continued to look up to him.

Not Keynter, though.

Keynter hadn't really been part of the command squad, though. Namal knew he should go talk to the man. He understood Keynter's fear and anger. They were all under a great deal of stress, and some of that was bound to spill out.

Still, Keynter had been insubordinate, and Namal knew Laita had to teach the young man a lesson. He'd go find Keynter this evening and make sure any punishment was having the right effect—motivate to do better instead of fostering resentment—just in case.

"Bor, how are you holding up?"

Bor put the lid back on the empty crate and thought about it.

"I'm okay, sergeant. I'm worried, of course. Just knowing the Church is out there and they know about us … it's not a comforting thought."

"No, it's not."

"But the commander has an idea, sir. If the Resistance is willing to do what we need them to do, then it could work. I'm just … I hope we can manage to walk that narrow line of convincing the Church that we're going to work with them while setting everything up behind their backs."

"You've done an excellent job so far, Bor. You and Saeda both. And you know that if you need someone to talk to, you just have to ask, right?"

Bor nodded at him.

"I know, but thank you, sir. After all, there is so much that can still go wrong. I believe in the commander. Like I said, she'll get us out of this, one way or another. I'm just worried about …."

"You're thinking about the soldiers," Namal voiced Bor's unspoken thoughts. "You're wondering how many of 'em are going to die here in Ythis. It's not an uncommon thought. I always go through that right before a battle. I think about the orders I need to give, even knowing that some of those I command are not gonna come back. But that's our job."

"Yes, sir."

"You're gonna make a fine sergeant, Bor."

"Thank you, sir."

Neither man pointed out that Bor's opportunity for promotion was now severely limited. He could never return to the Legion. His only path was with Laita, with whatever she decided her soldiers would do next.

They fell silent for a moment, and Bor returned to moving the empty crate to one side.

"Sir, was there something you needed today?" Bor asked when he had cleared the space in the middle of the floor.

"I'm here to meet Irako. Is he already here somewhere?"

"I haven't seen him, sir. He might be in one of the rooms on the ground floor."

Namal nodded and left, heading down the stairs. He found the soldier who guarded the door and asked him if Irako had already arrived.

"No, sir. He hasn't been here today."

Namal frowned. It wasn't like Irako to be late.

"Okay, when he gets here, send him up to the second floor. I'll be with Bor."

"Yessir."

Namal returned to the main room on the upper level.

"Bor," he said. "Irako ain't here yet, so I can help you organize this stuff or whatever you need."

Bor smiled at him.

"Well, sir, I was just about to have the boys bring down another couple of crates. If you'd like to help me get the next batch prepared …."

Namal nodded and they set to work. He threw himself into the logistics, something he didn't generally take a direct hand in anymore. Before he knew it, at least an hour had passed, and Irako still hadn't shown up.

"I don't like this," he said to Bor. "Being late is one thing, but with everything going on right now, a no-show gets my hackles up."

"You think something's happened, sir?"

"If he shows up here, tell him not to go anywhere. I'll be back. I'm gonna pass by his usual haunts and see if he's around, or if there's any signs of something wrong."

Namal stepped to the door and turned around.

"If I'm not back within two hours, get word to Laita that we're compromised. Get everyone out of this building and stay away from the White Eagle Inn. Irako doesn't know about that place, but if he's taken, then they may have also captured one or more members of the command squad."

"Yessir," Bor said, and Namal could see the worry on his face.

The decision may have just been made for us, he thought as he hurried back down the stairs. *It may already be too late for anything except fleeing the city.*

*   *   *

THE WHISKEY BOTTLE WAS ALMOST HALF-EMPTY, AND LAITA COULD feel the effects of the alcohol on her thoughts. Despite her reservations, she found Oriuna easy to talk to and enjoyed her company. The other woman was not some slavish devotee of Iathephos, or the Church and their methods. Instead, she seemed to see them as a necessary evil.

She couldn't blame Oriuna for her choices. Only the truly privileged could hold to their beliefs and values without compromise. For the rest, there were times when mere survival meant turning your back on what you had once held sacred.

Laita understood that. She had not made her decision to abandon her oath to the Legion for her own survival, of course, but still felt the weight of that decision.

And now, she knew that she would have to manipulate this woman, in order to get what she needed from the Church while preventing them from realizing their own goals. She also knew Oriuna would likely pay the price for her duplicity.

We all make choices, and everything comes with a price, she thought to herself.

Perhaps she was being callous, but too much hung in the balance for her to be kind. She couldn't gamble on Oriuna's own kindness with so many lives at stake. Laita might be selling the other woman short, but the risk was too great to give her the benefit of the doubt.

All of which was why she had agreed to accept the Church's help against the Emperor. As far as Oriuna and the priests would know, Laita had decided their control of the Empire was the lesser evil.

When they figured out her plan, it would be too late for them to do anything about it.

"So, how do we reach the Palace?" she asked.

"Did … Namal … tell you about the tunnels?"

Laita noted the strained note in Oriuna's voice as she said Namal's name. If it was all an act, it was quite a good one.

"Yes, he told me. But not how we get into those passages. Through the sewers?"

"No!" Oriuna said quickly. "You have to avoid the sewers completely. There are these … creatures that take care of the sewers. They live down there. Those tunnels are off-limits to anyone else."

"Creatures?"

"I don't know much about them. Apparently, they were brought to Ythis to build the sewer system in the very early days, and then, once the entire system was complete, they decided to stay. The city sent soldiers down there, to try to push them out. Only a handful returned, or so the story goes. Supposedly, the Emperor granted them permission to live in the sewers as long as they continued to maintain the system, as it wasn't worth fighting a war for a bunch of tunnels filled with shit."

Laita blinked at her, not sure if Oriuna was making it all up. It seemed almost too strange, even for Ythis. Then again, she thought back to that cave in the valley, and the horde of creatures that had attacked her soldiers. She knew better than to believe the world did not have its share of strange beings.

"Okay, I'll make sure to let my people know to avoid the sewers. But then how do we access these tunnels?"

"There is a very old building that is owned by the Church, though not openly. They discovered the passages when a part of the floor collapsed. I will give you the location once you are ready to proceed. You will be provided with a guide who take you under the Fortress and show you where you can break through into the Palace."

"A guide?"

"Someone who has done some extensive exploring down there. He won't accompany you into the Palace, though. Once you pass that barrier, you're on your own."

Laita nodded. She had expected that.

"Yesterday, you said something about guardians in the Palace. Tell me about them."

Oriuna hesitated, and Laita could see something in her eyes.

"What is it?"

"You're going to have to meet with someone. A priest."

A chill ran down Laita's spine and settled in her gut. The last thing she wanted was to be in the presence of another priest. The last priest she had met had slaughtered a bunch of her soldiers while in the thrall of his god's power before she killed him.

The priests were all mad. That meant they were also unpredictable, and supremely dangerous.

"Why is that necessary?"

"He will tell you about the things you'll face, but he'll also give you something you'll need to fight back. They won't give it to me to pass on to you, and that's fine with me. Just because I work for them, it doesn't mean I enjoy being in their company or handling anything that comes from their god."

Laita didn't like the sound of that, either. Anything touched by Iathephos was likely to have serious effects on the minds of normal people. Would her possession of such a thing, whatever it was, affect her own sanity? It wasn't a comforting thought.

"Laita," Oriuna said. "I can't tell you anything else until they hear you say it. The Church needs to know you're committed. They need to know you're not going to suddenly disappear with your soldiers, or use this information against them."

"What do they want from me?"

"They want you to swear an oath."

"What, that I'm going to kill the Emperor? You realize that I'm already an oathbreaker, right? What difference will that make?"

Oriuna looked down at the table and took a deep breath.

"You're not going to like this. I told them that this might be the thing that makes you decide not to go through with it. But they are demanding you do it or they'll refuse to help you."

"What do they want me to swear?" she asked and had trouble making her voice hold steady.

"It's not the 'what' but the 'how' that you won't like. You must swear an oath to do everything in your power to complete this mission to kill the Emperor, on your own life and the life of every soldier under your command. You must do it in the presence of a priest. And you must do it as part of a ritual."

Laita pushed herself back from the table and almost stood.

"A ritual? What kind of ritual?"

"One that will bind you to your oath. That if you turn away from your promise, the ritual will ensure the price is paid."

Laita did stand and kicked her chair back behind her. It fell over and Oriuna flinched at the sound of wood hitting wood.

"If you think … if *they* think I'm going to connect myself—and all my people—to some magical ritual that gives their god power over me …."

Oriuna looked up at her said nothing. Laita turned and paced back and forth a few times, clenching her fists and forcing herself not to scream. The price was too high. She could sacrifice herself willingly, but putting that on the heads of her people was beyond her limit.

"No," she said at last, turning to face Oriuna. "I will do it for myself, but not for anyone else. If that's not good enough for the Church, then they can withdraw their support. But I won't negotiate or budge on this."

Oriuna looked like she was trying to smile at Laita, but her face wasn't cooperating.

"I told them you wouldn't agree to it. You're too good a commander for that."

"Then what happens now?"

Oriuna also stood up.

"Now I go tell them your answer and hope they don't kill me for failing to convince you."

She said it lightly, but Laita could see the tension in her body, the fear in her eyes. Again, she wondered if it was all an act, to engender pity—and compliance—in Laita. But she had already made her choice. If it came down to sacrificing Oriuna or her own soldiers, Laita wouldn't hesitate to save her people.

"Come back here tomorrow just after midday. If I'm here, then they've agreed. If not …."

Laita nodded, not entirely sure which outcome she preferred.

Chapter Thirty-Three

THE VOICE OF MASTER ILISTI SEEMED TO COME FROM VERY far away and Phana ignored it. She was floating in the darkness, the black stone of the tower at her back and the endless campfires spread out before her. With a thought, she moved away from the tower and out into the night sky.

The historian called her name again, and she felt herself being pulled down toward the ground. But she didn't want to go down there. The ground was full of enemies and that was a fight for tomorrow. Right now, she just wanted to float.

But his voice called her name again and she began to plunge toward the ground, the lights she had taken for campfires becoming globes that shot past her on either side. And then she realized she wasn't falling toward the ground, but up into the sky as the stars began to blur around her.

"Phana!"

With a start, Phana's eyes snapped open and she lurched to her feet. It took her a moment to recognize Master Ilisti standing before her, though he quickly backed away a few steps, his hands up, palms out toward her.

"What happened?" she asked, her tongue feeling thick in her mouth.

"You fell asleep, my dear," Master Ilisti explained, concern in his voice. "It has been a very long day, and as much as I do not want to stop, I think we both need our rest."

Phana's brain finally caught up with her senses, and she took a deep breath that turned into a yawn.

"You're right, sir. I should be going."

"My dear, you are exhausted. There is no need to go anywhere. I asked Tyilly to make up one of the guest rooms. It's quite comfortable and you're more than welcome to stay for the night."

Phana couldn't help but smile at Master Ilisti's worried expression. She figured he was more concerned about whether she'd come back in the morning than he was about her walking home tonight. Still, his offer was generous and there were advantages to her staying here.

For one, Yarrian was probably out there searching for her. She didn't believe he wouldn't try to find her again and attempt to convince her to come with him away from Ythis. And she had no intention of leaving the city right now.

Especially since she had convinced the historian to help her. They had continued to search the histories for the rest of the afternoon, and Phana was able to provide details that even his most thorough scrolls and books did not reveal.

She believed he *did* want to help her, though today he had been the one to benefit from their time spent together. But some of what she revealed to him allowed him to start putting together a more comprehensive history—a puzzle with many pieces missing. The more she talked, the more connections he was able to make, and those connections opened up new memories in her mind.

And Phana didn't want to return to her apartment. Either Koral or Yarrian would surely find her there. And though she missed Koral, she wasn't ready to see him yet.

"Thank you, Master Ilisti. I appreciate your hospitality and I'll stay the night."

He smiled at her and stepped out into the hall, calling for his servant. A moment later, Tyilly appeared in the doorway, frowning at Phana. She was still clearly bitter about their encounter this morning, and likely angry that Phana had not only gotten her meeting with the historian, but would now be staying the night and taking up his time again tomorrow.

"Tyilly, please see the Lady Phana to the guest room and make sure she has everything she needs."

"Yes, Master Ilisti."

Phana bid the man goodnight and followed the serving woman down the long hall and up a flight of steps to the third floor of the mansion. Another hallway ran the length of the building, but Tyilly opened the very first door and motioned for Phana to enter.

The room was spare, with a bed, a dresser, and a small table the only furniture. A basin of water sat on the table, and a washcloth and towel were folded beside it. The bed looked well-made and comfortable—certainly better than Phana's own.

"If you get hungry in the night, you'll have to wait until morning. The kitchen is off limits to … guests."

Phana turned to the serving woman, surprised at her tone.

"Look, I understand we got off on the wrong foot—"

"I will be in the very next room, and I am a light sleeper. I expect all of the master's valuables to be right where they are come morning."

Phana was taken aback. This woman thought Phana was here to rob the historian. And the fact that she was so brazen as to state it aloud, to warn Phana directly, was surprising. Phana had seen that Tyilly was protective of Master Ilisti, but this was too much.

"I am a guest of your master," she shot back at the servant. "I don't appreciate being called a thief by a member of his staff."

Of course, Phana was aware of the irony in her statement. A thief was exactly what she was. But that was not why she was here.

"Master Ilisti can be too trusting. My job is to ensure that this house continues to run properly, and that his person and his belongings are safe. I do not know who you really are, or how you convinced him to help you with whatever it is you need, but I will make sure you do not bring trouble to this house."

Phana opened her mouth to retort, but then stopped. She realized that Tyilly was afraid. The sense of doom that smothered Ythis each night represented an unknown threat, something that the average citizen living in the city could do nothing about. Add to that her unannounced arrival on the historian's doorstep this morning, and his reaction to seeing her, and the serving woman was right to be worried.

And Tyilly didn't know about Yarrian, or Phana's difficulties with the Wolf, or her history of stealing from the noble estates of Ythis. She was right to be wary of Phana's presence, and she didn't even realize how much of a threat Phana really represented.

So instead of fighting, Phana took a deep breath and nodded.

"I understand. I'm not here to bring trouble to anyone. You have no reason to believe me, but it's the truth. Your master has agreed to help me uncover information, and that's it. We'll spend the day exchanging what we know, and then I'll leave, and you'll never have to see me again. And I have no intention of taking anything with me that I didn't bring in here."

Tyilly's eyes narrowed, as if she expected something further—some insult or declaration of intent to get the serving woman in trouble. When none came, she seemed surprised.

"I am going to sleep now," Phana told the woman. "I'm exhausted and wouldn't have the energy to get up to anything even if that was my intent. And I'm sorry I disrupted your house today. I wouldn't have come if it wasn't important."

The other woman's expression didn't change. She just stepped out into the hallway and pulled the door closed. Phana sighed and pulled off her shirt and trousers, laying them on the table beside the basin.

She was too tired for anything but sleep, and so she crawled onto the bed and pulled the linen sheet up to her waist. The shutters were open, and a warm breeze came wafting in. Phana closed her eyes.

An instant later they snapped open.

The window. It was large, certainly large enough for someone to enter the room from outside. Yarrian was out there, somewhere. The last thing she wanted was him coming in here while she slept.

She got up and pulled the shutters closed, latching them securely. The room would likely get very warm with no circulation of air in here, but Phana preferred her privacy. She moved over to the door and locked it as well.

Phana didn't expect the simple latches and locks would stop Yarrian if he really wanted to get in. But Phana was generally a light sleeper. The sound of the shutters opening, or the lock turning, would bring her out of sleep, and she would be ready if Yarrian tried to enter.

She hoped it wouldn't come to that.

Despite her exhaustion, her thoughts were a chaotic mess and it took her a very long time to fall asleep.

*   *   *

THE GUARD PULLED THE HEAVY WOODEN DOOR OPEN AND HINARA stepped through into the chamber beyond. Though two more Imperial Guards stood on either side of their prisoner, his eyes immediately focused on the young man secured to the chair in the center of the room.

Irako was bound with leather straps, both arms and legs, and was gagged with a rag tied over his mouth. His eyes were wide as he looked up at Hinara, and sweat rolled down his face.

Hinara smiled down at the other man, letting all the malice he felt toward these traitors pour from him in the twist of his mouth and in his eyes. He saw the effect his expression had, and reveled in the power he wielded here.

"I think you begin to understand your predicament, young man. In case you could not see through the bag over your head when they brought you in, you are in the bowels of the Fortress."

Irako lowered his head and began to weep.

"Yes, you *do* understand. There is no way out of here. No amount of heroics will get you free, no last-minute rescues are coming. There is just you … and us."

He turned to the guard at the door and nodded at him. The man closed the door with a solid thud and then they all heard the lock turn. It was the sound of Irako's life ending, and to Hinara it was sweet music.

He began to slowly walk in a circle around the chair. Irako tried to keep him in sight, but as Hinara spoke, the young man sank back in the chair and eventually just stared at the floor.

"Listen very carefully to what I am about to tell you, Irako. If you wish to have any hope of not just surviving to see another dawn, but surviving without spending the rest of your time in unimaginable pain, you need to listen, and you need to follow my instructions."

He continued to pace slowly around the chair.

"We know about your friends in the Resistance. We know that Laita Naschect is here in Ythis, along with the fools and traitors who follow her. There is no escape for her or for them."

He stopped in front of Irako and looked down at him. Irako slowly raised his head to look Hinara in the eyes.

"You cannot save her, boy. We will catch her, and she will be tried as a traitor and executed. There is nothing you can do to stop that from happening."

He gestured to one of the guards, and the man undid the strap holding the rag in Irako's mouth. Irako worked his jaws as it was released, obviously trying to ease the pain that must have set in during his time in captivity.

"But you are not completely helpless here, Irako. You have the power to save some of the others. I know not every soldier who follows her is a traitor. She is very good at manipulating her subordinates, getting them to believe that she knows best. They may be gullible fools, and they will never be permitted to rejoin the Legion, but they do not have to *die*. You can save their lives."

Hinara leaned down, his face inches from Irako's.

"If we can round them up before they commit any further crimes, the magistrates have agreed to be lenient. Those who only followed, who were fooled by Laita's lies, will be granted mercy. But time is running out for them. Their lives are in your hands, Irako. Do you have the courage to save them.?"

Irako looked into Hinara's eyes and smiled.

"Fuck you," he said quietly. "The Legion, the Imperial Guard, the magistrates—you don't even know what you're up against."

He spat on the floor at Hinara's feet.

"So fuck you and fuck the Emperor," he finished.

Hinara smiled. He had expected the man to resist. As much as he wanted to catch Laita, he had hoped Irako would give him a reason to get physical. He straightened and held out his hand to the second guard.

The woman pulled a pair of leather gloves from her belt and handed them to Hinara. He pulled them on, feeling the leather creak as he flexed his fists. The weights sewn into the leather over his knuckles were cold.

Time to warm them up, he thought happily.

Irako watched him donning the gloves, but Hinara gave him no time to ready himself for the first strike. As he was fastening the strap on the second glove, his right fist shot out and connected with Irako's cheekbone.

The captive's head snapped to the side and he let out a grunt. The skin split and the cut welled with blood.

"I like these," Hinara mused. "You will have to forgive me if I get carried away. This is my first time using anything like this. I usually prefer to feel my knuckles digging into my victim's flesh. But I have been told that these will help me keep going long after I would normally have roughed up my own fists."

He stepped forward and saw Irako setting his jaw, so he hammered blows into the other man's belly and chest instead. Irako grunted with each impact. Hinara didn't like the gloves. They didn't let him *feel* the damage he was inflicting. They dulled the creaking of Irako's ribs and made him unsure if he was hitting the organs exactly the way he intended.

Still, he figured he'd be here for a while, and he had to make sure he lasted longer than Irako did.

After some time, he stopped throwing punches and stepped back. Irako was gasping for breath, the skin of his face gone pale.

"I have to admit, I would prefer not to have to use these. Perhaps after I have softened you up, I will just take them off and then we can get down to some real pain. How does that sound?"

"It doesn't ... matter what you do ... to me," Irako gasped. "I'm not telling ... you anything."

"Everyone says that," he replied. "It just tells me you do not believe me yet. But there is one thing I do know, and that is that you just need more convincing. Everyone has their limit, Irako. And I will reach yours long before you reach mine."

"I'd rather die ... than help you find her."

"A noble sentiment, but one that will not help you or her. You are not going to die, Irako. Not until I decide you are of no further use.

And as long as you have information you can give to me, I will keep you alive."

He was stepping forward to begin beating Irako again when the sound of the lock turning echoed through the room. He spun as the door opened and Sergeant Danashy entered. He had another two Imperial Guards with him, and he motioned for Hinara to step out of the room.

Hinara ground his teeth together as he stepped out into the hallway. This interruption was the last thing he needed. It gave Irako a pause, and it gave him hope. All while he was working to strip away every ounce of the man's hope bit by bit.

"What is it?" he hissed at the sergeant. Danashy didn't look impressed, which angered Hinara even further.

"You're wasting time," the sergeant answered. "There are faster ways to do this. I thought you were in a hurry."

"I am in a hurry! This man knows how to find Laita Naschect and I am extracting information from him."

One of the two guards who had been in the room, the man who untied Irako's gag, joined them in the hallway. Sergeant Danashy turned to him.

"Any progress?"

"None," the soldier answered. "He's just beating on the prisoner for his own satisfaction."

Hinara turned to the man.

"What would you know about it? He is my prisoner. These things must be done carefully or—"

"When the Guard agreed to the Legion's request for assistance, they didn't tell us you were going to beat prisoners in our dungeon," Sergeant Danashy interrupted. "It's unreliable, it's slow, and it's unprofessional."

Hinara blinked at him.

"Unprofessional?" he repeated incredulously.

"Yes, unprofessional. We have Imperial Inquisitors who have the skills to extract information from prisoners properly. We don't beat captives like we're thugs."

"Torture is torture," Hinara snarled back at him. "You may be too squeamish to do it yourself, but I—"

"That's it," the sergeant interrupted again. "You're done here. This man will be taken to an Inquisitor and questioned properly. I thought the Legion had standards, but if you're an example of how they do things, no wonder they've got deserters and traitors in their ranks."

Hinara was still wearing the gloves and for an instant he felt his fists clench and he knew he was going to strike the sergeant. But just as his arm tensed, he managed—barely—to get control of himself. He was alone in the hallway with four Imperial Guards, with a fifth just inside the room. If he started a fight, he would give them a reason to beat him senseless.

He refused to give them the opportunity to visit such an indignity upon him.

"Fine! Take him to your Inquisitor. But I *will* be present—I have many questions and I will make sure your 'professional' does not miss anything."

Sergeant Danashy chuckled.

"You don't get to call the shots around here, Investigator. The Inquisitor will have a witness to the interrogation, but it'll be one of the Guard, not a Legionnaire."

Hinara opened his mouth to protest, but the sergeant cut him off.

"There's no point in arguing with me about it. The rules are set by the magistrates, so you can go make demands of them. But for now, you can leave."

Hinara spun on his heel and marched back to Irako, who obviously had heard some part of the discussion.

"It seems as if the matter has gone from bad to worse for you. If you have anything to tell me, this is your last chance. Once I leave this room, the Imperial Guard is going to hand you over to an Inquisitor. You know what will happen then, do you not?"

Irako's fear was visible on his face. He swallowed and then gave a curt nod.

"Well?"

Irako looked down at the floor and said nothing.

Hinara wanted nothing more than to start pounding on the man's face, head and body with his fists, but he knew the soldiers would stop him.

"Then to the Abyss with you," he spit at the young man. "I will get what I need from you one way or another."

Pulling off the leather gloves, he tossed them on the floor as he left the room.

Eighteenth day of Highsummer,
1 day to the Arrival

Chapter Thirty-Four

THE SUN HAD BARELY PEEKED ABOVE THE HORIZON WHEN Relael arrived in his carriage. It was going to be a rather warm day, but he wore a cloak over his priest's robes to disguise his calling. He didn't want to approach the house as a member of the Church—it would have more impact when he revealed who he was after introductions were made.

Relael had ordered two squads of Church soldiers to move into position on side streets near the house. He didn't want to use them, but felt safer with them nearby. He was being cautious, but considering the abilities that Phana was said to possess, he didn't want to take any chances.

His spies reported that the house belonged to a historian, and Phana had stayed the night in the large house. And while they had watched the house throughout the night, it was certainly possible that Phana had managed to slip away without being seen. She was quite skilled in that regard, and Relael couldn't rule out the fact that she was already gone.

He pulled the curtain aside and looked out at the house. His carriage was parked around the side near the servants' entrance and where deliveries of food and supplies would be dropped off. It was only a matter of time before someone arrived, and then he would move.

Relael didn't have long to wait. Soon enough, a wagon pulled up near the side entrance and a delivery man grabbed a small crate filled with loaves of bread, vegetables, and other foodstuffs. As the man approached the servants' entrance, Relael climbed from the carriage and crossed the street to the house.

A serving woman opened the door and the delivery man carried the crate into the house. Relael waited outside the door, his cloak closed and his hands at his sides.

A moment later, the door opened. The man stepped out and saw Relael. But he was looking over the man's shoulder at the serving woman who was about to close to the door.

"Madam," Relael said. The delivery man stepped around him and returned to his delivery wagon.

"Yes?" she said cautiously, pushing the door mostly closed.

"Madam, I would like a quick word with you, please."

"We are not looking for any new suppliers."

Relael wanted to move closer, but she looked like the type who would shut the door in his face if he tried to bully his way in. So he remained where he was.

"That's not why I'm here. I'm not selling anything. In truth, I'm hoping you can answer a simple question for me."

She paused, unsure. But the fact that he stood well away from the door gave her confidence.

"What is it?"

"I should tell you that I'm here on official business. And that this conversation must remain solely between you and I."

She frowned at him, and he reached up and unclasped his cloak.

"This is a Church matter," he said, opening the cloak and letting it fall from his shoulders. Her eyes went wide, and he was sure she was going to slam the door. If she retreated into the house, the serving woman would certainly alert everyone inside. And if Phana was still here ....

"Madam," he said in a calm but commanding voice. "You will come outside and answer my questions. Once I have the information I need, I will leave you in peace."

He could see her hands gripping the edge of the door, and her eyes were nearly ready to pop from their sockets. He waited, gambling on her fear to make her compliant.

Finally, he could see her swallow and she gave him a short nod. She glanced nervously back into the house and then opened the door and stepped outside. He beckoned her toward him as he stepped forward. She took two steps and then stopped.

He lowered his voice for her ears only as he spoke.

"Madam, you will speak truthfully and tell me everything I need to know. Once I am satisfied, you will be free to go about your normal business. Do not lie to me or attempt to conceal anything—I already know a great deal and will surely catch you out. Do you understand?"

She nodded at him quickly, birdlike.

"This is the home of the historian, Master Ziarithllo Ilisti, correct?"

The woman nodded again.

"How many serving staff are currently in the house?"

"Just ... just myself."

"Your master has no other servants?" Relael asked, letting a note of skepticism be heard in his voice.

"He has a carriage driver. But the man lives elsewhere and only comes when the master has arranged to leave the house. I manage everything else."

Her voice quavered with her fear. A single tear sat at the corner of her eye, not yet ready to break free and run down her face. Relael knew he needed to be careful. If she burst into tears, he would get nothing else from her here.

"You have a guest in the house, correct?"

The woman's eyes widened again, and he watched as a series of emotions passed across her face—shock, fear, *anger*.

"Yes," she whispered. "She ... she forced herself into the house yesterday."

Relael fought back a smile. Phana was still here.

"Tell me her name."

"She said her name was Phana. I don't know if she's lying."

"She is not," Relael assured her. "Why is she here?"

"She said ...," the woman started and then paused, swallowing again and fighting back the tears that still threatened to come. "She said she needed Master Ilisti's help. She claims she doesn't remember her past, and she thinks he can help her recover her memories."

Relael considered this new information. Why would she go to a historian to find out about her past? Phana was perhaps just past her twentieth year, or thereabouts. It didn't make sense.

"Why did Master Ilisti agree to help her? Did she pay him?"

The serving woman looked at the ground, her mouth shut tight. Relael spoke calmly and evenly, but there was iron in his voice.

"Do not make me repeat my questions."

Her head snapped up and this time he was sure he had pushed too hard and she was about to lose control. But he saw the muscles in her jaw tense as she grimaced, and then she shook her head.

"He said Phana looked just like a woman in one of his old paintings. He was curious if she might be related. I didn't trust her, but Master Ilisti—he trusts people. He would never do anything against the Church, or the Empire."

Relael raised his hand, palm out.

"I am not here to accuse anything of your master. This woman is clever and manipulative, and she has caused no end of trouble for otherwise innocent people. I am here to put a stop to that."

The woman nodded again and seemed to calm slightly.

"Where is Phana now?"

"She is upstairs in a guest room. Master Ilisti offered for her to stay the night. She told me … she told me that she would spend one more day here looking through the histories and then she would leave for good."

This time, Relael did smile.

"You and your master have done nothing wrong. But now you must cooperate to see this through to the end. You will say nothing to anyone about me and our talk this morning. Not even Master Ilisti must know. Phana is dangerous, and if she suspects something is wrong, she might hurt him. Better that he know nothing."

The woman looked into Relael's eyes and he saw her work through the implications. She would have to spend time in the house with Phana and not let on that she knew anything was wrong.

"I will come back as quickly as I can, though it may be an hour or more before I can return. The Church will deal with this woman, and you and your master can go back to your normal lives. When I return, you will cooperate with us and do exactly what we tell you.

Is that clear?"

"Yes," the serving woman said, nodding slowly. "I will do whatever you need. We didn't know who she was."

"I know," Relael said, letting his voice reassure her. "You've done nothing wrong. But we need you to keep this secret for the next few hours. And then everything will be fine."

"What if she tries to leave?"

Relael considered that, but he knew this woman wouldn't be able to lie convincingly to Phana to get her to stay in the house.

"Let her. The Church has the house surrounded. If she leaves, we'll know and will act accordingly. Now go back inside and prepare breakfast for your master and his guest. Stay out of Phana's way as much as possible. I will be back to deal with her."

With that, he turned and walked back across the street to his carriage. As he climbed inside, he glanced back to see that the serving woman had gone back into the house.

This was still a gamble. He had no way of knowing if she would reveal Relael's orders to her master, to Phana, or both. But there was little he could do at this point. An assault on the house would likely turn out badly for the Church soldiers, and Relael didn't want to escalate the matter if it wasn't necessary.

He knew where Phana was, and all indications were that she would spend the entire day in the historian's house. He had time to return to the Temple and report to High Counselor Untoleu. She could decide how to proceed from there.

The only question was whether he could hold himself together in her presence long enough to see this mission through to its successful completion.

*   *   *

PHANA AWOKE IN A POOL OF HER OWN SWEAT. SHE HAD THROWN the sheet away and lay naked in the darkness of the room, the air thick and cloying. She raised her head and looked around. Everything seemed to be exactly as she had left it when she went to bed.

She climbed out of bed and threw open the shutters, letting a breath of fresh air into the room. The morning air was cooler outside, and it raised chills on her sweat-damp skin as it came flooding into the stuffy room.

After washing herself with the tepid water in the basin, she dressed and opened her bedroom door. She could hear the faint sounds of someone moving about in the kitchen on the ground floor, and her stomach rumbled in response.

Though it had taken Phana some time to fall asleep, at least she felt rested. She didn't remember dreaming—perhaps her mind had been too exhausted once she had drifted off.

She walked down the stairs to the ground floor and followed the sounds to the kitchen. Tyilly was chopping vegetables on a wooden chopping block, her back to the kitchen door. Phana cleared her throat and the poor serving woman spun around with a squawk, the knife dropping from her hand and barely missing her foot as it hit the floor.

"I'm sorry," Phana said, holding up her hands to calm the other woman down. "I didn't mean to startle you."

Tyilly's eyes were wide and she was breathing heavily. She put a hand on her chest and took a deep breath.

"No, I am all right. I just did not expect you in the kitchen."

Tyilly looked down at the knife on the floor and back up at Phana.

"There is food in the dining room," she said as she bent down to pick up the knife. Phana saw her knuckles go white as she gripped its handle. She turned back to her cutting board. "Please help yourself. Master Ilisti is up and has already eaten. He waits for you in the same room you were in yesterday."

"Okay, I will hurry, then. I *am* sorry I startled you."

Tyilly waved off her the apology and didn't bother turning around. "I'm fine," she said, though her voice was anything but.

Phana shrugged and moved back to the dining room, where a selection of pastries and cheeses were set out on the table. She sat down and stuffed food into her mouth, chewing quickly and gulping down a couple glasses of water. Soon enough, she was up and heading for one of Master Ilisti's library rooms.

The elderly man was poring over a leather-bound volume as she stepped through the door. She knocked softly on the door frame, and he looked up with a smile.

"Lady Phana, good morning to you. How did you sleep?"

"Quite well, thank you. Your guest bed is very comfortable."

He beamed at her.

"It doesn't get used much. I don't have many guests—only the occasional scholar from another city who comes to view some of my collection. No one nearly as interesting as you."

Phana chuckled at his good humor. He was far nicer than she had expected, and she was grateful for all the time he had spent with her yesterday.

"I know you have other obligations, Master Ilisti, and I don't want to take up too much of your time—"

He waved his hands at her.

"Oh my, not at all. You have been a huge help to me in making connections between scrolls that I never realized were right there. Even the smallest detail can bring two seemingly unrelated pieces of information together to reveal a picture of our past that was previously missing. You have done me a great service. I only wish I could help you as much as you have helped me."

He stepped toward her and there was concern in his voice.

"Did you see anything new in your dreams last night? You seemed so very tired and I hoped that your mind let you rest."

Phana sighed as she sat down.

"Truthfully, I don't remember dreaming at all. It was a nice change. Perhaps I've wrung out every possible memory—or whatever it is—that was in my head."

She realized she didn't sound enthusiastic about that possibility. Nothing she had remembered told her anything about her time in Ythis. She still didn't know how she had come here, or what she had been doing before the last couple of years that she could recall.

Master Ilisti put his hand on her shoulder.

"Yesterday, those memories in your head started us on a path. There's a thread there, and now it's a matter of following that thread to see where it leads. We know it eventually leads to you and Ythis. And perhaps it will shed some illumination on your own history."

He turned back to the book on his table.

"This was written well after the events it describes. It claims to be a collection of first-hand accounts that were lost and then rediscovered. I had never given this particular volume much credit, as there was nothing to corroborate the stories within its pages. However, something you said yesterday jogged a memory of a detail I had read in this book, so I took a second look."

He motioned for Phana to sit down as he pulled the tome to face her. The writing was of a language she did not recognize, though something about it was familiar to her. Master Ilisti pointed to a passage about halfway down one page.

"There is mention here of three companions. One is described as a great bear of a man, with gray hair and a stern countenance. One is a handsome man who seems to prefer the shadows of night. And one is a woman."

He pointed to the charcoal sketch of the woman who looked exactly like Phana.

"The description fits the lady in the picture."

"Then it describes me as well."

Master Ilisti looked at her over the top of his spectacles.

"Well, yes. Except for the long hair."

He turned back to the book.

"And it tells of the three companions traveling across the continent. They go up into a mountain range, and then over and down into the plains of dust. Of course, that's where the account ends, as it says no one could live on those plains."

"The tower," Phana whispered.

"Yes, the tower. The only problem is that, while there have been a few references—both veiled and direct—about those plains of dust, they don't appear on any maps I've ever seen. Not on this continent, not in the south where the Charnai have their own empire, and I've never seen a reference to plains of dust in any writings of the far eastern continent."

"Maybe they don't exist anymore."

"That's a possibility, of course. There were some great upheavals when the new gods replaced the old. But if that's the case, then we'll never know for sure."

He pulled up another chair and placed it in front of her. Sitting down, he took Phana's hands in his.

"My dear, we keep coming back to this point. The tower, the three companions, and the army camped at its base—this is where your memories seem to end. And then it's nothing until a couple of years ago here in Ythis."

He leaned forward.

"Are you sure you cannot remember anything else? You said that the companions had planned to go out to meet the army in the morning. Picture it in your mind, the sun rising above the plains, the army probably formed up in endless ranks facing you. The three companions …"

… walk out from the base of the tower toward the waiting soldiers. A dozen misshapen giants tower over the squads arrayed around them, their heavy maces longer than two men laid end-to-end. A wooden platform has been built far back from the front ranks.

The betrayers are there, watching.

"Look," she says to her companions. "They think this army will protect them from us. They think they are safe back there."

The big man on her left says nothing. He is dressed in his war armor, dark iron covered in spikes. A sword that hums as lightning plays over its surface rests easily in his hand.

The man on her right laughs softly. He is dressed all in black and seems to absorb the light around him, as if the sun itself cast a shadow.

She is dressed in simple leathers. She needs no armor and carries no weapon. The cold builds up inside her …

… Phana gasped as the memory came back to her. She blinked at Master Ilisti and then …

… the screams of the dying surround her, a sweet music that fills her soul with joy. The final giant bellows in a voice that shakes

the earth as it topples, crushing countless soldiers beneath its falling body. Another great wave of dust rises into the air and rushes toward them, though the air is already thick, and she cannot see more than twenty paces in any direction.

"Where are they?" she screams, knowing her companions can hear her voice no matter how far away they might be across this endless battlefield.

Yarrian comes staggering out of the dust, clutching his head. He has no visible wound—no soldier has the skill to hurt him—and yet blood runs from his nose.

He looks up at her, his eyes wide. She sees something in his face that she has seen only once before, when they were forced to leave the city that had been built just for them but that they had lost forever—she sees fear.

"Run!" he screams at her, and his voice is raw and full of terror.

"Where are they?" she asks him, grabbing his arm. He shakes free and continues to stagger back in the direction of the tower.

"Run! They have ... we cannot win this day!"

She turns back in the direction from which he came, and a cloud of darkness rushes forth and engulfs her ....

Phana leaped to her feet, her lungs full and her mouth open to scream. Only Master Ilisti's grip on her hands anchored her to the present, and she clutched at him, the breath pushing at the inside of her chest. She felt as if she must let it out in a howl of terror and pain or her lungs would burst.

But Master Ilisti just said her name, over and over, and the sound of his voice relaxed her muscles just enough that she was able to exhale without forcing it out in a shriek. He grimaced, and she realized she was crushing his hands in her grip.

She forced her own hands open and fell back into the chair, breathing heavily.

"My dear, I'm sorry. I'm so sorry. I should never have suggested—"

She waved off his apology.

"No, you were right. There was one last memory. The battle ... something happened. We lost. They ... they did something to turn the tide and we were helpless against it. That's where everything goes dark. Whatever they did, that's where the memories end."

The historian sat back down in his chair and took her hands in his once more.

"Then this is where we will stop. I do not want to cause any further distress."

All of Phana's muscles were weak, as if she had just been through the battle in her head for real, but she forced herself to sit up.

"No, I can't give up. There are too many questions now. Before, I just thought that I was a normal person—well, not exactly normal but at least … I don't know how to describe it."

"You believed that something strange had *happened* to you, but that you yourself were just a regular person."

"Yes. But now I know that's not the case. Now I know there's more to it. But I have no idea how to get back what was taken from me."

Master Ilisti pondered it for a moment. And then he gave her hands a squeeze.

"We have only come at this from one direction, my dear. Something took all your memories after a certain point. But at another point, your ability to remember your recent past came back. You remember the last couple of years. What happened there to start your memory working again?"

He let go of her hands and stood up.

"I do not just study ancient history. I also keep extensive records of what happens in this city on a monthly basis. We have hit a wall coming from the past forward. So now it is time to start from now and work backward. But we'll have to go to another room where I keep my more recent histories."

Phana looked up at him. Her body was still weak, but that wasn't going to stop her. She pushed herself to her feet and followed him from the room.

Chapter Thirty-Five

L AITA STEPPED INTO THE ROOM AND LOOKED AROUND. ONCE again, her command squad was assembled to hear what she had to say about their course of action. She needed their feedback, she needed to see if what she had planned was reasonable. All their lives hung in the balance, and she wasn't going to make the decision for them this time.

They stood and saluted her as she entered, even Namal. His gaze was cool, and it pained her to see him look at her like she was simply his commanding officer instead of his friend.

"At ease," she told them. They returned to their seats as she moved to stand in front of them.

"I've come to a decision on what I feel we should do here in Ythis. But I want to hear what you think about it."

"You're the commander," Bor stated simply. "You set the plan and we execute it."

She smiled at him. He still looked at her like she was some kind of legendary hero.

"Thank you for your support, Bor. But I *need* to hear your views. This affects all of us, and I will not simply give orders this time. We need to make a decision, *all* of us together."

She saw Saeda and Addiru glance at each other, a tense look passing between them.

They're thinking about Keynter, she guessed. *He was starting to feel like one of us, but his behavior showed he wasn't ready for any command responsibilities.*

"I know that not all of the command squad is here. I'm worried about Ellend, too. And I sent Keynter back to his own squad because it needed to be done. He was letting his anger get the best of him. None of us can afford to do that, not here and not now. His behavior the day before yesterday told me that I can't trust his judgement about this."

Bor nodded, Saeda and Addiru exchanged another glance, and Pilayni kept still. They weren't giving her much to work with this morning.

"Before I begin my briefing, is there anything you need to report?"

Namal stood up and cleared his throat.

"Irako missed his meeting with me yesterday. I went by his work and the taverns we know he frequents. No sign of him. I don't know where he lives, but if you give me the location, I'll check out his apartment as soon as we're done here."

Laita swore under her breath. Irako was normally reliable. She didn't want to imagine him in the clutches of the Imperial Guard or the Legion.

And then it struck her that perhaps the Church had grabbed him to help encourage her cooperation. No, that was unlikely. Oriuna knew that would only push Laita farther away from being willing to work with them.

"Okay, I'll give you directions once this meeting is over. He lives in the Warren, so be careful. Take a couple of the soldiers with you when you go."

"I can move more easily out there during the day if I'm by myself. No one looks twice at me, but three of us will get noticed."

Laita hesitated. She knew he was probably right, but she didn't want to risk him getting captured if Irako had already been taken. But she couldn't really argue his point, and she had to show him she trusted him.

"Okay, just you, then."

Namal sat down and she turned to the others.

"I've been thinking about this since our meeting two days ago. And yesterday afternoon I had another meeting with Oriuna."

She noticed the slight grimace on Namal's face at mention of the woman's name. He wasn't ever going to forgive Oriuna for her duplicity, and Laita couldn't really blame him.

"I simply cannot leave the Church in control of the Empire. If I do that, if *we* do that, then we may as well just give up now. There is no point in removing the Emperor if another group that is just as bad comes in and takes over. We'll have accomplished our mission for nothing."

She paused to let that sink in. There were no glances between them now. Each was thinking about it in personal terms, deciding what they were and were not willing to do.

Finally, Bor looked up at her.

"You've got another option, though, don't you, commander?"

She smiled at him with what she hoped was a reassuring expression.

"It was just an idea I threw out at our last meeting, but I think we can do it. I intend to find a candidate among the noble families who can get the Imperial Guard and the Legion to back them as a new Emperor."

She held up her hands to forestall Namal's protests.

"I know you don't believe it will work, Namal, but things are coming to a head, here. We must commit to something. And you *know* I won't leave Ythis until this is resolved one way or another. It's a risk, a huge one, but we've risked everything just coming here. I think the only way out is to keep moving forward and out the other side."

She lowered her hands.

"But it's not just my decision. I want to hear from you, all of you."

She looked at Namal and smirked.

"Even Namal, though we all know what he's going to say."

"Laita," he began and coughed and cleared his throat. She thought she could see the glint of a tear in his eye.

"Sorry, commander. I mean to say, you're right that I think we should run. But you have a goal and if I know you, you've already got at least a rough plan. And if everyone here feels we should stay the course, then I'm behind you. I've seen you pull off the impossible before. I'd be a fool to miss seeing it happen again."

Laita's chest ached and she wanted to grab him in a hug and not let go. No matter what had happened between them over the past few days, he still believed in her. She had to fight back a tear as she nodded at him.

"That's a ... well, it's the best endorsement I've ever received."

She saw Saeda wipe her eyes and couldn't hide her smile. This was not just a command squad. This was her family.

"I'm with you, commander," Bor said. "I hate to leave a job unfinished."

Saeda held up her hand and muttered "Me too" before turning away to hide her tears. Pilayni nodded.

Addiru, however, didn't look convinced.

"Commander, with all due respect, I disagree."

Everyone turned to look at him, and Laita motioned for him to continue.

"I want to hear your thoughts, Addiru."

He looked at the others, one by one, before returning his attention to Laita.

"We came here to remove the Emperor. He's a threat, and we sacrificed everything we had in choosing this path, but it was the right one and I don't regret what choice I made."

He sighed and slowly shook his head.

"The odds were against us when we just had the Emperor to deal with. But now you're planning to betray the Church. Even if you succeed, they're not just going to let that go. *Especially* if you succeed.

"The Emperor is one man. Yes, he is a powerful man, and he has the the Legions and the Guard to protect him. But at the end of the day, we can remove those threats by eliminating him. The Church is a different story entirely."

"So you want us to run?" Bor asked him.

"No, I want us to complete our mission to kill the Emperor. But *then* we run. Namal was right when he said there's no way to beat the Church. They don't just have their own soldiers, they have a god. Fuck, they have *nine* gods. If we do this, if we anger the Church, it isn't just our lives they will take."

Everyone sat silent, considering his words. Finally, Pilayni spoke up.

"I'm terrified," she said into the silence. "I want nothing more than to run and hide somewhere the Legion will never find me. But ... that's what others do. Not us. It doesn't matter how scared we get, how tired we get, how wounded we get. We keep fighting for the Empire. Not the Emperor, or the Church, or even the nobles. We fight for all those who can't, all those people who make up this Empire."

She turned to Addiru.

"You're a Legionnaire, Addiru."

"Not anymore," he replied quietly.

"Yes, you *are*. We all are. We can't rest until the job is done, until the mission is complete. Killing the Emperor is only half the mission. We just didn't know about the other half when we started on this road. Now we do."

She reached out and grabbed Addiru's hand.

"We're all afraid. We all know what's at stake. But we're together and we have the commander leading us. Don't let fear turn you into something you're not. You're a Legionnaire. We've been hiding so long that we've forgotten the pride that should come with that name. It's time we take that back."

She turned to Laita, who couldn't hide the tears that had welled in her own eyes.

"Commander, I'm behind you completely."

Laita saw Addiru look up at her and slowly nod.

"Okay, I'm with you, commander. But I ask you for one thing."

"What is it, Addiru?"

"If the Church comes after us, kill me before they take me. Don't let my soul end up in the clutches of the gods."

Laita swallowed before answering him.

"You have my word."

*   *   *

NAMAL CLIMBED THE STEPS TO THE TOP FLOOR OF THE TENEMENT and paused to catch his breath. He could feel his heart beating heavily in his chest and the tips of his fingers tingled. He gripped the railing and closed his eyes, taking deep breaths and letting them out slowly.

Once he felt that both his heart and his breath were under control again, he proceeded to the second door on his right. He raised his hand and knocked softly.

The door swung open at his touch.

He stepped back and had his knife in his hand in an instant. He froze, listening for sounds from the other three doors in this short hallway. If this was an ambush ....

But nothing further happened, and he could see the small room through the partially opened doorway. No one was visible.

Irako had said that he would be returning home in the late afternoon from his job at the warehouse. It was possible he hadn't returned yet. But then, he wouldn't have left his door unlocked.

Namal looked at the very simple lock on the door and realized that wouldn't stop any determined thief.

That's probably it, he tried to reassure himself. *Someone has broken into Irako's apartment to steal his valuables.*

But Namal couldn't convince himself that was true. He glanced down the hallway at the other doors. If this was an ambush of some kind, the time to launch it was when he first knocked on the door. There would have been someone inside the apartment, someone on the floor below to block the stairs, and at least a couple of others in another apartment on this floor.

But there was no sound other than the normal street noise from outside.

He stepped to the opening and peered in. The room was a mess. Holding his knife in his right hand, he pushed the door fully open with his left. He could see the entire room from the doorway, and there was no one here.

But it was also immediately clear that this hadn't been some simple burglary. A struggle of some sort had taken place here. The cot was overturned and the table on was its side. But the clothing in one corner hadn't been disturbed. A thief would have tossed the entire room, looking for any hidden coins or other treasures.

No, a fight had most likely taken place here.

Namal stepped into the room and examined the scene more closely. He saw the broken latch on the door and figured it must have been forced open. But the lock was still intact.

That means Irako was here when it happened.

A cold lump of lead settled into Namal's stomach. Someone had come here and grabbed Irako. But when?

He sheathed his knife and returned to the stairs, pulling the door closed behind him, though realizing it probably didn't matter. Regardless of who had him—the Legion, the Imperial Guard, the Church—Irako was as good as dead. The odds of him ever returning to this room were essentially nil.

Namal considered his options and then turned to the closest door across the hall from Irako's room. He knocked twice and then listened.

The faintest sound of movement was audible from the other side.

He knocked again.

"Hello, is anyone in there? I'd just wanna ask you a question."

No further sound came from the room beyond.

"I have coin. I can pay you for an answer. I just wanna know what happened here."

He waited, but no one came to the door. Whoever was on the other side had probably heard the abduction and wanted no part of it.

Namal returned to the stairs and proceeded down to street level. Emerging from the rear door into the alley behind the building, he looked around, but no one was visible.

Looking up and down the narrow alley, he realized that whoever had taken Irako must have transported him somewhere else. That mostly likely meant a wagon, or at least a spare horse. Whoever had done it couldn't have used these alleys.

And if they had used the streets, then someone had seen it.

He moved a few buildings down the block to the first alley connecting to the street on the other side. Stepping out onto the cobblestones, he looked around at the people moving about their business.

Across the street and up a short way, at the mouth of another alley, three men stood around. They were thin and weaselly, with an air of menace about them. They eyed the passers-by, as if evaluating them as targets.

Thieves and cutthroats. Good enough for his purpose.

He began to walk over to them, and one of three, the shortest, noticed him approaching. The man elbowed his companions and muttered something to them, but Namal couldn't catch what he said.

"Afternoon," he called out to them. "Would you like to earn some coin?"

A few heads turned at his words, but those quickly turned away when they saw who he was addressing.

The locals know these men are thugs, he realized. But they were the only good candidates to have possible seen Irako's abduction.

The shortest of the men stepped forward as the other two began to step around Namal. Instead of letting them surround him, he put out a hand and stopped the tallest.

"You don't wanna do that," he growled at the man.

The third man did step around behind Namal, but Namal turned and put his own back toward the wall.

The shortest man glowered at him.

"You don't tell us what we want. We tell you."

"I'll tell you that I'm gonna pay you for information. And you'll answer my questions and end up richer than you were before I arrived. Then we'll all part company happy."

The tallest of the men frowned at him.

"No, you're going to give us your money and then you fuck off."

Namal knew he might have to kill one or more of these men. At least they were in the Warren and he didn't have to worry about any members of the Watch coming after him.

"Dead men can't spend their coins."

The tall man stepped forward, trying to look intimidating. Namal's fist shot out and he buried his knuckles in the man's solar plexus. The man's eyes went wide as his breath left him and he staggered back.

Before the others could react, Namal grabbed the short one by the throat and squeezed. The short man's hands grabbed at Namal's wrist in an automatic reaction, which meant he didn't go for his knife.

The third man *did* draw his knife. Namal couldn't reach him and still hold onto the short one, so he pulled his own knife and aimed the point of the blade at the short man's left eye.

He was counting on the third man to not attack anyway. If these three didn't like each other, Namal's threat wouldn't amount to anything and he'd be in trouble.

But the third man, his knife in his hand, crouched in a ready position but didn't move forward to engage.

"Like I said, I'm gonna ask you some questions and pay you for your answers. Don't be stupid and die for nothing."

The short man was slowly choking in Namal's grip. The tallest of the men was on his knees in the street, holding his chest and trying to draw a breath. The last man looked back and forth at his companions, not sure what to do.

"Someone got taken out of that building over there, probably some time yesterday. You guys look like you hang out here a lot. Tell me what you saw."

The man with the knife glanced back at the tenement where Irako had lived and turned to Namal with his eyes wide.

"Yesterday?" he asked, and Namal saw in his face that he knew something.

"Young guy lived there. What happened to him?"

"Five guys," the man said. "Soldiers."

"Legion?" Namal asked him, and he shrugged.

"Don't know. They was dressed normal ... like us. But they was soldiers, for sure. You can always tell a soldier."

"So what happened?"

"They walked up with two horses. Some of 'em went inside. Then they came out with a guy—all tied up and a bag over his head. They put him on a horse and he and one guy rode off together."

"Where did the other four go?"

The man with the knife looked at his companion in Namal's grip. The short man's face had gone red and was slowly turning purple.

"You really gonna pay us?"

"Yes. Now answer my fucking question!"

"They walked off together, back the way they came."

"Last question," Namal told him. "When did this happen?"

The man with the knife shrugged.

"Yesterday, I think after midday."

They had Irako, whoever they were. It could have been the Legion.

The Imperial Guard probably wouldn't have bothered to hide themselves, but then again, they might not want to come into the Warren without a large force, and that could have alerted Irako before they reached him.

And Namal also had to consider the Church as a possible culprit. They might have grabbed Irako as a bargaining chip to use against Laita.

There was no point in speculating. He had to get back to her and tell her what had happened. With Irako in someone's custody, all their people were at risk, along with the other members of the Resistance.

"Toss your knife over there," he told the man. "I'll give you the money once I know you're not gonna stick me."

The man looked at his companions once more then tossed his knife away.

Namal pulled his own knife away from the choking man's face, and then hammered him in the nose with his fist. He let go of the man's throat and watched him fall to the street, barely conscious.

Then Namal grabbed a handful of coins and tossed them at his feet.

"Next time, when someone offers to pay you for your troubles, don't get greedy."

He backed away, keeping his eye on the three men, but the third man was focused on collecting the coins, and the others were in no condition to follow Namal.

In minutes, he was well away from the area.

I must reach Laita, he thought. *If they've got Irako, they've got us all.*

Chapter Thirty-Six

THE DOOR OPENED AND SHUYAJA STOOD IN FRONT OF RELAEL, barring entry.

"You were ordered to report first thing this morning."

Relael smiled at him, though there was no humor in it.

"I know what my orders were, and I know it's no longer morning. I'm here. The High Counselor will wish to hear my news *immediately*."

Shuyaja just looked at him and sneered.

"Will she? I think that will be up to her to decide. She is already angry with you for your tardiness."

Relael was out of patience and time was of the essence. He wasn't going to waste it getting into a pissing contest with this lackey. He stepped close to Shuyaja, and though the other man was slightly taller, Relael didn't let that affect his confidence.

"I am here to report to the High Counselor, and that's precisely what I am going to do. Delay me further, and I will look forward to overseeing your escort to the chamber below when you are given over to our god."

He stared into Shuyaja's eyes and did not blink. The other main stared back for a moment, but what he saw in Relael's gaze was enough for him to realize that he had pushed too far.

"I look forward to overseeing your punishment for failing in your duties," Shuyaja said, but the power of his words were diminished as he stepped back out of the way.

Relael pushed past the man into the chamber beyond. A heavy door, bound in iron, stood closed on other side of the room. Despite the barrier, he could feel High Counselor Assirra Untoleu's presence on the other side. He felt his hands begin to tremble, and he clenched his fists and tucked them into the sleeves of his robes.

As he moved to stand before the door, it opened, revealing the High Counselor's office. It was a large room, one wall lined with racks holding books and scrolls. A desk of rich, dark wood sat in the middle of the room and Assirra Untoleu stood behind it.

She beckoned Relael to enter and waved him to one of the seats opposite her desk. As he stepped in, the door closed behind him with a solid thunk. The power radiating from the High Counselor nearly rocked him back on his heels. There was no expression on her face, but the air was warm around her and he realized he was feeling her anger.

"I have found her," he blurted before he reached the chair. "I know where she is right now."

The High Counselor did not move, but something in her bearing changed at his words.

"Why have you not come before now?" she asked, and her voice resonated within him. Despite the cold tone, he could feel his body reacting to the sound of her voice as passion welled up within him. He tried to control his emotions, but even at his best, he was nearly helpless in her presence.

"I ... she has been difficult to find, High Counselor. She is secretive and careful, and she keeps her home hidden even from those she calls friends. But once I discovered her identity, it was only a matter of time before we found her."

"*We?*"

"I have used my own spies to search for her, though none know the reason why. The woman is involved romantically with the Wolf's right-hand man. They assume that is why I want her."

At the mention of the Wolf, the High Counselor's mouth twisted in distaste. It was the most emotion he had ever seen from her. He realized that he was still standing, but was now unsure if he should approach the chair and sit, as she had first ordered him to do, or if it would look insolent if he did it now.

His hands continued to tremble in his sleeves, and he wondered if there were any other visible signs of his distress at being in her presence.

"Does the Wolf know you hunt her?"

Relael shook his head.

"No, High Counselor. The Wolf is not involved. In fact, the Wolf has declared that she is not permitted within the tavern where he makes his residence. I believe that the Wolf is not happy with his servant's relationship with the woman."

Her eyes bored into Relael's, and the heat radiating from her dissolved away. He almost stumbled forward, as if he had been pushing against some kind of resistance and it was suddenly gone.

"He knows," she said in a low voice. "But he also knows to stay out of my way. He is still the coward."

Relael realized she wasn't really talking to him, but rather expressing her thoughts aloud. He had never seen her behave this way before. Whoever this Phana woman was, her presence had certainly affected the High Counselor.

"What name does she currently wear?"

The phrasing of the question was strange to Relael, but he answered immediately.

"Her name is Phana. I have discovered no family name."

"And where is she now?"

"She was seen at a mansion near the fortress, and I confirmed her presence there this morning, and that she stayed overnight. I do not believe she is planning to leave anytime soon. In fact, I have just come directly from there. It is the home of Master Ziarithllo Ilisti, a historian—"

"By the Abyss!" the High Counselor snarled. The door behind Relael swung open.

"Yes, High Counselor," Shuyaja answered.

"Get my carriage," she ordered, already moving toward the door. "And grab two priests as well. Relael, you'll ride up front with the driver. Take the most expedient route."

Relael hurried after her as she strode through the outer chamber to the hallway beyond. Other priests and acolytes in the hall nearly threw themselves out of her way as they recognized the High Counselor and saw the look on her face. Shuyaja literally ran ahead to ensure the carriage was ready when she arrived.

Relael followed two paces behind her.

"I have squads of soldiers stationed on side streets near the house, and spies watching it from every side."

"It doesn't matter. She knows. Now it's a question of how much she's managed to recover before we get there. How long has she been with the historian?"

"She was seen entering the house yesterday morning, and no one has seen her leave."

They had reached the main staircase and began ascending toward ground level. Relael heard the High Counselor sigh as they headed for the entrance where the stables and carriages were kept.

"Your soldiers won't matter. Nothing will matter if we don't get there in time. If she manages to …."

She trailed off, and Relael knew better than to ask for an explanation of her concern. Obviously, there was a possibility that Phana might find out some important piece of information from the historian, and the High Counselor didn't want that to happen. But what could the historian tell her that would make Phana … do whatever it was she might do.

"Will we need more soldiers?"

The High Counselor didn't respond at first as they crossed the great hall.

"No," she said finally. "I will deal with this. She can't remember everything, or she'd have fled the city already. Or she'd have come here looking for me."

Relael blinked at her words. They had reached the entrance to the street beside the stables. Relael's carriage still stood at the curb, waiting for his return. One of the acolytes saw the High Counselor and went white.

"Your carriage is coming, High Counselor!" he squeaked.

She looked at the acolyte, turned to Relael, and then looked at his carriage.

"Every moment counts," she said and turned toward the carriage that was immediately ready. His driver fumbled at the door as she approached and managed to get it open just as she reached him. She climbed in and he looked at Relael.

"I'm riding with you," he told the driver. The man blinked at him and then shut the door and climbed back up to his bench at the front. Relael joined turned to the acolyte.

"Send the priests in the counselor's carriage—the home of Master Ziarithllo Ilisti at the north end of Merchant's District."

He climbed onto the carriage beside the driver.

"Make haste back to the historian's mansion, but remember who your passenger is," he told the man.

The driver nodded, his eyes wide. He flicked the reigns and Relael glanced back as the carriage pulled away from the curb. The High Counselor's own carriage was just emerging from the building where it was kept.

Relael shrugged and faced forward. He wasn't going to question the High Counselor's urgency. He also tried to not think about the reasons why she was so concerned. If the High Counselor was worried, Relael figured *he* should be *terrified*.

*   *   *

JISKA CHARGED INTO THE ROOM, LETTING THE DOOR SLAM AGAINST the wall. Hinara's muscles tensed in shock at the sudden and unexpected intrusion into this office, not to mention the noise. He shoved himself to his feet.

"Sir, you must come at once," Jiska panted at him. The man had obviously been running.

"What is it?" he snapped at his aid. He took a deep breath, ready to berate the other man for his rude entrance.

"Sergeant Danashy demands your presence in the yard. He received the report from the Inquisitor and now the Imperial Guard are mobilizing."

"Mobilizing for what?"

"To capture the rebels, sir."

Hinara swore, loudly and with great creativity, as he grabbed his uniform jacket and strode into the hallway, heading for the main staircase. In moments, he emerged from the Fortress to see the soldiers of the Imperial Guard forming up in ranks in the main yard.

Sergeant Danashy was surrounded by a group of aids and messengers, giving orders. Hinara marched over to him, but was frustrated in his attempt to reach the sergeant by the bustle of people around him.

"Sergeant!" he called, and Danashy turned to see him and frowned. The sergeant gave one last order to a messenger—to take two squads and assign them to The Forest—and then stepped past the others toward Hinara.

"Investigator, you're just in time. You may accompany one of our groups this afternoon, and I'll let you choose which one you want to witness personally."

"What are you doing?" Hinara demanded. "Where is the report from the Inquisitor?"

Sergeant Danashy motioned to one of the aids and was handed a rolled-up parchment. He passed it to Hinara.

"You can look at it as we ride. I assume you'd prefer to participate in the capture of Legion deserters?"

"Wait, you are raiding them now?"

Hinara unrolled the parchment and began scanning the Inquisitor's report, trying to pick out the key details while the sergeant turned back to the others and began asking questions and issuing orders again.

It took him almost two full minutes before he picked out her name on the pages. Reading rapidly, he saw what Irako had eventually admitted regarding Laita Naschect.

I was right, he thought triumphantly. *She is here in Ythis!*

As he continued to read, he saw, however, that there were no further useful details. She had met with a group of Ythis locals, sure, and was planning to take action against the Emperor himself. But nothing related to where she was hiding. She might be at the tenement on the edge of the Warren, but she didn't normally stay there.

He almost crumpled the paper in his fist, but realized that would make it significantly harder to read. Looking up, he saw a high-ranking member of the Imperial Guard approaching, obvious by the embellishments on her armor and the red cape hanging from her shoulders.

Attempting to the seize the initiative, he stepped forward into her path.

"Centurion," he began, but one of the Guardsmen accompanying her stepped forward to block him.

"Step aside!" the man yelled in his face, and Hinara involuntarily took several steps back. The Centurion marched past him, straight to the cluster around Sergeant Danashy. The sergeant saluted her and immediately began talking.

An incandescent rage began to build in the back of his head, a white-hot star that would soon explode if he did not get some control over this situation.

"That is *enough!*" he screamed across the yard, and for an instant Sergeant Danashy, the Centurion, and all the aides stopped talking, heads whipping around, eyes seeking him out. He took advantage of that momentary focus and drew himself up his full parade-ground stance.

"These deserters belong to the *Legion*," he snarled at them. "You are welcome to participate in their capture, but I represent the Legion here, and I am in charge of this operation."

The Centurion blinked at him, and then he saw the corner of her mouth turn up as she glanced at the sergeant. With a wave her hand, the aides stepped back and she strode over to Hinara. She was taller than he was, and muscular. He didn't doubt that she still trained vigorously with her soldiers, despite her rank.

"I assume you are Investigator Hinara."

He opened his mouth to respond but she cut him off.

"Let me explain something to you, Investigator. The Imperial Guard was happy to lend you hand when all it seemed you were hunting for was a bunch of deserters. If that was all this was about, you would be given a few squads of Guards to go round them up yourself."

She held up a hand as he tried to speak and simply spoke over him.

"But that is no longer the case. The Inquisitor discovered a much greater threat than some deserters. There is a rebellion growing in this city, Investigator, one whose goal it is to overthrow our Emperor. And your deserters are working with these rebels directly."

She looked down and saw the scroll in Hinara's hand.

"Have you not read the Inquisitor's report?"

Once again, Hinara had to force himself not to crumple the pages in his fist.

"I just received it. Your sergeant saw fit to keep this information from me."

"Untrue. He's had it not much longer than you. But we in the Imperial Guard move fast, Investigator. Unlike the great unwieldy club that is the Legion, we are a scalpel. We strike quickly and with precision.

"This is no longer a Legion matter. There is a direct threat to the Emperor in Ythis. We are in charge of this mission now. I believe the sergeant offered you a chance to accompany one of our units on today's operation. It is up to you if you want to participate, but we are going to capture the rebels and your Legion deserters both."

"Centurion," Hinara said, trying to keep his voice even. "With all due respect, I need time to notify my superiors in the Legion ...."

"There is no more time, Investigator. The prisoner gave us the identities of the rebels, the location of multiple groups of your former soldiers, and the location where they are storing and distributing their weapons and gear. We are going to hit those locations in less than an hour."

"But Irako did not give you the location of Laita Naschect and her command squad," he argued. "She is far more important than any dozen of those soldiers. You risk losing her if you jump too soon."

The Centurion looked around the open yard at her forces preparing for their assault, and then back to Hinara.

"It does not matter. We will capture enough of them that some will know where she is hiding and will give that information to us. She will not escape the city."

She turned and walked away and Hinara saw Sergeant Danashy grin at him and then turn back to his group. He clenched his fists and spat a curse at the sergeant, though the man did not hear him.

Laita Naschect was *his* to capture, not these strutting peacocks with their gleaming armor and oiled bodies. The Imperial Guard were not true soldiers, and the woman should be apprehended by those she deserted and betrayed. Besides, they did not know her like Hinara did. He understood her mind, and was not fooled by her tricks and misdirections.

It would be a week at least before he could get messages to his superiors and receive any instructions back. By that time, this would all be over. Either Laita would be in the custody of the Imperial Guard, or she would be gone from Ythis, most likely gone from the Empire, for good.

He had an hour to send whatever messages he could, and then he would have to make a choice on whether to accompany the Guard on their raids. He would most certainly participate, and he would go to the location where they were distributing the weapons. That was the only place he was likely to find Laita, and if she was there, then he would be present when she was captured.

He cursed Sergeant Danashy once more as he spun on his heel and marched back to his temporary office.

Chapter Thirty-Seven

THE SOFT KNOCK AT THE DOOR INTERRUPTED PHANA'S TRAIN of thought. She had been reading about the arrival in Ythis of the Tsojim, a race of creatures that had moved into the city to build the sewer system that ran underneath the streets and buildings. The work had caused many disruptions, especially when it was discovered the Tsojim had built their own settlement in tunnels under and around the sewers and the city steward at the time had tried to have them forcefully removed.

Phana was trying to imagine Ythis back then, the changes to the city streets as the work was conducted, the fear as people heard about the Tsojim's intent to permanently live underneath the city. The details weren't familiar to her, but she hoped something she read might nudge one of her hidden memories and open it up in her mind.

Assuming the memories were hidden and not entirely erased.

She looked up to see Tyilly at the door and realized that it was midday. She was suddenly hungry.

Master Ilisti looked up from the pile of books on the table in front of him.

"Yes, Tyilly?"

"I have prepared a lunch for you both, Master Ilisti. It is set in the dining room."

Phana turned to the historian.

"I just realized that I'm starving. Maybe we should take a break."

She looked back at Tyilly and noted that the serving woman did not so much as glance in her direction. Her eyes were fixed on Master Ilisti and her hands were clenched together at her waist. Phana thought the woman looked nervous.

"Please bring some food up here," Master Ilisti told her. "I'd like to keep reading while I eat."

Tyilly paused for a moment, blinking at him.

"But … but it's a bit messy. You don't want to get anything on your books."

The historian looked at Tyilly over the top of his reading glasses.

"I believe I can take care of my books, Tyilly."

She nodded at him.

"Yes, Master Ilisti. It's just … I've set out a bit of a spread. It may be faster for you to come down and select what you want to eat, and then I'll bring it up."

The historian sighed, but Phana stood up and stretched. She didn't understand why Tyilly wanted to serve them in the dining room, but perhaps this was just her way of regaining some control over the household. And Phana didn't want to battle with the woman.

"I could use the break, honestly. And I'd like to stretch my legs."

Master Ilisti waved Phana toward the door.

"Please take whatever time you need, my dear. Tyilly, please just prepare a plate and bring it up here. I'm going to keep working."

Tyilly's eyes glanced in Phana's direction and then flicked back to her employer.

"Yes, Master Ilisti."

She turned and walked back into the hallway, and Phana followed her. As they walked down the stairs to the ground floor, the woman's head kept twitching sideways, as if she wanted to turn to face Phana but was forcing herself not to look back.

Phana ignored the serving woman's behavior. Tyilly was obviously still angry at Phana's presence and was trying to ignore her … or something. She didn't feel like trying to unravel the other woman's issues.

As they approached the doorway to the large dining room, Tyilly fluttered her hand in that direction.

"The food is in the dining room," she said, her voice nearly squeaking. Then she picked up her pace, hurrying past the door toward the kitchen as if she was afraid Phana was going to knife her in the back.

Phana watched the woman go and frowned at Tyilly's rapidly receding back. She reached the door and stepped into the dining room. And stopped.

A woman was seated at the far end of the dining table, facing Phana. Beside her stood a man in the robes of a priest.

They were obviously waiting for her.

She looked at the woman's face and gasped ….

She stands on a stone platform above a crowd of men and women kneeling on the ground, their arms stretched out as they bow up and down, chanting in a tongue she can almost understand. To Phana's left, a beautiful woman—her friend, her lover, her family—stands beside her, a golden goblet in her right hand. Assirra's long blond hair stirs in the cool breeze coming across the clearing as she takes a sip from the goblet.

Phana turns to look out over the heads of the worshippers and sees a thick forest ringing the clearing in which sits the sacrificial altar. The torches mounted on spears throw flickering light over the kneeling supplicants.

Assirra hands the goblet to Phana, and she takes a sip of the dark liquid, the copper taste filling her mouth. She swallows and the liquid burns pleasantly as it slides down her throat. This is something special that Assirra brews when it is time for the rites.

Phana hands the goblet back to her companion and wipes her hands on her long white gown. She grips the sides and lifts it over her head, tossing it aside as she stands naked before her worshippers.

"Shall we begin?" Assirra asks her.

Phana nods.

"It's time to reap," she replies with a smile.

Phana felt her balance give out as the floor tilted under her. She lurched forward and grabbed the back of a chair to steady herself.

"Hello … Phana," the other woman said in a voice that was low and throaty. Phana felt passion well up within her, but it was quickly overwhelmed by a surge of hatred toward this woman that boiled her blood.

"You … you're the woman in my memories."

She did not know *why* she hated this woman, only that it was immense and consuming.

"I am Assirra Untoleu. I have been searching for you for a very long time. I'm here to help you."

The other man, the priest, was holding himself rigid, as if afraid to call attention to himself. Phana looked into Assirra's eyes and was acutely aware of that great black curtain in her own mind. She believed her memories were on the other side of that curtain. Everything she had seen. Everything she *was*.

"Help me how? Can you restore my memories?"

Assirra smiled at Phana, but there was no warmth in her eyes. They were cold, calculating. Phana knew she couldn't trust her.

"I can help you … recover … much of who you were. What was done to you … I do not know if I can show you … everything."

"You're not the first to be 'worried' about my memories. About what was done to me. But no one seems to want to tell me *who* did it."

Assirra frowned.

"Who *was* the first to be worried, Phana?"

Phana said nothing. If this woman was there in her past, then she likely knew of Yarrian. And he was concerned about his identity being known by those who lived in Ythis.

"The Wolf?" Assirra asked. "Was he the catalyst for the return of your past?"

"Yes," Phana lied. She had no loyalty to the Wolf anymore. She didn't have any loyalty to Yarrian, either, though she remembered fighting at his side, at least.

"How much has come back to you?"

Phana considered how much to tell this woman. She decided to ignore the question and ask one of her own.

"Whose memories are they? And how did they get into my head?"

Assirra's frown was replaced by a radiant smile. She was unnaturally beautiful when she smiled, and once again Phana felt lust stirring in her heart. She ignored it.

"They are *your* memories, Phana. You lived through the events you see in your mind, just as I did."

She put a delicate hand on her chest.

"I am not fully human, my dear. I am more than human, and I am *ancient.*"

She reached out her hand in a gesture to Phana.

"And so are you."

*   *   *

LAITA PULLED THE DIRTY CLOAK AROUND HER SHOULDERS AND drew the wig over her hair. Midday had just passed, and it was time to return to the Wandering Horse and see what the priests had decided. If Oriuna was there when she entered, then she would know they had agreed to only require her own life as insurance.

If a priest was waiting for her ....

There was no guarantee of anything if the priests had decided to take an active hand in dealing with her. It might mean Oriuna was dead and the priests were there to capture Laita and turn her over to the Legion. It might mean they intended to intimidate her into agreeing with their demands. It might mean they had agreed to hers and wanted to conduct whatever ritual they were going to perform to bind her to her oath right then and there.

It's impossible to predict the actions of the mad, she thought to herself.

She left the room and snuck up the stairs and out of the inn, avoiding the staff and the few guests who had not left the city to avoid the oppressive dread that continued to increase each night.

The streets were busy, and she blended in easily as she headed toward the section of the city where Oriuna had set herself up. The heat of the day was at its peak and Laita sweated under her thick wig. She hated the thing—it clung to her skull and trapped the heat—and she felt almost claustrophobic under it at times.

But it also helped protect her identity, and she couldn't move about Ythis freely without both it and the dirty clothes she had been given. No one looked twice at her when she walked the streets of the city. She was just another poor and wretched figure in a city full of them.

It took her less than a full bell to cross the distance between the White Eagle Inn and the street where the Wandering Horse Tavern crouched in its nondescript nook. As she turned the corner, she spotted Saeda—also in disguise as a simple servant—hurrying toward her on the street. Saeda spotted her, and Laita glanced over at the mouth of an alley between two buildings just ahead of her.

Saeda slowed and let Laita reach the alley mouth first. Laita slipped inside and moved down from the main street into the dim shadows. A minute later, Saeda turned and entered the alley. Her step quickened as she moved to Laita.

"We have an emergency," she said in a low voice as soon as she was near. "The Imperial Guard just raided the tenement where we were storing our weapons."

Ice water ran down Laita's spine.

"How do you know this?"

"I was on my way there. Another few minutes, and I would have been inside when they arrived. A force of about twenty soldiers rode up in those transport wagons they have. Some went down the alley around the back while another group smashed in the boards over the front door and entered the building."

"Bor?" Laita asked.

"I don't know. They left a handful outside and I didn't think it wise to get any closer. I kept walking so as not to draw attention to myself, so I couldn't wait around to see if they brought anyone out. I figured I should find you as quickly as possible."

Laita's mind raced. How could the Guard have found the building? *Irako.*

He hadn't shown up to meet Namal yesterday ….

"Namal! He was going to find Irako at his apartment."

The look of horror on Saeda's face told her she had just come to the same conclusion.

"What do we do, commander?"

"We need to warn the others. If Irako was captured, he's going to reveal everything he knows—he won't be able to resist their torturers. That means the Guard now has the tenement with our equipment, at least two or three locations where our soldiers are staying, and ...."

She looked Saeda in the eyes as it hit her.

"The entire Rebellion. He knows their identities, all of them."

Saeda glanced back at the mouth of the alley and back to Laita.

"That includes Oriuna. The Guard could be on their way here right now."

Laita motioned for Saeda to follow and she turned toward the other end of the alley and began to walk.

"It may already be too late, Saeda. If the Guard just hit the tenement, they'll have split their forces to hit the others at the same time, so that if someone escapes, that person won't have time to warn anyone else."

"If I remember correctly, Irako will know the location of about thirty to forty of our people. The rest were either settled by Bor and me, or as part of our agreement with the Wolf."

Laita pulled up short and turned to face Saeda.

"The Wolf. We're assuming Irako was captured, but what if the Wolf turned us in? He knows far more of our locations than Irako does. If this is his doing, then the bulk of our people are in immediate danger."

Saeda's skin was white in the shadows of the alley, as if all her blood had been drained.

"Commander, if that's the case, then we're finished."

"Not necessarily. There are a limited number of Imperial Guards and no Legion soldiers to back them up. I would guess they have a hundred, perhaps as many as one hundred and fifty. They must split their forces to make sure they throw an overwhelming force at each location. Assuming they're splitting up into standard squads, say three squads each gives us about twenty-four soldiers per group."

"So they can hit four to six locations at once."

Laita nodded.

"I'm guessing here, but the numbers make sense. They'll want to capture instead of kill, so they can torture the prisoners and get more information. That takes more time, which gives us a window to warn the others."

"Where do you want me, commander?"

"Start with the closest locations and work outward. You go southwest and I'll go southeast. As we reach our people, get them to spread the word as well. Give each runner a single location to warn, so we keep our security, just in case anyone gets picked up on the street."

She considered her options.

"Tell each group to find somewhere new to hide for the rest of the day and overnight. Tomorrow, each group should send a single soldier to the area in the northwest corner of the Market square. I'll have someone ready to make contact there and give them further instructions."

Saeda saluted Laita, obviously forgetting where they were.

"Careful," Laita reminded her. "I know this is frightening, but we need to keep our wits about us. It's the only way out of this, and the only way to save our people."

Saeda lowered her head.

"I apologize. I forgot—"

"No need—or time—for that. Just be careful. Now go."

Saeda left the alley, heading down toward the Bay of Ythis. Laita glanced back at the other end of the alley, leading out onto the street where Oriuna might be sitting in the tavern, waiting for her. She had the opportunity to warn the other woman.

Of course, Oriuna might not even be there. And if a priest was waiting for Laita, it might be a whole different threat. Then again, if Oriuna was captured, she would eventually reveal the role of the Church in this affair, which could lead to even greater problems for Ythis.

You don't have time to reason out all the possibilities, she reminded herself. *You must make a decision and act.*

Her ultimate responsibility was to her people. And her people were being rounded up by the Imperial Guard.

Turning her back on the far end of the alley, she stepped out onto the street and headed in the direction of the closest group of her soldiers.

Chapter Thirty-Eight

T HE WORDS HIT PHANA LIKE A HAMMER TO HER CHEST. Her heart was racing, and she felt the strength draining out of her legs. She pulled the chair out from the table and slid into it. At the other end of the table, Assirra and the priest watched her calmly.

"No," she said in a whisper.

"Tell your brother I will kill him if I see him again," the big man rumbles. Assirra stands in front of him, proud and beautiful.

They stand in the foothills of a vast mountain range, the peaks soaring above them into a blue sky that seems somehow muted compared to where they had just been.

"He did what any of us would have done, given time," Assirra snarls back at him.

Phana stands to one side, watching. She is angry with Assirra's brother … Ashiru. He is the cause of their fall from grace. But she cannot blame the woman in front of her. They have been so close for so many years.

The big man growls at Assirra and she takes a step back.

"You damn us all, and refuse to learn the lesson of our banishment. Perhaps in time, the two of you will see the truth, while the rest of us share in your punishment."

Assirra looks at him and raises her chin, as if looking down on him though in truth he towers over her.

"We will stay out of your way, and you can stay out of ours, Rotos. But don't presume to give us orders or tell us how to live

our lives. What we do with the people of this world is none of your concern."

Assirra turns away from the man—Phana realizes his name is Rotos and that she has always known this—and as she does so Assirra vanishes from sight.

"Well," she says. "We've lost our home and we're back where we started."

Yarrian steps between her and Rotos and rests a hand on each of their arms.

"No," he says to the two of them. "This was our home. It's where we came from. I feel the loss as much as anyone, but we still live. And we have a whole world out there. Let us go, let us travel across this world. There are many places we have never seen, and we have as much time as we need."

Rotos considers his suggestion and then nods at Yarrian. Phana is still angry, but she also realizes she had been bored in their city. A paradise is not what she has ever wanted. This world at least presents opportunity for … amusement.

"Yes, I will come with you," she says. "And there is no way to ever go back there, anyway."

She sees a look on Rotos' face as he glances at the mountains. She can tell he knows something. But it doesn't matter right now. There is adventure to be had.

"No!" she shouted as the memory released her.

Assirra raised her hands, palms toward her.

"Please, do not be afraid. I am not here to hurt you. You have been through so much already. Do you not remember me as a friend?"

Phana *did* remember the bond between the two of them, but for some reason she also hated the other woman. There was no memory to go along with that feeling, however. Whatever Assirra had done to her to make her feel this way, the memory of it was still buried.

"Yes, I do remember us being together as companions," she said tentatively. She had no intention of revealing to the other woman her true feelings.

At least, not yet.

"You say we're not fully human. What are we? Who am I, really?"

Assirra lowered her hands to the table and gave Phana another of her cold smiles.

"I want to tell you everything. But as I said, we must go slowly. What did the Wolf do to you? How much do you remember?"

She shook her head, playing up her confusion, buying herself time to think this through.

"It's all so jumbled, coming in flashes. I don't ... I didn't have any memories older than about two or three years ago. I was looking for help."

She looked Assirra in the eyes.

"How did you find me? Was it the—?"

She waved her hands without specifying what she meant. As if she expected Assirra to know exactly to what she was referring. She wanted to see how much Assirra knew about her before she revealed anything else.

"Yes, Phana. When you used your ... power ... it called to me. I couldn't believe it was you at first, but I knew it had originated from within Ythis. So I began to search for you."

"You ... you're part of the Church," she said slowly. "Are there more like me, like us, in the Church?"

Assirra looked at her and Phana saw her eyes narrow ever so slightly. She could tell the other woman didn't really trust her. And Phana was asking more questions than she was answering.

"There are few of us left," Assirra told her. "Many of the others are dead. Who do you remember?"

Again, Assirra was pushing to know how much of her memory she had recovered. She decided to give the other woman something so that she could continue to push her own questions.

"I remember a huge man with dark gray hair. And another man, always dressed in dark clothing. I remember you and I being together as people knelt around us."

Assirra smiled and it was the first expression that looked genuine.

"It was a simpler time, then. Before we were given the city—"

The smile disappeared as she stopped. Phana wasn't sure which city Assirra meant and wondered if it was the one she had thought about in the memory that had just come back to her. A city that was supposed to be some sort of paradise. A city created just for them.

"What city?" she asked Assirra. "Ythis?"

Assirra looked at her, but kept her own face blank.

"Perhaps it's best if we work our way to that. I expect it may be too much, too quickly. I don't want to cause you any more distress than you have already experienced."

She leaned forward.

"What happened when you met the Wolf? What did he say to you? Did your memories start coming back right away?"

She paused, not sure what to say. This woman obviously knew the Wolf, and anything further she said might reveal the lie. She now wanted to go talk with Yarrian and find out what he knew about Assirra. But she expected the woman would not let her so easily leave now that she had been found.

Still, she had to say something. She decided to tell the truth, but alter and leave out some details.

"I wanted to meet the Wolf, hoping that he might be able to tell me something about myself. They say he knows more secrets than there are stars in the sky. I thought he might know who I was, or who my family had been. But getting to see him was more difficult than I expected it to be."

She took a deep breath, as if this was difficult for her to explain.

"That night, when I finally met … him … I fainted. A jumble of memories came flooding into my mind. I didn't wake up until the next morning."

Assirra was watching her face carefully. She knew she had to be cautious about what she revealed.

"That memory of you and me with the people kneeling around us … that was the first thing that came back. And a memory of living in a great tower with the large man and the other one. But none of it made sense."

"And what else has come back since then?"

"More of the same, really. When I first saw you, just now, I remembered traveling in the foothills of some mountains with those two men. But it was just that, walking through the wilderness with the peaks above us."

Assirra waited for her to explain further, but she put a hand to her head and grimaced, as if thinking about it gave her a headache.

"Phana, I am here to help you. I am a powerful figure in the Church. You have nothing to fear from them. Come with me, and I can help you. Just you and I."

A feeling of dread and revulsion filled her heart. She knew it came from a memory that she couldn't recall, this anger and fear toward the other woman. But it was real.

Assirra was the enemy. And she had the power of the Church behind her.

"I ... I don't know if I'm ready to do that yet," she said in a small voice. "Something was done to me, that much I know. Some*one* did this to me, took my memories from me. I don't know who I can trust."

Assirra looked at the priest beside her.

"Leave us," she ordered. "Close the doors."

He looked from Assirra to Phana and back again. He opened his mouth as if to protest, but then closed it and nodded. He turned and went out into the main foyer, pulling the dining room doors closed as he left.

Assirra watched the priest leave and then turned back to her. She got up and walked over to the other end of the table where Phana was sitting. She sat down beside her and spoke in a low voice that wouldn't carry through the doors into the hallway.

"You and I were ... we were family. We were ... lovers. We did great things together and we reveled in our power. We were worshiped and we were feared, and it was wondrous."

She heard Assirra's words and knew they were true.

"But I did something terrible. I caused us all to lose access to a place that was created just for us. It was a mistake, and one I've regretted for countless years. For centuries. You and I ... well, it was difficult for anyone to forgive me. And I don't blame you or the others for that. But I lost you. I've tried to make amends, but our people scattered after that and then ...."

She waited but Assirra didn't continue.

"What are we?" she asked the other woman. "I need to know who I am."

Assirra took a breath and laid her hand on Phana's thigh. Her touch was electric and once again she felt that surge of lust.

"We were here before the founding of the Empire. We were here even before the coming of the new gods. That war, when the old gods were driven out and the new gods took our world—we watched it happen. We were many in those days, and we fought the invaders on behalf of the old gods. But most of us were slaughtered. There are only a handful who remain now."

She could feel the ice in her core responding to Assirra's words. She didn't want to believe it, but she knew it was true. But it was only part of the story.

"Back in the early days," Assirra continued, "the old gods would manifest avatars of flesh and blood. The rites of worship gave mortals the chance to touch the very essence of the old gods. And sometimes, a woman would come away from that encounter with a child in her belly. If she was very strong, and the stars were right, she and the child would survive through the pregnancy. And a child of the gods would be born into this world."

Her heart was beating like a wild thing. She didn't want to hear this, but couldn't stop Assirra's words from penetrating her mind and driving into her thoughts. This was beyond anything she could have possibly imagined.

She wanted to believe Assirra was lying to her. But the way the cold in her blood was responding, she knew it was all true. And the knowledge of it filled her with despair. Everything she knew about her recent life was all just a charade.

Even her relationship with Koral was built on nothing but smoke and lies.

"You see now why we fought on the side of the old gods. They were … they are … our parents."

"You said the old gods were driven out. I thought they were destroyed."

"That is the Church's official story. But they are out there, somewhere. Locked away from this world, certainly. If they could reach anyone on this world, it would be us. But there has been nothing, all this time."

"You … you *work* for the Church."

"Yes, I do. You don't remember the founding of the Empire. The new gods were … they fed on us indiscriminately. They wiped out entire civilizations. The original purpose of the Church was to … contain them. Give them a reason to allow humans to survive. Give them what they needed, satiate them. I believed in that purpose, and I still do. I didn't want to see all life on this world consumed. So I joined the Church. I founded a sect within the Church that does not commune with the gods, so that my priests are not driven mad. With this, I can limit the worst excesses of the Church, and no one questions my loyalty."

She looked at Assirra and had a nearly overwhelming urge to grab the other woman by the throat and choke the life from her. She didn't know if Assirra was lying, or if she believed this justification of her actions ….

But what had Assirra done? That was still maddeningly blank. Her mind went back to the memory of the battle on the plains before their tower. What was the cause of that black cloud that had rolled over her? She felt that was the moment she had lost who she was.

Was it Assirra who had done that? Were they already at war with one another?

Assirra stood up and turned her back on Phana, slowly pacing across the room before turning back to her.

"It has been a very long and difficult time. But I have done what I could. I did not know who survived, mostly. On rare occasions I would feel someone use their abilities, somewhere out there in the world. But I couldn't leave to find them, and as I said, most still held a grudge against me."

"Is that why I hate you?" she asked Assira. She hadn't meant to blurt it out, but the disgust she was feeling at Assirra's words had overwhelmed her caution.

Assira paused, facing her.

"You hate me," Assira said, and her voice was flat. "But you do not even know why."

"I know much of what you told me was true," she said, also standing. "But I also know that you … you are trying to manipulate me."

As she said the words, she realized that, too, was true. That was what the ice in her blood was trying to tell her. She hadn't been doing it consciously, but she was resisting Assirra. The other woman was trying to do something to her with her words.

Assira was trying to seduce her. It was … what she could do.

And the woman realized at the same moment that her ploy hadn't worked.

"You try to justify what you've done," Phana said to her. "But it's really just about you. You'll do anything to be the one holding the reins of power, won't you?"

She was surprised when Assirra laughed in her face.

"Oh, Phana. You have no right to judge me. I have saved countless lives by my actions. You would have let it all burn and reveled in the death and destruction."

Assirra stepped forward.

"Your memories haven't yet revealed to you who you really are, have they? Rotos may have been the Warlord, the commander of armies and the facilitator of endless battles and wars between the peoples of this world. But at least what he did was practical. You … you *enjoyed* it. Your endless violence was purely for your own pleasure."

She wanted to deny Assirra's words, but her throat wouldn't let her speak. She could see it coming, and was powerless to stop it.

"Phana isn't your real name, of course. I don't know when that was applied to you. No, your real name is Issra. But I think perhaps you should be called by your title."

For the third time, Assirra gave Phana that cold smile.

"You were known as the Reaper."

She gasped as her blood surged in response to the title.

Issra dances among the worshippers, her blades flashing. Blood sprays across the clearing as she slices through flesh, carving out organs and throwing them up to the sky in an offering to her father and the other gods.

She laughs and grabs a mortal, sinking her teeth into the woman's neck and tearing a great chunk free. The woman screams, no longer caught up in the power of the rite and suddenly aware of her pain and the rapid approach of her death. Her torn artery fountains blood into the air, and Issra spits out the woman's flesh and bathes in the stream of warm liquid.

Dropping the woman, Issra turns to the others and raises her arms above her head, howling in pleasure. She eviscerates a man and grabs his head so that she can watch the dawning horror in his eyes as his mind is released from the ritual and he comes back to himself. She drops her knives and drives her thumbs into his eye sockets as he screams.

Issra turns and sees Assirra on the stone platform. Their eyes meet.

"Join me!" Issra calls to the other woman. "Join me!"

She grabbed her head and screamed as the memories, the sensations, the *joy* came back to her in a rush.

At the sound of the doors to the dining room being yanked open, she opened her eyes to see the priest from before, a second man in priest's robes, and a half-dozen Church soldiers ready to leap in between her and Assirra.

But Assirra held up her hand to forestall their interference.

"I offer you help, Reaper. I give you this chance. Last time you were a fool, and you have paid for your rebellion for centuries. But now you will submit to me. Refuse, and this time I will take far more than just your memories."

She could feel the cold in her blood bubbling up, and tried to release it. But something stopped it. She couldn't summon it to the surface. She turned to Assirra and the other woman was watching her but didn't seem worried.

She knew that if she allowed the Church to take her, she would become Assirra's slave. And she refused to be a slave to anyone.

But without the power of the ice inside her, she couldn't fight her way free of all these people.

She acted as soon as the thought came to her, moving before anyone could guess what she was going to do. The heavy draperies were closed even here, and she didn't know exactly where the windows pierced the outer wall. But she had no choice.

She was running across the room before anyone could react. She heard Assirra shout as Phana leaped and flung herself at where she hoped a window hid behind the curtain.

Her body hit the drapery and then there was the sound of shattering glass and she fell through the opening. The drapery protected her from the broken glass, but it got caught up on the shards and she was left hanging in a pocket on the outside of the wall.

She could hear the soldiers rushing toward her across the dining room. She grabbed her knife and yanked it out of its sheath. Stabbing it through the drapery, she ripped it downward, opening a hole for her to slither out of her trap as if she was being born once again. She hit the dirt of the flowerbed below the window.

An instant later, she was on her feet and past the gate. She saw another group of Church guards approaching from a side street, so she spun in the opposite direction and ran away from the guards, from Assirra, and from the house of the historian who had tried to help her.

*   *   *

BOR WATCHED THE THREE SOLDIERS LEAVE THE ROOM AND THEN he turned back to the crate. It was boring, repetitive work, but he knew what he was doing was vital. While he could have tasked anyone with distributing the weapons and armor, he wanted the soldiers to have a chance to talk to someone from the command squad.

Most of the young men and women who came here to collect their equipment had little to say. He forced himself to make some small talk with them, to ask them how they were holding up, if they were getting enough food, and so forth. He could see in their eyes that it made a difference to them, that it helped them feel connected to the rest of the force while they hid in isolation.

Others had an endless supply of questions for him. He couldn't them any details about the mission, of course, but he provided them with what they really needed—reassurances. As long as they knew the commander was out there planning the mission, making arrangements, looking out for them, they would be okay.

And then, despite all his preparations, all his training, when the shout came he stood there stupidly for a moment, waiting for another sound, another alert to tell him it was real and not just a mistake.

The man's scream—clearly someone in terrible pain—finally got him moving. He slipped his arm through the straps of a shield and grabbed the nearest sword, and then moved to the doorway as more shouting came from downstairs.

They were being attacked.

"Form up on me!" he shouted, as the three soldiers in the other rooms on this level emerged into the hallway. He heard the pair of soldiers on the floor above coming down and moved to the head of the staircase leading down to the ground floor.

The door crashed open and he saw a cluster of armed men and women on the other side.

"Imperial Guard! Surrender at once!"

The Guard soldiers boiled through the door, and Bor heard the sounds of battle as the four soldiers on the ground floor engaged the invaders.

How did they find us? he thought, and then pushed that away and focused on the situation in front of him. If the Guard was here, then the building was surrounded. The weapons and armor were certainly lost, and now the only goal was to save as many of his people as possible.

"The roof!" he ordered to the soldiers behind him, not loud enough for the Guard soldiers below to hear. "Scatter to the adjoining buildings and try to get free. Alert any other soldiers you can find."

They looked at him, their eyes wide, as the Guard began to ascend the stairs toward him.

"Go!"

All but one bolted for the stairs to the upper level. This young man, Ludhon, shook his head.

"They need more time. I'm with you."

Bor gave him a quick nod and crouched, using his shield to protect his legs. The Guard soldiers could only come up the narrow stairs one at a time, and would be facing two opponents on solid footing. They paused, halfway up the staircase.

"You cannot escape," the man in the lead said to him, not unkindly. "Surrender and you'll survive this day. You'll get a trial and maybe the Magistrates will take mercy on you."

"I can't do that," Bor replied.

"We already have soldiers on the other rooftops. No one is getting free, and we do not need to rush. Save yourself and drop your weapons."

Bor looked at Ludhon, and the young man met his eyes.

"If I get wounded, you have to kill me."

"What?"

"I can't be captured. Do you understand? If I go down, you have to finish me. The mission depends on it."

He could see the fear in Ludhon's eyes. The soldier had wanted to be brave and support his commanding officer in a fight, but it had just become much larger than that.

Bor silently cursed his choice to protect the others. He should have prioritized his own escape, because he knew too much. If he was captured, the Inquisitors would get everything from him.

At least I don't know where the commander is hiding.

Still, he knew the locations of at least five other buildings where soldiers were staying. His decision to stay and delay the Guard could cost the lives of far more than he had just "saved."

The sounds of battle on the ground floor had ceased, and Bor knew that those soldiers were either captured or, more likely, dead. He gripped his sword and turned back to the man waiting below him.

"I'm prepared to die. Are you?"

The man grinned up at him.

"Then let's see what you've got."

He moved up the stairs, the others holding back and giving him room. But a crash from above interrupted his advance.

A single shout, suddenly cut off, and then the thump of booted feet hitting the floor above.

The man on the stairs looked disappointed as Bor realized that more Imperial Guard soldiers had just breached the building from the roof.

Whether the others had escaped or not, Bor was now in even greater danger of being captured. They could rush him with their shields and pin him to the wall, preventing him from fighting.

As the Guard soldiers came down the other staircase in a rush, Bor dropped his sword and drew his dagger. He put the point over his own heart and the man below him opened his mouth as he realized what Bor intended.

"Make sure I die!" he ordered Ludhon as he tightened his grip and took his final breath.

Chapter Thirty-Nine

I T WAS OVER.

The mission, the rebellion, was finished.

Laita stood and watched the handful of Imperial Guard soldiers standing near the wagons as the rest of their force flooded through the tenement, grabbing her people. The sounds of fighting from inside the building came to her and she clenched her jaw as she heard a woman scream.

In moments, the clash of swords on shields began to subside, until she heard no more. It was over. Those who had fought back were most likely dead, and the rest were in the hands of the Empire.

She felt tears welling in her eyes and she withdrew back into the alley from which she had watched it all happen. A dozen minutes, that was all she needed and her soldiers in that building would have been gone by the time the Guard had arrived. But she had missed her chance.

A dozen minutes.

Blinking back her tears, she spun on her heel and headed back to the last cross-street. There were still others nearby and perhaps she could save them. She knew she was risking everything by going herself. If she was inside one of the locations when the Guard arrived, she would be captured as well.

Unless I fight back and make them kill me, she thought.

She considered the option. If she died in a raid, the Imperial Guard would likely relax in their efforts to find every last one of her people. She knew there was no love lost between the Legion and the Guard. They wouldn't care about people they considered simple deserters.

And it would be a slap in the face of the Legion if a bunch of soldiers were never captured.

Still, she wasn't ready to sacrifice herself just yet. Her people still needed her, and she would do everything she could to save as many of them as possible.

And then what?

There was no way to accomplish her mission now. She expected the Imperial Guard would round up the members of the Resistance. Her heart hurt to think of Galla in the clutches of an Inquisitor. Tasius would likely take his own life rather than let himself be captured. Ennius and Zita would not fare well, and Xuthos … if she was being honest with herself, she couldn't bring herself to care too much about his fate.

But Irako, the thought of him a prisoner of the Guard pierced her to her core. He was a good man, and he deserved better than torture and inevitable execution. Of course, if he hadn't been captured, it meant the Wolf had betrayed her, and even more of her people were at risk.

As she walked quickly along the side street, she saw a couple of servants looking at her and moving to give her a wide berth as she passed. For a moment, she worried that they had seen through her disguise.

But then she realized her jaw and her fists were all clenched, and she was walking as if marching to a battle. She slowed her pace, slumped her shoulders and forced her face and hands to relax. The last thing she needed right now was to draw attention or arouse suspicion.

How many of her people were going to be taken today? How many would die fighting back? Those who had already received their equipment would be more likely to resist. But it was only a matter of time before they were overwhelmed by superior numbers. The Imperial Guard would simply fall back and maintain a perimeter around a building until more of their force could arrive from other locations.

Any resistance her soldiers put up would be temporary and achieve nothing.

Right now, it was vital to get the word out and get her people away from their current hiding places. She had no doubt that more would be rounded up throughout the evening and overnight. There were many places to hide in the city for a small handful of people. But she had almost two hundred. They would no doubt draw attention, and the Imperial Guard would immediately mobilize at any rumor of something suspicious.

By tomorrow, there was no way to guess how many would be prisoners of the Guard, or dead.

Furthermore, the Guard now knew about her mission. Security around the Emperor would be doubled or tripled. The Palace would become another Fortress. And if Oriuna was captured, they would soon discover her plan to enter the Palace through the tunnels.

There was no way to succeed anymore. She needed the members of the Resistance to help her. She needed Oriuna and the Church. It was all gone, disappearing like smoke.

Had they ever really had a chance? Or was this all just a futile gesture, driven by her desire for revenge?

She turned the corner of a cross-street and saw another set of small apartments above a row of shops where two squads were currently being housed. She looked around, but the traffic on this street seemed normal—regular people out on their daily errands.

She moved to a flight of wooden stairs at one end of the row and ascended to the rickety walkway that ran the length of the rear of the building. She knocked on the first door and waited, listening for the sound of wagons coming in this direction.

"Yeah?" said a muffled voice from the other side. She put her face up to the edge of the door.

"It's Commander Naschect," she said in a low voice.

There was a pause. Laita expected they were probably expecting a knock in a particular pattern, but she didn't know the codes—she had always accompanied Saeda to visit the soldiers, and her aide knew all the codes.

"It's an emergency," she said to the door. "I don't know the code."

"Don't know any Naschect," said the voice.

"Soldier, open this fucking door or I will kick it down!" she commanded, using her normal voice. There was no time for subtlety or secrecy anymore.

The young man on the other side pulled it open a crack and peered out. Laita yanked off her wig and revealed herself. The man's eyes went wide at the site of her.

"The Imperial Guard are coming for us," she told him, and she heard a gasp from further inside. She stepped forward and shoved the young soldier backward so she could open the door and see the others.

"One of our people was captured, and we're all compromised. You need to get out of here right now. The Imperial Guard could arrive at any time. Find a place to hide until tomorrow. Then one of you come to the northwest corner of the main market square tomorrow at noon and we'll make contact."

The handful of soldiers in the room looked at her with blank expressions, as if it were all too much to take in at once.

"Move!" she commanded them, and they snapped out of it and began to grab some possessions.

"Take only what you can carry openly without calling attention to yourselves."

She turned to the young man who opened the door.

"You know the code. Go alert the others on this row, right now."

He saluted and hurried out and down the walkway to the next door.

"What are we going to do?" one of the soldiers asked her.

"There's no time for that. Get out of here and hide somewhere else. I'll give you all further instructions tomorrow."

She grabbed two soldiers who were ready to go.

"I need the two of you to help alert others."

She pulled one of the soldiers to the side and gave her instructions to another location, before sending her on her way. Then she did the same with the second soldier.

Turning to look down the walkway, Laita was relieved to see her people filing out of multiple apartments and heading toward the staircases at either end of the row.

"Stay safe," she said to those in the first room who were now ready to leave.

She placed her wig back on her head, draped her shawl over her hair, and then returned to the stairs and descended to the street. There was still no sign of the Guard. Perhaps this was not one of their target locations, or they were too tied up at others.

She thought again of the fighting she had heard at the last building. How many lives had they possibly saved by delaying the Guard with their resistance? She was determined not to let their sacrifice be in vain.

Laita left the street and headed to the next location, in a race against time.

Over the next two hours, Laita reached three more buildings and warned the soldiers there, pulling two from each location to go warn others. She figured by this point that she was probably overlapping with Saeda, but she wasn't going to risk missing anyone.

She was deep in the Warren, somewhere near the shore of the Bay of Ythis by the smell of saltwater in the air. There were no other hideouts near here, and nothing further east.

For the first time, she considered what to do next. Could she return to the White Eagle Inn? Only a few of her people knew about it. But she was only confident that Saeda was still free.

Namal might have been taken when he went to check on Irako. Keynter was back with his original squad, and they had not been one of the groups Laita had spoken to today. And she didn't know if Addiru or Pilayni were at the building where they were storing their weapons when the Imperial Guard soldiers arrived.

Her thoughts turned to Bor. He had been staying at that building around the clock as he was responsible for distributing the gear to everyone. There was little chance that he had escaped. He was either in custody of the Guard, or he was dead.

Laita had to swallow down a sob as she thought of him dying under the swords of the Guard soldiers. He had shown such faith in her. This is how she had repaid him.

Which brought her full circle to the White Eagle Inn. Bor hadn't know about the inn, nor had the rest of the command squad. And Laita thought about Cedaro, another good man who didn't deserve to be captured or killed by the Guard.

She couldn't simply leave him to his fate. She had to warn him, at least. That meant going back to the inn and hoping the Guard wasn't keeping it under surveillance, waiting for her return.

It took her a while to reach the area north of the market square where Cedaro had his inn. As she approached, she felt her whole body tensing up. If she was going to be captured today, this was the most likely place for it to happen.

She decided to walk past the inn and see if she could spot any watchers. She proceeded up the street and was about to pass an alley when she heard three low whistles coming from above. She shuffled toward the alley and then ducked into the opening.

Looking up, she saw Pilayni crouched on the roof of the one-story building beside her. Pilayni lowered a rope and climbed down to the floor of the alley.

Laita couldn't help herself. She grabbed the young woman and hugged her tightly.

"Commander," Pilayni whispered, and Laita heard the raw emotion in her voice.

Letting Pilayni go, Laita stepped back and took a deep breath.

"I'm so glad to see you're okay," she told her.

Pilayni smiled sadly.

"We were so worried that you had been captured, commander. That would have been the end of us."

Laita tried not to think that the events of this afternoon already *were* the end of them. She was still free, still alive, and so were many of her soldiers. And there was still a great deal of work to be done to keep them that way.

"What's happened around here?"

"Saeda got word to us at one of the hideouts. Addiru and I have been watching the inn for the last couple of hours. No one suspicious has come near. If there *is* a spy watching the building, he must be invisible."

"Namal?" she asked, dreading the answer.

"He came by less than half a bell ago."

Laita nearly gasped as her heart gave a great lurch. Namal was still alive and hadn't been captured. The relief from the news nearly knocked her off her feet.

"I spoke to him. He said Irako was taken by some disguised soldiers yesterday afternoon. Namal tried to reach you here, but you had already left to meet with Oriuna."

"Where is he now?"

"He went back out to check that all of our hideouts were abandoned. I think he also wanted to see if he could find you."

"That's what I've been doing for the last couple of hours, myself. I think we've reached everyone we could. Any further word from Saeda?"

Pilayni shook her head.

"She hasn't been here since we started watching."

"Keynter?"

"No, commander. I haven't seen him. But he'd most likely stay with his own squad, wouldn't he?"

"I expect so. But he's the one other person who knows where we were staying. I passed by the building where his squad was holed up. I didn't see any signs that they were captured, but there's no guarantee he's not in custody."

Laita looked over at the inn, looking peaceful in the afternoon sunlight.

"I need to go inside and talk to Cedaro. I need to warn him."

"Commander, I should go instead. If the Guard does show up here, and you're inside …."

"There's no way for you to warn me. I understand. But Cedaro took care of me for years. I can't send someone else to tell him he might in danger that I brought to his doorstep."

"You can't risk it, commander. Everyone is relying on you. Especially now that they are actively hunting us. We need you more than ever. Only you can get us out of this mess."

Laita tried to dismiss Pilayni's words, but the other woman had a point. She had a responsibility to Cedaro, certainly, but she also had a greater responsibility to her own soldiers. They had followed her here to Ythis.

As much as she wanted to see Cedaro, to apologize to him for getting him into this mess, she couldn't risk her own life. Pilayni could warn him as well as she could. And the horrible reality was that Pilayni was expendable, at least when it came to Laita's survival.

She hated the reality of the truth, but she couldn't deny it. A good commander needs to recognize their importance, even if they don't revel in it.

"Then get over there and tell him what danger he is in. And then get back out. As much as you need me, I need all of you."

Pilayni grabbed Laita in a quick hug, and then stepped back and saluted. Before Laita could say another word, she was gone.

*   *   *

THE BLOOD WELLED UP AS THE PRIEST'S TEETH SANK INTO THE flesh of his own fingers, the skin tearing, his lips pulled back in a rictus grin.

Relael motioned for two of the Church soldiers to help him as he grabbed the priest's arm and tried to pull the man's hand free from his own jaws. The priest let out a low, panting moan as he tore at his flesh, his eyes bulging from their sockets.

The soldiers grabbed the priest and held him, but Relael realized that pulling the priest's arm would end up tearing his fingers from his hand. There was no way to get the priest to release the pressure of his jaws, his teeth now grinding against the bones of his fingers.

"Relael."

Assirra's calm voice cut through the struggle and Relael turned to the High Counselor.

"Let him be," she told Relael and the soldiers. "There is nothing we can do for him now."

The soldiers immediately released their hold on the priest and stepped back. Relael turned back to the man's face and looked into his eyes. There was nothing in that gaze but bleak madness.

Reluctantly, he let the man's arm go and stepped back.

"Take him back to the Temple," Assirra ordered the soldiers. "Relael, come with me."

Assirra turned and walked out the front door to stand on the flagstone walkway. There was no sign of the soldiers who had been stationed out here. The pursuit of Phana had quickly moved away from the historian's house.

Relael followed her, his heart beating like it wanted to escape from the confines of his chest. His fists were clenched to hide any trembling and his skin felt cold and clammy despite the warmth of the day. He was afraid if Assirra turned her full gaze on him he would collapse in a fit as his own madness took him.

"They will not catch her," Assirra said to him, looking out at the street, the citizens of Ythis already once more going about their normal business. "You must continue the hunt."

Relael couldn't help but glance back as the soldiers guided the priest out of the house. The man had torn off two of his own fingers, and blood covered his chin and neck. A soldier had grabbed a cloth and wrapped it around the priest's hand, but it was already dark with blood.

"He will live long enough to return to the Temple and be given to Iathephos," Assirra told Relael. The soldiers all started at her calm statement of the god's name. Even those who worked for the Church did not casually name Iathephos for fear of attracting its attention.

Relael felt his left eye twitch, and he turned his face to the flagstones at his feet to hide it from the High Counselor.

"He served his purpose, Relael," she explained, and he realized that she assumed he was uncomfortable with the man's sacrifice. "He channeled the power of our god to block Iss … Phana's access to her own power. I had hoped she would submit to me once she understood that I controlled all aspects of the encounter."

The High Counselor took a breath and let it out in a long sigh, something that Relael had never witnessed before.

"Her stubbornness is just as strong as ever."

"Will she flee the city?" Relael asked, trying to keep any sign of weakness out of his own voice.

"Not yet. She has made connections here, and her loyalty to those few who had earned her respect was always her weakness."

"Koral Creyss," Relael said. "But he is with the Wolf."

"Yes. That complicates matters."

"Phana cannot go to the Wolf, though. He will not permit her inside the Wolf's Den."

Assirra spun to face Relael. Involuntarily, his head snapped up to meet the woman's gaze.

"You said that earlier, didn't you? What do you mean?" she demanded.

"The ... the Wolf has forbidden her to enter the Wolf's Den. He did not force her out of his ... guild. But she cannot go to see the Wolf. From what I have been able to discover, this happened more than a week ago, but I don't know exactly when."

Assirra's eyes narrowed. He tried to look away, but he was unable to move. He could feel her eyes boring into his skull. His whole body began to tremble, and he knew it was over. There was no way to hide that seed of madness that had taken hold in his mind.

She knew *everything*.

He gasped as she turned away and started walking to her carriage, which had pulled up just outside the open gate. His legs were weak, and he wasn't sure he could take a step without falling. But she began to speak, and he knew he would have to follow her.

He lurched forward and was surprised when his legs supported him, and he remained upright.

"Find her, Relael. Surround the Wolf's Den with watchers. If Koral Creyss leaves to go meet Phana, our people will be there as well."

Relael tried to speak, but no sound came out. He cleared his throat and tried again.

"I have people there already. But it's likely the Wolf has secret ways underground and through the surrounding buildings. Koral Creyss might already be out in the city somewhere, and there's no way for us to know."

Assirra paused as she reached her carriage. The driver held the door open for her and visibly tried not to hear her instructions to Relael.

"Your mission is no longer a secret. Use whatever Church resources you need, under my name, to find Phana. She is not to be attacked. She is not to be hurt. Do not try to capture her. Find her and summon me. I will deal with her myself."

She looked into his eyes once more.

"Your success in this matter will determine what happens when this is all over."

He nodded dumbly as Assirra turned and climbed into the carriage. The door was closed, and the driver took his station. As the carriage lurched into motion, Relael let out the breath he hadn't realized he had been holding.

She knew.

She had seen it, the touch of madness in his mind. Of that he was absolutely sure. But she was leaving him in charge of the search for Phana. And she was offering him ... something. Not hope, surely, for there was no hope in the Church. A clean death, perhaps?

He didn't want to die, but a simple death was preferable to being given to the god in the great cavern under the Temple.

Then again, Assirra hadn't really promised him anything. She had suggested there might be some benefit to his success, but that could just as likely be the avoidance of some punishment, some torture, than any actual reward. He had concealed his madness from her, and that was a betrayal of the Hidden.

Was he a traitor to the Church? It was not a question he wanted to explore. And his own thoughts on the matter were irrelevant. High Counselor Assirra Untoleu had looked into his mind and seen the corruption there. But she had chosen to leave him in charge of the search for Phana.

She would not have done so if his descent into madness appeared to be imminent. He had some time, at least. And she still trusted him to focus on this task and see it done successfully. What happened afterward would be out of his control, regardless.

For now, there was work to be done.

He turned back to the soldiers who were still occupying the house. There was the matter of the historian and his servant. Perhaps Phana had mentioned something personal about herself to either of them, something that would help them find her in this vast city.

One way or another, he would soon find out.

Chapter Forty

KORAL STOOD UP FROM THE COT AND, ONCE AGAIN, TRIED to pace back and forth. But the room was too small for him to take more than a few steps in each direction. He eyed the door, trying to will someone to come for him, but it remained closed.

He had been confined to this room since shortly after arriving at the Wolf's Den. When he managed to escape his pursuers yesterday morning, he had been taken inside and straight to Nid's office.

The manager of the Wolf's Den was surprised at Koral's appearance and had questioned him at length about what had happened. He left Koral in his office, watched over by one of the large men who protected the Wolf's Den from trouble, and went to see the Wolf.

Koral had waited in the office for nearly an hour before Nid returned.

"The Wolf is busy right now," Nid explained. "He said he'll see you when he's free. But you'll stay here for now."

And then Koral had been escorted to this small room. There was nothing here but a cot pushed against the wall and a stool in the corner. He had been brought food but was forced to consume it in this room. A guard stood outside his door, and he was not permitted to leave. The sole exception was when he had to relieve himself, and then the guard would accompany him.

It felt like incarceration.

More than a day and a half had passed and there was still no sign of the Wolf. Phana was out there, somewhere, and the Church was moving against the Wolf's guild. Koral wanted to be involved, doing whatever was needed to protect his people. Instead, he was stuck in this tiny room, waiting for a meeting that might never come.

Eventually, he heard footsteps approaching in the hallway outside his room. He forced himself to sit down on the stool and compose himself.

The door opened, and Nid stepped in.

"He's ready to see you."

Koral stood but Nid held up a hand.

"Do yourself a favor, Koral. Don't go in there and start talking, don't tell him what needs to be done, don't demand to be part of what's happening. Listen to him and wait to hear what he has to say."

Koral nodded but Nid didn't move.

"I mean it. There is more going on than just what you've been involved in. I don't know the half of it, but I know the Wolf is dealing with something that's a lot bigger than just what you and I have seen. He's always ten steps ahead of any one of us. Remember that and act accordingly. You're a decent man, and I don't want to see you tossed out on the street to be snatched up by the Church."

Nid lowered his hand.

"But he doesn't have any patience for horse shit right now. Your history doesn't matter. Step carefully."

"I understand," Koral replied. "Thank you for the warning. I know I can be a bit …."

"Just keep yourself under control and let him talk, and everything will be fine."

Koral nodded again and Nid motioned for him to follow.

A few moments later, Koral stood outside the door to the Wolf's office. His stomach fluttered and he realized how nervous he was about how this was going to go.

Nid opened the door and motioned for Koral to enter. As he stepped across the threshold, the first thing he noticed was the two bodyguards standing on either side of the room. The second thing he noticed was the man sitting at the Wolf's desk.

Though the man wore a face that Koral had never seen before, with closely cropped grey hair above skin the color of walnut, he knew instantly that the Wolf was looking out at him from those dark, deep set eyes. Koral's thoughts fluttered from the bodyguards—something the Wolf had never needed in their meetings before—to his new face. He didn't know what it all meant, and a hundred questions ran through his mind in that moment.

The Wolf gestured to the chair facing his desk. Koral took a deep breath and seated himself. The Wolf leaned forward in his chair, resting his elbows on his desk and clasping his hands under his chin.

The Wolf didn't immediately speak, and Koral felt the urge to open his mouth and start talking. But he remembered Nid's advice and held his tongue. The silence stretched out between them.

Finally, the Wolf sat back in his chair and lowered his hands.

"The … conflict … with the Church will soon be over. By tomorrow, I expect things to settle back to our mutual avoidance of each other."

Koral felt his heart beating hard in his chest. He had so many questions he wanted to ask, and he had to force himself to clench his jaws to keep from speaking.

"I am not happy with what happened. My displeasure will be made clear, and I expect restitution for my people who were taken. But that is between me and the Church. We will not engage in any acts of vengeance against them, nor escalate the matter into any kind of confrontation."

The Wolf raised one eyebrow.

"Is that clear to you? They chased you and tried to capture you, and they failed. You will not make any petty attempts at revenge. In case you do not fully understand me, this is not a request."

Koral nodded.

"I understand."

"I am not sure you do, at least not yet. But you must accept it, regardless, because what I am about to tell you will cause you to question everything. It will make you want to take rash action, and I will *not* permit that."

A knot of dread formed in Koral's stomach. He knew he didn't want to hear the Wolf's next words, knew it was going to be something that would destroy him. But there was nothing he could do.

"I know what the Church was after," the Wolf continued. "I had hoped it wouldn't happen, but even I cannot control everything in

Ythis. They are after Phana, and I believe they may already have her."

Koral felt his blood go cold. The air in the room thinned out until he could no longer take a full breath. A numbness spread through him as he realized that he would never see her again.

"No," he whispered.

"There is far more to Phana than you were ever aware. I do not know what is going to happen to her—it is unlikely they will kill her because of who she is—but you must accept the fact that she is lost to you forever. There is nothing you can do. And as I said, I will not permit you to throw your life away, and cause me more difficulties in the bargain, on a futile attempt at rescue or revenge."

Koral realized he was gripping the arms of the chair so tightly that the wood creaked. He heard the two bodyguards behind him shift position slightly. They were ready to grab him if he moved so much as a muscle.

"Can … can you tell me why they wanted her? Was it what she had done … the ice?"

"That is a small part of it, of who she is. But otherwise, I am not involved and have no intention of inserting myself further into this matter. They took our people in order to gather information about Phana. It is why they went after you. I will deal with that."

Koral bowed his head and tried to blink away the tears in his eyes.

"I need some time alone," he said in a low voice. "I can't just be okay with this."

"I know. You will stay at the Wolf's Den until I can be sure you won't do something stupid. Deal with your grief, and then we will talk again about your own future. I am giving you a chance that I would not give perhaps anyone else. Do not make me change my mind."

Koral nodded and understood that he was dismissed. As he stood, one of the bodyguards stepped forward to guide him back to the door. He didn't look back at the Wolf as he stepped out into the hallway. The other man who had been guarding the door to Koral's room escorted him back the way they had come.

He returned to his small room and the door was closed behind him. He took a deep breath and then sat down on his cot, his head lowered, his hands limp in his lap. There was a chance someone was watching him—the wooden walls were full of cracks and knotholes that could be used to spy from an adjoining room. He wanted to give the impression that he was defeated and grieving the loss of Phana.

But inside his head, he was calmly planning his escape from this building. If the Church was after Phana, they would have their hands full. She wouldn't just let herself be taken, and he had faith in her ability to outwit and outmaneuver her opponents. The Wolf didn't know if the Church had captured her yet, and that told Koral that she was probably still free.

The Wolf may have decided not to get involved any further, but Koral wasn't going to simply let her go. She was strong and smart and powerful, but she was facing the might of the Church. She'd need friends and allies, people she could trust. Right now, that was Koral.

But he couldn't help her from in here. And time was not on his side.

*   *   *

HINARA WATCHED AS THE HEAVY WAGON ROLLED THROUGH THE gates of the Fortress, escorted by two squads of Imperial Guard soldiers. It was full of prisoners, and Hinara looked for Laita Naschect's face among those he could see. He moved closer to get a better look, carefully avoiding the mounted Guards who were more focused on watching the wagon than where they were riding.

Earlier in the day, he had accompanied the squads targeted the building where the traitors were storing their weapons and other equipment. He figured his best chance to find Laita was at such a location, and he wanted to be present when she was apprehended.

The Guard had told him he wasn't permitted to enter the building until they had it fully secured, and he had worried that Laita might die resisting the Guards while he waited outside. The sounds of fighting from inside the building had set his teeth on edge and he nearly charged in more than once as he heard someone scream from what was most likely a fatal wound.

But eventually, one of the Guards had come out and motioned for him to enter. He looked carefully at each of the half-dozen dead bodies he saw on his way through the building, but Laita was not among them. Nor was she among the other dozen traitors, those who had been injured in the fight or who had surrendered.

None of them were old enough to be Laita Naschect's sergeant, either. He didn't know what the other members of her command squad looked like, but he figured the Inquisitors would get the identities out of these prisoners soon enough. He certainly hoped at least one of her direct subordinates was among the living.

After the raid, he had spent nearly an hour examining the crates and noting that well over half of their weapons and armor was still in this building. That meant only perhaps fifty to sixty of Laita's soldiers were fully equipped. This was good news indeed.

Even if the Imperial Guard didn't apprehend or kill her entire force today, they would be mostly unarmed when they were eventually found.

It was the only good news he was to get the rest of the day.

By the time he was done in that building, it was too late to link up with any other Imperial Guard forces. Instead, he returned to the Fortress to await the groups of prisoners and the dead. They began to arrive shortly after he did.

But Laita's face was not among the living or the dead. Neither was her sergeant.

After such an effort to capture her, she was still out there in Ythis. On the run, most likely, but still free and, knowing Laita Naschect, plotting her way to victory despite the setbacks of the day.

Even though about fifty deserters had been captured today, with another twenty or so dead at the hands of the Guard, Hinara didn't feel like he had won yet. None of these common soldiers mattered. Only Laita Naschect and her command squad counted for anything.

He could certainly be commended for his efforts—not to mention his correct assumptions about her movements despite the false trails she had laid—but there would be no immediate promotions or other boosts to his career if she was not among those captured or killed. She was the key to his rapid advancement in the Legion.

The sound of more horses broke his reverie, and he turned to see three more black carriages, also escorted by mounted Imperial Guard soldiers, come rolling into the inner yard. The carriages came to a stop, and a pair of Guards opened the door on the first carriage and pulled out a figure.

For moment, Hinara's hopes surged, but the figure that stepped out was obviously male, dressed in military-cut trousers and jacket. A black cloth bag had been pulled over his head.

A second figure was taken from the carriage. A small woman in an expensive dress, she also had a bag over her head. She was followed by another man and a pair of younger boys, similarly covered.

Hinara began to walk toward the group, but a pair of Guards stepped into his path.

"That's close enough," one of them said.

"I must see if that woman is one of the prisoners I am looking for," he said in his most commanding voice. It had no effect on the Guards.

"It isn't," the man answered. "Keep back."

The door to the second carriage was opened and another man was pulled out, followed by a woman. They, too, had their identities hidden behind cloth bags.

He looked between the two Guards who were blocking him and realized the two woman were not soldiers, that was obvious. The first was wailing in a high-pitched voice, crying and repeating "please" over and over.

"Who are they, then?" He asked the Guards in front of him.

"Traitors to the Undying Emperor."

And then Hinara remembered the notes from Irako's questioning he had skimmed this morning. These must be members of the resistance movement and perhaps their families, citizens of Ythis who had lent aid to Laita Naschect.

"I will need to see the notes from their questioning," he told the Guards. "They could give us leads to Laita Naschect and the rest of her people."

He saw the two Guards exchange glances, and one grinned at him.

"I wouldn't count on it," he replied. "They're not Legion soldiers. This is a matter for the Guard."

Andrew J. Luther

Hinara ground his teeth and tried not to scream at the two men.

"As long as Laita Naschect is free—"

"Yeah, you should talk to Sergeant Danashy. No point in arguing with us, we don't make those kinds of decisions."

"Of course not," Hinara snapped, and spun on his heel.

As luck would have it, he immediately spotted the sergeant dismounting from a horse near one of the wagons that had brought in the prisoners, who were now being herded into the Fortress to the dungeons below.

"Sergeant!" Hinara called out as he marched over. He saw Sergeant Danashy look up and see Hinara, and his face darkened into a heavy frown.

"Not now," he said wearily as Hinara reached him.

"Sergeant, you have just brought in—"

Hinara's words were choked off as the sergeant grabbed him by the throat. He leaned in, and Hinara saw flecks of blood on the other man's face.

"I said, 'not now!'" he snarled in Hinara's face. "I don't give a shit about whatever you want. Fuck off before I bash your fucking brains in."

He let go of Hinara's throat with a shove, and Hinara tripped over his own feet and hit the ground hard. He reached up to his neck and took a ragged breath.

How dare he lay his hand on me!

Since he had arrived in this accursed city, Hinara had been treated with disrespect by the Imperial Guard, by the Watch, even by the fucking criminals. And now this man had grabbed him by the throat and threatened to beat him.

Hinara had reached his limit. A red haze filled his vision. He pushed himself to his feet and faced the man.

Sergeant Danashy had turned away to get something from one of the saddlebags. Hinara grabbed the knife at his waist and yanked it free. Stepping forward, he grabbed the sergeant by the shoulder and drove the knife toward his kidney.

The blade never connected. The sergeant trapped Hinara's hand on his shoulder and spun, twisting Hinara's arm and throwing him off balance. Danashy's other fist came up and hammered into Hinara's face.

The shock of the punch sent stars through Hinara's vision. He was yanked upright and the sergeant struck his forearm with his armored bracer. The knife dropped from Hinara's hand as his entire arm went numb.

He felt the grip on his hand disappear and he tried to step back and protect his face, but another fist hammered into his cheek, snapping his head sideways. And then a quick follow-up struck him on the chin and the ground came up and hit him in the back.

"Investigator!" he heard a voice yell in the distance. He wanted to look, but all he could do was blink up at the darkening sky above him.

"Take your fucking investigator and get him out of my sight. I see him again, I put him in the dungeon."

"But you attacked him!" Hinara heard the other voice accuse, and he realized Jiska was there. As embarrassing as that was, he was impressed that his aide had the guts to confront Sergeant Danashy.

"I lost good soldiers today!" Danashy yelled back. "*Real* soldiers. Better men and women than this asshole. He's lucky I didn't take his knife away and gut him with it."

The sergeant came into Hinara's view, and spit on him. Hinara's senses were starting to come back to him, but he still wasn't sure he could move his body with any control.

"I mean it. Keep him out of my sight or he's going to disappear into the Fortress, along with any Legion personnel with him."

The sergeant walked away, and Jiska knelt beside Hinara.

"Oh, sir. Let's get you back to your office and cleaned up."

Hinara could do little but agree.

*   *   *

RELAEL FELT THE CARRIAGE PULL TO A HALT AND A MOMENT LATER the door opened. He climbed out and looked around, noting that they had stopped on the eastern side of the city, just north of the Warrens.

A Church soldier—a sergeant—stepped up and saluted Relael and he nodded to the man.

"Sir, we have established a cordon around approximately five blocks. The target is in that area."

"Has the Watch or the Imperial Guard gotten involved?"

"No, sir," the sergeant replied. "There's been no sign of either."

Relael was pleased, though he wondered at the lack of response from the Guard. There were too many Church soldiers out on the street tonight, and while the two organizations worked in tandem to address threats to Emperor, neither really trusted the other. He would have expected at least a few observers to have shown up by now.

Phana had gone on the run, but the Church soldiers, mounted on horses, had managed to keep pace with her and limit her options. Away from the priest who had been channeling their god, Phana would be able to draw on her supernatural abilities, and Relael was surprised that she hadn't slaughtered her way past the soldiers.

The pursuit had lasted the entire afternoon, and Church soldiers had blanketed the streets in an attempt to keep her contained. It was now full dark, and for the first time the soldiers believed they had managed to fully surround her.

But five city blocks was still a significant area to search. The fact that most citizens had retreated into their various residences to avoid the attention of the Church at least worked in their favor. The streets were almost entirely clear.

Relael considered sending a message back to the High Counsellor, but decided against it. Phana could be hiding anywhere in this area, and it could take hours to narrow down her hiding places. Better to send a message when they knew where she was.

"Tell your men on the other streets to hold their position and let no one through. We'll start our sweep from this side and work our way up, building by building."

The sergeant saluted again and turned to make the arrangements. Relael looked down the street nearest to him. It was a mixture of three- and four-story tenements with rows of apartments above shopfronts. The search could take the entire night.

Relael felt the hairs on the back of his neck stir and a shiver ran down his spine. Somehow, he knew someone was watching him. He looked around, but there were only soldiers moving with purpose, getting into position to begin their sweep of the area.

Something drew his gaze upward. He lifted his head to scan the rooftops and saw it.

A swirling cloud of darkness was perched on the roof of a shop above him. It was a darker mass against the night sky, the inky blackness slowly twisting and churning without sound.

He could see no figure within the cloud, but he knew there was someone inside, and that being was focused on Relael. He opened his mouth to call out a warning to the soldiers, but he couldn't make his throat work, and nothing came out except a slight gasp. He imagined the cloud descending from the rooftop to envelop him, knowing he was about to die.

"Sir?"

The sergeant's voice shocked Relael, breaking the hold the creature above had put on him. Relael threw his hand up toward the cloud as the glanced at the sergeant, and shouted, "There!"

The sergeant and a few nearby soldiers turned to look where he pointed and Relael looked back up at the roof.

Whatever had been up there was gone.

"Sir, what is it?" the sergeant asked him as a few soldiers with crossbows rushed over and took aim at the roof line.

"I don't know," Relael answered in a whisper.

"Was it the woman?"

Relael shook his head.

"No, it wasn't her. Perhaps a trick of the shadows, perhaps nothing."

Relael now realized that something else was looking for Phana, and it wasn't an ally of the Church. But he wasn't going to worry the soldiers about it.

"Or perhaps an omen," he said, regaining control over this voice. "Phana is a threat to Ythis and we must capture her tonight. There can be no mistakes. She cannot overcome us, and so she will try to run. We cannot let her escape."

Andrew J. Luther

The sergeant saluted and turned back to the other soldiers, barking orders and getting them back into their formation.

Another carriage approached and was waved through by the soldiers guarding the street. The driver jumped down and pulled open the door to reveal two more priests. Relael didn't know either man, but understood immediately why they were here. From what Relael understood, Phana would slaughter the soldiers if she could draw on her abilities. One of these men would sacrifice himself to his god to ensure that didn't happen.

Relael exchanged greetings with the two men.

"The High Counsellor has explained why we are needed, and precisely what we need to do," the older priest told him. Relael nodded and motioned for them to proceed.

The older priest closed his eyes and began to mutter under his breath. The younger priest took his arm and began leading him forward.

A group of twenty soldiers approached the first storefront and surrounded it. The lead soldier kicked in the door and rushed in, followed by a dozen more. Relael waited, not really expecting to find Phana in the first handful of buildings they searched.

Minutes passed before the soldiers began exiting and forming up in front of the second storefront. The operation was repeated again and again, while Relael waited and watched the night creep onwards. The stores were easily searched, as most were one or two rooms with the occasional cellar. The apartments above were not much bigger, though they were mostly occupied with terrified couples or families.

But the first couple of hours of searching passed without incident. When they reached the first of the tenements, Relael knew each of these buildings would take significantly longer to search. He also knew that at least a few citizens would put up resistance to the soldiers' intrusions. No doubt some lives would be lost this night to the swords of the Church soldiers.

Relael mentally shrugged it off. He would do whatever was necessary to serve the High Counsellor.

He was contemplating returning to his carriage to sit down to wait when the piercing shriek of a signal whistle caught everyone's attention. A second blast helped pinpoint the direction—the next block over on the south side.

The sergeant shouted out an order and the soldiers on the street charged toward the sound of the whistle, which suddenly went silent. Relael ran after them, worried that they might kill Phana before she could be captured.

They rounded the corner and the lead soldiers slowed, their swords out and shields up. Relael could see nothing from his vantage point at the back.

"Don't kill her!" he shouted.

And the formation broke apart as the soldiers moved forward to establish a perimeter around the bodies that lay on the ground at the next intersection. Relael saw five men and women sprawled out on the ground, motionless. A sixth soldier moaned and clutched at his thigh as a pair of soldiers began performing first aid on him.

The sergeant began checking the others, but Relael marched directly for the injured man.

"What happened?" he demanded.

He saw that the soldier had been stabbed through the thigh, just above the top of his greave. The man groaned as the soldiers attending him wrapped a belt around his upper thigh and pulled it tight. Relael knelt and grabbed the man by his collar.

"What happened?" he yelled into the man's face.

"She came at us out of the darkness," the man sputtered as the two soldiers stopped their work to watch. "She was so fast ... she was among us before we could react."

Relael heard the sergeant yelling at a few soldiers off to one side.

"We tried ... to stop her. But she had ... she just carved them up."

Relael let go of the man's collar and stood up to see the sergeant approaching him.

"Sir, the target broke through the picket."

"I know that!" Relael snapped at him. "Your people failed."

The sergeant nodded and gestured to three soldiers who had been stripped of their weapons and were now surrounded by a half-dozen others.

"I am charging those men with cowardice," he explained. "The woman was more skilled than we had been told, and when they heard her laughing as she killed our people, they held back. I've ordered the horsemen back into pursuit, but it's night and we don't know what direction she took."

Relael stood facing the man, trying to control his anger but unable to face the fact that he had failed.

"Those men are to be given to Iathephos," he snarled and felt a certain satisfaction as the soldiers around him flinched at the open naming of their god.

He gestured to the injured man at his feet.

"This one, too."

The man screamed "No!" as Relael turned and started walking back to his carriage. He knew he would likely be joining them before the day was out.

Chapter Forty-One

DUCKING INTO AN ALLEY, NAMAL STOPPED AND WAITED. He figured one of the others would soon come to meet him here. He had walked past the White Eagle Inn, and kept going for another block before turning into this alley.

He knew Addiru and Pilayni had set up vantage points by the inn, but it would take them at least a few minutes to leave their spots and reach him. He leaned against the rough wall and heaved a sigh. He felt like he could never get a full breath anymore.

What would happen if he needed to fight for his life? It was likely to happen sooner rather than later.

He heard someone approaching and he pulled back farther into the shadows. Night had fully come, and the alley was almost pitch dark behind him.

A figure stepped into view at the mouth of the alley and quickly moved into the shadows. But Namal had identified her as soon as he saw her.

"Pilayni," he called out in a low voice. As his eyes were already adjusting to the darkness, he was able to make out her figure as she turned toward him.

"Sergeant," she said with obvious relief. "I'm glad you came back safely."

"Any sign of enemy movement?"

"Nothing yet."

She hesitated, and then said "Keynter?" tentatively.

"He's fine. I made contact with his squad, 'cause a couple of them were watching their old place, and it was never hit. But they've gone into hiding somewhere else."

"So the Guard only knew a few locations?"

Namal shook his head slowly and then realized she probably couldn't see the gesture.

"Irako. From what I can tell so far, they only hit locations Irako knew about."

Pilayni didn't respond, and he knew she was holding back tears. The thought of what had probably been done to the young man ....

He reached out a hand and laid it on her shoulder.

"Pilayni, we're gonna get through this."

She sniffed, and put her hand on his.

"Yes, sir. I know we will, sir," she replied in a shaky voice. "We should go over to the others. Addiru and the commander are on the opposite side of the inn from here. I'll lead you around the back way, just in case."

Namal pulled his hand away and said, "lead on."

They cut through three different alleys before coming to a small intersection behind a quartet of buildings. In the darkness, he was able to make out two more figures.

Pilayni whistled twice as they approached, and the figures stepped forward.

"Commander, Namal is here."

He was just able to make out Laita's face as she stepped up and grabbed him in a tight embrace. There was no mistaking the stress she wore like a mask over her normal expression.

"You old bastard," she muttered in a voice thick with emotion. He wrapped his arms around her and squeezed her just as tightly. They stood like that for a moment, letting all the conflict that had been between them over the last few days melt away in the face of what was now ahead of them.

Finally, Laita released her hold and stepped back.

"Any word about the rest of the command squad? Bor?"

"Nothing, commander. Bor was ... he was probably there when they hit the building. As much as I wish it, I just can't think of a reason why he would have been anywhere else."

They all fell silent, their thoughts with their compatriot.

"Keynter is okay," Pilayni said eventually.

"Yes," Namal confirmed. "Their building was never hit."

"Okay, we've got some planning to do before midday tomorrow. We need a place to hide as well. Even if it appears to be safe for now, it's too risky to stay at the White Eagle, at least for the next couple of days. If it doesn't get raided and there is no sign of surveillance, we can come back."

"Agreed," he replied. "Saeda told me about a warehouse near the docks where we can stay for a few days at least. Gave me directions when I saw her a few hours ago."

"She told Addiru and I about it as well," Pilayni said. "We'll keep watch here until she returns and then the three of us will meet you there."

Laita nodded her agreement.

"Be careful and stay safe. I want to see all three of you by dawn."

Addiru and Pilayni saluted her, but she reached out and clasped each of them on the arm.

"We'll have time to go back to formalities soon enough. Right now, it's okay to just need each other."

She let them go and turned back to Namal.

"Let's go."

He set off beside her, heading south once more. He wondered how far he had traveled today. It was different than when on a march, when you could look at a map and gauge the distance.

They kept to the alleys where possible, moving out onto the streets when they were sure there were no patrols of Imperial Guards near-by.

"You meet with Oriuna today?"

He tried to ask it casually, but he couldn't keep the accusing tone out of his voice. But Laita didn't seem to care. She reached out and brushed her hand down his arm.

"I never got the chance. Saeda found me just before I reached the tavern. I had to decide whether to risk warning her or try to reach my own people."

"She's got her own protection," he said. "Assuming she was even there."

"That's what worries me. What if the priests had decided my demands were too much? What if they are after us now, as well?"

Namal shrugged.

"They'll gain too much if you succeed. They'd be fools to turn on you just because you have your own demands."

"Namal, they're all mad! Every time I try to think it through logically, I have to remind myself that they use their own form of logic."

Namal chuckled despite himself. For some reason, he found the absurdity of it all funny at that moment.

"Laita," he said seriously. "I owe you an apology."

"No, you don't. You were saying what you needed to say, and I attacked you for it. And I'm sorry, Namal. You didn't deserve what I said. I was trying to be hurtful, and I should be better than that."

"You can't always be the perfect commander, Laita. You're human, too. I was angry at what you said, but I got over it pretty quickly. I'd still rather serve with you than with any other commander I've ever known. That never changed."

"Thank you," she said in a choked voice. She coughed to cover it up, and once again Namal was astounded by her strength.

"So what's next?" he asked.

"We have to decide if we're going to give up or not."

He looked over at her to see if she was joking, but her face was deadly serious.

"Give up?"

"Yeah, give up. Abandon the mission and run."

"Why would we do that?"

Now, out of the corner of eye, he saw Laita turn to look at him.

"Have you forgotten what happened today?"

"I know exactly what happened today. They found one of us, and that let them find a bunch of us. We lost good soldiers, good people. But they didn't defeat us. Not yet."

"I don't know how we can win, now. It was going to be difficult before. Now it feels impossible. We lost all our weapons, all our armor."

She walked on a few paces and he could tell she was thinking it through.

"They got Irako. That means they got the entire Resistance. Ennius, Tasius...*Galla*. I can't stop thinking about Galla. Imagine, at her age, being taken to the dungeons below the Fortress. Behind handed over to the Inquisitors."

She took a deep breath before continuing.

"But even looking at it dispassionately, this means they also dismantled our entire support network. We lack equipment, we lack funding, we lack places to live while we prepare."

"We still have the Wolf and his people."

"And we were using Galla's money to pay him for his services. With the money gone, you can expect his support is going to dry up."

Namal shrugged.

"Even if we leave Ythis, we've still gotta get all our people out. The Guard will have soldiers at each of the gates. Getting into the city was easy compared to how hard it will be to leave."

"And getting more than hundred people onto a ship without being discovered might also be nearly impossible," she replied. "They'll be watching the docks. Plus, we would need to find a ship captain willing to take us and not just turn us in for the reward."

Namal gave her a serious look.

"Is running what you really wanna do?"

"Of course not. I want to complete the mission. But we must evaluate our options. If completing the mission is no longer possible, than I need to get our people out. We can reevaluate once we no longer have a sword hanging over our necks.

"And the Legion is going to receive a message in days at most. That means a full contingent, at the least, will be on its way within a week. Give it another week or two to arrive, depending on how far away they are. That's our window to accomplish the mission. Once the Legion arrives, then they'll start sweeping through the city to find us, and there will be nowhere to hide."

"That puts a box around our logistics, then," Namal said. "We need to keep our people fed for about two weeks."

"True, but that also puts time pressure on us. Remember, we don't have weapons or armor for most of our people. And we don't have the money to buy it, assuming we could manage to find someone able to outfit more than a hundred soldiers with a full kit within two weeks."

"Okay," he said slowly. "So, our first priority is keeping everyone hidden and fed. Our second priority is getting equipped."

"Well, that brings us to the Church. If they really want to see us succeed, then they might be able to help us solve our logistics issues. They have their own soldiers, which means they have weapons, armor, all kinds of equipment. And they were intending to provide us with the means to get past some of the … guardians … they said we would face in the Palace."

She saw the look on Namal's face and it was her turn to shrug.

"Yes, that's part of the problem. It means we are relying entirely on the Church. If they weren't involved in tipping off the Guard about Irako, then we don't even know if they have cut us loose after the events of today. It's possible that they simply want to wipe us out so that we can't reveal their involvement."

"Fuck!" Namal suddenly grunted, and Laita looked around wildly, sure that they had blundered into an Imperial Guard patrol. She saw nothing unusual and looked back at him.

"What is it?"

"Bor," he said. "Bor knows about Oriuna and the Church's offer of help. The entire command squad knows. If he, if any of them, gets questioned by their Inquisitors …."

She felt her blood run cold. What would the Emperor do once he discovered the Church was trying to have him killed? What *could* he do? He couldn't gather his sorcerers and go to war with them, could he?

Bor's capture might bring everything to a head all at once.

"By the Abyss, Namal, I can always find a way to beat 'difficult.' But 'impossible' is beyond my capabilities."

And as much as he had faith in her, he had no answers, either.

*　　　*　　　*

PHANA CROUCHED ON THE ROOFTOP, LOOKING OUT OVER THE street below. The Crown and Coin was quiet—she had seen no one enter or leave for the hour she had been here watching. It was late, granted, but there still should have been a few patrons coming and going.

She knew she was taking a great risk coming here. The Church soldiers were still hunting her across the city, and this was an obvious place for her to come for help. The fact that she had seen no one so far indicated that something unusual was happening at the tavern. Perhaps it was already filled with soldiers, waiting for her to show up.

The last thing she wanted was for the people at the Crown and Coin to suffer because of her. She had already decided to leave Ythis so that the Church wouldn't have reason to come after those who had known her. In fact, Phana had almost reached the North Gate when she stopped and reconsidered fleeing the city this very night.

The fact that she had no supplies and no idea of where to go was not the main reason she had changed her mind. It was the thought of Koral, of leaving him for good without a chance to say goodbye, of leaving without addressing the last time they had seen each other.

She couldn't leave things like that. She cared about him too much to simply disappear from his life in such a manner.

And perhaps he would agree to come with her ….

No, that was foolish, and she pushed that thought away with nearly physical force. Koral was sworn to serve the Wolf, and nothing would change that. She wanted to see him one last time, and that was it. There was no holding onto any hope that he would leave this city with her.

The streets were nearly empty this night. The malice that hung over the city was growing ever greater, and there were Church soldiers out in force tonight. Word spread quickly, and few were willing to brave the night unless they had no other choice.

In fact, that may be why no customers had come to the Crown and Coin this evening. Perhaps Phana was being too careful. Perhaps Koral was in there right now, and she was wasting time perched up here, being overly cautious. It was folly for her to come back to a place where she was known to frequent, and the woman from the Church—Assirra—would know that.

But that woman also apparently knew Phana, knew how she thought. Phana had to assume that Assirra would anticipate Phana's actions, at least to a degree. But that meant Phana should leave this place as quickly and quietly as possible and never come here again.

She couldn't do that if she wanted to see Koral.

To say goodbye. Yes, just to say goodbye.

Phana almost believed her own thoughts on the matter.

Almost.

The road here wasn't terribly wide, and Phana would be able to cross over to the far side without having to go down to the street below. She took one last look at the front entrance of the Crown and Coin, but nothing had changed. There was a second entrance from the alley in the back, but if the Church was here, they would be watching that as well.

Phana moved off over the rooftops, down the row of buildings until she reached a rooftop that hung out farther over the street. Taking a deep breath, she took off at a sprint and leaped as she reached the edge. For a moment, she hung over the three-story drop to the cobbles below, but then she landed on the lower rooftop on the other side.

She rolled as she landed, trying to avoid making too much of a crash that might be heard from the rooms below. An instant later, she was moving back up the row of buildings toward the roof of the Crown and Coin.

The tavern was a two-story affair, with the apartment of Elmther on the second floor. She knew he had a window on the back wall that led into his bedroom. If she could slip in there, she might be able to listen to the sounds from below and determine if there was a trap laid for her.

Unless there were soldiers in Elmther's apartment as well.

She reached the roof of the tavern and moved to the edge over the alley that ran behind the building. Lying flat on the roof, she looked over and saw that the window shutters were open, but no light came through from inside.

Would the soldiers be waiting in the dark? Perhaps, but she had no way to know.

Once she swung herself down and into the window, however, there would be no way back up. If she had to escape, her only route would be back out the window to the alley below. And if they had soldiers waiting, it would be easy to trap her in the alley by blocking the entrances.

They wouldn't be so cautious this time, either. She had killed at least two of the soldiers when she had escaped earlier. They would be ready for her this time.

For a moment, Phana considered that Koral might not even be here. She might be risking her life for nothing. But she had no way of knowing either way, and she wasn't going anywhere until she had a chance to speak to him.

She spun around and lowered her legs over the edge of the roof. Hanging by her hands, she swung her legs toward the window and let go. An instant of free fall, and her feet caught the bottom of the windowsill and she grabbed the sides to steady herself.

The inside of the room was dark, but her eyes adjusted with un-canny speed and she saw the apartment was empty.

She climbed in and lowered herself to the floor. Moving over to the door, she listened carefully. She could hear nothing from the tavern below.

Was the building empty?

She eased the door open and stepped out onto the landing at the top of the wooden stairs. The thunk of a tankard hitting the surface of a table came to her. Someone was in the tavern, and that person was drinking. It was very unlikely to be a Church soldier making that noise.

Phana eased herself down the stairs, placing her feet on the outside edge of each stair to reduce any creaking that might give away her presence. She reached the bottom without hearing any further noise.

Stepping into the kitchen, she saw the door to the alley was closed and barred with a thick plank of wood in metal brackets that had been newly attached to the outer frame. The light from a candle flickered through the doorway to the main room. She moved to the kitchen entrance and slowly peered around the corner.

The front door leading out to the street was similarly barred. The single candle barely illuminated the large common room, but she could see the single figure sitting at one table, a tankard before him.

Elmther.

The door to Koral's office was closed, but if this was a trap, no more than four or five soldiers could possibly be hiding in there. And no reinforcements were going be coming from outside.

She stepped around the corner and held up her palms in a non-threatening gesture. Elmther looked up at her, showing no surprise at her appearance.

"Phana," he said by way of greeting, giving her a small nod.

"Elmther," she replied. She looked at him.

"Were you expecting me?"

"I wasn't sure you'd show up here. Don't know how much you know about what's been going on. But I figured there was a pretty good chance I'd see you tonight."

Phana gestured to the barred front door.

"I've been a bit out of touch. Is the Crown and Coin shut down?"

Elmther stood slowly, stretching his back, and walked toward the bar.

"For now. I've been told it will be back to business as normal in the next day or two. I assume you're here to see Koral."

Phana gave him a nod as he grabbed a bottle of whiskey and carried it back to the table, along with a second tankard.

"Have a seat and take a drink with me before you go."

"Koral isn't here," Phana said.

"No, he's not here. He's being kept at the Wolf's Den."

The man's choice of words raised the hairs on the back of Phana's neck.

"Could you explain what you mean by 'kept'?"

Elmther gestured to the chair again and poured a generous helping of whiskey into the second tankard. Phana pulled out the chair and sat down but didn't take the drink.

"As you obviously know, the Church is looking for you. They took a few of our people, trying to track you down. We assume those people are dead now. They tried to take Koral, but he made it to the Wolf's Den before they could catch him."

Phana gasped. She had no idea the Church was going after people near her.

"Who was taken?"

Elmther waved off her question.

"Don't matter now. The Wolf now knows the Church just wants you, and he's told us to stay out of the way until they have you. We're not to get involved. Of course, we all know that isn't going to sit well with Koral, so he's being held at the Wolf's Den until this is all over. The Wolf doesn't want Koral causing more trouble with the Church than we've already had."

Elmther's words hit Phana like a punch to the gut. The Wolf had not just pushed her away, he was trading her life for peace with the Church. And he was confining Koral so that the one person who cared about her couldn't help her.

Phana clenched her fists and stood up.

"I've had enough of the Wolf. I'm going to see Koral, and the Wolf better stay out of my gods damned way."

Elmther sighed and took the tankard that he had offered to Phana. He tipped it back and drained it and then set it carefully back on the table.

"I know. And you're going to get yourself killed."

"The Wolf doesn't know what I can do—"

"He *does* know. He knows everything. He knows what you can do, and you'd better believe he knows how to take you down with no risk to himself. The Wolf isn't just some crime lord. He's something else entirely. I've heard about your … abilities. You think you're the only one who can do something special in this city? The Wolf will stop you, one way or another, even if he has to sacrifice Koral to do it."

That took the wind out of Phana's sails. She was ready to kill to free Koral, but the Wolf was also willing to kill the very man she wanted to rescue.

She looked at Elmther and saw the pain on his face. He had been waiting for her and was now trying to stop her from getting herself—and perhaps Koral—killed.

"Why are you telling me all this? What's in it for you?"

Elmther pushed himself to his feet once more.

"I've known Koral for many years now. He's like a son to me. Most people blame you for everything that's happened, as if you *wanted* things to turn out this way. But Koral loves you, and I've never seen him so happy as when he's with you. And I've seen you enough to know that, no matter what scary things you can do when you're defending yourself, you're not a bad person."

Your endless violence was purely for your own pleasure. You were known as the Reaper.

Phana pushed that thought away as tears came to her eyes.

"What are you saying?"

"I'm saying that if you go the Wolf's Den, too many people will die, maybe you and Koral among them. That's why *I'm* going to go to the Wolf's Den and free Koral."

Phana gripped the back of a chair and leaned on it wearily.

"How can you—"

"I'm currently acting in the role that Koral previously held in the Wolf's guild. If anyone can get to him, it's me. You need to choose a place to hide out so that I can tell Koral where to find you."

"Elmther, the Wolf will have you killed."

He smiled at her.

"Young lady, I've lived in this city for almost sixty years. I've had a lot of time plan my exit if I ever needed to disappear. By the time the Wolf realizes what I've done, he'll never find me."

Nineteenth day of Highsummer,
Day of the Arrival

Chapter Forty-Two

THE REMAINS OF A HUNK OF CHEESE SAT AMID THE CRUMBS on the platter that was perched on the stool. Koral knew it to be early afternoon only by the meals they brought to him. He drained the watered wine in his cup and placed it back on the small platter.

Heaving a sigh, he stared at the door, his mind going over the last few weeks again and again, trying to find where he could have done something to alter this course of events. It was a pointless exercise, he knew, but it was the only thing keeping him sane while he waited, helpless.

Out on the streets of Ythis, the Church hunted Phana with the blessings of the Wolf. Or perhaps they had already found her. *That* thought brought a pang of fear to his chest. If they had managed to catch up with Phana, she might already be dead.

The Wolf had said he doubted they would kill her. But Koral knew Phana. She would never willingly give herself up to the Church. She would fight them with everything she had, and they would have no choice but to kill her.

And he could do nothing to help her.

His mind went back to their last time together. He had been so angry with her, at her inability to understand his position with the Wolf. Koral wasn't anyone special. And he posed a potential threat to the Wolf. Which was exactly why he was trapped here in this room. The crime lord wasn't going to let him out until the matter with the Church was settled.

And perhaps not even then.

He had been loyal to the Wolf, but things were not what they used to be. Koral loved Phana and couldn't just accept that she was being given to the Church simply to keep the peace.

Not that his opinions on the matter had any bearing on how things would turn out.

Phana would eventually be captured … or killed. The Wolf would hold Koral prisoner until he inevitably decided that he could never trust Koral again. So Koral would also die, quietly and without fuss. He would disappear and that would be the end of it.

He clenched his hands. Perhaps he should act now, instead of just waiting. Perhaps, the next time the door opened, he should try to get free. They wouldn't be expecting it—he would have the element of surprise.

Before he could formulate any kind of plan, he heard footsteps outside his room. He pushed himself off the cot and made ready to lunge for the door. Two voices were talking in the hall outside, but they were too muffled for him to be able to understand what was being said.

The lower voice was the guard. The other voice was male, familiar. Probably Nid. The voices continued, back and forth, and as the tone of the voices changed, he realized they were arguing.

Finally, the lock on the door rattled and he tensed up, ready to spring at whoever entered the room. Perhaps he could grab the first person, get his hands on a weapon, and use them as a hostage.

The door swung open and he saw Elmther standing in the hall. The guard filled the doorway, and he knew he wouldn't get a chance this time.

"Ask him your questions," the guard told Elmther.

The tavern keeper spoke in a calm voice, all the more threatening for it.

"Then get out of my fucking way."

The guard was a big man, all muscle and barely restrained violence. Elmther was old, his belly hanging over his belt, and at least half a head shorter. But everyone knew Elmther's reputation.

He had been a brawler in his youth. He was one of those nasty fighters who always won, and never cleanly. Quite a few men who picked fights with Elmther had lost an eye, or ended up with a busted kneecap or elbow. Elmther handed out injuries that took a long time to heal, and often left their victim with permanent limits on their mobility or strength.

The guard met Elmther's eyes and Koral saw him tense up. Reputation or not, the guard saw him as an old man whose prime fighting days were long gone.

Koral wasn't sure Elmther could win if they came to blows, but it would certainly provide a distraction for the guard. This might be his chance to escape.

But then the guard relaxed his shoulders and took a step to the side to let Elmther speak to Koral. He must have seen something in Elmther's eyes that told him the older man might still have a good brawl or two left in him yet. Koral cursed inwardly. As much as he liked Elmther, he had just lost his chance to get free.

"Koral," the tavernkeeper said to him. "I have a couple of questions for you. Stuff that you dealt with a few months ago."

He was about to fling himself back down on his cot and almost missed seeing the strike. Elmther spun on the ball of his foot, his fist coming up and connecting with the guard's jaw. The momentum Elmther put into that punch was enough to snap the guard's head sideways, and the man's legs locked up as he tipped to the side and hit the floor, hard.

An instant after the guard dropped, Elmther was on him, grabbing both the man's short sword and his dagger. He tossed one and then the other to Koral.

"Put those on and let's go."

He stared at Elmther for a moment, not believing what had just happened.

"Your girlfriend came to visit me last night. She was looking for you. She wants to see you."

His heart lurched at the other man's words.

"She's still alive?"

"She was last night. And she had lost the soldiers who were chasing her. So I expect that she's been hiding out. I told her I'd come to get you out of here."

Koral couldn't believe what he was hearing.

"The Wolf … he's going to—"

"Koral, I've been a criminal since long before the Wolf ever set foot in this city. I've got my own plans, my own arrangements. I'm going to disappear, and he'll never get near me."

The guard was starting to stir, and Elmther knelt and slipped an arm around the man's neck, squeezing as the guard's eyes popped open. He tried to put up a struggle, but in seconds he was unconscious. Elmther let his head drop back down to the ground, grabbed his feet, and dragged him into Koral's small room. Once they were both in the hallway, Elmther shut and locked the door.

"He'll be unable to call for help for a few minutes at least. Let's go."

"Where is Phana?" Koral asked him as the older man led the way through the twisting hallways.

"She is going to be at a particular place at dusk tonight. She asked me to tell you this: go to the place where your mutual friend first showed everyone who he was."

They came around a corner and Koral suddenly realized where in the complex they were. Elmther began to head for the passageway that led toward the common room of the Wolf's Den.

"Wait," Koral told him. "There are other exits. Less take one with fewer people."

He took the lead and made for a side exit that would lead to the street from a building down the block from the main entrance to the Wolf's Den.

They had almost reached the door when they passed another hallway at right angles to them. Two guards were coming down that hallway and spotted him immediately.

"Stop!" one yelled as they both drew their short swords. He was about to bolt for the door, but Elmther charged toward the guards, drawing a simple dagger.

Koral followed on his heels, the short sword and dagger Elmther had given him in his hands. An instant later, they engaged in the tight confines of the hallway. The guards were large, and strong, but Koral was far more skilled with a blade. The man facing him tried to use his size to his advantage and came at Koral with his sword out and pointed at Koral's chest.

He spun his own sword up, knocking the other man's weapon up just enough to slide underneath and plant his dagger straight into the man's heart. He was knocked backward, however, by the guard's momentum and spun to the side to barely avoid being pinned to the floor by the man's body.

Elmther shouted and he turned to see the other guard's short sword buried halfway up the blade in Elmther's side. Elmther had dropped his dagger and he hammered the guard in the face with his fist. Blood spurted as the tavern keeper's thumb drove into the man's eye socket.

The guard let go of the blade and staggered back and Elmther turned to Koral.

"Go! I can't run with this sticking in me."

Koral leaped forward and grabbed his friend's arm.

"Don't be fucking stupid!" Elmther snarled at him. "I just took a sword for you. Make it count for something."

Koral looked his friend in the eyes and then turned and ran back down to the doorway. He lifted the bar and tossed it aside and then pushed the door open a crack. He was nearly blinded by the afternoon sunlight, much brighter than the widely spaced lanterns in the hallways.

But he could make out normal traffic on the street beyond. He glanced back, but could not see Elmther around the corner in the other hallway.

Shoving the door open, he stepped out into the street, and then burst into a run. He was at the first cross street a few seconds later, turning down the avenue and crossing between wagons and carriages to reach the other side.

He ducked into a shop he knew, bolted through the front, and exited through the rear door into an alleyway that took him on an angle away from the Wolf's Den. He could see no one chasing him, but knew pursuit would not be long in coming.

He knew there was no way Elmther would escape now. Even if the wound wasn't mortal, the Wolf would have him captured. No doubt Elmther would die for betraying the Wolf and freeing Koral.

But first, the Wolf would keep him alive long enough to make him reveal the message from Phana. Koral wondered if the Wolf would know what building she had described.

He had known right away the place she meant. Back when their friend Jadir had joined the Wolf's guild, he had been taught how to fight at a warehouse near the docks. After everything that had happened with Jadir and his sister, the Wolf had pulled everyone and everything out of that warehouse and had sold it off to some merchant.

But that was where Jadir had been the night that Marilsa had been threatened by an assassin. And Jadir had somehow known, had been called by Marilsa to come save her, and had raced across the intervening blocks to save her life.

That had been the moment when they all realized there was a lot more to both Jadir and Marilsa than anyone had thought.

That warehouse was where Phana was going to be a few hours from now. At dusk.

He could only hope that, if Elmther was still alive and under questioning by the Wolf, the crime lord wouldn't figure out that location as well.

*　　　*　　　*

WOODEN CRATES FILLED THE FLOOR OF THE WAREHOUSE, STACKED just high enough to block the view of anyone wandering the alleys between them. Phana stood in a dark corner, listening intently for the sounds of anyone entering.

The wealthier merchants hired guards to stay within the warehouses at night in an attempt to prevent the theft of their goods. Most others paid for roving guards who patrolled from one warehouse to the next, checking to ensure that locked doors remained that way and that no one was making off with the entire inventory.

Phana had entered through the roof, where she knew the boards were loose and could be lifted with minimal noise to make a hole large enough for her to lower herself through. It had not been found nor repaired when the new owners took possession of the warehouse from the Wolf.

Phana hoped Koral remembered it—there was no other easy way into the warehouse without leaving evidence for the guards to find, such as a picked lock on the chain across the main doors.

She forced herself to unclench her hands. This all depended on Elmther successfully freeing Koral from the Wolf's Den, by no means an easy task. If he failed, Phana wasn't sure how else she might reach him. Would she be forced to leave Ythis without saying goodbye?

A slight creak on the rooftop told her someone was up there. Her heart swelled with hope as she heard it—it could only be Koral up there. A moment later, the loose boards shifted and were pulled up.

Though there was no light in the warehouse, Phana eyes didn't need torches to see Koral lower himself through the hole. He hung there for a moment before wrapping his arm around one of the support pillars and climbing down to the floor.

"Koral," she whispered. "I'm over here."

He moved cautiously out of the alley between the crates, able to see only vague shapes in the darkness of the warehouse. She stepped forward and took his hand.

"It's me," she said.

"Phana," he whispered, and pulled her toward him. She threw herself into his arms and kissed him deeply as he grabbed her and lifted her off the floor.

It was some moments before they were able to separate long enough to speak.

"Phana, I'm so sorry for what I said—"

She put her finger over his lips to stop him.

"You were right, Koral. I should have seen how much danger you were in, and how little choice you had in what was happening. I'm just so happy you're here."

He frowned at her words.

"Elmther …."

Phana tensed up. It was obvious something bad had happened.

"Tell me he's okay."

Koral shook his head.

"He was stabbed helping me escape. He gave himself up so that I could get away."

Phana gasped and gripped Koral by the shoulders.

"Is he alive?"

"He was when I left him. But that means the Wolf has him. He'll question Elmther, get him to repeat your message to me."

"We can't stay here, then. The Wolf will figure it out."

Koral dropped his arms and stepped back.

"Yes, we should go right away."

Phana led him back to the pillar and started climbing. He followed her and moments later they were both on the roof.

"The Wolf will send someone after you, won't he?"

"I killed one of the guards while escaping."

Koral carefully placed the boards back over the hole.

"Yes, he'll send someone to kill me. As I told you before, I know too much about his operations. He can't risk leaving me alive. And the fact that I'm helping you definitely seals my fate as far as he is concerned."

They moved over to the edge of the roof, looking for any sign of the patrolling warehouse guards. Lantern light was visible in the alley three buildings down, slowly coming in this direction. They crossed to the opposite side and climbed down the corner to the street below.

"Where now?" Koral asked her.

"They'll expect us to flee," she told him. "To get as far from this meeting place as possible."

She turned and pointed at another warehouse further along the docks.

"So how about there?"

Koral grinned at her, and then became serious.

"What happens when morning comes?"

She grabbed his hand and they moved from shadow to shadow toward the other warehouse. When they reached the alley that ran beside it, Phana leaned over and whispered to him.

"I scouted out a bunch of other warehouses earlier to be sure there were no Church soldiers waiting in any of them. This one is empty, and the amount of dust says it has been for some time."

She moved to a small door in the side of the building and in moments had picked the simple lock and stepped inside. Koral followed her into pitch darkness. He pushed the door closed behind him and relocked it.

"I can't see a thing," he told her.

"Take my hand."

Phana led him deeper into the warehouse and helped him to a chair that sat beside a small desk in one corner.

"Shouldn't we be fleeing the city?" he asked her.

She swallowed before answering. She hadn't been sure how this would go between the two of them.

"Are you sure you want to do that?"

"When the Wolf told me last night that the Church was after you, and that he was going to stand back and let them have you, I wanted to kill him. Only the pair of bodyguards standing over me prevented me from doing that. I realized then how important you are to me. I should have seen that sooner."

He reached out and she gave him her hand.

"I'm done with the Wolf. I decided that before Elmther came to release me. I had prepared myself to attack the next person who came into my cell, and I was ready to fight my way out to reach you."

Phana smiled at his words—though he could not see it—but she said nothing. Koral was a good man, and he cared deeply for her. She had wanted to see him again, at the very least to say goodbye before she left Ythis. She had hoped he would offer to come with her.

Now he was here, and she was genuinely happy to see him, to have his arms around her. But seeing him here, she was reminded that there was something vastly different between them. She sat in the darkness, able to see with clarity. She was not fully human, if Assirra's words could be believed.

Koral was mortal. Vulnerable. He had nearly died a few months ago after getting stabbed. What else was out there in the world? What might they face if they left here and fled together? Yarrian would no doubt try to follow her. Would he try to remove Koral from her side?

Would she be the cause of Koral's death if he came with her?

She gritted her teeth and forced herself to concentrate. What was the point of all these questions? Koral could no more stay in Ythis any longer than she could. At least they could face the road together.

And once Koral was safely away from Ythis, she could decide what to do about the two of them.

"We do need to leave Ythis," she told him. "But we need supplies. Ideally, we would have horses, but we can't exactly walk through the gates. We might be able to buy passage on a ship and leave the city that way. Even the Church isn't going to be able to stop all trade while they look for me."

"Where do you want to go?"

Phana shrugged and then realized he still couldn't see her.

"Ultimately, I'll have to leave the Empire. Anywhere there are Church priests, there will eventually be someone looking for me. I've been thinking of going south. There are whole other continents I've never seen."

Or perhaps I have, but just don't remember it.

Phana leaned on the desk and took Koral's face in her hands.

"But before we make our plans, there are some things I need to tell you about me."

"You already told me—"

"No, what I told is what I knew at the time. But the last few days have been … eventful. I need to tell you everything. You need to know what you're getting yourself into. You need to know who I really am. So I'm going to tell it all to you. And you'll have until tomorrow night to decide how you feel about it and what you want to do."

Koral put his hands on hers.

"Nothing you tell me is going to change how I feel about you."

"Wait until you've heard what I'm going to say," she told him, and completely failed to keep the sadness out of her voice.

*   *   *

NAMAL TOOK A DEEP BREATH AND LOOSENED HIS KNIFE IN ITS sheath. He didn't know what the response would be when he entered, but he had to find out what their status was with the Wolf. And if they decided to leave the city, they would need a way out.

He pushed the door open and stepped inside. The owner, Schurk, was leaning on the bar, but the table where Danz and the others had usually been found was now empty. A couple of sailors sat at another table, drinking quietly.

Schurk saw him enter and stood up straight. He didn't look friendly now, but then Namal had never seen him look friendly.

He approached the bar, and Schurk's right hand dropped below the level of the bar. Namal kept his hands open and away from his body as he stepped forward. He reached the bar and carefully placed his palms on the surface.

"Is Danz around?" he asked in a low voice.

Schurk looked him over before answering.

"Never heard of him," he said evenly. "Never seen you before, either. This tavern is for regulars only."

Namal paused. Was Schurk giving him a message that the Wolf wanted nothing more to do with Laita and her people? Or was he simply paranoid and worried that the Guard was about to come charging into his tavern to round up everyone they found inside?

"I wasn't followed," Namal said quietly. "Yesterday was—"

"That's enough," Schurk said and came around the bar. Namal turned to face him, and Schurk grabbed him by the shoulders.

"You don't listen, you're getting the treatment," he said and yanked Namal toward the back of the tavern. He heard the sailors chuckling as Schurk pulled at him.

Namal didn't fight back. He wasn't sure if it was an act, or if Schurk was going to try beating him in the alley behind the bar. He figured he'd play along and defend himself if it came to that. He was gambling with his life, but he didn't feel he had much of a choice.

He didn't know why Danz or at least one of the others wasn't at the Red Flag. Had the Imperial Guard raids caused the Wolf to pull his people out of their usual haunts?

Schurk marched him to the back door and shoved him into the alley. The former pirate stepped into the alley and pushed the door closed. Stepping forward, he grabbed Namal by the front of his tunic and pulled back his fist.

Namal was about to block the strike and kick the other man in the kneecap when Schurk spoke in a low voice.

"What the fuck are you doing here? You trying to bring trouble to my bar?"

Namal looked the other man in the eyes.

"I said I wasn't followed."

"You think everyone who comes into my bar works for the Wolf? What kind of moron are you?"

Namal fought down his urge to punch the man in the mouth.

"I just need to speak to Danz."

"He ain't here. None of them are here. The Wolf ordered them to stay home and watch each others' backs."

"Because of yesterday?"

Schurk blinked at him.

"You don't know?"

"How the fuck am I supposed to know anything if you assholes won't speak to me?" Namal spat back at him.

He felt Schurk's fist on his chest tighten up, but the man still didn't throw the punch.

"Someone has been taking the Wolf's people. Danz' girlfriend got taken, we think. After yesterday, it looks like it was the Imperial Guard."

Namal and Laita had already been through that line of thought.

"That can't be it," he replied. "They got their information from someone else, someone who only knew about the building where we had the weapons, and a few other places we had found ourselves. The Guard didn't hit any of the other places the Wolf gave us."

He saw Schurk considering it.

"Then who has been taking the Wolf's gangers?"

"How the fuck would I know? But if it was the Guard, then we would have lost a lot more people yesterday."

Schurk released Namal's tunic and lowered his other arm.

"So what do you want with Danz, then?"

"We need to arrange passage on a ship out of Ythis. The rest of us are leaving, and we don't know how to get past the Guard."

"If you were leaving anyway, why the weapons?"

Namal hesitated, caught off guard by the question.

"What do you mean?"

"I'm not an idiot. You were planning something in Ythis. If you were just going to leave on a ship, you would have just transferred all those crates to the ship that was going to take you away."

Schurk leaned in toward Namal.

"So what were you planning?"

"Nothing you need to know about," Namal replied.

"Then I guess the Imperial Guard shut you down yesterday. And now you're running."

Namal shrugged.

"You do what you have to."

Schurk eyed Namal, waiting for him to supply anything more, but he had no intention of sharing any further information with the man. He was too nosy for his own good.

"You got money?" Schurk asked finally, his eyes narrowing.

"Enough to pay for passage and the arrangements."

Schurk thought it over.

"I might be able to help you. How many of you are left?"

"About one hundred and twenty, give or take."

"Where do you want to go?"

Namal shrugged.

"Out of the Empire, ideally. South. But for now we'd settle for a ship that will get us far enough from Ythis that we can make it the rest of way on our own. Can you contact the Wolf?"

Schurk shook his head.

"I don't work for the Wolf."

Namal was surprised to hear that.

"But Danz and the others use your tavern for the Wolf's business."

"Yeah, and he pays me for the privilege. But I'm Lassadar Schurk. I've always been my own man, and that'll never change."

Namal hesitated. As far as they could tell, the Wolf had kept to his word and not betrayed them. Schurk, however, was an unknown. He didn't have the Wolf's reputation for honorable dealing.

In other words, he was exactly what they needed.

"If you can get us out of the city, then you've got our business."

Schurk grinned, and it wasn't a comforting look.

"Oh, I can get you out of the city. I know more ship captains than anyone."

"It has to be someone you can trust not to sell us out. We'll pay them well to take us away from Ythis—more than the reward for our capture—but we don't want anyone who will settle for a lesser reward just to avoid the work."

"Yeah, I've got it. Smuggling people into and out of the city is more common than you think. I know just the captain."

"How long will it take?"

"Give me three days to make the arrangements. Come back then, just after dusk, but come to the back door and knock. I don't want you seen entering my tavern again."

Namal nodded.

"Three days."

Schurk grinned at him again, and then returned to his tavern. Namal stood in the alley, considering the man's offer.

It was, of course, a gamble as to whether the former pirate would turn them into the Guard for the reward or fulfill his promise. All Namal could do now was hope the man played his part properly.

Chapter Forty-Three

ADDIRU REMOVED THE BAR AND PUSHED THE WAREHOUSE door open. Saeda entered and Addiru closed it behind her and barred it again. The late afternoon sunlight was still brighter than the light from the small lantern that illuminated the interior of the warehouse, and Saeda paused for a moment as she blinked at the dimness.

Laita had been discussing options with Pilayni while Saeda had been out meeting with the soldiers and Namal was off setting up her plan.

"Commander," Saeda said, saluting while she moved over to the desk. Laita waved off the salute and clasped her arm.

"How did it go?"

"No incidents, though I did see a bunch of Guard patrols on my walk. More than I've seen before. They're out looking for us."

Laita smiled. It was, in truth, a good sign—they obviously had no idea where the rest of her people had gone. Patrols could be easily avoided. Raids were far more dangerous.

"And our soldiers?"

"I met with six squad sergeants today. It seems that we have eleven full squads, but some of the squads have stuck together and they only sent one sergeant to the meeting place."

"Smart," Laita commented. "No point in sending out more than is necessary."

Saeda nodded.

"They're worried, of course. And concerned about those who were captured yesterday. A couple of them expected to receive orders to withdraw, and were surprised when I told them to hold steady. But only three of our eleven squads have their equipment. The rest are unarmed, other than knives."

Laita tried to keep her emotion off her face, but it was obvious Saeda saw her sorrow as she thought about those who had put up a fight yesterday afternoon. The Imperial Guard had eventually won out, and most likely anyone who had fought back had died in battle.

They had probably had their equipment, or they wouldn't have tried to resist. At least one more squad with equipment didn't show up to the meeting today. The probable explanation was they were captured or had been killed.

Saeda reached out and put her hand on Laita's shoulder.

"Commander, we'll do right by them."

Will we? Laita asked herself. *And what good will it do them now?*

She tried to give Saeda what she thought was a reassuring smile.

"You're right. We will. But for now, we've got plans to make and a time limit hanging over our heads."

Someone knocked on the door, a pattern that they had set up last night once they had all gathered together. Laita felt some of the tension leave her when she heard it—Namal was back safely.

Addiru removed the bar and pushed the door open, and Namal entered. He came over and nodded at each of them.

"It's done," he said.

"Let's hope it works," she replied.

He told them about Lassadar Schurk and the revelation that the former pirate didn't work for the Wolf.

"I don't trust him," Namal finished. "I get the impression he's the kind of man who would sell his mother for an easy profit."

Laita smiled and nodded approvingly. Pilayni looked from Laita to Namal and back.

"That's bad, right? If we can't trust him …."

Laita chuckled.

"He'll play the part we need him to play. At least it may relieve some of the pressure off us for a few days."

Namal looked at Laita with an expression that she knew well, and she stood up.

"Excuse us, Namal and I need to have a word."

Pilayni and Saeda moved to the door to talk to Addiru, while Laita and Namal walked the far side of the warehouse.

"I'm going," she said before he could open his mouth.

He stopped and blinked at her, obviously flummoxed that she had known what he was going to say.

"Laita … just hear me out."

She looked at him, at the concern in his eyes, and nodded.

"Okay. Tell me what you're thinking."

"I agree that one of us has to go meet with Oriuna. Or, at least, see if we can make contact with the Church through the Wandering Horse. I don't like it, but I agree that there isn't really any other choice."

"There isn't."

"All right. But we can't risk you going. Think about it. If you get captured, then the mission is really over. Without you, there *is* no mission. And no one else is going to be able to lead everyone out of Ythis and keep them safe."

"That's where you're wrong, Namal. You're that leader."

He snorted, dismissing her words.

"Don't do that," she told him. "Stop trying to pretend you aren't just as much the leader of our people as I am. Everyone looks up to you as much as they do me."

"That's not true and you know it," he replied.

"Okay, maybe not quite as much, but *you* know they would follow you if I wasn't here. You could take our people away from Ythis and keep them safe just as well as I can."

He looked at her and in the dim light from the lantern she thought his eyes were watering.

"Laita, I can't … I can't do it. There's something wrong. With my health, I mean. I haven't said anything, but I've been getting these pains in my chest. Any time I have to exert myself."

Laita frowned.

"But you were fine on the march."

"That's not true. I struggled to keep up with the rest of you. You all saw it."

"Sure, you get winded faster—"

"Laita, it ain't about stamina. More than once I thought my heart was going to give out. I can't lead our people. I can't lead 'em if I can't even keep with 'em. And my days are numbered."

"All our days are numbered, Namal."

He gritted his teeth, obviously frustrated.

"You're not listening. If we lose you, our people need a leader they can rely on, who is going to be around long enough to see this through. They can't rely on me. My health is a liability. Right now, I'm the most expendable soldier we've got."

"Don't say that!" Laita said, and the others paused in their conversation, but then quickly resumed so as to give Laita and Namal their privacy.

"It's true, Laita. You know who needs to take over for you if you get captured or killed. And it ain't me."

Laita turned to look at the three remaining members of her command squad. She saw how Saeda kept the others engaged, how they looked at her when she spoke.

Namal was right. They did have someone who could take over if anything happened to her. Someone well respected among the soldiers. Someone who had done more to keep the force together in Ythis than anyone else.

She turned back to Namal.

"Okay, you're right. I'll give Saeda a field promotion right now, so she has the rank to go with the responsibilities. But that doesn't change what I have to do tonight."

"I'm expendable, Laita," he repeated. "I should be the one to go."

"Namal, you want to kill Oriuna."

He nodded wearily.

"Yeah, I did. But I know now what's happening here. I'll never trust her, sure. She works for the Church, and you shouldn't trust her, either. But I can get past that for the mission. I'll go meet with her."

Laita considered his words, but finally decided that she couldn't put this on him.

"I'm sorry, Namal, but I have no choice. The priests want me. They want me to swear an oath, and they won't settle for anyone else. Oriuna might not even be there. It may be a priest waiting at the tavern. And if anyone but me shows up, things could go very bad, very quickly."

"Laita …."

"No, Namal. I'm sorry. I love you, you old bastard. And I appreciate what you're trying to do here. But it must be this way. Nothing else will work."

He looked as if he was going to try to argue further.

"That's an order, sergeant," she said with a smile.

He let out his breath and nodded slowly.

"I had to try."

Then he straightened up.

"Yes, commander," he said, smiling back at her. This time, she was sure his eyes were wet.

She grabbed him in a quick hug, and then turned to the others.

"Saeda," she said. "I have something to tell you."

*   *   *

THE CARRIAGE WAS PARKED ON A SIDE STREET NOT FAR FROM THE Wolf's Den. There was nothing to indicate the identity of its owner, or who might be sitting inside. Out on the main thoroughfare, a steady stream of customers made their way into the busy tavern. It was still too early in the evening for anyone to be coming out.

A lone figure stepped out of the alley that ran along the western side of the building and crossed the street, avoiding the main entrance to the Wolf's Den and the patrons converging there. The figure proceeded down the block and turned onto the side street. As the man approached the carriage, the driver hopped down from his perch and pulled open the door.

Relael sat on one upholstered bench and watched the man climb inside to take the seat opposite. The man glanced nervously at Relael as he seated himself and ran a hand down his face.

"Where is she?"

The man gave a slight start at Relael's voice. His bald pate shone with sweat in the light of the single candle. He took a deep breath before answering.

"The Wolf is not happy with this … with what's happened."

Relael wanted nothing more than to grab this man by the throat and choke the life from him. The High Counselor had tasked him with finding Phana, and every delay increased the chance that she would slip through his fingers. He wasn't going to fail. He couldn't allow himself to fail.

"That," he said through gritted teeth, "is between your master and mine. You are here to tell me where she is. Spit it out, and then get out of my fucking carriage."

The man twitched at his words, and then glowered at Relael. This man was not used to being spoken to this way. He was high up in the Wolf's guild and expected a certain amount of respect. He had been initially afraid to deal directly with agents of the Church, but now his back was up.

Relael didn't care.

"Listen here, you son of a bitch—"

Relael spoke over him.

"You will tell me now where I can find Phana, or I will have you taken to the temple and given to Iathephos."

The man flinched at Relael's naming of the god of Ythis. A chill wind swept up the street—noticeably unseasonable at this time of year—and rattled the carriage. The man gripped the bench and looked like he was going to throw himself out through the carriage door whether it was open or not.

Relael saw that his words, and the resulting effect, had adequately rattled the man across from him.

"Where is she?" he repeated in a low voice. It was clear by his tone that he would not ask a third time.

"She's at a warehouse near the docks. She's meeting Koral Creyss there. They will probably hide out there until tomorrow night and then try to escape from the city."

"Where is this warehouse?"

The man gave detailed directions and Relael nodded, satisfied.

"The Wolf should know that if Creyss is with her, he will not be spared."

The man nodded as if he already expected that would be the answer.

"You may leave now, Nid."

The man flinched a final time as Relael called him by his name, and then he pushed the door open and nearly flung himself out onto the street. The carriage driver climbed down and stuck his head into the carriage.

"Get us over to the West River Road," Relael told him. "Find the soldiers waiting there—I must speak with them immediately."

The driver nodded and shut the door, and a few seconds later, the carriage jolted forward. The man up front understood the urgency and wasn't afraid to jostle Relael around to get him where he needed to be as quickly as possible.

A few minutes later, the carriage rolled to a halt and Relael shoved the door open, not waiting for the driver. A dozen mounted Church soldiers were waiting at the mouth of a side street.

Relael strode over to them as their sergeant dismounted.

"We have her location. Send one of your riders to the temple to advise High Counselor Untoleu immediately. Send another to alert the other squads. The rest of you will follow me. We need to cover the streets around a warehouse near the docks."

Relael gave the two messengers the location of the warehouse while the sergeant waited. When they rode off, he stepped forward and spoke.

"Sir, what she did to our soldiers earlier …."

"You're not going to make any attempt to capture her. In fact, I don't want her knowing we've discovered her hiding place. The High Counselor has advised me that she will deal with the woman directly. Your job is to be ready to give pursuit if she runs."

The look of relief on the sergeant's face irritated Relael.

"Your cowardice is noted, sergeant," he said to the man. "Perhaps someone else should take command of your squad. Or do you think you're still up for the job?"

The sergeant stood straight and saluted Relael.

"I am, sir! I was only concerned for the safety of the soldiers under my command, sir."

"I'm *not*," Relael snarled at him. "You are soldiers of the Church, sergeant. I shouldn't have to remind you of what that means. If I must throw every one of your lives away to capture that woman, that is exactly what I'll do. I will not fail the High Counselor, and the very thought of doing so should never even enter your mind."

The sergeant stood at attention and Relael noted that all the mounted soldiers sat very still, looking directly ahead and not at the dressing down their sergeant was currently receiving.

"My apologies, sir."

"Save it," Relael snapped. "I want us to stop at least two full blocks away. Your squad will spread out on the main streets until the others arrive to cover the rest of the alleys and roads that lead into and out of that area."

He turned away as the sergeant saluted once more. As he climbed back into his carriage, his hands started to shake. He shoved them into the sleeves of his robes to hide their trembling as the driver shut the door behind him. The carriage very shortly jerked into motion.

Relael sat in the carriage, one hand caressing the hilt of the knife in the sheath hidden in the sleeve of his robe. He had carried this small dagger for years and never needed to use it. For a moment back there, he had imagined drawing the knife and dragging it across the sergeant's throat.

He drew the knife now, holding up the blade in front of his face and staring at the edge in the light of the lone candle in its glass holder. He touched his thumb to the blade and held it there, close enough to feel it but not enough to break the skin.

But then his hand spasmed and his thumb ran down the blade. It sliced into his flesh and the sharp pain made him drop the knife to the floor of the carriage. His blood dripped onto his robes and he quickly wrapped his sleeve around his hand to stem the flow.

He hadn't intended to cut himself. He just wanted to feel the edge. He just wanted to feel it sliding through flesh. He just wanted ….

Relael realized that he had picked up the knife once more. He carefully slid it into its sheath in his other sleeve and forced himself to let it go.

Tonight, Assirra would capture that woman and it would be over.

He would be successful in his mission. He could ask the High Counselor for help, confident that she was pleased with his efforts.

As he rode toward the warehouse, he tried to convince himself that he wasn't doomed.

*   *   *

HINARA'S CHEEK WAS BRUISED AND SWOLLEN DESPITE JISKA'S attempts last night to treat his injuries.Now, his aide stood near him, waiting to jump at any order he might give.

Quaest stood beside the door to Hinara's borrowed office. He stared straight ahead, trying not to show his likely pleasure at seeing his superior in pain.

Hinara knew his aides hated him. He didn't care. He treated them as they deserved. It would either make them strong and show them how to rise in the ranks of the Legion, or they would become like Jiska, doomed to be just an aide for the rest of his career.

After being helped back to this room last night, he had penned a series of messages to his superiors in the Legion and had them sent with all speed. Despite his pain, he had taken great satisfaction in informing them that his suspicions about Laita Naschect had been correct all along.

She was here in Ythis, along with her entire force of deserters. Some had been captured by the Imperial Guard, he had written, but the Guard had botched the job by jumping too early, and Laita herself was still at large. She was trapped in the city for now, but Hinara lacked the resources to perform a full sweep to find her.

He knew his request for soldiers to come assist him would be approved. The Legion High Command would want her captured and tried as a deserter and a traitor. She had besmirched the Legion's honor, and that could not stand.

Hinara would get his soldiers, and then he would scour Ythis until she was found. He would personally present her to his superiors, and then receive the accolades that he deserved.

But that could not happen for another two to three weeks. In the meantime, the Imperial Guard was keeping watch at each of the city gates, as well as the docks. Still, they lacked the soldiers to prevent that woman from slipping away if she really tried to escape.

His only hope was that she wouldn't try to leave Ythis yet. She had come here for a reason, after all. Of course, that reason was to overthrow the Emperor—a ridiculous notion that had been doomed to failure from the start, as far as Hinara was concerned. But Laita Naschect was some kind of idealist. She might still believe she had a chance, as silly as that idea was.

There was a knock at his door, two short raps. Quaest opened the door to reveal Ukaunee, one of the four aides who had accompanied Hinara to Ythis. Other than Jiska, the aides had spent their time out in the city, at the gates keeping watch or buying drinks in taverns near the docks, trying to uncover any hint of Laita and her people.

Jiska had sent messages to recall them to the Fortress earlier when the Guard advised him that they were now covering the city gates. Hinara hadn't told him to do that—it was on his own initiative. As usual, Jiska had tried to anticipate Hinara's needs, and completely botched it. By the time Hinara knew what had happened, they had already arrived.

Ukaunee was a quiet man, thin and unassuming. When he was not dressed in his Legion uniform, no one would know he was a soldier. His appearance was ideal for this sort of work, and he had developed some skill in ferreting out information.

As of yet, however, Ukaunee had done nothing to help the investigation in Ythis. Hinara was not feeling charitable at the best of times, and this was most certainly not the best of times.

"Well, more of my useless underlings, come to watch me suffer."

Ukaunee saluted and stepped into the office, which was now feeling too crowded with four of them in here.

"You should not be here," he told Ukaunee and Quaest. "Jiska was trying to be clever, so of course he fucked up. Get back out there and do your jobs. Your failures are starting to wear on me."

Quaest reached for the door, but Ukaunee stood impassively.

"Sir, I believe I may know where Laita Naschect can be found."

Everyone in the room froze at his words. It was the last thing anyone had expected to hear.

"You had better not be mistaken," Hinara told him, which was by no means an empty threat. He wasn't about to put up with any more incompetence.

But Ukaunee pulled out a single parchment and handed it to Hinara.

"Sir, I was down in the Imperial Guard offices just now. I—"

Hinara held up a hand.

"What were you doing down there?"

"Acting just like any other regular messenger, sir," he said matter-of-factly. "It was the best way to see if I could find out any information from the interrogations, sir."

Hinara picked up the parchment and quickly skimmed the notes. This had been taken from the Inquisitor's report on Irako.

"I have a copy of this entire report already," he snarled at Ukaunee. "Great work, bringing me something I already have. I am cursed with a bunch of idiots!"

He slammed his hand down on the desk and Jiska flinched, which only served to increase his anger. He almost didn't hear Ukaunee's next words.

"This wasn't in your copy of the report, sir."

Hinara stopped and looked at the page again. It was about the group of Ythis citizens who had formed a Resistance movement ....

He looked back up at Ukaunee.

"My copy did not have any names in it."

"No, sir. But the prisoner gave up the names of six individuals. They captured three of those individuals yesterday. I was able to identify the three that remain at large, a man named Xuthos Chazan, a woman named Galla Javadi, and a woman named Oriuna whose family name was unknown by Irako when he was questioned."

"Okay. And how, exactly, does that help us find Laita Naschect?"

"I expect that she will attempt to contact the Resistance for help, sir. Half the group have been captured, and she likely doesn't have money to pay off the local criminal element. That just leaves these three. The Guard raided the homes of Galla and Xuthos, but both had already gone into hiding. And despite being her lover, Irako knew almost nothing about Oriuna."

Hinara shook his head at Ukanee.

"So what? We do not know how to find these people, either."

"Sir, I do know where she might be. Over the past nine days, I've spent every evening in the taverns, going from one to the next, gathering information. There is a small tavern in Ythis called the Wandering Horse, and it is owned by a woman named Oriuna."

Hinara was on his feet in an instant.

"Do the Imperial Guard know this?"

"I don't believe so, sir. It's not in the notes from Irako's questioning, so it looks he didn't know about it, either."

"It might not be the same woman," Hinara said, knowing that he couldn't ignore this possibility.

"Perhaps not, sir. However, we know about it, and the Imperial Guard doesn't."

Ukaunee let that hang in the air.

"Where is Wholbur?"

Hinara saw the corners of Ukaunee's mouth quirk up, ever so slightly.

"I sent him to fetch a carriage and keep it about a block from the Fortress, sir."

"Get your kits," he told the others. "We are going to do this ourselves."

He was taking a risk by not bringing additional soldiers from the Imperial Guard, he knew. But he was not going to beg for help from Sergeant Danashy, not to mention the fact that Oriuna was one of their targets. If he told them about her tavern, they would prioritize capturing her over catching Laita Naschect.

No, Laita would not bring more than one or two of her people as backup if she went to the Wandering Horse. Any more would draw attention.

Hinara and his aides would be more than enough to catch her themselves. Tonight, Laita would finally be in his hands.

Chapter Forty-Four

THEY HAD SPENT THE DAY IN SILENCE.

She watched Koral sitting in the shadows, thinking about everything she had told him last night. Even in the darkness of the empty warehouse, she had been able to see the expressions on his face as she told him about Yarrian, about Assirra, and about everything she had learned about herself.

He hadn't really been able to see her as she talked—even with his eyes adjusted to the lack of light, she knew she had been little more than a shape in the shadows. And so he hadn't attempted to keep that neutral expression he was so good at maintaining when he was being watched. She had seen it all on his face.

His fear had been the worst for her. Nothing else made her feel less human than seeing the fear on his face as she told him about her visions and what it meant.

They had started with him holding her hands, but as her story was revealed to him, his grip had slackened until their grasp fell apart. He had covered it by shifting in the chair as if he was trying to get more comfortable. But he hadn't reached for her again once he was settled.

She had told him she wished it wasn't true. That she had never wanted this.

As if that changed anything.

He had taken a deep breath before finally speaking.

"I … I don't know what to say, Phana. This is far beyond anything I ever expected to hear. I've been so worried about you, about who or what was after you. I never imagined something like this. You and I, we …."

She waited for him to finish his sentence, but he had lapsed into silence once more.

Eventually, he had said he needed time to think about it and so she had left him to his thoughts, and eventually he had fallen asleep. Despite all she had been through yesterday and throughout the night, she didn't feel tired and so had stayed awake as the daytime sounds of industry rose on the streets and in the warehouses around them.

Koral had awoken in the early afternoon and gave her a guilty look.

"Sorry, I hadn't intended to fall asleep."

"You were exhausted," she told him. "You needed it."

"Did you sleep?"

"No. I'm not tired."

He opened his mouth as if to say something, but then closed it again. She knew how unusual she was for continuing to function normally despite her lack of rest since yesterday morning.

But Koral had avoided the topic of her abilities and had instead brought up the difficulties they would face trying to leave the city. Phana had gone along with it, not wanting to force the issue, but she felt that it was a sign that he couldn't quite accept who—or what—she was.

"I've never tried to leave Ythis," she told him. "At least not as far back I can remember. I don't know any ship captains or smugglers who can help us get out of the city. And you can't risk going to anyone who works for the Wolf. So, what are our options?"

"My thought is that leaving by ship is probably the best way to get out. I know a fair number of ship captains, but there are only a few who would consider helping me if the Wolf has put word out that he wants me caught. I'm not sure if any of them are currently in port. I'll need to get out onto the docks and see who is here."

"We should be able to leave here once it gets dark," Phana told him. "The Church is unlikely to still be sweeping the streets by now—it will bring too much attention to them and interfere with the business of the city. By now, they must be unsure if I'm still inside Ythis and they will have to send patrols out of the city to check the surrounding area, just in case I'm out there. We'll have a better chance of moving along the docks without being noticed after dusk."

"I don't suppose you've got any food stashed away in here?"

Phana shook her head.

"No, I didn't have time to stop and buy something with the Church soldiers chasing me."

She smiled as she said it, but she couldn't keep the annoyed tone out of her voice. They would both have to go without food and water until they left the warehouse. It wasn't ideal, but they had no other options.

They lapsed into silence once more, Phana not knowing what else to say. She was no longer sure she had made the right decision to try to see Koral one more time. If she had simply left Ythis last night, Koral would still be held by the Wolf, but at least he'd be safe after some time had passed. And Elmther wouldn't now be injured, or perhaps even dead.

And the way Koral was acting, she was starting to believe he couldn't handle the revelations she had given him about her origins.

The next few hours passed in uncomfortable silence. Eventually, the sun set and the slivers of light in the warehouse that came from the gaps between the boards faded until the interior was nearly pitch black once more.

She was just about to stand up and take a look outside when Koral spoke up.

"Phana, listen. I—I'm sorry about—"

"Stop," she told him. "No more apologizing. We're past that point. Say what you have to say, but just stop being sorry for whatever you're thinking or feeling. I want honesty, not platitudes."

"Okay," he said. "This is difficult for me. I know it's hard for you, too, and I want to be there for you. But I don't know *how* anymore."

Phana was unable to keep the frustration out of her voice.

"The same way you would be there for me before any of this happened, Koral. Learning about my past doesn't suddenly make me a different person. I'm still me, and I still need to know you have my back."

"I do have your back," he told her, a hurt expression on his face. "I've willingly given up everything for you, turned my back on one of the most dangerous men in Ythis, and ran to help you against the gods' damned Church! How can you question that I have your back?"

She could feel herself getting angry, and she knew it was partially because he was right. No matter how he felt about the things she had told him, he had come to her aid no matter the consequences.

So what did she want from him? And did she have the right to demand anything more from him? And, more to the point, did she actually *want* anything more from him? Would it be easier if he left Ythis with her and stayed by her side? Or was she not-so-secretly hoping that he would decide to go his own way and leave her free to do whatever she needed to do without having to worry about his safety?

"You're right," she told him. "You have done everything you could for me. And I want you to know that I'm grateful for that. It couldn't have been easy to abandon the Wolf."

"It was far easier than you realize. When he told me that he was going to stay out of the Church's way and let them take you, I knew right then there was no way I could remain with him. Yes, it was a decision that scared me, but it wasn't one I had any choice to make."

He frowned at her in the darkness.

"He will kill me if he gets a chance, Phana."

"Then we won't give him the chance."

"How do you keep doing it?" he asked her, sitting back in his chair.

"Keep doing what?"

"Your confidence. Just yesterday you found out that you're not even hu—"

He stopped, realizing what he had been about to say. It was too late—they both knew what his next word would have been had he not caught himself.

He doesn't think I'm human anymore.

As much as she had learned, the one thing that Phana had held onto was the fact that at least her mother had been human. Phana was born of this world, no matter what her father might have been, no matter her lineage or abilities. That humanity was what she felt. She believed it was what made her who she was.

But now she knew Koral had begun to think of her as something else. Something *not* human.

"I'm sorry," he said. "What I meant was—"

"I know what you meant," she said in a firm voice. "And I guess you're right. I'm not human, and I suppose I never was. Maybe that's what is allowing me to deal with all this—that I already knew it, and it was only the memories that were locked away."

"Phana, please."

"I don't know what I expected of you, Koral. Maybe I had hoped you would hear my story and tell me none of it matters. Maybe I wanted to hear that someone who cared for me would keep doing so no matter what was sitting in that dark place where my memories should be. But that was silly. Your reaction is normal, and I shouldn't have expected anything else."

Koral reached out, searching for Phana's hands, but she pulled them away.

"I'm sorry I got you into this, Koral. If it wasn't for me, you'd be safe in the Wolf's protection."

"Phana, I ... I'm not going to lie to you. This is a huge shock to me. I need a bit of time to come to grips with what you've told me. I listen to your voice and I hear the Phana I know, but the Phana I know is only a part, maybe a very *small* part of who you really are. Your memories are coming back to you, and I have to wonder if that means you're going to become someone else as it happens."

"Someone you need to fear."

"I'm not afraid of you, Phana. But I'm certainly afraid of this High Counselor you told me about. And I've always had a healthy fear of the Wolf. And I'm pretty sure I should be afraid of this Yarrian person. I'm just a regular man. Your enemies could kill me without breaking a sweat, and I'm not so sure your friends wouldn't so do by accident."

Phana was glad the darkness hid her face so that he couldn't see what his words were doing to her. She knew he was right, and that was the worst part. She couldn't even be angry with him. What future did the two of them have together, really?

Only now she was responsible for him, at least until he was safely out of Ythis. He had turned his back on the Wolf for her, had not only given up everything but had made an enemy of someone who would exterminate Koral just to protect his own interests.

She now wished she could just leave, but she would have to stay by his side, at least until they were both safely away from Ythis. And that would hurt worse than a clean separation.

She forced herself to change the subject.

"Phana, I don't love you any less than I did last week, or last month, or the day we became a couple. I want nothing more than to be with you. I literally killed someone to get away from the Wolf so that I could be here, to see you. And I did that knowing I was giving the Wolf a reason to hunt me down and take my life. That's how important you are to me."

She opened her mouth to say something, but he couldn't see her face and kept talking.

"I'm ready to go wherever you go, just to be with you. And it's not because the Wolf will kill me if he finds me. It's because I'm crazy about you. But I can't pretend what you told me doesn't matter. It matters to you, it affects you, and so it affects me, too. And I'm going to need some time to come to grips with all of this."

"We don't *have* time, Koral. I don't know what I'm going to remember tomorrow and what it might do to me, never mind what I might know a month from now, or a year. Assuming I live that long."

She knew he loved her, but she couldn't stop herself from wondering if his feelings were genuine. More than one man had become obsessed with her over the past few years that she could remember. Perhaps her nature influenced mortals to experience strong feelings of attraction.

Maybe Koral was under her power and she didn't even know how to turn it off.

"Koral, we need to figure out how we're going to leave Ythis. That's more important than anything else right now."

"Getting out of the city is easier than you think, Phana."

The voice came out of the darkness and Phana spun to see Yarrian emerge from a patch of shadows in one corner of the warehouse.

"Leave this mortal, and we can be gone within the hour."

Phana stepped in front of Koral as Yarrian approached across the warehouse floor.

"Stop where you are," she told him, holding up her hands toward him. She drew on the ice in her blood and could feel it fill her veins.

Yarrian stopped and held his arms out from his sides.

"I'm not here to hurt you, Phana. I'm trying to help you. I can get us both out of this city and we'll be long gone before Assirra realizes it."

Phana flinched at the woman's name on his lips.

"Phana, who is that?" Koral asked her. She put one hand behind her and gripped his arm.

"Stay behind me," she told him.

"She's got her soldiers out on the streets searching for you," Yarrian told her. "They won't find you here—I had enough difficulties finding you even with my abilities. But the longer you stay, the more likely she'll get the priests to use their foul magics to pin down your location."

Phana took a deep breath. She knew how dangerous Yarrian could be, and he cared nothing for mortals. He would kill Koral casually and without remorse, just to remove him as a complication.

"I'm trying to help you, Phana. When you ran away from me the other morning, I could have chased you, I could have interfered. But you obviously wanted to be alone and so I did not bother you. I would have been able to help when Assirra found you at the home of the scholar, but I got there too late to do anything."

"I never asked for your help, Yarrian. I never wanted any of this."

He looked hurt at her words.

"Have you not recovered any more of your memories? Do you not know who I am? We were close companions for countless years, Phana. We traveled across the breadth of this world and saw things that no mortal has ever seen. When I felt you use your power and realized you were in Ythis, I feared that Assirra had taken you prisoner. But I came anyway. I put myself in danger to help *you*."

"Yes, I know who you are. But the woman you traveled with isn't me. That was someone I used to be, and I'm not that person anymore."

Yarrian took a step toward her, and she clenched her fist and aimed it at his chest. He stopped where he was.

"You are that person, Phana. You always were. You just don't re-member. But it's obvious that Assirra opened up more of your mem-ories, and now I can help you open up the rest."

Phana was about to answer him, but was interrupted by the sound of chains rattling as they fell from the warehouse doors to the cob-blestones outside. She spun as the doors opened to reveal Assirra standing in the street, surrounded by Church soldiers.

Phana's breath caught in her throat. How had the woman found her? She had tried so hard to get away, to hide, but it was all for naught. And she knew she would have to protect Koral—neither Yarrian nor Assirra would bother to spare him if it came to a fight.

Assirra calmly strode into the warehouse, and the Church soldiers pushed the doors closed behind her. As the light from the lanterns carried by the soldiers was cut off, she began to radiate a soft white glow that illuminated the warehouse interior. Koral squinted his eyes at the light and looked back and forth at Yarrian and Assirra.

"My dear Yarrian," the woman said as she approached. "It has been … too long."

"I would say it's not nearly long enough," he replied.

She turned to Phana.

"You were dishonest with me. You said it was the Wolf who opened up your memories. I never would have guessed it was Yarrian."

"The Wolf?" Yarrian asked.

"But I suppose it worked out for the best. The Wolf and I were hardly on speaking terms for quite some time, but your activities have reconnected us."

"The traitor," Yarrian snarled. "This Wolf person is the traitor, isn't he?"

Assirra nodded at him.

"I suppose you would call him that. I consider him a rather useful tool who performed exactly as I wished at the time. Tell me, Yar-rian, are you still scurrying alone around the world from shadow to shadow, trying to find a purpose to your existence? Or have you convinced your large friend to come out from his hiding place?"

Phana saw a look of grief cross Yarrian's face.

"Rotos is … dead."

"How could that have happened?" Assirra asked him, and Phana heard the tremor in her voice as she spoke. His words made Phana unaccountable sad, and she wished she remembered more of the big man who had been their third companion.

"I do not know yet. I was not there, but I felt it happen. I will find out once I am done in this accursed city."

"How did you find me?" Phana interrupted.

Assirra turned to look at Phana and smiled.

"Your friend there left a loose end when he escaped from the Wolf, and the Wolf passed that information on to me. But when I got to that warehouse, I knew you were not inside. But you could not have gone far, and so I tried to sense you. I might have missed you if you were alone, but with Yarrian also here, it was like a beacon."

She spread her arms to take in all four of them.

"But now we must get down to business. Yarrian, I am sorry to hear about Rotos. Truly, I am. He and I were not friends, but I respected him, nonetheless. His strength, and his determination were … inspiring. I have no further quarrel with you, and I do not wish to reignite our previous conflict. You are free to leave Ythis."

Yarrian glowered at Assirra.

"I don't recall asking your permission—"

Assirra ignore him and turned back to Phana.

"Issra, this warehouse is surrounded not just by Church soldiers, but by priests as well. They are ready to call down the wrath of their god on you, and only I can prevent that from happening. I do not wish to see you destroyed. You and I were so very close for so long. I understand that you disagreed with my choices when the new gods arrived, but look at the world we have. It is better this way than it would have been with all civilization wiped out."

Assirra has come to them, to beg them to join her.

"The war is lost," she tells them. "Our gods are being driven out, and these invaders are consuming any mortals they can find. We must do something or there will be nothing left."

"What can we do?" Yarrian asks her. "Rotos' armies have been

wiped out, and he barely survived."

"Let us go to these new gods and appease them," Assirra says, and Phana laughs at her suggestion.

"Appease them? You want us to turn our backs on the gods? How can you betray them like that?"

"I am not betraying anyone! We cannot stop them, not through force. But we can...give them a reason to trust us. We can get close to them, in a way that no mortal ever could. We could serve them, for a time, until we find a way to destroy them or drive them out of our world."

Yarrian frowns, and Phana takes Assirra by the arm.

"I will slaughter anyone who serves these invaders. Do you understand me? I will not let them have our world. Do not make this choice, Assirra. I love you, but I will kill you if you join them."

Assirra looks down at her feet and Phana sees the fight go out of her.

"You are right, both of you. I will go find Rotos and help him in any way I can. We will talk soon."

Assirra turns and disappears, and Phana feels the hilts of her knives fill her palms.

"This war isn't over," she says to Yarrian.

"You ... you did this to me," Phana said to her in a low voice. "You turned your back on all of us, and when we wouldn't submit to you, you took my memories. You made me forget who I was."

"I saved your life," Assirra snapped at her. "You would not stop fighting, and the gods would have destroyed you."

"You wanted to get close to these new gods. Serve them until you could find a way to destroy or banish them. But what have you done, Assirra? You still continue to serve them, because all you care about is your own power."

Phana could feel the ice churning in her blood. She wanted to lash out at this woman who had stolen her mind. She wanted to hear Assirra scream, and the thought sent a rush of pleasure through her body.

"You ... had ... no ... right!" she growled at the woman.

For an instant, Assirra looked worried. But then she relaxed and smiled at Phana.

"You are starting to remember who you were. But that person became a threat and I have no desire to deal with her again."

Like water draining out a basin, Phana felt the cold flow out of her body, leaving her trembling and empty. She tried to hold onto it, tried to pull it back, but it slipped away from her and was gone.

Her legs started to go limp, and Koral lunged forward to grab her and keep her from falling.

"How touching," Assirra said to them. "The Wolf will be very happy when I hand you over to him. And Issra, I realize now that just taking your memories was not enough. This time, I will *reshape* your memories and create the companion I have missed having with me all these years. I look forward to seeing you serve me throughout the centuries to come."

Phana tried to hold onto consciousness as Assirra's smile filled her vision.

Chapter Forty-Five

THE STREETS WERE MOSTLY EMPTY AS LAITA MADE HER WAY toward the Wandering Horse tavern. As if the strange pall hanging over the city wasn't enough, Imperial Guard patrols marched or rode down the main streets. The citizens of Ythis were used to them staying in the area near the Fortress, or focusing their efforts on keeping the Nobles' District safe.

This must be a strange sight for most of them, she thought. *No doubt rumor about the raids yesterday have already made their rounds, growing with each telling.*

So far, she had encountered little difficulty in avoiding those patrols. They stuck mostly to the major thoroughfares, which allowed her to move across the city along the smaller, narrower streets, without having to flit from alley to alley. The last thing she needed tonight was to encounter any thugs or cutthroats in the darker places of the city streets.

She reached the end of a block and crept out to look up and down. The sound of booted feet marching double-time came to her, and she withdrew back into the shadows of a storefront as the group of what could only be Imperial Guard soldiers approached.

Both of the other patrols she had seen tonight were marching at a normal pace, and she wondered for a moment if they had found one of her squads somewhere and were heading to launch another raid. If so, there was nothing she could do for her people right now. She didn't even know where most of them were hiding.

The patrol reached the corner where she was tucked into the shadows and continued past. The soldier at the head of the column carried a lantern, and she nearly gasped aloud when she saw the troop following him.

These weren't Imperial Guards. They were *Church* soldiers.

What were Church soldiers doing out in the streets at this time of night? They were heading south, toward the docks, but she couldn't think of any reason why the Church would send soldiers out to that part of the city at night. There wouldn't be any ships coming at this hour.

Unless ….

Had the Church given her up to the Imperial Guard? Were they helping to hunt her down?

She hesitated. If the Church had betrayed her, then she was probably walking into a trap. But there was no way to know. It was just as likely these soldiers were involved in some other event taking place tonight. Ythis was a big city—there was no telling what was going on that didn't involve her.

It was no easy choice. If she didn't make contact, then even getting out of the city would be more difficult. She needed resources, and right now the only option was allying with the Church. But if they were waiting to capture her ….

She took another glance around the corner, but the soldiers were now far down the street and she crossed quickly and ducked into another narrow lane that wound between tall tenements that loomed over the cobbles.

There was little choice. Saeda would make a fine leader, especially with Namal to advise her. He had wanted to come with Laita to the Wandering Horse, to help keep an eye out while she went inside. But if it *was* a trap, she couldn't risk both Namal and herself. Saeda would need him, need his guidance and support.

And it would help the rest of the soldiers to accept the transition if Namal demonstrated that he stood behind the new commander. Saeda would do the right thing, and would get her people out of the city if the Church did turn on Laita.

She reached the correct street, a few blocks south of the Wandering Horse. There were no signs of the Imperial Guards, but that didn't mean anything. If they were watching the tavern, they wouldn't do so from out in the street.

Moving up the street, she peered around, looking for any flicker of light in a window, listening for the clink of metal, the sound of a booted foot. But there was nothing.

She had no way to approach the tavern entrance except by moving along the street, completely exposed to anyone watching. She passed the last alley entrance, and took a quick look inside. But even with her eyes adjusted to the darkness of the night, the shadows blocked her from seeing any further than a few feet.

The tavern entrance was about thirty paces away. She hesitated beside the alley, and then took a deep breath and let it out slowly. One pace, then another, and she moved toward the door to the Wandering Horse.

She was about halfway between the tavern entrance and the door when she heard a man's voice behind her.

"Laita Naschect! Stop and hold in the name of the Imperial Legion."

Up ahead at the next cross street, she saw two figures step out from around the corner and block the road. She spun to see two more down at the last cross street.

She froze, expecting a squad of Guard soldiers to come boiling out of the tavern, but no one else appeared.

The voice said Imperial Legion, she thought. *Not the Guard.*

But wouldn't the Legion and the Guard be working together to capture her?

She didn't have time to figure it out. The two figures to the south began to walk toward her. One of them spoke up again.

"Stay right where you are. There is no escaping this time."

She glanced at the alley mouth. She was closer to the opening than they were. But surely, they wouldn't have left her such an easy way out of their trap.

Unless they want me to head in that direction.

The alley was narrow, and if they blocked off both ends, she would certainly be trapped.

She had another couple of seconds to make her decision, and then it would be too late to make a run for it.

"Fuck," she growled as she threw herself forward. If the alley was a trap, she was going to run right into it. But it was a greater risk to face two soldiers with two more coming up behind her. They would only have to delay her for a moment to give the others time to surround her.

The two men down the street saw her run and immediately charged toward her. She was sure the two behind her were giving chase as well. The alley mouth drew toward her as she pushed herself forward, running full out.

A fifth figure stepped out of the alley entrance, a truncheon in his hand instead of a sword. They weren't going to risk killing here—the Legion wanted her alive.

Unfortunately for them, she had no such restrictions.

The man at the alley entrance stepped forward and swung his truncheon at her head as she charged at him. He was expecting her to block or dodge, like any trained soldier would normally do. But she didn't have time to get into a real fight with him. The others were approaching too quickly.

She ducked her head and barreled into him. His arm glanced off her shoulder as she moved inside his swing and then her other shoulder caught him in the chest. She had crouched slightly just before she connected, and now she pushed up with her legs, lifting the man off his feet.

Her own feet didn't stop moving, and she carried him two full strides before they collided with the wall of the alley with a bone-jarring thump. His head cracked off the wooden beams as he let out an "oof" as her shoulder drove any remaining air out of his lungs.

Laita let herself bounce off his body, and she spun away to keep moving down the alley, her legs churning. She glanced back as the man fell away from the wall and stumbled to his knees, just as two of the other soldiers reached the alley mouth. The first barreled into the man she had hit, and they both went tumbling to the ground.

"No!" she heard the other man scream, his voice filled with rage.

She reached the other end of the alley and plunged out into the street. To her surprise, no squad of soldiers was waiting for her. The street was empty.

They only sent five men to capture me?

It didn't make any sense to her, but she didn't have time to think about it. The pounding of boots in the alley behind her told her that the others were now in pursuit.

Laita took off running, desperately trying to think of a way out.

Cutting right, then left, she tried to get just enough of a lead that she could turn a corner and have a chance to slip into an alley or cut back without immediately being spotted. She glanced back over her shoulder and saw that she had a lead of barely more than second or two.

The next time she cut around the corner, she threw herself into the mouth of an alley between two buildings. She slowed and moved quietly down the alley, ducking into the darkest shadows.

An instant later, one of the men ran right past the mouth of the alley. She leaped up and charged further down the alley, heading for the cross-street. But just as she was about to emerge, she heard pounding footsteps as another of the pursuing men came down this parallel street.

They're trying to cut me off, she thought, crouching and hoping that the man wouldn't see her as he ran past.

But shortly after he passed her, she heard a shout behind her. Glancing back, she saw that another figure stood at the far end of the alley and had spotted her silhouetted by the lanterns on the opposite street.

Flinging herself forward, she turned and cut back up the street, back toward the Wandering Horse tavern. She could only hope that the others had already passed her by.

Spotting another man up ahead, she ducked into another alley and stopped again. She had no good plan to lose them. They knew she was nearby, and they called to each other and began to draw closer once more.

For the next hour, Laita continued to alternately run and hide. But her pursuers managed to follow her with dogged persistence. When she hid, they would spread out and begin to sweep the area, and she would be forced to run once again. And at least one of them would spot her and the chase would continue.

Now, Laita crouched in the shadows, listening carefully. They were out there, on the streets, searching for her. She tried to get her breathing under control, tried not to give away her location.

She knew they were nearing her hiding place again. They continued to call out to one another, making sure that she couldn't ambush one of them and get some distance without the others immediately knowing where she was. And Laita was a soldier, not an assassin. She didn't have the training to pick them off one by one.

As she turned to make her way along this alley to the next street over, she heard hooves—as if from a group of horses—on the cobblestones ahead. She froze, wondering which direction would be better.

"You!" a voice called out, and the sounds of the horses slowed. "Stop and identify yourselves."

It was an Imperial Guard patrol. No doubt these men would ask for their assistance in catching her. There was little chance of her escaping an entire patrol. She clenched her fists and tried to decide if she should make a run for it before the men revealed who they were and what they were doing.

The man who was obviously in command of those five who followed her spoke up.

"I am Investigator Hinara Angumu of the Imperial Legion."

His name sounded familiar, and Laita thought she might have encountered him at some point in her career. But she couldn't quite put a face to the name. She began to move back away from these men. Her only chance would be to head in the opposite direction.

"What are you doing out on the streets at this time of night, Investigator?"

"Legion business."

There was a pause, and Laita hesitated.

"And what business is that?" the Guard soldier asked.

"None of yours," Hinara retorted angrily, to Laita's surprise.

"What did you say?"

"My business is not the concern of the Guard. You know why I am here in Ythis. You have your duties and I have mine. I do not need your assistance, so you may go on your way."

He's not asking for help, she thought. *Why not?*

The Guard soldier chuckled out loud.

"Sergeant Danashy was right about you," the man said. "No wonder the Legion is full of deserters and traitors."

This Investigator Angumu is not popular with the Guard. Is that why he isn't telling them I'm right in their vicinity? Is it so important for the Legion to catch me that he's willing to risk me getting away?

She reached the opposite end of the alley, but two of the Legion soldiers were out in the main street, keeping watch. If she ran now, the Guard would no doubt decide to join the hunt whether the Investigator wanted them to or not.

"Are we done here?" she heard him ask.

The Imperial Guard soldier didn't respond, merely clicking his tongue to get his horse moving, the rest of the soldiers following him up the road. In another minute, they were gone.

But Laita would soon be found. She was readying herself to make another run when she heard booted feet approaching quickly, and then a scream.

She moved to the corner as the clash of steel on steel echoed in the street. Glancing around the edge of the building, she saw two figures fighting, a third sprawled out on the ground. The two fighters parted for a moment, and she realized what was happening.

It was Namal. He was fighting with the Legion soldier.

She heard Hinara and the other two shouting as they ran in this direction. Yanking her own knife free of its sheath, she sprinted toward Namal and his opponent. The Legion soldier heard her coming at the last second and tried to move away, but Namal was on him, forcing the man to defend against his sword thrusts.

Laita was able to circle around behind him, and she drove her knife into his back all the way to the hilt. The breath was driven out of his lungs and his legs gave out. She gripped the hilt tightly, pulling it out of his body as he fell.

"What are you doing here?" she asked Namal.

"I followed you ... shortly after you left. I wanted to keep watch ... while you were inside ... but I got there right after you ... ran. I've been ... trying to catch up ... ever since."

"I gave you a direct order to stay with Saeda, sergeant."

"Looks like you … needed the help," he gasped, trying to get his own breath back.

The Investigator and his two remaining men rounded the corner and slowed as they saw their comrades on the cobblestones. Laita and Namal faced them. She knew she couldn't run anymore. Namal would be unable to keep up.

She was angry with him for following her. She had no choice but to fight, now. Namal had a sword, but all she had was her knife. And they were still outnumbered, though the odds were certainly much better now.

"Laita Naschect and her loyal sergeant," Hinara Angumu sneered. "Nice work. You probably think you have a chance, now."

"You should have asked … those soldiers for help," Namal growled at him. "The three of you ain't enough to take us."

Laita watched Hinara smile grimly.

"I only need her," he said, pointing the tip of his sword at Laita. "You have no additional value alive, sergeant. I'm going to enjoy the look on her face when I gut you."

She looked at the faces of the two other men, one standing on each side of Hinara. One looked calm, ready for whatever was about to happen. The other looked terrified. His eyes were wide, and he was sweating profusely.

Reaching up, she pulled the shawl and the wig off her head and tossed them to the ground.

"I guess I don't need this anymore," she told them. "Hated that thing. But now you can see the real me and know who you face."

"Oh, I know you, Laita Naschect. I know you so well that I came here to Ythis because this is where I knew I would find you. You fooled some of the others with your false trails. But not me."

"You're not going to take me alive," she told him.

"Yes, I would prefer to hand you over to the Legion High Command in chains, but still breathing. Your death is a risk. But it is one I am willing to take—"

He was interrupted by Namal charging forward and was forced to defend himself from the sergeant's quick strikes.

Laita drove forward at the man facing her. He squealed and backpedaled, his sword out but not doing much to block. She glanced at Namal and saw the third man engage him. In an instant, he was on his back foot, parrying the other men's attacks and giving ground.

She spun and lunged toward Hinara. He turned to meet her and swung his sword, keeping her at a distance. He began to advance toward her.

"Get her!" he barked at the man who had retreated from her attacks. The man moved forward tentatively. Laita was just moving to keep both Hinara and the other man in front of her when Hinara spun away.

At that moment, Namal knocked the third man's sword to the side and stepped forward, driving his own blade into the man's chest. But Hinara slashed down low and caught the back of Namal's thigh. He grunted as the blade bit deep.

"Namal!" Laita screamed and moved toward Hinara, ignoring the last man and hoping he was too timid to suddenly drive forward and take her down.

As Namal staggered sideways, Hinara swept his blade in a circle and caught Namal's wrist. Blood spurted as his hand parted from his wrist, and both hand and blade hit the cobbles. Hinara grabbed Namal by the shoulder and spun him around, putting the edge of the blade to his throat.

Laita froze, and then the wind was knocked from her lungs as the last man tackled her to the ground. Her elbow hit the hard surface of the road and she lost her grip on her knife, the blade skittering away across the cobblestones.

"I did it!" the man holding her shouted excitedly. "I really did it."

Laita looked up into the eyes of Hinara and saw victory there. She had well and truly lost everything.

Chapter Forty-Six

KORAL HELPED PHANA INTO THE CHAIR AS THE LETHARGY stole through her limbs. She could not stop trembling from the emptiness that yawned in the core of her being. This was worse than yesterday, when the priest had blocked her from using the cold inside her. It had still been there, just below the surface.

But now it was entirely gone, as if it had been removed from her body. She wanted to scream, but lacked the energy to make more than a soft moan.

"Phana, look at me!" Koral said to her, holding her face and staring into her eyes.

She looked at his face, so close to hers. He was going to die, and it was her fault. She had asked Elmther to free him. The old tavern-keeper was most likely dead by now, and Koral would soon join him. All because she had wanted to see him again before she left.

How many people had Phana slaughtered in her long life? How many lives taken with her own hands? She had been the Reaper, and she remembered the joy, the pleasure, from the freeing of all that blood.

Perhaps she was finally getting what she deserved.

Koral didn't deserve it, though. He tried to be fair to everyone, tried to keep his people safe. The Wolf would kill him and that would be the end of it. He would be forgotten soon enough.

Phana would surely forget him, once Assirra reshaped her memories. She would forget everything except what Assirra wanted her to remember.

Perhaps that was for the best. She had been the Reaper for so long, and then Assirra took her memories and Phana had somehow become a decent person. She needed to believe that she had turned into someone good. She needed to believe that was the true core of her being, when everything else was stripped away.

She had helped others, like Jadir and Marilsa. She had found love with Koral. And she had had friends, for a time.

But she had lost all her friends. She had used her powers, and that had been the beginning of the end for her in Ythis.

Perhaps the Reaper was the real person after all, and Phana was just a dream. Nothing more than a temporary illusion.

She stared at Koral's face as he talked to her. She could no longer hear his voice. Her head was filled with a buzzing drone. Flashes of memory flitted across her consciousness. She saw once more Rotos and Yarrian standing with her at the top of the tower, looking over Assirra's army spread out below them.

They had been happy in that tower, in their exile. She had started to see herself as something other than the Reaper. The old gods were gone, locked away from this world and unable to feel her worship. So she had stopped worshipping them. Stopped sacrificing to them.

But that hadn't mattered, either. Assirra had shown up with her army, and Phana had picked up her knives once again. Thousands of lives had ended on her blades that day.

Despite all their efforts, Assirra had used her priests to summon the power of their gods. Yarrian had managed to escape. Phana didn't know what had happened to Rotos. And her own mind had been wiped clean.

What did it mean? There was a time when Phana believed in the fate that had been given to her by the old gods. She understood that they had a plan for her, and she was willing to fulfill her part in that plan. And then they were defeated.

Did that mean she had become the pawn of the new gods? Or perhaps there was no such thing as fate, and she had been fooling herself all along. Or maybe she was being punished for failing when the old gods needed her the most.

Her gaze drifted past Koral's face to see Assirra and Yarrian standing together. They were speaking, but the buzzing in her head drowned out their words. Neither of them looked happy, and Phana thought they might be arguing about something.

About *her*.

Yarrian wanted things to be the way they had been during their travels. He was alone—he was *lonely*—and he wanted to return to that time. Assirra wanted Phana to be the person she had been before the coming of the new gods.

But that was the past. Phana had been revisiting the past in her mind over the last few days, and it wasn't a welcoming place. It was full of blood, and darkness, and war. It was full of betrayals, and conflict. It was a place of loss.

Somehow, Phana had made a new life here in Ythis. She had found her way here, right under Assirra's nose, and managed to remain hidden all this time. And she had a life. *Her* life.

They had taken that away from her, just as they had taken away her old life.

So who was she?

Issra?

The Reaper?

Phana?

Or was a person's being all just based on what they remembered? Was a person nothing more than their memories? Change the memories, change the person.

If she hadn't lost her past to the darkness, would she still be the Reaper? Or would she have become something else?

Which one was real?

Yarrian might be putting up a show of resistance, but he would yield to Assirra. He had never been one to keep fighting when the battle was lost. He would do nothing to save Koral. And he would let Assirra have Phana if it meant he could escape alive.

Yarrian would look for a future opportunity to free her, but that might take years. Decades, even.

She looked back at Koral and saw something in his face. His eyes roamed over her face as if he was seeing her for the last time. She could see tears in his eyes as he gently let her head lower and pulled his hands from her face.

She watched his hands move down to her waist.

To her knives.

She knew what he was going to do. He was going to take her knives and try to kill Assirra, in the hope that it would free her. He was going to sacrifice himself for her.

And he knew that he was going to die in the attempt.

But that wouldn't stop Koral. He had given up everything to come to her. And now he was willing to sacrifice all he had left on the smallest chance to help. He didn't know what Assirra could do, but even if he did it wouldn't have mattered.

She wanted to tell him to stop, but her mouth wouldn't cooperate. She saw him grip the hilts of her knives and slowly begin to draw them out so as not to make any noise. Assirra and Yarrian were occupied with each other, and Koral thought he could get to them.

It wouldn't work. He wouldn't even reach them before they killed him. Yarrian would drop him with a thrown dagger. Or Assirra would crush his mind. And Phana would just sit here, staring at her own lap, unable to hear his last words to her.

The knives were nearly out of their sheaths. She tried desperately to move her hands, to grab his wrists, but she could only make her fingers twitch slightly. She felt him lean forward to kiss the top of her head, and then he pulled the knives out and settled them in his palms.

She wouldn't even be able to say goodbye.

*　　　　*　　　　*

NAMAL LOOKED DOWN AT LAITA, HIS FACE PALE, BLOOD DRIPPING from his thigh, his severed wrist cradled in the crook of his other arm, Hinara's blade at his throat.

Laita looked up at him and despair filled her heart. Namal was going to die here on the streets of Ythis. Laita was going to be chained and brought before the Legion High Command, where they would pronounce their sentence. Nothing but pain and blood awaited her in what little remained of her future.

She would be tortured, slowly, as an example to others. It would go on and on, until her body could take no more and she died.

Her soldiers would be left to fend for themselves. They would need to flee the city, the Empire, and no doubt more of them would be captured or killed in the attempt.

Laita had lost. It was over for good. She had brought them all here to accomplish the impossible, her own desire for vengeance, her arrogance taking them out of their lives to do something that could not be done. And she had always believed, deep down, that she would find a way to succeed, no matter the odds.

But she was wrong. And how many would suffer for it, had already suffered? Those who were killed in the raids, those who would feel the Inquisitors' hands on their bodies until they were wrung of all their secrets, before they were executed as traitors and deserters. Their only crime was in believing in her.

She had failed them all. And her own suffering would never be enough to make up for what she had done to them.

The joy on Hinara Angumu's face nearly lit up the dark streets on its own. And it came to her then, where she had seen him before. He had been at the training grounds while she was stationed there. He had made a terrible soldier, and would have been an even worse officer. But he was intelligent and had a keen eye for details. She recommended that he be assigned as an aide to an Investigator so that he could be trained, and his particular skills would not go to waste in the Legion.

She had set him on this path, and now it had come full circle. Another mistake to be laid at her feet. Namal would die because of choices she had made, events she had set in motion, years before.

We're all just wandering in the darkness, she thought. *Thinking we have control over our fates, thinking we can see the future ramifications of our decisions. But we have no control. We know nothing.*

She had tried to save Kied, and had failed. He had died without even a chance to say goodbye. She had loved him, *still* loved him, and he was gone. In another moment, she would be forced to watch Namal die, all so Hinara could relish his victory over her. All so he could punish her directly before he gave her to the Legion.

She thought of Bor, the young man who had believed so strongly in her. She still didn't know if he had died in the raid on the tenement in the Warren, or if he was chained up in a cell under the Fortress. Either way, there was nothing she could do for him. He would be questioned by the Inquisitors and then executed. There was no mercy coming for Laita's command squad.

She silently wished Saeda well. The woman was strong, and smart, and might just succeed in saving at least some of the soldiers who had followed Laita to Ythis. But it was out of her hands, and she would never know the fate of her loyal soldiers.

Namal looked down at her, the pain of his wound plastered across his face. He met her gaze.

And then he *winked* at her.

She glanced from his face to Hinara and back. Only a couple of seconds had passed since she had hit the ground. Namal eyes twitched down and back up to her face, and he winked again.

Namal's sword, his severed hand still gripping the hilt, was sitting on the cobbles at his feet. And she knew what he intended.

There was no way out for him. Hinara was about to kill him, and he knew it. But he was going to give her a chance. It would be up to her to take it and make the most of it.

The man who had tackled her was looking up at Hinara, smiling with excitement. He had found a moment of courage at just the right instant. But Laita could see his attention was focused on the Investigator, perhaps looking for some sign of approval from his superior.

Regardless, even though she had lost her knife, she certainly hadn't lost her ability to fight. And instead of pinning her arms or trying to flip her over onto her stomach, his attention was elsewhere. This man was no soldier, and Hinara had lacked the skill to teach him everything he needed to know.

Laita wasn't finished yet. It was easy to give into despair. It was easy to give up. It felt as if the entire world was against her, and what hope did she have against such power?

But she *wasn't* alone. As much as she felt the weight of responsibility on her shoulders, as much as she felt as if she alone needed to solve all the problems her soldiers were facing, it simply wasn't true.

She was surrounded by those who believed in her. But, just as important, they were willing to do whatever was necessary for her to succeed. Because they knew she could bring them through this mission like no one else.

Laita Naschect didn't give up. No matter the odds, she continued to fight. She couldn't save everyone, and some losses would tear her heart asunder, or haunt her forever. But if she was the leader they needed, then she had to be ready to accept a willing sacrifice by those who served her.

A sacrifice for the greater good.

She felt it keenly in heart as she readied herself for the moment. Namal was going to give his life, not just to save her, but so that she could save everyone else. They all needed each other. It was the lesson that so many other leaders in the Legion had never learned.

It was why almost two hundred Legionnaires had followed her into danger and darkness and death. Because, together, they were fighting for something greater.

She saw Hinara narrow his eyes as she turned back to the man crouched on his hands and knees over her. He claimed to know her, to know how she thought. Perhaps he did.

And if his claims were true, there was no more time to waste.

Her eyes met Namal's one last time, and she saw the love in his gaze. She saw how proud he was of her.

She tensed her body as Hinara began to say something.

"Don't …."

Chapter Forty-Seven

KORAL SLOWLY STOOD UP, THE KNIVES IN HIS PALMS. PHANA desperately tried to reach the cold in her blood, but it remained out of her reach. She wanted to scream in frustration at her weakness. This power in her veins, her heritage, had done nothing but cause her trouble. She had been better off without it.

She saw her hand tremble again and her fingers twitched.

All she wanted to do was stop Koral from throwing his life away for nothing. She didn't need anything magical for that. She just needed herself.

Fuck whatever is in my blood! I don't need it!

Her fingers curled into a fist.

And then Phana understood.

She *didn't* need her power to stop Koral. She didn't need her power at all. Half of her was still human. So let her be human. Let her give up this unwanted heritage, this unwanted power.

It wasn't enough to just bottle it up inside her. She had to get rid of it.

With all her will, she rejected her heritage. She pushed it away from her—mentally shoving it out and closing herself off to it. Her limbs began to tingle, but it wasn't enough.

She needed more.

Phana imagined the source of her power as something within her blood. She usually kept it contained, closed up tight within her body. And when she used it, she felt as if she was opening up something within her and letting it out, to flow through her blood.

Now, she imagined that source as a lump of ice in her chest, beating alongside her own heart. Connected to her heart, but a separate organ. Something that she didn't need to survive—something she could live without.

In her mind, she lifted her hand from her lap and touched her own chest. She pulled open her shirt and felt her skin over her heart.

Phana closed her eyes, fixing the image in her mind. She dug her nails into her skin, and imagined the blood welling up as she forced her hand to claw open a hole in her flesh. She tried to feel the pain, to make it as real as possible as she dug her fingers into the hole, ripping it open as she forced her hand into her chest.

She could feel the beating of her heart, and just beside it, an icy chill told her where to look. Phana saw herself drive her own hand into her chest cavity and reach for that cold core. Her hand brushed it, the chill burning the tips of her fingers. She pushed harder, feeling the pain—forcing herself to experience the agony—as she wrapped her hand around that lump of ice inside her being.

Phana wanted to scream as she gripped that second beating heart but there was no air in her lungs. She forced herself to take a deep breath and then she wrenched her hand away, ripping that icy heart away from her real heart, tearing it out from her body.

A bright, blue glow surrounded her fist, throbbing with its beat. This was the source of her power and the source of all her pain and trouble.

With a shout, she cast it away from her into the darkness. She watched as the glow faded and disappeared …

… and her eyes snapped open, her hand shooting up to grip Koral's wrist as he turned to face Yarrian and Assirra.

Phana raised her head and stood up behind him. He looked back at her, his eyes wide.

"Phana …."

She put a finger on his lips to silence him. And then she stepped around him to face the others.

Yarrian noticed her first, and Assirra turned at his look. For a moment, just an instant, Phana was sure she saw fear on the other woman's face.

"Issra, what are you—"

"My name is Phana. I don't give a shit what you once called me. That's the past and it's over."

"Did your priests release her?" Yarrian asked in a low voice.

"No, they did not," Assirra answered without taking her eyes off Phana's face. "How are you even standing? What have you done?"

"You cut me off from my blood heritage. Took my power away. You thought it would weaken me, and it did at first. Because I let it."

Phana took a step forward.

"But I've realized I don't need it. It's not who I am. So I rejected it. I tore it out of myself and cast it away. It's gone, and you have no hold over me, anymore."

Assirra frowned and Yarrian looked confused.

"Phana," Yarrian said slowly. "That's impossible. It's part of you, your birthright. You could no more remove it from you than you could cast out your own heart and live."

Phana simply raised her arms out to either side of her to show him that she now had control over her body again.

Assirra laughed out loud, and Phana's confidence slipped. Assirra was always so sure of herself, and Phana had forgotten so much.

"You've learned a few new tricks, Reaper. You were so unimaginative before. You never would have done this in the old days. You would have just fought tooth and nail to reach your powers and it would have kept you trapped. But casting it away? That was clever."

And suddenly Phana understood. The priests hadn't really taken her power away from her. That would have been impossible to do without killing her. It was a mind trick. They had blocked her, set a trap in her mind to spin her in circles and prevent her from commanding the power inside her.

And she had escaped, not by strength or savagery. She had escaped by turning away from that power and giving the mind block nothing to grab, nothing to hold.

"But you still don't have your power, Reaper. You are only as strong as any other mortal. And you still cannot stop me."

But Phana understood what the priests had done. And she knew now that the mind trick—no longer containing her will to reach the cold in her blood—had dissolved away into nothing. They might be able to re-establish the block if she thought about it.

So Phana didn't pause to think.

She saw Assirra's eyes widen as the other woman realized what she was about to do. Yarrian didn't understand, but Assirra knew her like no one else ever had. The decision was made in an instant, before the priests could erect the walls in her mind once more.

In that instant, Phana looked into Assira's eyes and saw the fear once more, hidden behind a veil of confidence and disdain, but always there.

The fear of the Reaper.

Phana felt the rush of ice in her blood, and she let the cold erupt out of her in a wave. It exploded forth, shattering the wooden pillars that supported the roof, tearing up the earth under her feet, and bursting the crates piled around them.

Assirra tried to raise her hands but it was too fast. She was hammered to the ground with a blunt spear of ice that caused the ground to tremble. Yarrian was thrown backward, his body punching into the piles of shattered crates and disappearing into the frost-covered debris.

The earth groaned as tendrils of ice ran through the foundation and up the walls, causing the boards to rip apart. The pillars toppled in pieces as the ceiling crumbled and fell.

Phana spun to Koral and reached out to him as the ground gave way beneath the warehouse and they dropped, the warehouse collapsing above them. She pulled him toward her and tried to shield him.

They fell, farther than she would have thought possible. And then she caught a glimpse of an underground cavern lit by great phosphorescent trees and she realized the warehouse had been built over ground that was too thin and fragile for what she had done.

An instant later they landed heavily on wet dirt. The breath was knocked out of her and she heard the snapping of bone as they impacted the ground of the cavern.

Phana looked up to see a pile of earth and wood from the hole above rushing toward her.

She managed to get one arm up before they were buried under an avalanche and she lost consciousness.

*   *   *

AS HINARA'S AIDE BEGAN TO FROWN AT HINARA'S GROWING LOOK
of alarm, Laita's hands clapped his head on both sides, her thumbs
driving into his eye sockets. Before he could pull back out of her
grasp, she twisted his neck and spun him sideways.

The howl of his voice was just rising as she reversed direction and
rolled to her hands and knees, just in time to see Namal's final act.

He hooked his toe under the blade of his short sword and flicked
it up toward her. The blade skittered across the cobbles and she
clutched at it, feeling the warmth of his flesh as she grasped his severed hand and pulled it away from the handle.

Namal swung his fist up and tried to connect with Hinara's head.
For an instant, Hinara reared back and Laita's heart surged with hope
that perhaps Namal might win free. But his strike merely glanced
across the side of the Investigator's head.

With a savage jerk, Hinara yanked the blade of his sword across
Namal's neck.

Laita has known it was coming, but still she froze for an instant
as Namal's eyes went wide, his throat opening in a bloody gash. She
wanted to scream his name, to run to him and somehow stop the
bleeding. But it was too late for him.

He had made the ultimate sacrifice for her. For her and for all
those who followed her. She wouldn't let it go to waste.

The aide screamed as he writhed on the ground, blood seeping between his fingers. She doubted that she had blinded him permanently, but he was now effectively out of the fight. By the time he would
be able to recover, either she or Hinara would be dead.

Hinara shoved Namal away from him and she saw her friend drop
to the cobbles, his wounded leg giving way while he clutched at his
throat. She could hear him choking, and the sound tore her heart
apart.

She faced the man who was responsible for so many deaths. He
plastered a smile across his face, but she could see the worry in his

eyes. When this had started, the odds were five to one in his favor. Now it was just the two of them.

"Listen to him dying, Laita. Such a quick movement with my blade, and now he bleeds out on the ground. So simple, and so final."

She tried to control her breathing and watch Hinara's movements as he slowly came toward her. He was trying to get her to act in anger, to attack in vengeance, to lose control.

"I have to admit, I was beginning to doubt you had come to Ythis. No one could find you or your people."

He leaned forward and spit his next words at her.

"Until you were betrayed by one of your own! Once a traitor, always a traitor."

He was lying. Even if someone was willing to betray her, they wouldn't betray their own comrades.

"You think they all support you, but they most certainly do not. They realize now what they have given up to follow you. You have managed to keep them in the dark about most things, but how do you think I found Irako?"

She hesitated. Had one of her soldiers told Hinara about the young man who had connected her to the Resistance? Had all of this been set in motion by someone trying to turn her in?

More important, though, did it matter? He was trying to undermine her confidence. Make her angry, make her hesitant, make her despair. It was all the same trick.

As much as he claimed to know her, he knew nothing. Someone like him would never truly understand her. Her motivations were alien to him.

He saw her attachment to her people as a weakness. One he could exploit.

Hinara Angumu couldn't have been more wrong.

She lunged forward with a clumsy thrust, baring her teeth at him. He stepped back and batted her sword away, and she saw his smile tighten as he focused on this life or death struggle.

She kept coming, trying for another lunge. Once again, he moved out of her way and knocked her sword to the side. But he didn't reverse direction and come back at her. He was testing her, looking for a weakness.

Looking for a pattern.

She switched it up and came at him with a side swipe of her blade and he blocked it and thrust at her. It was a half-hearted attempt, and she turned the point of his sword easily.

But she continued to advance as he slowly retreated. Another swing, and another, and he continued to parry and slowly retreat.

It was time.

Setting herself up, she moved forward suddenly, aiming for a thrust at his heart one more time. She saw the victory in his eyes as he recognized what she was doing. Instead of stepping back, he moved to the side and forward, his own blade coming across toward her shoulder.

She wasn't there, of course.

Ducking her head, she dropped under his swing and drove her shoulder into his stomach. Letting go of her sword, she hooked the backs of his legs with her hands and shoved forward.

He was unable to maintain his balance and she took him down the cobbles with a bone-jarring impact. His heavy grunt as he hit the ground told her she had the upper hand for one or two seconds at best.

She pulled her legs up over his and, straddling him, dropped her weight down as she drove her elbow across his face. His head snapped sideways, and he tried to roll under her.

It was exactly what she wanted him to do.

Letting him expose his back to her, she snaked her arm under his and wrenched it upwards as her other arm wrapped around his neck. Gripping her arm with her other hand, her forearm settled across his throat.

He tried to wave his sword around in the hopes of connecting with her, but she merely increased the pressure on his throat, and he dropped the blade. Every part of his attention focused on his inability to take a breath.

"You weren't as clever as you thought, you son of a bitch," she murmured in his ear as he struggled. "By coming after me, you just killed yourself."

He tried to pull her arm away with his free hand, but she had the leverage and his strength was waning fast.

"You failed, Hinara. Die with that in your mind."

His own hand slowly dropped away, and she wrenched even harder on his neck. When the life left his body, she was still gripping him so tightly she felt it through her arms and chest.

Slowly, she unwrapped her arms from around his neck. She checked for a pulse, just in case, but he was dead. His aide still lay on the ground a dozen paces away, moaning softly and holding his eyes.

Laita moved over to Namal and rolled him onto his back. His sightless eyes stared up at the dark sky above Ythis. Once again, she had lost someone she loved without being able to say goodbye.

She looked around, just in case anyone had heard the battle and was coming to look. But the streets were still empty. She moved over and picked up the Namal's sword, turning to the blinded soldier.

"Give me one reason not to kill you," she told him. He jerked at the sound of her voice and his moan turned into a whimper.

"Puh … please. Don't kill me. I … I … I'm blind."

Laita looked down at him.

"You killed my people. You stopped me from saving my friend. Why should I let you live?"

She wanted to kill him, and so she was forcing herself to talk to him. She knew she should let him live, but her desire to end his life in revenge for Namal's death was nearly overpowering. Perhaps he could say something to let her walk away without another death on her conscience.

But fate wasn't going to let her off that easily.

The man started screaming for help, his high-pitched voice echoing off the walls of the buildings around them.

"Shut up," she ordered him, but he didn't hear her and just kept screaming.

She silenced him with a single thrust of the blade in her hand. His screams cut off as he gasped, shudders running through his body. She pulled the sword from his heart and wiped the blood off on his trousers.

In the distance, she could hear hooves on the cobblestones. Her eyes went back to Namal. She wanted to take him with her, but she knew it was impossible. She couldn't carry him all the way to the warehouse, and she didn't have time to find transportation.

Dropping to her knees, she gently closed his eyes and kissed him on the forehead.

"I won't fail you, my friend."

She stood and moved off into the shadows of the night.

Chapter Forty-Eight

PHANA AWOKE TO COLD AND DARKNESS. HER HEAD WAS pounding, and she felt as if she was lying on a bed of ice. Koral's face was beside hers, his eyes closed, his breath steaming.

They were surrounded by a cocoon of solid ice.

Panic hovered at the edge of her mind as she realized where they were. They had fallen from the warehouse, through a hole in the ground, into a small cavern below. The warehouse had collapsed upon them, the ground and ceiling falling through the hole to bury them.

Phana had managed to protect them with this sheath of ice. But now she wondered how deeply they were buried.

There wasn't room to sit up, and she had no idea how much debris was on top of them. She somehow knew she could dissolve the ice by concentrating on it, but it might be the only thing keeping a crushing weight off their bodies.

And then she heard the scraping noise coming from above. She realized that noise was what had awakened her.

Someone was outside, digging through the debris. Probably searching for her.

She didn't know how long she had been unconscious. Could the Church soldiers already be down here? Were they searching for her? Or perhaps they were searching for Assirra.

Phana figured the woman was most likely dead. She had hit Assirra with everything, and she had seen her fall under the weight of an ice pillar as large as a tree trunk. No doubt Assirra's body had fallen through the hole and was likely buried under this debris as well.

And Yarrian—he might also be dead. She hadn't wanted to kill him, and he had been knocked away by her blast. It was more likely that he had survived. They had been friends once, though he had done nothing to stop Assirra in the warehouse. His fear for his own safety had overridden any loyalty he might have had to Phana.

She hoped he had survived, though she also hoped he would choose to leave her alone now if he still lived.

The scraping noise came again, and the ice above Phana's face brightened. There was light on the other side of her cocoon.

The air inside this pocket was getting stale, and as much as Phana didn't want to face another fight, she knew she had little choice. They couldn't stay in here, and Koral might be hurt. Phana flexed her own muscles and moved her arms and legs. She didn't think anything was broken, but she had heard bones snapping when they hit the ground.

A soft tapping came on the ice in front of her face. She summoned the cold in her blood and held it ready. And then she concentrated and the ice above her melted into water.

Phana and Koral lay under about a man's height of debris from the hole above. No light filtered down from that hole, and it seemed as if it was still covered over with the remains of the warehouse.

The debris had been dug away on one side, and a single figure stood here, outlined in the dim light of the huge phosphorescent plants that grew in the dirt here. It was vaguely man-shaped, though the head was asymmetrical, and the arms looked more like tentacles hanging from its shoulders.

The figure stepped forward and Phana saw it clearly. It was no man. The thing's skin was pitch black and looked as if it was made of tiny stones stuck together. The legs had two bends, as if they held an extra pair of knees.

It had no nose and a slit for a mouth. Only the eyes appeared human, and Phana found that disturbing in such an alien face.

It made a hissing noise with its mouth, and a strange, high-pitched whistle formed what sounded like words.

"Humans in danger," Phana heard. "Humans must come."

The creature stepped back from the hole and gestured with one of its arms. Phana saw that the arm was indeed some kind of tentacle that did not end in a human hand.

She held onto the cold, ready to lash out, but the creature made no threatening move.

"Humans in danger," it repeated. "Humans must come."

Phana sat up and looked down at Koral. He lay on his left side, and his left arm was twisted unnaturally beneath him. It appeared to be broken in two places.

She wished she had some ability to heal injuries. She stroked Koral's face and called his name. His eyelids twitched and then opened. Before he could move, she put her hand on his shoulder and held him in place.

"We're okay," she told him. "But you were injured in the fall so don't move."

Looking back at the creature, she spoke to it.

"His arm is broken. Can you do anything to help him?"

The creature just stared at her.

"Humans in danger. Humans must come."

It motioned again, more vigorously, and Phana looked at where it was gesturing. She saw a tunnel leading from the cave. Looking around, she saw two more tunnels leading out in other directions.

Figuring the creature didn't understand her words, she stood up carefully to make sure she wasn't also hurt. She had bruises everywhere, but she seemed otherwise okay.

"Phana … I'm in a lot of pain."

"I know. It's going to hurt much worse when you move. Your arm is broken and you're lying on it. But we've got to move. The Church soldiers are going to come down here eventually and look for us."

Koral nodded slightly and gritted his teeth.

"Then let's get this over with."

She slid one hand under his neck and gripped his right arm with the other.

"Ready?"

"Don't have a choice. Let's go."

She lifted him up and he gritted his teeth to keep in a scream. His moan was loud and long.

"Humans be silent," the creature said to them. "Ksathash will come."

Koral had his eyes tightly shut, but he opened them and looked at the creature standing a few feet away. His whole body started in surprise, and he grimaced.

"What in the Abyss is that?" he asked her, and she could hear a note of panic in his voice.

"It's okay. I think it's one of those creatures that built the sewers. It seems like it wants to help us."

He kept his eyes on the figure but gave her a small nod.

"Fuck, I can't remember what they're called. If it's one of those things, though, it's probably not hostile unless we threaten it. Be careful."

Phana grabbed Koral's good arm and helped him to stand. He nearly fainted when he stood up, his broken arm swinging freely.

"I don't have anything to make a sling or a splint. And your arm will have to be set first, anyway. Can you walk?"

"What about … your ice. Can you freeze my arm?"

Phana considered it.

"I honestly don't know. I don't have precise control. I might hurt you."

"I'm already hurt. If you can put some ice around it, keep it from moving, it'll help us go faster."

She hesitated, but he was right. She touched the wrist of his broken arm and closed her eyes.

"Hold still," she told him.

Phana drew her on power and tried to focus it, letting only a small amount of it flow from her onto his arm.

Koral gasped and said "Stop!"

She opened her eyes and saw that frost covered his entire arm. It wasn't a sheath of ice, and it wouldn't hold his limb immobilized. But his lips were turning blue and he began to shiver.

"My arm is numb. But I can't take any more—it's starting to freeze my whole body."

The creature motioned for them again and moved over to the tunnel entrance.

Phana helped Koral move to the tunnel, and the creature went off ahead of them. They had no choice but to follow.

They traveled for about five minutes before they came to a small opening. The smell of sewage from the hole was nearly overpowering. The creature slipped through and Phana took a peek. The opening led onto a ledge that ran along a sewer tunnel, a few feet above the thick sludge that flowed toward the Bay of Ythis.

It was slow going getting through the small opening, but Koral managed it and they walked for another few minutes before they reached a series of metal rungs set in the wall leading up to a grate in the ceiling.

"This is going to hurt," Koral said, eyeing the ladder uneasily.

Phana climbed the rungs and looked up through the grate. The sky was still dark, though she could tell that dawn was not far off.

She pushed the grate up and poked her head out. They were on the west side of the Dock Ward, near the outer city wall. The grate was on a side street at the mouth of an alley. No one was in sight.

"How do you want to do this?" she asked Koral.

"You go first, and I'll do my best. I'll need your help when I reach the top."

Phana climbed out onto the street. Koral pulled himself up onto the first rung. Then he grabbed the next rung with his good hand and climbed up. He repeated this until he reached the top. Phana took his good hand and held him steady as he walked up the last few rungs to the street.

She looked back down into the hole to thank the figure for its help, but it was gone. She closed the grate and she and Koral moved into the alley.

"We need somewhere to hide out," she told him. "Do you know anyone not connected to the Wolf who could help you with your arm?"

Koral considered this and shook his head.

"No, we're on our own as far as that's concerned. But I know a couple of places where we can stay that I've never told anyone else about. We can make it to one of them before dawn hits."

"Where is it?"

"It's an inn called the White Eagle. There's a concealed room in the cellar. The owner is not connected to the Wolf, and if we can get in there early enough before the inn gets active, they'll never know we're there. The owner probably doesn't even know the room exists."

Phana took his good arm.

"Then lead on."

They proceeded north toward the White Eagle Inn.

*   *   *

RELAEL WATCHED AS THE CHURCH SOLDIERS FRANTICALLY DUG IN
the collapsed ruins of the warehouse. His whole body was numb, and
he couldn't believe what he had seen.

Assirra Untoleu was dead.

She would have had you killed.

The voice hissed in his mind, as if someone stood behind him,
whispering.

*You're tainted, and you can't hide it anymore. They will kill you if
they find out.*

Relael felt a shudder roll through his body, though there was no
chill. It was as if his flesh belonged to someone else, and he was only
a passenger. That was fine with him. He didn't want to feel any real
emotions at that moment.

You can't return to the Temple.

He paused, considering the words that had been whispered into
his mind. Relael had been a member of the Hidden for many years.
He had enemies within the Church, those who he had betrayed or
manipulated to succeed at his own missions in the past. The High
Counselor was his protection—he was known to be one of her fa-
vored agents.

But with Assirra dead, there was no one to protect him. Someone
else would step into the role, but for the next dozen nights, knives
would flash in the dark and schemes set up perhaps years before
would be released to eliminate the rivals for her position.

If Relael still had all his wits, all his mental capabilities, he would
look forward to such a challenge. He knew he had once had a good
chance of coming out on top. Of becoming the next High Counselor.
There were few as cunning as he.

But that was no longer the case. He was ... distracted. He had difficulty concentrating on the problem at hand. His enemies would outthink him, which meant they would also outlive him. He had no wish to die at the hand of an apprentice wielding a dagger in some dark passage beneath the Temple.

Or worse, being framed for a crime against the Church so that he could be given to Iathephos.

You must hide, for now. You will have your chance, but you must not let them take you.

Relael didn't know who was giving him this advice, but it was sound.

He looked around himself and saw that no one was paying any attention to him. He casually stepped back from the frantic soldiers as they tried to move heavy wooden beams and piles of cut stone to get to what Relael was sure would be the dead body of Assirra Untoleu.

It took only a couple of moments for him to reach the mouth of an alleyway, and he spun and darted into the shadows. He burst into a full sprint and was shortly at the next main street.

Don't go too far. You have work to do here.

He paused and considered the voice in his head. He wasn't sure what he was supposed to do, but perhaps that would shortly become clear. He considered where he was and thought about places he might hide and wait out the coming day. There were countless bolt holes and makeshift "living spaces" in the Dock Ward, occupied by the destitute and desperate. Relael was now desperate. He couldn't return to his own office—it would shortly become a trap once word got back to the Temple that Assirra was dead.

So for now, he would hide out on the streets. The first thing he would need to do would be to get rid of these priest's robes and find some other clothes. Tomorrow night, he would consider his options.

Things didn't look good right now. But who knew what might change tomorrow? And Relael had always been a survivor.

*   *   *

LAITA SAT IN THE WAREHOUSE WITH SAEDA, ADDIRU AND PILAYNI. None of them were ready to speak. The news of Namal's death had hit them hard. Laita gave them the silence they needed, each lost in his or her own thoughts about Namal, about Ythis, about everything that happened to them.

But they were together. Laita knew now that nothing could stop them.

What if we were betrayed from the inside?

The thought intruded, cutting through everything else. Had someone given up Irako in an attempt to give her over to the Legion or the Guard? If so, what else would they do?

She mentally gave herself a shake. Hinara had probably been lying when he told her that. He was trying to throw off her concentration. He would have said anything. There were other ways he might have found Irako.

But she remembered the Inquisitor's face when he said it. He wasn't just taunting her. He had taken a perverse joy in telling her about the traitor.

Aren't we all traitors, anyway?

She didn't want to think about this right now. She wanted to remember Namal as he had lived. She wanted to remember him giving advice and support to the soldiers under her command. She wanted to remember all the times he had been there when she needed to rant about the Legion bureaucracy, or the orders that didn't make any sense.

Pilayni wiped away a tear and took a deep breath.

"It's not going to be the same without him."

Addiru reached over and took her hand.

"But we'll do his memory proud. When we accomplish this mission, it'll be for him."

"It'll be for *all* the people of the Empire," she told him kindly. "That's what Namal would want. It's what he spent his whole life fighting for."

Addiru nodded and looked down at the floor to hide the tears in his own eyes.

Laita wanted nothing more than to see Cedaro again. It was likely that their hiding place at the White Eagle Inn was safe and hadn't been revealed to the Imperial Guard. She would give it another day and then take her people back to the inn.

Saeda turned to Laita.

"Do you think he told anyone else about the Wandering Horse? It seems like the Guard didn't discover that from Irako."

Laita shrugged.

"I don't believe Irako knew that's where Oriuna spent her time when not at the Resistance meetings. If Hinara didn't tell the guard—and I think he kept it a secret so he could catch me himself—then it's probably safe."

"So that means you're going to go back there and see if you can make contact with Oriuna and the Church, doesn't it?"

Laita looked into Saeda's eyes, and then at each of the others.

"Yes, sergeant," she replied. "That's exactly what I'm going to do."

*   *   *

AMBASSADOR ZARTAY SEAPHON FINISHED READING THE PARCHMENT. He rolled it up and slipped it back into the parchment case.

"I thought there were witnesses to where he was buried," he said to the soldier who stood at attention in his front hall. "None of them could find the grave?"

"No, Ambassador," the soldier replied.

Zartay adjusted his robe and leaned on the wall. Kied Leele was a martyr in the eyes of those who had deserted the Legion and followed Laita Naschect. Zartay would have preferred to have the man's body, to return it to Ythis and publicly burn it as a symbol that no one could resist the Emperor.

The delay in finding that woman and her fellow traitors was terribly inconvenient. Zartay himself had been questioned at length by the magistrates, and he had worried at one point that they were going to hand him over to an Inquisitor to make sure his story was not missing any vital details.

He had managed to come out of it with his reputation damaged and his career barely intact. The mission for the Emperor had failed spectacularly, with not just one, but two commanders betraying their oaths. And he had been there to manage both of them.

He was lucky to still be alive, never mind still have his job as Ambassador.

The next assignment was likely to be awful—not only a punishment for failure but a demonstration that the Emperor no longer had any confidence in him. He had hoped recovering Kied Leele's body would at least help a little.

Now he had one more failure to report. And he had even been woken up before dawn for this. For once, it was a message he had wished could have waited for later.

"Perhaps wild animals dug him up and ate him," the soldier suggested.

"That does not do me any good. I needed his body. We can't exactly round up all the animals in that valley and check their shit for bits of the man, can we?"

"No, sir," the soldier said in a subdued voice. "Is there a return message?"

"I just woke up," he told the man, not even trying to suppress his irritation. "Come back later. Just before midday. I'll have a message for the Legion then."

The soldier gave him a sharp salute and let himself out. Zartay turned to his servant.

"You might as well start preparing something to eat. I won't be getting back to sleep after this."

He returned to his bedroom, his mind already churning. If he was going to regain his status, he had much work to do.

*   *   *

THE SOLDIER SLOWLY WALKED PAST THE TORCH, THE FLAME flickering in the light breeze. The spaces between the torches seemed so much darker than normal. The pall of doom that filled the air each night just continued to get worse and worse, and tonight it felt as if a great weight hung poised over the city, on the precipice of falling and crushing them all.

Dawn wasn't far off, and the soldier counted his paces and wished the sun would hurry up already. He reached the edge of the bright torchlight and quickened his pace. He wanted to spend as little time away from the flames as possible.

He silently cursed the new commander. Apparently, there was some kind of hunt going on in the city, and his commander had decided to lend a bunch of soldiers from the wall to assist. After all, the man had said, no force capable of attacking Ythis is going to get within a month's march of the capital of the Empire without us knowing about it.

So now the wall patrols were one man alone instead of paired up. With this … dread … hanging over the city, that somehow made sense to the new commander.

The soldier was almost at the halfway point between the torches when he heard a soft scrape, as of something sliding against stone. He stopped, his hand going to the hilt of his sword as if it had a mind of its own.

He heard no further sound, just the whisper of the night breeze.

Taking another step, he watched the edge of the wall. Even in the dimness between the torches, there was just enough light to see … something … up ahead.

He stopped again and squinted at the small, dark object that lay on the parapet a dozen paces ahead of him. It was pale and resembled a large insect.

A spider?

He drew his sword and took another step, and then another.

The soldier realized that it was a hand just as the figure pulled itself up over the edge of the wall. He got a glimpse of pale skin and dark hair, and the smell of earth filled his nose as the figure rushed toward him.

The soldier managed to get his sword up, but the figure knocked it aside and grabbed him by the throat, cutting off his air.

The last thing he saw, as he was lifted from the ground, was the face of man, twisted in rage.

And then the soldier's vision went dark and he knew no more.

~ End ~

The Undying Empire: Rebellion *story concludes in book 3,* The Revenant and the Reaper.

Thank you for reading The Traitor and the Thief. If you enjoyed this book, please tell others about it. Honest reviews are also greatly appreciated and are the best way to help other readers discover new authors.

About Andrew J. Luther

Andrew J. Luther lives in Burlington, Ontario with his wife and son. He currently works as a communications professional in his day-job, but spends his spare time playing tabletop roleplaying games and writing.

You can keep up-to-date with Andew by joining his mailing list at www.andrewjluther.com or on Twitter @andrewjluther.